+
$27.99

P9-DGY-457

DISCARD

Collusion

LARGE PRINT

GIN	Gingrich, Newt
	Collusion
APR 30, 2019	

The Pacific War Series

Pearl Harbor

Days of Infamy

To Make Men Free: A Novel of the Civil War
(with William R. Forstchen)

A Nation Like No Other

Real Change

5 Principles for a Successful Life
(with Jackie Gingrich Cushman)

To Save America

A Contract with the Earth (with Terry L. Maple)

Breakout

Drill Here, Drill Down, Pay Less

APR 3 0 2019
920

Collusion

A Novel

Newt Gingrich
and Pete Earley

HARPER LUXE

An Imprint of HarperCollinsPublishers

DISCARD

FAIRPORT PUBLIC LIBRARY
1 VILLAGE LANDING
FAIRPORT, NY 14450

This is a work of fiction. Names, characters, places, and incidents are products of the author's imagination or are used fictitiously and are not to be construed as real. Any resemblance to actual events, locales, organizations, or persons, living or dead, is entirely coincidental.

COLLUSION. Copyright © 2019 by Newt Gingrich and Pete Earley. All rights reserved. Printed in the United States of America. No part of this book may be used or reproduced in any manner whatsoever without written permission except in the case of brief quotations embodied in critical articles and reviews. For information,, address HarperCollins Publishers, 195 Broadway, New York, NY 10007.

HarperCollins books may be purchased for educational, business, or sales promotional use. For information, please e-mail the Special Markets Department at SPsales@harpercollins.com.

FIRST HARPERLUXE EDITION

ISBN: 978-0-06-288801-3

HarperLuxe™ is a trademark of HarperCollins Publishers.

Library of Congress Cataloging-in-Publication Data is available upon request.

19 20 21 22 23   ID/LSC   10 9 8 7 6 5 4 3 2 1

We dedicate this book to the poison victims and others who have been murdered by Russian president Vladimir Vladimirovich Putin's regime.

Russia never lost the Cold War because it never ended.

—VLADIMIR VLADIMIROVICH PUTIN

Contents

Cast of Characters

PART I

The Bear Shows Its Claws

Those who "abjure" violence can only do
so because others are committing violence
on their behalf.

—George Orwell

One

Two Years Earlier

The jihadist seemed to rise from the underworld. Crawling across the Cameroon terrain when he'd reached them before dawn. Navy SEAL Brett Garrett could see the color of his black eyes. Boko Haram. The missing twentieth fighter whom everyone except for Garrett had believed dead. He'd followed them from the bloodbath in his camp. Patiently waiting, watching them board the helicopter, waiting until liftoff, knowing it was his best chance to maximize deaths.

He shouldered his weapon at the same moment Garrett raised his rifle from his seat inside the open cargo door. Garrett fired and in that same instant saw the rocket-propelled grenade flying at the cockpit.

A bright yellow burst. Instant loss of hearing. Instant concussion. Instant confusion. The machine fell. Its shell smacking into the earth, throwing Garrett free but on fire.

Still conscious enough to roll over, over, and over again. What of the others? He didn't know. He'd disobeyed a direct order. He was responsible for what was now happening. But he'd done it for the right reasons.

Hadn't he? Surely, they would understand. He'd wanted to save the children.

Two

Current Day

A shrill alarm pierced the darkness. A hulking figure stepped outside the building into the minus-twelve-degree temperature cradling an unconscious woman in his arms. Roof floodlights illuminated the snow-covered grounds. Svetogorsk, Russia. A facility hidden outside the town in a dense forest.

The man trudged through a foot of snow toward a 1980s-era, rusty Lada parked alongside a half-dozen other tired Soviet-era vehicles. It was a twenty-yard trek to the car. The man almost made it halfway before a thin line of blood trickled down from under the protective mask covering his nose and mouth. His breathing became gasps. Two steps more before he fell to his knees still holding the listless woman. His wife.

He struggled to remain upright; he gazed forward at the parked Lada as if he were picturing himself reaching it. So close. His heart stopped. He fell, covering his wife's corpse.

The alarm ended but the spotlights continued to shine, causing the snow to glisten. Twinkles of bright and faint ice diamonds.

Two figures. A man and a woman in hazmat suits. Like space travelers, they emerged from the building, following the man's footsteps to where he and his wife were motionless. Disfigured snow angels.

With thick-gloved hands, the man leaned down. Inspecting the bodies.

"We must incinerate the corpses before we contact Moscow," he said through a microphone to the woman with him.

"General Gromyko will be angry," she replied.

"We cannot to be blamed!" the man snapped. "Accidents happen."

"Accidents? This was no accident."

"Don't be a fool. Immediate cremation. For everyone's protection."

"They have a child," she said. "Peter. A mute."

"The boy is of no consequence to us. General Gromyko will deal with him."

The woman stared down at the dead couple. "Her father holds a high position in the Foreign Ministry," the woman said.

"Which is why we must burn these bodies quickly and report their deaths as an accident."

The man stood, turned his back to her and the dead couple, and began making his way through the snow to the building. The woman hesitated, glanced over her shoulder to be sure he was not watching, and made the sign of the cross.

Her lips moved. A prayer for the dead.

Three

Two years earlier

*E*lsa Eriksson couldn't sweat.

Dehydration. The body loses 10 percent of the water it takes in every day through sweat. That's what the nursing instructors in Sweden had taught her.

Lying in the fetal position on the hard ground, she guessed it was at least a hundred degrees. She'd asked her kidnappers for water, but they wanted her weak, compliant—not dead. She was worthless to them dead. One bottle of water per day—sixteen fluid ounces— handed to her bound wrists for her to lift underneath the loosened black hood slipped over her head.

With her bare feet—they'd taken her shoes—she'd felt the bare ground beneath. Extending them out, she touched the mud walls of what she assumed was an

African mud hut. She decided to stand and was met with a sucker punch to her abdomen. She fell back to the floor. Someone was guarding her.

She had no one to blame but herself.

The Nigerian army commander had told her not to leave the compound. Thirteen-foot-tall pieces of corrugated metal—each four feet wide—protected "New Banki City" in this northern province—although it was hardly a city by any definition. Cities had municipal services, order, normality. New Banki was a refugee camp.

Eriksson had been warned before leaving Sweden. Still, she was shocked when she'd first arrived three months ago. Trash-strewn dirt paths, bombed-out concrete buildings, flimsy tents. Inside the camp were children, women, and old men. No males of fighting age. They'd been herded sheeplike into trucks for transport to Nigerian army detention centers. Outside the enclosed compound, Boko Haram was in control. Islamic extremists. Kidnappers. Murderers. Rapists. Suicide bombers in training eager to claim their celestial virgins. She'd entered a human toilet bowl edged by IEDs—a cesspool of disease and death unlike anything she'd witnessed.

The Nigerian commander had confiscated all the medical supplies that she'd brought from her employer, a Swedish humanitarian NGO, and only after her repeated threats to report him to the Swiss and Americans had he returned less than a third of them, selling the rest on a thriving black market. Having a Swedish father and American mother gave her twice the diplomatic clout.

She had stuck out. A too-thin, unmarried, thirty-year-old Christian woman in an ocean of uprooted Muslims. The army soldiers took bets about how long she would stay.

The explosion had come at dusk. An IED tripped by one of two women who'd left the compound at dusk to gather firewood. One had returned staggering. Cuts, bruises, and totally confused. The Nigerian soldiers had smirked. They showed no interest in searching for the other woman.

Eriksson had gone out with a medical bag. A recent Christian convert, Abidemi, which translated to "girl born when father was away," had accompanied her.

Eriksson, Abidemi, and Jesus wandered in the darkness. Outside the camp, they'd proven easy prey.

Now captive in a Boko Haram hut, Eriksson could hear Abidemi screaming nearby. Fourteen. Unlike the foreign NGO worker, Abidemi was not worth a ransom.

"Please, God, save us," Eriksson whispered. "Please, send someone, Jesus, someone to save Abidemi and me."

Four

Current Day

Yakov Prokofyevich Pavel glanced pensively from his upper-floor window at the Ministry of Foreign Affairs of Russia, one of Moscow's seven landmark Stalinist skyscrapers. It was Nikita Khrushchev who'd recalled Stalin's words: "We won the war . . . foreigners will come to Moscow, walk around, and there are no skyscrapers. If they compare Moscow to capitalist cities, it's a moral blow to us." Stalin had demanded his architects build them. Posturing for the world. Necessary after World War II, even more so now. Stalin had asked for forty stories, but twenty-seven was as high as they could reach in 1953. His builders' limited skills were a national secret—like so many others. Heavy steel frames with concrete ceilings necessitated a slab foundation that was more than twenty-two feet thick. Even with it, twenty-seven floors was the max. Pavel was on the twenty-sixth with its premium views.

Pavel had been told earlier this morning that General Andre Gromyko was coming. He spotted the general's jet-black Mercedes-Benz S600 Pullman limousine—a gift from the Russian president—as it turned into the ministry's circular driveway. When Pavel was a party member, no high-ranking Communist would have risked driving a foreign luxury car. But that was before.

The seventy-two-year-old Pavel remembered the past, unlike the junior diplomats scampering around him. Before the end of the Soviet empire, President Vyachesian Leninovich Kalugin had been considered a mediocre KGB agent at best, not considered particularly bright and with little potential for advancement. How then had such a man seized control?

Like so many of his fellow Russians, Pavel had welcomed the end of the old Soviet Union but had been unprepared for what had followed. A drunk Boris Nikolayevich Yeltsin had been swept into power only because of a single courageous act—standing on a Soviet tank defying the KGB's 1991 aborted August coup. It had been Yeltsin who had first opened the corruption floodgates, permitting the looting of the country's vast resources, giving birth to both the Russian mafia and money-grubbing oligarchs.

The Americans were not blameless. They had emasculated Russia, stripped it of its pride—declaring themselves the world's only superpower—creating resentment. Looting Moscow became the new rule for the powerful.

Vyachesian Kalugin had seized the moment, tapped into the centuries of distrust. Fueling the bitterness, he'd taken advantage of a nationalistic wave, a need for restored pride. The old guard had badly underestimated him. The ambition. The ruthlessness behind the grin. His insatiable greed. A Russian Gordon Gekko with a gun. Not a literary symbolic wolf of Wall Street but a genuine wolf trained by the KGB. A bribe or a bullet. What man would refuse to kneel?

The Kremlin was now a kleptocracy. Western intelligence estimated Kalugin's personal wealth at $80 billion, magically accumulated while being paid less than $200,000 per year on his government salary. Where were the cries of corruption? Where was the demand for an accounting? Critics were jailed or murdered. Others were fellow pigs feasting at the trough. Or, like Pavel, they remained silent.

President Kalugin had chosen a brutal lackey of limited intellect as his closest advisor. General Andre

Gromyko's military rank and chest filled with colorful medals were as fraudulent as his toothy smile and too-firm handshake.

A hurried knock on his office door snapped Pavel to attention. His secretary stepped in.

"The general and his aides have entered the lobby. Should I serve vodka or water with gas?"

"Vodka." The one constant in Russia.

"Cookies?"

"You decide."

A look of trepidation fled across her face. She was older and from a generation that remembered the dangers of the simplest, most innocent error. Pavel's mother had once told him a story about when she had worked for Lavrently Pavlovich Beria, the brutal secret police chief and overseer of gulag labor camps. After the war, she'd been assigned to Beria's secretarial typing pool. One day he'd entered and asked in his charming voice, "Girls, who typed a letter for me yesterday addressed to our party leader in St. Petersburg?" No one had raised a hand. Silence. "Come, girls," Beria repeated softly, "I've lost my copy of the letter, and there is a small detail I need to recall." A young typist stood and, when he asked, provided the missing detail.

Pavel's mother had never forgotten what had happened next. Two men dragged the girl away. Beria's mood had changed from pleasant to cruel. "You girls are to type letters. You must never read them."

Brutality. Yet another constant. Another carryover from the past.

"Bring cookies," Pavel said, moving from the window to his desk. He would not be standing to greet General Gromyko. A Beria still in diapers.

His secretary announced them. Gromyko paraded inside like a peacock with an attractive, much younger woman following him. Pavel glanced up from his desk. Neither offered a welcoming hand. Gromyko sat in a chair facing Pavel. The woman on a stool behind him.

"Yakov Prokofyevich, I'm sorry to report bad news," the general announced, although his voice and facial expression registered no signs of sorrow. "Your daughter and son-in-law."

Pavel's jaw tightened.

"An unfortunate accident. Both are dead."

Gromyko spoke with the empathy of a babushka dropping a hatchet across a chicken's neck.

Pavel's secretary entered with a silver tray that she placed on Pavel's desk before excusing herself.

"When and where?" Pavel asked.

"They died serving our motherland. There is little else I can tell you. Both were chemists, were they not?"

His question was insulting.

"Honor graduates from MIPT, and both were working for you."

"Ah yes, the Moscow Institute of Physics and Technology," Gromyko responded. He glanced at the unopened vodka and sugar cookies. Leaning forward from his chair, he helped himself to a cookie. "A decent school, I've heard. If I recall, you graduated from the Moscow State Institute of International Relations, our Russian Harvard."

Pavel didn't reply.

"And yet here I sit," Gromyko continued, glancing around Pavel's office. "Your superior—a simple former KGB officer who attended the St. Petersburg Mining University, but for only a brief period. I found school rather unchallenging."

Again, Pavel remained stone-faced.

Dismissively tossing half the cookie back onto the silver serving tray, Gromyko licked crumbs from his fingers and said, "Shall I assume you had no communication with your daughter and your son-in-law?"

"I was told their work required secrecy," Pavel said.

"Always the clever diplomat. Your reply does not answer my question. When was the last time you spoke to your daughter?"

"I have not been in communication with her since she and her husband began working for you."

"Come now, you're a widower. Your only family is your daughter, her husband, and your grandson—Peter, isn't that correct?—and not a word from any of them in two years?"

"It is a price we willingly pay for the benefit of all, is it not?" Pavel said.

Gromyko let out a short sigh. "Again, the answer of a diplomat. Yakov Prokofyevich, both of us know rules can be bent, especially for someone such as you, a high-ranking, senior diplomat."

Momentary mutual stares.

"General Gromyko," Pavel said, "I assume you have made arrangements for my grandson to be brought to Moscow to live with me. When should I expect him?"

"Tomorrow. I will have a car bring him to your office."

"And the remains?"

"Cremated. If you like, your grandson can bring them with him."

Awkward silence.

"General Gromyko," Pavel said, "is there more we need to discuss? I have a meeting, a matter of great urgency to the ministry, and I am late."

"A meeting, but my dear Yakov Prokofyevich, you should be in mourning. Do you not wish to take a day off?"

His voice was taunting.

"The work of the state continues," Pavel said.

"I will not think about leaving until after we have a toast in memory to your daughter and her husband. It is the only decent thing to do."

He motioned to his female aide, who summoned Pavel's much older secretary. The elderly woman opened the vodka with shaky fingers, pouring two shot glasses.

"Your girl here is like a frightened rabbit," Gromyko noted. "I can send you a replacement, one of my prettier assistants, even this one. She would be a compliant and an eager companion now that you have lost your wife."

Pavel glanced behind Gromyko at the young woman standing behind the general. Her face was blank, betraying nothing. Empty eyes.

"Thank you, General, but my secretary has served me well for many years." Pavel nodded toward the door, and the older woman hurriedly excused herself.

"As you wish," Gromyko said, raising a shot glass. "I am so sorry for the bird."

Gromyko's words were a reference to a 1960s Russian comedy *The Caucasian Prisoner*, a tale about a flock of birds headed south for the winter. One small, proud bird broke away and flew straight for the sun. It burned its wings and fell to the bottom of a deep gorge. In the story, the narrator said, "Let us drink to this: let not a single one of us ever break away from the collective, no matter how high he flies!" At that point, one of his friends had begun sobbing. "What is it, my friend?" his host had asked. The friend had said, "I'm so sorry for the bird!"

Old Soviet humor didn't always travel well outside its borders, but among Russians, it was a well-known toast used to break tension. A poor choice, however, offered in memory of the dead.

Pavel drank his vodka.

"Yakov Prokofyevich," Gromyko continued, "the days of the collective are gone, but the Kremlin remains a flock of birds soaring together. It still is dangerous for a single bird to break away from those leading the flock. To risk having their wings burnt. You are from the past. Your ways of thinking are from the past. This is no fault of your own. All men reach a point of uselessness in their lives. It is time for you to reap the rewards

FAIRPORT PUBLIC LIBRARY
1 VILLAGE LANDING
FAIRPORT, NY 14450   9 20

of your many years of service, especially now that your grandson will need your full attention. I have discussed this with our president, and we believe it would be best for you to consider retirement."

"Does the president intend to fire me?"

"The president simply said—after the loss of your daughter and son-in-law—you might wish to retire. It was my recommendation to him."

"Good day, General," Pavel said, placing his shot glass on the serving tray.

"Good day, Yakov Prokofyevich, and please think about what I have just said."

Five

Two Years Earlier

*T*he specially outfitted Lockheed C-130 four-
turboprop aircraft cruising above Africa had been
made quieter than standard U.S. military planes. Inside,
Petty Officer 3rd Class Richard Stone elbowed Chief
Petty Officer Brett Garrett was seated next to him.

"My old man told a joke at the Pentagon the other
night," Stone said.

All fourteen of the Navy SEALs inside the C-130's
bowels were keenly aware that Stone's father—Cormac
Stone—was a U.S. senator from California. All could
hear the younger Stone talking through their linked
headsets.

"My father tells these generals that a new Army
recruit lost his M-4, so the Pentagon charged him six

hundred and fifty dollars to buy a new one. Then my father says, 'That's why in the Navy, the captain always goes down with the ship.'"

A few SEALs groaned.

"Hey, it's an old joke," Stone said, defensively, "and I know it sucked."

"But every general laughed, didn't they?" Garrett replied.

Stone nodded his head, "You bet they did."

"Hey, Senator," which was Stone's nickname for obvious reasons, "here's a joke for your old man to tell the next time he gives the brass a speech at the Pentagon." It was Malcolm Moss, aka Sweet Tooth, a play on his M&M initials. "It's about a Navy chief."

Everyone looked at Garrett. "Go ahead," he said.

Brett Garrett had made chief petty officer in fourteen years. That was normal. What wasn't was his age. Thirty-two. That was young.

"You got ten guys clinging on to a rope dangling from a helo," Sweet Tooth began.

"What kind of helo?" a fellow SEAL, nicknamed Bear, interrupted.

"What? It don't matter what kind it was," Sweet Tooth replied indignantly.

"'Course it does," Bear responded. "If you got ten guys hanging on a rope from a helo, it sure as hell matters what sort of helo it was."

"It's a joke," Sweet Tooth said. "Now shut up and let me tell it."

"Go ahead, but it would matter."

"Point taken," Garrett said, ending their argument. "Go ahead. Finish your joke."

"Okay, this rope—it's bound to break unless someone lets go. The guy who lets go is going to fall and certainly die. So, these ten guys are holding on for their lives, and they begin arguing about who should be the one to drop off. Finally, the chief says he'll do it because chiefs are used to doing everything for the Navy. They never see their families, work all those hours—all without getting nothing in return."

"Suck up," Bear said.

"Shut the hell up," Sweet Tooth snapped. "Now, this chief decides to give a little farewell speech before he lets go. I mean, he's earned the right to say his final words. He talks about his great love of country, the importance of sacrifice, and his complete devotion to his men, and when he finishes, why, the other nine guys hanging there, they are so moved, so emotional, they all begin clapping."

Sweet Tooth broke out laughing. Even Garrett smiled.

"I don't get it," Bear said.

"The other nine started clapping, stupid," Sweet Tooth explained. "That means they let go of the rope. Only the chief kept hanging on to it. That's why the chief is a chief, and you're just another E-4."

"What kind of helo was it?" Bear asked, goading him.

"Enough," Garrett said. "Get focused."

Before he'd become a chief petty officer, Garrett's nickname had been Hillbilly, a reference and insult to his Arkansas roots. He hated it, but no one picked their own nicknames during SEAL training. An instructor had tagged him when he'd been doing push-ups in the rain and mud in a courtyard called "the Grinder."

Garrett didn't particularly like having a U.S. senator's son on his team—even though Richard Stone had never sought special treatment and Garrett wouldn't have given him any. If anything, the opposite was true. Senator had assumed everyone knew. His father was constantly on the news. One of the country's most outspoken liberals. That being the situation, Richard Stone—the SEAL—had talked openly about his dad from the start and had done everything to prove he wasn't riding on his old man's coattails. Did more than what was expected—and those expectations were already too high for most.

Garrett eyeballed his crew, silently checking their gear, searching each man's face for tells. Was Senator different from the rest of them? Yes and no. Every SEAL had a personal reason for becoming one. Including Garrett. But this was Senator's first mission. Being an overachiever in training was impressive. It might not carry over in combat, though.

Garrett pushed his worries from his head. Only four things mattered. His men needed to follow his orders. Each needed to complete his assigned task. Each needed to be willing to die for the man next to him. And all of them needed to trust Garrett. He was their chief. His job title didn't include being their father, confessor, or shrink, even though he'd played all those roles at different times. It did require him to be one of them, yet not one of them. The "goat locker." That's what the Navy called it. He ate when they ate, drank when they drank, fought when they fought, died when they died. That's what petty chiefs did. But Garrett was ultimately responsible for their lives.

"We've entered Cameroon airspace," the pilot said. "Prepare for drop."

Boko Haram had underestimated U.S. technology. The kidnappers had used Elsa Eriksson's cell phone to call her boss in Sweden: $25 million ransom or body parts in the mail. The terrorist had switched off

Eriksson's cell phone, but not discarded it. A critical error. Boko Haram hadn't been aware of "the Find," a sophisticated NSA-enhanced satellite locator device capable of tracking a cell phone even after it has been switched off.

A surveillance drone had been dispatched. Photos of a permanent camp. Eight primitive mud huts. At least twenty male terrorists. Easy to count because of their morning prayers, all on their knees facing Mecca, Kalashnikovs next to prayer mats. Eriksson was in a hut designated by the CIA as Alpha-1. Jumping in three klicks away. That's 3.1 miles of hiking at night. Garrett's orders: snatch the Swedish-American humanitarian worker in the morning darkness. Limit full engagement. Cameroon's northern leaders had elected to allow the terrorists to operate without much interference. Why rattle that cage? In and out.

Rescue operations were the only type of military assignment dependent on complete surprise. That's what Garrett had read in a SEAL School training manual—Gazit, 1980, pages 118–22. Garrett wasn't certain why that reference had stuck permanently in his head, but it had. If alerted, a terrorist could kill a hostage. It took only seconds to pull a trigger, detonate a bomb. Dealing with Boko Haram was dicier than most kidnappers. Jihadists had nothing to lose. That *gave them an edge. Set off a suicide vest. Kill yourself and hostages. Virgins and eternal glory were assured.*

The most difficult task Garrett faced was assuring his team they were invincible. It mattered. No one was going to die today. The slightest doubt jeopardized the mission and their fellow SEALs.

Focus. It was time. Out the door. Falling. Everyone landing, everyone assembling, everyone hurrying toward the Boko Haram camp where Elsa Eriksson was being held hostage.

Six

Current Day

A casual look backward at the chase car on Sikorsky Street caused U.S. ambassador Stanford Thorpe to pause before he slid into the leather seat of the embassy's armored Cadillac.

Thorpe prided himself on remembering faces and names. A key to his successful diplomatic career.

"What the hell is that former Navy SEAL doing in my protection detail?" he demanded.

"Brett Garrett is a private contractor now," John Harper, the U.S. chief of mission in Kiev, replied. "Where better to bury someone than in Ukraine?" He chuckled.

Thorpe wasn't amused. "After that screwup in Cameroon, he's toxic. Private contractor or not. Get rid of him."

"He's on a short leash."

"It should be a noose."

"Sending him home won't be easy. An ex-Navy pal owns the company with the security contract."

"You don't get paid to do easy. Call Washington. Throw your weight around. I want Garrett on a plane out of here tomorrow."

The three-car caravan entered Mykhaliv Square in central Kiev, arriving outside the Ministry of Foreign Affairs. By the time they stepped onto the sidewalk, Harper was on his cell phone ordering the regional security officer to keep Garrett and the other five private security guards outside with their vehicles. Only the two-person State Department protection detail assigned to Ambassador Thorpe would enter the building.

From the chase car passenger seat, Brett Garrett watched as invited dignitaries and news reporters quick-stepped into the six-story Ukraine Foreign Ministry with its five-Roman-column façade—a communist-era building commemorating the defeat of the Nazis in World War II. Now it was the communists who had fled.

Patience. He looked at the security guard in the driver's seat next to him. Donald J. Marks. He was a habitual smoker. Give him a few more moments. He'll leave the chase car.

"Screw this sitting here," Marks said as if on cue. "I'm grabbing a smoke."

Mental telepathy? No, Garrett understood addictions. As soon as Marks lit up outside, Garrett removed two thin rectangles from a prescription packet in his jacket. Both went under his tongue. Instant relief.

Inside the grand ballroom, Ambassador Thorpe greeted other diplomats as he walked to the portable stage raised some two feet above a white marble floor. John Harper settled into a reserved front-row seat to watch his boss. U.S. and Ukrainian flags were positioned at each corner of the raised platform. Thorpe's two State Department bodyguards stood like bookends near the podium. Sunglasses worn indoors. Military haircuts. Flesh-colored earpieces. Jackets unbuttoned.

"I'm proud to announce that our two great nations have reached a new level of cooperation under the U.S. Generalized System of Preferences Program, which allows Ukrainian exporters and U.S. importers to take advantage of duty-free treatment for nearly four thousand products from Ukraine," Ukraine's foreign minister announced, officially starting the news conference.

From the stage, Thorpe half listened, scanning the crowd for a pleasing face, possibly a redhead this time, someone half his fifty-nine years, someone in awe of his position or perhaps seeking a special favor. Impeccably dressed and coiffed, he was ending his sixth year in Kiev, twice the average posting for a career diplomat and, in his mind, an obvious sign of his importance. No president or secretary of state would dare to dole out such a strategic ambassadorship as a political plum—not with the ongoing fighting in eastern Ukraine against Russia-backed insurgents. No, Ambassador Stanford Thorpe was special. Educated at Groton, the private Episcopal preparatory boarding school that had graduated Franklin D. Roosevelt. On to Harvard College, the guaranteed entryway into the State Department. Ambassador Thorpe fit the decades-old stereotype of an anglophile statesman, and he was proud of it.

His comments today would be brief, delivered with measured enthusiasm, but with little actual meat that could bind him or the United States to any legal commitments beyond handshake promises. Then off to a leisurely lunch, hopefully with the twenty-something whom he'd just spotted seated in the second row, wearing a bit too much red lipstick and too short of a cheap wool skirt. Definitely Eastern European. Yes, he would mention her to John Harper. Have him extend a personal invitation to a private lunch with the ambassador.

But only after Ukraine's foreign minister finished publicly kissing up to the United States. Finally, Thorpe's turn. He rose slowly. Dignified. Buttoned his jacket. Shook the Ukrainian minister's hand while posing for obligatory photographs and finally stepped behind the oak podium.

"Good morning, my distinguished friends," he said, smiling, glancing again at the redhead.

The main doors at the back of the rectangular ballroom flew open. Looking directly down the aisle between rows of seats, Thorpe saw it all. Three figures. Ski masks. Kalashnikovs. Their gun barrels aimed toward the stage.

With a burst rate of a hundred rounds per minute, the bullets slammed into the wooden podium and swept across the stage, hitting both Thorpe and Ukraine's foreign minister.

Screams. Panic. A State Department bodyguard drew his Glock 19. The other, a Heckler & Koch MP5 submachine gun from inside his jacket. In the mayhem, both aimed at the same attacker, leaving the other two free to continue shooting.

The assailants had assumed the bodyguards would be wearing bullet-resistant vests. Head shots for a kill. The exchange ended quickly. The State Department detail critically wounded one assailant, who collapsed at the rear of the room onto the polished floor. Both Americans fell where they stood. Chief of Mission Harper lunged from his seat, bravely intending to throw himself atop Ambassador Thorpe. Bullets struck his back, killing him before he could reach the platform.

One of the masked terrorists fired indiscriminately into the panicked crowd. Two hundred attendees fighting to exit through a single side exit. The other terrorist helped his wounded comrade stand.

Brett Garrett entered the grand ballroom at the same moment the three assailants were about to exit through an unmarked side door directly opposite him that had been overlooked by attendees trying to escape. The first attacker ducked through it out of sight while Garrett raised his SIG Sauer P226 pistol. People hurrying by him blocked his view. He shifted to his left, finding a momentary gap, and squeezed off two rounds. His first missed, striking the door's molding near the two attackers. His second round hit the intruder helping his already wounded companion walk. Garrett's bullet pierced the assailant's right arm, forcing him to drop his buddy. He bolted through the open doorway to save himself. The attacker left behind was now motionless on the floor.

By now, Garrett's fellow private security guards had joined him. Two dashed across the ballroom in pursuit of the fleeing shooters. Garrett hurried onto the stage.

Vanity had kept Ambassador Thorpe from wearing the bulky protective vests that the State Department had made available, but the seasoned diplomat was no fool. Before arriving in Kiev, he'd flown to South America for a private fitting by the famous "Armored Armani," who hand-made bullet-resistant clothing for Latin American presidents and American entertainers, mostly gangster rappers. Thorpe had ordered a half-dozen suits, nearly indistinguishable from those tailored on London's Savile Row. His protective wear had blocked several of the 7.62x39 mm rounds, but the fabric had not stopped all of them. Three had penetrated the protective weave. One was now next to his heart. The ambassador was conscious but bleeding out.

Garrett had been with wounded men who were dying. He understood what Ambassador Thorpe was thinking. Surprise mixed with shock and anger. This was not supposed to be happening, not to him.

Through pleading eyes, Ambassador Thorpe stared at Brett Garrett kneeling over him. His final sight of a man whom he'd wanted sent away.

"My jacket," Thorpe whispered.

Garrett reached inside.

"No. Other side," Thorpe cajoled, coughing up blood.

Garrett removed a computer flash drive.

"The president," Thorpe said. "Promise me."

"A password?" Garrett asked. "Is there a password?"

There was no response. Ambassador Stanford Thorpe was dead.

Seven

Valerie Mayberry stepped off the Washington & Old Dominion Trail, which once had been a railroad track. A 1960s urban planner had decided that converting the right of way into a walking, biking, and running course would be a better use. Fast-forward fifty years. Local municipalities were spending millions constructing an aboveground subway line less than a mile away. Why hadn't bureaucrats thought ahead? They could have used the original train path for the subway line. Mayberry noticed such things.

Her ultralight running shoes left prints on the January-morning frost covering the swath of dried grass and weeds that separated the trail from the high-density Reston, Virginia, Town Center complex, some twenty-two miles east of Washington, D.C. Entering

Explorer Street, she jogged by PassionFish—all one word—a Millennial hot-spot eatery tucked among the mix of high-rise offices and condos.

Mayberry cared about history.

Some people heard music playing in their heads. A looping tune. Mayberry retained an unending tsunami of facts, most only found useful at trivia nights. Founded in 1964, Reston was the brainchild of Robert E. Simon Jr., who sold New York's Carnegie Hall to afford his vision of an urban utopia on 6,750 acres of farmland. Without restrictions based on race or income, he plotted a city composed of cozy villages each with lower- and middle-class and higher-end homes built together. Promising on paper, but troubled in reality. The nature paths turned dangerous to walk after dusk. The less expensive neighborhoods had become more expensive. Poorer families had been pushed into neighboring Herndon. That village was named after a Virginia naval officer who went down with his ship during a hurricane off the coast of Cape Hatteras.

A photographic memory and Adderall. A combination of four salts of the two enantiomers of amphetamine, a nervous system stimulant of the phenethylamine class. It helped her focus—although taking brain-enhancing drugs was generally not something the Federal Bureau of Investigation looked on favorably.

Mayberry's six-mile morning run had lifted her mood. Self-generated endorphins. She needed them. Each morning she awoke sad. Technically, it was called "persistent complex bereavement disorder," although psychiatrists couldn't agree whether it was a legitimate mental illness, stating only in the fifth edition of the *Diagnostic and Statistical Manual of Mental Disorders* that it was "under study" for possible later inclusion. She called it missing Noah. He had accepted her ADHD. She had accepted his constant need to save the world, right wrongs, and fight injustices. Her pragmatism versus his idealism. They had been a good fit.

Pit-pat, pit-pat—the sound of her shoes hitting the sidewalk slowed to a walk as she entered the Midtown, Reston's most exclusive condo building. Monthly HOA fees ran as high as many nearby house mortgages. Shiny ornate lobby. Valet parking. Doorman. Swimming pool. Owner's gym. Big-screen-television party area. The works, including views of the Blue Ridge Mountains from her sixteenth-floor unit.

"Good morning, Mrs. Williams," a perky recent community college grad with cascading blond hair and perfectly polished teeth chirped from behind the lobby's front desk.

Williams had been Noah's surname. She'd not legally

changed hers from Mayberry after they'd married, but she was identified on the condo's register of residents as Williams. It had made Noah happy and provided her with a thin veil of security if someone snooped into her professional life as an FBI agent. She still wore her wedding ring, although that had nothing to do with hiding her identity. There was something definite about taking it off—a final admission—that she wasn't yet ready to make.

"Good morning, Summer," Mayberry replied, silently wondering what kinds of parents name children after seasons.

Her cell phone rang while she was in the shower thinking of Noah.

Her wet feet hit the bathroom's heated tile floor. "This is Valerie."

It was her counterintelligence boss, Sally North.

An assassination. Kiev. Ambassador Thorpe dead.

"There's a briefing at nine," North explained. "The director will attend. Be on your best behavior. Think before you speak."

Mayberry dressed quickly. A burgundy structured blazer over a long-sleeve white J.Crew blouse with horizontal stripes and Paige Denim ankle-peg skinny stretch jeans, set off with a chunky gold necklace and black Ralph Lauren short heels. Her mother had been a stickler for style. She died without owning a pair of sweatpants or an article with a sports logo.

The mirror reminded Mayberry of her condition. Down exactly 17.2 pounds since Noah's death. An old copy of *Ultimate Jogging* magazine she'd read noted that world-class athletes weighed two pounds per inch. She was under that now, under what a five-foot, six-inch world-class runner should weigh. A dusting of makeup and downstairs to the underground parking garage to her silver Jaguar F-type R coupe; 550 horses. Zero to sixty in 3.9 seconds. The sound of the exhaust alone was worth its hundred-grand-plus price tag. Like cannon fire. A luxury she'd bought after Noah's death. He would have disapproved.

When CIA traitor Aldrich Hazen Ames had been caught spying for the Russians, the agency had been heavily criticized because no one at Langley had asked how a CIA employee could afford to pay cash for what was then a fifty-thousand-dollar Jaguar coupe—equal to his annual salary. The only eyebrows that her Jaguar had raised were jealous ones. Everyone in the FBI knew she had a trust fund. Word of such things spread quickly.

It took an hour to reach FBI headquarters on Pennsylvania Avenue. Congress had been arguing for decades about where to move the bureau. The 1975 building was crumbling. Fabric nets strung outside some upper floors had been installed to catch falling pieces. It had been an eyesore from the start. A gaping hole where a second floor should be. That was intentional to keep protestors from using ladders to break into the oddly shaped structure. An empty moat along one side. Again, designed to limit entry by demonstrators. It had been the late 1960s when the design was accepted. Rioting students. Vietnam. J. Edgar Hoover had been paranoid. No offices or windows on the street level. Instead, thick concrete support slabs. A courtyard. Rumor was Hoover had wanted spikes installed in the trees planted outside to keep them from being climbed.

Mayberry entered the director's conference room ten minutes before 9:00 a.m. Breakfast snacks. A clear signal that FBI director Archibald Davidson—Mack to his friends—would be attending. She didn't bother with any coffee, tea, or pastries.

She was the only woman present until Sally Norton entered precisely at nine accompanied by Davidson. He was old-school. Former chief of the Los Angeles Police Department. A political appointee but he knew his stuff. Gruff. Spit and polish. A lifelong law-and-order type.

"We believe Ambassador Thorpe was the main

target in Kiev," North announced while nodding at a large monitor. Everyone's eyes followed hers.

"When the shooting began, the television news crews filming the press conference ran for the exits," she said. Smirks by some listening to her. "This video is from permanent security cameras mounted in the Ukrainian Foreign Ministry's ceiling. Their government has asked for our forensic help."

The monitor split into four screens, each a different vantage point. Ambassador Thorpe could be seen poised behind the podium on one screen while three intruders shown on another burst into the ballroom.

Mayberry's eyes darted between images. Thorpe and Ukraine's minister hit by gunfire. Chief of Mission John Harper and two State Department bodyguards falling dead. Scrambling attendees. More gunfire. Three assailants hurrying toward a side door. One assisting another. Clearly wounded. An armed man appearing on the opposite side of the ballroom. Two pistol shots. One miss. The other causing the attacker holding his buddy to drop the injured assailant on the floor. Two escape. More security guards arrive. One makes his way to the stage, kneels above Ambassador Thorpe. The camera showed his face. Wait. Mayberry recognized him. Brett Garrett. His photo had been on every television network newscast during a Senate inquiry into Cameroon. A botched mission. A senator's son killed. Garrett was responsible. What was the former SEAL doing at a Ukraine press conference?

The monitors went dark.

Mayberry scanned her fellow agents in the briefing. Surely they had recognized Garrett, too. She had questions but remembered North's warning. No one dared interrupt Sally North during a briefing—unless it was the director. They were there only to listen, not question or comment. *All animals are equal, but some animals are more equal than others.* George Orwell and federal protocol.

Stay focused. Don't let your mind wander.

North continued: "The most logical suspects are Donetsk-based separatists being backed by the Kremlin. This has President Kalugin and General Gromyko's fingerprints all over it, but, so far, no direct links. Our best clue is the left-behind shooter."

Photos of a dead frozen face now appeared on the monitors. "INTERPOL identified him as a French national. Gabriel de Depardieu, whose address is a flat in Paris's Latin Quarter. Neither our people nor the DGSE has any records about him. No known ties to Russia or the separatists. Nothing on Facebook or social media. The French are leading the deep probe since he was one of their own."

A new face appeared. "French authorities have identified this American as someone of interest. Aysan Rivera, a twenty-six-year-old from Baltimore. Her name surfaced when the police were questioning Gabriel de Depardieu's landlord. Rivera and De Depardieu shared the same apartment for about a year. She stopped coming there six months ago when the landlord began hassling them for more money because De Depardieu was only paying for one tenant. The landlord knew her name because Rivera occasionally received mail from her family at De Depardieu's flat."

Director Davidson grunted. "Ms. Rivera has no interest in being cooperative," he said.

North continued, "Agents from our Baltimore field office paid her a visit. As soon as they mentioned Gabriel de Depardieu's name, she handed them her father's business card."

Another photo appeared on the monitor. A distinguished-looking fifty-something male posing with a similarly aged, striking woman. Both dressed in black-tie evening wear. "Rivera's father, Gregory Rivera, is an international lawyer and president of the American branch of a Turkish shipping company headquartered in Baltimore. His wife, Sirin Nadi Rivera, is the sister of the second-richest businessman in Turkey and a close friend of the Turkish president.

Neither of them or any of their four children have criminal records. No ties to terrorists or Moscow."

Director Davidson again jumped in. "Sirin Rivera called the Turkish ambassador after our agents showed up. The ambassador called the State Department and the White House to complain. Both called me. The Turkish ambassador is insisting we leave Aysan Rivera and her family alone. The family claims Rivera has not seen De Depardieu in the past six months. A mere college acquaintance."

North continued: "Aysan Rivera reportedly met Gabriel de Depardieu at the Ecole Normale Supérieure in Paris. For those unfamiliar with the ENS, it is the highest-ranked university in France and ranked among the top fifty universities in the world. It's within walking distance from Depardieu's flat. Rivera graduated last spring with a degree in philosophy. Since returning to Baltimore, she's lived in the Four Seasons condo building at Harbor East, overlooking Baltimore Harbor. Condos there sell for an average of a thousand dollars per square foot."

A few under-the-breath but audible *whews*.

"To summarize," Director Davidson said, "we have a twenty-six-year-old woman from an incredibly wealthy family with strong political connections. She has no history of criminal activity and neither she nor her family has any interest in being questioned about her dead French terrorist 'acquaintance.'" He stood. "The family already has hired a team of Washington lawyers to prevent us from interviewing Aysan Rivera. I have a meeting with the attorney general. Sally will take the point on the agency's role in the ongoing Kiev investigation."

North spoke for a few minutes after Davidson was gone, then asked Mayberry to stay behind while everyone else left.

"Valerie, I want you to go after Aysan Rivera. Be discreet."

"What's that mean, exactly?"

"Undercover. Befriend her. You're rich. She's rich. You just happen to bump into her. Off the books. A convenient coincidence. Get her to talk about De Depardieu."

"Rich families do background checks when someone suddenly pops up in their social circle, especially when their daughter is under suspicion of bedding a terrorist."

"Your family is well known. You're legit. You can walk the walk."

Mayberry was quiet for a moment. "What was Brett Garrett doing in Kiev?"

"You recognized him."

"Anyone who didn't should be fired. Is Garrett working for the agency or was he there as an actual security guard?"

"Why don't you ask him?" North said. "He's scheduled to land here later today. See what you can get out of him about the Kiev shooting. Human intel is always better than security footage."

Eight

With his right hand, Brett Garrett gently ran his fingers across his left side, moving downward under his armpit to his hip. Even through his plaid flannel shirt, he could feel the bumpy scars. Was there anything more painful than being burned? In the old days, medics had jabbed a shot of morphine into a wounded soldier. In 2011, the military began using a new wonder drug. "The lollipop." Such an innocent name. Medically OTFC. An acronym for oral transmucosal fentanyl citrate, 400 micrograms on a white stick that indeed was a lollipop.

"The fentanyl lollipop offers our medics a faster way to ease the pain of a battlefield injury because the drug can be absorbed more rapidly through a lozenge in the mouth than from a needle injected into a muscle," the Pentagon announced.

Apparently, no one had paid attention to its key ingredient: fentanyl. Only after the national opioid epidemic erupted had that drug become familiar to the public.

He turned uncomfortably in the narrow seat of the KLM Airbus A330 about to touch down at Dulles International Airport, west of downtown Washington, D.C. He'd never been afraid of dying. What was the phrase? Some run away, while others run forward. He'd not been afraid when Senator Cormac Stone had ordered him to appear before Congress for a pre-determined public humiliation about Cameroon. But the intense, physical craving, the constant need for painkillers, that had broken him.

Garrett unbuckled his seat belt so he could reach into the front right pocket of his denim jeans while sitting and withdraw his prescription. Two thin pieces of film quickly tucked under the tongue. Not fentanyl. Suboxone. The bitch's twin. The unintentional addict's pharmacological best friend. Buprenorphine and naloxone. It was supposed to offer salvation for the opioid addiction created during his months of hospitalization at Walter Reed Medical Center for treatment of burns and bullet wounds. The bullet holes had healed, and so had the burned skin. But his need for powerful painkillers had lingered. Suboxone was his best shot at getting clean, but he was still weaning and privately unsure if the cravings would ever end. It had started with a medic sticking a cute lollipop into his mouth while being airlifted out of Cameroon.

Relief.

Garrett always traveled light. Everything he needed, with one exception, was inside the backpack stored in the aircraft's overhead bin above him. His SIG Sauer P226 pistol was the exception. Most others had switched to Glock 19s, but the SIG had been a gift from Garrett's Navy SEAL instructor, a master chief petty officer—the same one who had given him the hated nickname Hillbilly. It had been the instructor's last SEAL class. Retirement. The SIG had been his combat weapon. Handed down with much respect. Garrett preferred a weapon that had already drawn blood. A buddy who flew military transport planes to Joint Air Base Andrews had promised to deliver it stateside. Garrett was traveling commercial. Too much hassle to explain it.

Garrett was coming home, but he didn't think of it like that. More like returning to a base camp. He'd bought a one-bedroom condo in Rosslyn not far from a metro stop. Two suits, one black, one gray, both off-the-rack, hung in its closet. Five collared shirts—three whites, two light blue. One tie. Red. Running gear, several pairs of denim jeans, T-shirts, boxers, and military fatigues. No car, but he owned a Norton Commando Interpol motorcycle—made in 1975 by the Brits for police use only. He'd recovered it from a barn in Belgium and personally rebuilt it. His daddy had taught him about engines and motorcycles, just like his daddy had taught him about shooting.

The Norton helped him unwind. When Garrett couldn't sleep, when the memories, second-guessing, and cravings became too much, he'd ride west at night along Highway 50 until he reached the right turn just outside Aldie, Virginia, onto the Snickersville Turnpike—although calling that winding bit of un-marked asphalt a turnpike was a grand embellishment. The two-way weaved through scenic Virginia hills that took travelers across a 180-plus-year-old stone bridge that enemies Robert E. Lee and "Fighting Joe" Hooker had both crossed at times. It wasn't Civil War history that called him. In a vanishing countryside being over-run with subdivided tract houses, Snickersville was one of the last rural stretches still defined by waist-high stone walls and pastures. There were no stoplights. As he leaned into the curves, the Norton's headlight would cast its beam only twenty yards into the curving blackness. Glowing eyes. A scampering raccoon. A fear-frozen deer. No time to react. No time for error. That was when the music started, as his favorite author, Hunter S. Thompson, had described it. The dance with fate. Pushing life to its edge. A patch of sand. A greasy spot. The slightest miscalculation. Catastrophe. Was he suicidal? No, it was a way for him to become completely focused. To drive out the distracting demons. The second-guessing that never ended. Some nights Garrett couldn't say. Maybe it was suicidal. All he knew was he could sleep soundly after those late-night runs. He could momentarily forget the brown tabs now dissolving under his tongue and the dishonorable-discharge papers that he kept at the bottom of a foot locker in his condo closet.

Besides the Norton, Garrett's other prized possessions were tools of his craft. A stainless-steel, nearly indestructible watch fitted on his wrist with a compass and altimeter and water resistant to a thousand feet. Behind a false closet wall in his condo, sixteen high-quality firearms, ranging from a modified M79 40 mm grenade launcher to a sniper's Mark 12 Mod 0/1 Special Purpose Rifle to a semicompact polymer Jericho 941 semi-auto pistol—a gift from a Mossad officer. He also owned a Glock 19, just because.

"Coming home?" the woman next to him asked as the KLM's wheels touched down on the Dulles runway. Garrett guessed she was eighty, with gray hair coiled tightly into a bun.

"No," he replied in a kind voice. "I'm from Arkansas." It wasn't a lie, although he'd not lived in that state since graduating from high school. The DMV—shorthand for the District, Maryland, and Virginia metro area—was considered a stopover for many who lived there—even those who'd spent decades in Washington.

"Arkansas," the woman repeated with a wrinkled smile. "I have a niece who lives in Fayetteville."

"Tusk. The Big Red," he replied.

A confused look.

"University of Arkansas. School mascots. Razorbacks."

"Oh," the woman replied, "no, my niece moved there. She graduated from Black Hills State up in South Dakota."

"Then she's a Yellow Jacket."

"You certainly know your college mascots."

Garrett's father had been a high school baseball coach who'd dreamed of moving up to the college level from his Genoa High School team—the Dragons. East of Texarkana, off Highway 196. His old man had started grooming him as a pitcher as soon as Garrett was old enough to hold a baseball. Pressuring him, making him spend hours practicing, convinced his boy would make the pros. In high school, he'd held the record for an Arkansas high school kid throwing the fastest pitch ever—nearly a hundred miles per hour. His mother had been quiet, a librarian. Both killed when his inebriated father had plowed their car into a tree late one Friday night. Garrett was out with friends, having just graduated from high school. He'd not thrown a baseball since then. Nor had he gone back to Arkansas. Now he was an addict. Just like his old man.

"It was nice speaking to you," the older passenger said as she maneuvered herself into the aisle to deplane.

Garrett spotted the four of them waiting in the terminal as soon as he exited the gangway. Who but federal agents could greet an international passenger prior to Customs and Immigration?

One was wearing a blue Transportation and Security Administration (TSA) shirt; two others wore coats and ties, and the lone woman a gray pantsuit. She flashed a U.S. State Department credential as he approached; the tallest man showed an FBI badge, the third simply said he was "Ted," a tipoff that he was CIA. The TSA worker was merely an escort whose name was of no consequence.

"We've come for the flash drive," Ted said, thrusting an open palm out like a neighborhood bully demanding another child's Halloween candy. His curtness irked Garrett. As a SEAL, he'd learned to study faces, interpret voices, spot tells like tea leaves in the bottom of a cup read by a fortune-teller. Garrett looked at Ted and saw contempt in his eyes. Judgment. Cameroon. But more. Ted was selling wolf tickets, talking tough without the cojones to stand his mud. A desk jockey.

"Back off," Garrett said. "Thorpe asked me to give it directly to the president."

Ted smirked.

"We understand," the State Department woman said, playing conciliatory. "That's what you said in Kiev after you first reported receiving it and then refused to turn it over. But you are here now, and we'd like to have it."

"Get real, Garrett," Ted said. "The president isn't going to meet someone like you. Now, hand it over."

Maybe it was a lack of sleep. Maybe it was the Suboxone. But it probably was Ted's attitude.

"I think I'll hold on to it. You don't look like the president," Garrett said.

"Listen, smart-ass," Ted replied. The blue veins in his neck were beginning to surface.

"Let's not make a scene," the woman interrupted in a hushed voice.

Garrett glanced around the gateway. His elderly seat-mate had hesitated a few feet away and was watching, as were many of the passengers still walking off the flight. It would be only a few moments before someone pulled out a cell phone and began recording.

Garrett had never believed the president would meet him personally. Still, he didn't like being treated as a mere errand boy, even if that was his only role. It wasn't only his ego that had kept him from surrendering the flash drive in Kiev. The three attackers had escaped through an unmarked exit. Maybe they'd simply been lucky. Maybe they'd done due diligence. Or maybe someone had *helped* them. Gotten them inside early. Told them about the side exit.

"Mr. Garrett," the State Department woman said quietly, "your promise will be kept. The White House sent us here and the president is appreciative, but this flash drive is now part of an international murder investigation, and the three of us have been delegated by our agencies to secure it on behalf of a joint federal task force."

"That doesn't include you," Ted said.

"Then put it in writing," Garrett replied. "Give me a receipt."

"You're joking, right?" Ted scoffed.

"Chain of custody," Garrett replied. "Doesn't need to be too detailed. For you, Ted, we can keep the words simple—'One flash drive given by Ambassador Stanford Thorpe in Kiev to Brett Garrett who is now surrendering it to me, as an official of my respective agency with my personal guarantee that it will be delivered to the president of the United States.' That will do nicely."

"I'm not giving you any damn receipt," Ted snarled.

"Mr. Garrett, I'm not entirely clear why you need a receipt," the woman said.

"If what's on this flash drive somehow leads to a congressional investigation, I want a paper trail. I've already had a target on my back once. In fact, let's include something about how I have no knowledge of the flash drive's contents."

"We don't know that though, do we?" the woman said. "You could have opened it."

"You just asked me to trust you," he replied. "I guess you'll have to trust me now? Besides, it's password protected."

"Then you have looked at it," Ted said. "Hand over the damn drive now."

Garrett let his backpack slip from his fingers onto the carpet. His hands were freely hanging at his side. Ready.

"Gentlemen, none of this macho posturing is necessary," the woman whispered. Reaching into her purse, she removed a notepad and began writing. She signed it and handed to the FBI agent to read. He signed it and passed it to the TSA officer who was standing next to him.

"Hey, man, I got no idea what this is about," the TSA worker said. "They told me to escort you to the gate. I'm not signin' nothin'."

Garrett said, "I don't need your signature." He looked at Ted.

Ted ripped the paper from the TSA officer's hand. "I'm not signing this, either."

The woman started to say something, but Garrett cut her short. Plucking the paper from Ted, he said, "Ted, right?"

Garrett wrote: "Also present, Ted—CIA." He then slowly folded the note and tucked it in his back pant pocket. "Two signatures should be enough."

From his backpack, he removed the flash drive, ignored Ted, who was still standing in front of him, and gave it to the woman.

"Thank you," she said. "You'll need to be debriefed."

"Later, after a warm shower," Garrett said. "But not by Ted. I'm a civilian now. I might need to check with my lawyer to see if I can cooperate."

Ted glared at him as the others turned to go. "You're a national disgrace," the CIA operative said.

Garrett watched Ted rejoin the others. Twenty minutes later, Garrett emerged from the airport's terminal and spotted a black Mercedes-Benz GLS 550 SUV parked next to a sign that said NO STOPPING and NO LOITERING.

Thomas Jefferson Kim stepped out from behind its wheel.

"If you're so damn important, why don't you have a driver?" Garrett asked, tossing his backpack into the SUV's rear and slipping into the front passenger's seat.

"Don't you start ragging me about my driving. It's racist just because I'm Korean."

"It's got nothing to do with your ethnicity. It's got everything to do with you almost getting me killed every time I ride with you."

Kim grinned and pulled away from the curb directly in front of a car whose driver had to swerve.

"I sent you to Ukraine to keep you out of the public eye and what do you do?" Kim said, completely unaware of what had just happened. "Senator Stone called State this morning. You got any idea what my embassy contracts are worth?"

"What'd you expect?"

"There's an old Korean expression—'It is a world

where people will cut off your nose and eat it if you close your eyes.'"

"What's that mean?"

"It's a dog-eat-dog world."

"Then why didn't you say it's a dog-eat-dog world? And in this scenario, who's the dog eating?"

"All subtlety is lost on you."

Garrett was Kim's employee, but they didn't act like it. Their roles had been reversed when they first met in Asadabad, Afghanistan, near the eastern Pakistan border. Kim had been fresh meat, a computer geek sent by the Navy as part of a "reconstruction team." Most Americans didn't realize the Navy had people in-country. They thought they were only aboard ships. Kim's job was winning the hearts and minds of a fledgling Afghan provincial government. Garrett's job was killing Islamic jihadists. Both were good at what they did. Three months in, an ambush. IEDs. RPGs. Garrett dragged a wounded Kim to safety. His injuries were his ticket home. A Purple Heart. An honorable discharge. Within a year, he'd become Washington's newest cyber-security wunderkind. Gobbling up other Beltway bandits with juicy government contracts, expanding into the ex-military security guard business at embassies. U.S. Marines were there to destroy all classified information if under local attack. State had protective details assigned for each ambassador and top aides. But the first line of defense outside the embassy grounds was the host country—only, dialing 911 didn't do much good in nations hostile to the U.S. That's where Kim's private ex-military force plugged the gap. Civilian warriors. Modern-day mercenaries. Recent world tensions had made that gap much wider and much more lucrative. At thirty-two, Kim had become a multi-millionaire running a global company from his Tysons Corner sanctuary. Brett Garrett had taken a much different path after their stint together. After Cameroon, it had been Kim who'd rescued him when he'd become an untouchable.

"Senator Stone is a vengeful—" Kim cut short his own sentence as he smashed his palm against the SUV's horn at a driver who'd cut him off.

Garrett chuckled. "Seriously. You need a driver."

"Don't be that guy. He cut me off."

"Just saying, with all your money—and stop crying about Stone. You knew about him and me, but you hired me anyway."

"It sucks to be you. My lawyers will deal with Stone and State. Kiev might actually be good for future business."

Kim honked at another motorist, this one for moving too slow. He swerved around the car and let loose with a string of Korean words. The other driver raised his third finger.

"You're not doing much to change ethnic stereotypes," Garrett said.

"Time is money, and there's a guest waiting in my office. FBI special agent Valerie Mayberry. My secretary told her to come at three o'clock, but she showed up at two."

"Why? The bureau, agency, and State already greeted me at the gate."

Kim shrugged. "She knew I was picking you up. Said she needed to speak privately to you. ASAP."

"Did it ever cross your mind that I might not want to speak to her? ASAP?"

"Play nice. I've got contracts with the bureau, too. Besides, you are single and lonely and don't have any friends except for me, and she's attractive."

"You've already met her? And you're my boss, not my friend."

"Looked her up. Twenty-eight, no Facebook page, no LinkedIn, actually little public on social media."

"For a cyber expert, that's pretty weak."

"Which is my point. Someone's cleaned up after her."

"Undercover?"

"My guess."

"Okay, let's not drag this out. If you didn't meet her and she's not on Facebook and she's working under-cover, how do you know what she looks like?"

"A photo. She's *pungbuhan* and a widow."

"Wealthy."

"Your Korean is getting better."

"*Neoui sumgyeol-i agchwiga nanda.*"

Kim laughed and hit the steering wheel with his palm at Garrett's bungled mispronunciation. "I believe you just told me my breath smelled bad."

"Then my Korean is getting better. A widow?"

"A photo at her husband's funeral posted by a friend."

"That's the photo? You saw a picture of a widow at a funeral, and you thought she looked hot? You need treatment."

Kim chuckled. "Her husband was a magazine re-porter who got himself killed in the White Mountains."

"A real reporter or agency?"

"C'mon, you know CIA rules prohibit their em-ployees from posing as reporters."

Garrett grunted.

Kim said, "He was a legit journalist and an unlucky one. He talked his way onto a supply helo making a delivery in the mountains. Wrong day. Wrong flight. A green on blue. Afghan commando, who we'd trained, blew an entire Sea Knight to pieces with a vest. Un-lucky bastard."

"A Sea Knight?" Garrett said. "You sure. I thought we dumped them years ago."

"I tell you about this reporter being blown to pieces, and you're concerned about the helo? You're the one who needs treatment."

Kim drove his Mercedes onto State Route 7. A mile later, he entered a side street that dead-ended at an eleven-story steel-and-glass building bearing the letters IEC. Kim entered an underground parking garage protected by a steel door. His parking spot was marked: THOMAS JEFFERSON KIM, PRESIDENT, INTEL-EYE-CHECK.

"Delivered safe and sound," Kim announced proudly. "You can apologize now about my driving."

"Intel-Eye-Check is a really stupid name," Garrett said, unbuckling his seat belt.

Nine

An office can say much about its occupant. From her seat on a chrome-rimmed white leather couch inside IEC president Thomas Jefferson Kim's outer office, Valerie Mayberry gazed at the only piece of artwork hanging on the room's bone-white walls. A 1932 Pablo Picasso painting. *Le Rêve*, French for "The Dream." Why had Kim chosen it? If an original, it cost at least $60 million. Showing off? Insecure? Or could he simply like the painting? Sometimes a cigar is just a cigar.

"The Picasso," she said aloud to the two Korean women seated across from her behind matching chrome-and-glass desks. "A limited print?"

"No," the one to Mayberry's right answered. "My husband doesn't buy imitations."

"Your husband," Mayberry replied and instantly thought about Noah. They could never have worked together. She was persnickety, left-brained. He was disorganized and said whatever thought popped into his head. She was nagged by worries. He didn't fret about anything. They had filled the holes in each other's personalities, creating a better-balanced person. At least most times.

Her mind continued to wander. Her decision to join the FBI had not pleased her parents, which made it more appealing to her. Earning money had never interested her, largely because she had never been without it. She had initially flirted with becoming a psychiatrist. However, the idea of listening to the worried well complain about not having friends, or their third marriage breakup, bored her. Dealing with schizophrenia was more of a neurological issue than a personality one. Forensic psychiatry held limited appeal. Most prisoners had the same cookie-cutter backgrounds—childhood trauma, drugs or alcohol addictions driving their criminal activity, or simply antisocial disorders such as narcissism mixed with a lack of empathy. Working in the spy-versus-spy game was much more challenging. It required understanding human behavior, trickery, and intellect. She enjoyed wandering in what poet T. S. Eliot described as a "wilderness of mirrors." She'd studied the life of James Jesus Angleton, the legendary American spy hunter who'd overseen counterintelligence operations for twenty years during the Cold War. It had been Angleton who'd looked for hidden meanings in the KGB's actions, suspecting everyone, always searching for that unidentified inside man, the double agent, the ultimate traitor. His paranoia had paralyzed the agency, ruined careers, and ultimately condemned him as a mole hunter who'd stared too long into the abyss and had been swallowed up by it.

Mayberry had read the complete Eliot stanza: "In a wilderness of mirrors / What will the spider do." Yet another quote came to her. One from her favorite novel, *The Spy Who Came in from the Cold*. John le Carré. "Counterintelligence people are like wolves chewing dry bones—you have to take away the bones and make them find new quarry. . . ." Mayberry felt comfortable wandering in the mirrors, chewing on new bones.

She'd chewed every bone of Noah's death to powder. "Recovery" was not a straight line, her therapist had said. Mayberry was stuck in anger.

She recognized Brett Garrett as soon as he entered with Thomas Jefferson Kim. Standing, she extended her hand. First to Kim, who was closest to her, and next to Garrett. She sized up Garrett knowing he was doing the exact same to her.

Garrett's first impression: not so much beautiful as arresting. No high cheekbones, porcelain skin, or long, flowing locks. Garrett studied her eyes. Windows into the soul, right? He sensed melancholy, or was he projecting that onto her because Kim had mentioned she was a widow? No, it was there. He was good at reading people. Mayberry could hide the down-curve of her lips, conceal the sadness, but grief was a dogged antagonist.

When it came to assessing Garrett, Mayberry had the upper hand. She'd studied his FBI file, at least the pages available to her. She'd read about his Arkansas roots. His father's alcoholism. How his parents had been killed when his father crashed their car while drunk. How Garrett had refused baseball scholarship offers. Choosing the United States Naval Academy. Multiple tours in Afghanistan. SEAL training. His last assignment: the CIA's Special Activities Division, Special Operations Group—the most secretive special operations force in the country. No one made it to that level without being mentally and physically tough. It was difficult to separate SEALs from the movie stereotypes: married to work. More at ease playing flip-cup and bench-pressing with their bros than spending a night at a Kennedy Center performance or learning to discern the five characteristics of a fine pinot noir. Unable to commit to more than a one-night stand.

Uncommunicative. Sentences in grunts. Obedient to orders. Love of country. Based on Garrett's close-cropped military haircut, signs of a broken nose, and muscular build, he checked all the predictable boxes. Certainly, he was nothing like her Noah, who hadn't been in a physical altercation since fourth grade, when he'd gotten his nose bloodied by a bully. Mayberry tried to look behind the Hollywood clichés. Like him, she was searching for clues. His face betrayed nothing. His background records showed that Cameroon had been a tipping point in his life. He'd been on a career fast track that had run off the rails in Africa. He'd had a fiancée, but after that, she'd left him. He'd begun seeing a psychiatrist and then had disappeared for several months. No one had known where he'd gone. And then he'd resurfaced, and Kim had hired him.

"Pleasure to meet you, Mr. Garrett," Mayberry said, releasing his hand.

"Likewise," he replied.

"Let's take this conversation into my inner sanctum," Kim suggested, leading them between the two secretaries' desks toward a solid, stainless-steel door. Kim touched a biometric fingerprint door lock and stepped aside, allowing Mayberry to enter first.

Unlike the pristine, Spartan outer office, Kim's "sanctum" was in disarray. Piles of papers stacked in rows on the royal blue carpet. Two golf bags. A dead plant. Books with yellow paper slips jutting from their pages. On the wall to their left were a dozen flat-screen monitors showing muted news channels. On their right was a massive floor-to-ceiling window made of specialty glass that was both bullet resistant and (through advanced technology that IEC had patented) impenetrable to outside snooping devices. Positioned behind Kim's desk, which they were now facing, were photos of Kim with Washington dignitaries and entertainment celebrities. Three computer screens were positioned on his desk with yellow reminder sticky notes in English and Korean stuck along their edges. Two desk items caught Mayberry's eye. The first was a *Big Lebowski* talking bobblehead doll. Actor Jeff Bridges molded in plastic. *"I do mind. The Dude minds!"* it declared in a recording of Bridges's voice when Kim dropped his clasped hands onto his desktop, causing it to shake. Next to Kim's ten-dollar re-creation of the Los Angeles slacker was what appeared to be a live hand grenade.

"Reminders," he said, nodding at the grenade and plastic Dude.

"Of what?" she asked.

"The absurdity and fragility of life."

Garrett showed a half smile. "He just likes his toys."

Mayberry chose the only seat facing the desk without papers on it. Garrett shoved the papers from another chair.

"What brings you here, Agent Mayberry?" Kim asked.

Mayberry removed a photograph from her front-flap satchel.

"This is Gabriel de Depardieu. A Frenchman. Do either of you recognize him?"

Kim gave a shake of his head no.

"He's the dead terrorist," Garrett said. "The last time I saw him, he was prone on a marble floor in Kiev."

"Did you ever see him before the terrorist attack? Loitering outside the foreign ministry—before the press conference? Entering the building?"

Garrett thought back to that morning. Waiting outside in the chase car for Don Marks to take his cigarette break, slipping the Suboxone tabs under his tongue. Was it possible he'd missed something?

"Mr. Garrett," she said in a demanding voice. "Did you see anything suspicious?"

"Agent Mayberry, I did not see three men carrying Kalashnikovs walk into the ministry wearing black ski masks."

Kim said, "The terrorists were probably already inside when Ambassador Thorpe arrived. Any lapse in security was on the Ukrainians' part, not my people. They're all ex-military. Highly trained and excellent at their jobs."

"Then why didn't you and the other private guards go into the building to help protect Ambassador Thorpe?" she asked.

Garrett didn't like her tone. "We were told to remain in our cars. You'll have to ask the RSO why—that's shorthand for regional security officer."

"I know what an RSO is," she said.

He assumed that she did but had said it anyway.

"It might interest you to know the RSO told our agents in Kiev that Ambassador Thorpe didn't want any IEC employees inside because of you. He was afraid someone in the media might recognize you."

"Hold on," Kim said. "Garrett isn't to blame. If anything, he was a hero in Kiev."

"Just being thorough and factual," she said, staring at Garrett, waiting for him to react.

"If that's what the RSO said, that's what he said," Garrett replied. "And if he said that, he is even more stupid than I suspected. If we had been inside, Ambassador Thorpe might still be alive."

"When the shooting began," she continued, "everyone inside panicked and began running toward a side exit—"

"No," Garrett said, interrupting. "Not everyone ran toward the exit."

She seemed confused.

"Ambassador Thorpe, Ukraine's foreign minister, two State Department protective detail employees, and John Harper didn't go anywhere because they were dead," he said.

She frowned. "The three terrorists didn't exit through the ballroom's rear doors. Instead, they used an unmarked exit across the room from the side doors, isn't that correct?"

"Mahogany," Garrett said. "The entire interior wall was covered with mahogany panels. Post–World War Two construction. The only indication an exit door was there was its doorknob."

"Which explains why the crowd didn't run toward it," she said. "Yet the terrorists knew about it. Moving on, neither you nor any of the other IEC private security guards were watching that exit, were you?"

"We arrived at the front of the ministry. From that vantage point, there was no visible gap between it and the buildings next to it. That door—the one the terrorists used—was located at the back of the ministry. It opened into a narrow walkway where trash cans were kept. None of us could have seen it."

"But you would have seen it if your team had stationed someone at the back side of the ministry, rather than having everyone sit outside the front entrance."

Addressing Kim, Mayberry said, "Isn't it standard practice for IEC security guards to be aware and cover every possible entrance and exit when an ambassador enters a building overseas? Seems rather rudimentary."

"Why are you trying to blame this on Garrett and my IEC guys?" Kim asked, clearly offended.

"I'm not blaming anyone. I'm simply trying to understand what happened. If Mr. Garrett and your people made mistakes, then we need to know what they were."

"Your buddies at Dulles said I would be debriefed later," Garrett said. "I've never been debriefed by a single FBI agent. You guys always travel in pairs. So why are you really here?"

Mayberry reached into her satchel and removed a photo of Aysan Rivera. "Did you ever see this woman in Kiev?"

Garrett studied Rivera's enlarged passport photo.

"Who is she?" Kim asked.

"That doesn't matter."

"No, I never saw her there."

She tucked the photo back into her bag.

"Are you certain the three assailants were men?" she asked. "Weren't they all wearing ski masks?"

"I only saw two of them well," he said. "I saw the dead one and the one I shot in the arm who dropped his buddy and fled. The third one had already exited when I entered the ballroom, so I can't fully answer your question."

"Mr. Garrett, let's assume you were one of the terrorists. Would you have been the first out the door or would you have stayed behind and provided cover fire while your wounded buddy was being helped through it?"

"I'm not a terrorist."

"I'm asking for your opinion."

"I thought you wanted facts," he replied.

She sighed. "Call it analysis, then."

"Someone with professional military training, who hadn't been wounded, would have provided cover fire. Unless his assignment was to be the first one out of the building to put down any security guards waiting for them."

"There's a third explanation," Mayberry said. "If the first terrorist was a woman, she might be used to going through doors first."

"Seems like a stretch," he said. "You did ask for my opinion."

"You don't open doors for women?"

"Not when I'm shooting people."

Kim joined their Q-and-A. "Can't you tell from security tapes if one of the terrorists was smaller than the others?"

"Not all women are petite," Mayberry said.

"Or tactful," Garrett added.

Mayberry picked up her satchel. "Gentlemen, thank you for your time. Because this is an ongoing investigation, please keep our discussion private."

Kim rose from behind his desk. "I didn't hear nothing that was said." He pushed an app on his watch, unlocking and opening his electronically controlled office door.

She started toward the door but stopped.

"Is there something else, Agent Mayberry?" Kim asked.

"'I didn't hear nothing?' You used a double negative."

"English is my second language," Kim replied, smiling. "I prefer Korean."

After she was gone, Garrett said, "You prefer Korean? What was that about?"

"Mayberry's smart," he replied.

"And where does that get her?" Garrett asked.

"Some people like that in a woman. Especially a hot one."

Ten

The presidential limousine, aka "the Beast," rode northeast from the White House en route to the Basilica of the National Shrine of the Immaculate Conception. Ambassador Stanford Thorpe's funeral was today, three days after his assassination.

"Our best can't open the flash drive," CIA director Harold Harris said.

"Brett Garrett hasn't a clue?" President Randle Fitzgerald asked.

"None."

"Where's Garrett now?"

"Cooling his heels in his Rosslyn condo."

The president gazed through the heavily tinted passenger window. "I've never liked funerals."

"No one does, sir."

"Especially when one of the bastards attending either knows or was involved in murdering Thorpe. I'm talking about the Russians."

"Knowing and proving, sir," Harris replied.

The day was overcast, and the president had awakened in a foul mood. A murdered ambassador. It made him look weak. It made America look weak. The Brits might have bodies of former Russian spies poisoned by the Kremlin stacking up, but America was not Great Britain. He needed to put an end to this—now. Or another attack would happen.

He glanced forward as his motorcade entered the basilica's manicured grounds. President Fitzgerald was Southern Baptist. He didn't know much about the basilica or really care. He'd never bothered to tour it or learn it was the largest Catholic church in not just the United States but all North America, one of the ten largest churches in the world, and the tallest habitable building in Washington, D.C. Just the same, it was not the nation's official "National House of Prayer," an honor bestowed by Congress on its religious rival, the Washington National Cathedral, a neo-Gothic Presbyterian church where the funerals for most prominent national luminaries, including presidents, usually were held.

"Didn't see Thorpe as Catholic," Fitzgerald said as the motorcade stopped outside a side entrance.

"A bit hard to picture him as an altar boy," Harris replied in a soft voice.

"Now, now, let's not talk ill of the dead," Fitzgerald said, chuckling.

The president was seated inside. Next to Thorpe's only son and relatives. In chairs placed in front of the church's permanent wooden pews. Closer to the altar. After a priest blessed the casket and sprinkled it with holy water, an organist began playing "O God, Our Help in Ages Past" and President Fitzgerald's mind wandered. He thought about his own funeral, and who would attend it. Probably depended on how far he was from power when he passed. By the time the organist had finished, he had moved on. Russia. What could he do?

It became apparent that he would have plenty of time to ponder options. The full mass dragged on for two long hours, during which time the president nervously tapped his foot. He had work to do. Finally, a liturgist, under the watchful eyes of his eminence the archbishop of Washington, delivered a final send-off. "In peace let us take our brother to his place of rest."

Thorpe's son had requested privacy at the burial site—thankfully. No need for the president to go graveside. Outside, he shook hands with the son. Spoke obligatory words about how great Thorpe had been.

How he had faithfully served his nation. Then back inside the church. By the time the hearse pulled away, a reception line had formed. Washington was returning to the now. Press flesh. Cut deals. Plot. Conduct the nation's business. No matter how great the fallen, they were the past and pushed to the side.

Secret Service agents separated dignitaries from curiosity seekers at the reception doorway. Only foreign diplomats, members of Congress, other senior government officials, and lobbyists were allowed inside where the president was holding court.

President Fitzgerald was a big man. Once handsome, now with drooping jowls. Once an NFL quarterback. Twice MVP. Once in shape. No longer. Being a quarterback required quick decision making. He'd retained that ability. He was from an era when a handful of quarterbacks still called plays. They were team leaders. He was one of them. He wasn't a follower. His football fame led to an easy election win, first into the House, next the Senate, representing the good people of New Hampshire. Finally, the White House. At age sixty-seven, he remained a dominating presence. A Washington reporter had compared the president's blue eyes to the color of a calm mountain lake on a chilly winter morning and his temper to that of an angry charging bull wounded with banderillas. A bit too flowery, but Fitzgerald had loved it.

A State Department aide stood behind him at the reception, whispering names of foreign dignitaries approaching in the receiving line. He needed no reminder when he noticed Yakov Prokofyevich Pavel, Russia's deputy minister of foreign affairs.

"Mr. President, I was there in Kiev," Pavel said, shaking the president's hand. "As a guest attending the news conference."

"Clearly you weren't a target," Fitzgerald replied.

"Yes, I was most fortunate. My bodyguards shielded me, and we were seated close to the side exit. But enough about this horrible event." Pavel leaned in close and whispered: "A good glass in the bishop's hostel in the devil's seat. It's the password to the flash drive."

Fitzgerald said loudly, "Thank you."

The Russian diplomat continued down the receiving line.

Back in "the Beast," returning to the White House, President Fitzgerald and Director Harris analyzed what had happened.

"Yakov Pavel made a point of telling me that he had been in Kiev at the press conference," Fitzgerald said. "Next, he told me a password for the flash drive."

"The natural conclusion is that Pavel gave the flash drive to Ambassador Thorpe in Kiev before he was murdered and now Pavel wants you to open it."

The flash drive, an IT expert named Oscar Lopez, and a new portable computer freshly removed from its box were waiting for them. Harris had ordered a new computer be brought to the White House. Its network connectivity had been disabled out of the box to prevent the building's Wi-Fi from kicking in. He wasn't going to risk inserting an unknown drive from the Russians into the White House's system.

Fitzgerald and Harris watched as Lopez typed: "A good glass in the bishop's hostel in the devil's seat."

Incorrect password.

He repeated it without spaces.

Incorrect password.

He tried no capitals.

Incorrect password.

He tried with all capitals.

Incorrect password.

"Mr. President," Lopez said, "this password doesn't appear to be working."

"Try it again."

He did. It didn't work.

"I know what I heard," the president grumbled.

"It's a phrase," Harris said. "Probably from a movie

or poem. Oscar, please use a computer with Internet access to do a search."

Lopez left them to use a different computer before returning moments later.

"It's from 'The Gold Bug,' a short story by Edgar Allen Poe. The story contains a cryptogram that Poe challenged readers to decipher."

"A cryptogram," Harris repeated. "Pavel used an old Poe cryptogram as a password. Clever."

"In the book, the cryptogram contained the directions to a buried treasure hidden by Captain Kidd. I've copied all the information about 'The Gold Bug' off Wikipedia." He showed them a sheet of paper. "Here's the actual cryptogram that Poe's readers had to decipher."

```
53‡‡†305))6*;4826)4‡.)4‡);806*;48†8
¶  60))85;;]8*;:‡*8†83(88)5*†;46(;88*96
*?;8)*‡(;485);5*†2:*‡(;4956*2(5*—4)8
¶  8*;4069285);)6†8)4‡‡;1(‡9;48081;8:8‡
1;48†85;4)485†528806*81(‡9;48;(88;4
(‡?34;48)4‡;161;:188;‡?;
```

Continuing, Lopez said, "If you decipher the first sentence of Poe's cryptogram correctly, it reads: 'A good glass in the bishop's hostel in the devil's seat.'"

"That's the exact phrase Pavel said!" President Fitzgerald exclaimed. "See if the cryptogram's first line works."

Lopez typed:

53‡‡†305))6*;4826)4‡.)4‡);806*;48†8 ¶60))85;

The flash drive opened, revealing a single file. "Only for the eyes of President Randle Fitzgerald" was marked on it.

"Great work, Oscar," Harris said. "You can wait outside now." Addressing the president, he added, "Do you want to open this file alone or should I stay here."

"Don't be ridiculous. You stay. Now let's see what these Russian bastards are up to."

He clicked on the file, and a video recording of Pavel appeared.

Eleven

Yakov Prokofyevich Pavel exited the Tupolev Tu-134 twin-engine jet aircraft minutes after it landed at Ostafyevo International Airport, on the southern outskirts of Moscow. The 1960s-era airplane was nicknamed "Crusty" when it first appeared in the West. An aeronautical insult because it was considered substandard. After a 2011 crash killed forty-seven, the Kremlin said all remaining Crusty planes would be grounded. Russia, being Russia, still used them, although they were generally assigned to transport lower-level government officials, not someone of Pavel's status.

General Andre Borsovich Gromyko had arranged for the Tu-134 to carry Pavel to Washington, D.C., for Ambassador Thorpe's funeral. It was an obvious slight.

Pavel had been in line to become Russia's foreign minister, but that was before Gromyko had targeted him. Gromyko was orchestrating a power takeover. Most of Pavel's peers already had been forced out. Pavel had stubbornly stayed. He still had important connections, but for how long. The general was merely dancing on Russian president Vyachesian Kalugin's strings.

Pavel had detested Kalugin since his arrival in Moscow from St. Petersburg. It was contempt at first sight. An uncouth personality. Extreme grandiosity. A Visigoth had become president and Pavel had watched it happen and, more important, understood why.

After the Soviet Union had been broken into fifteen separate countries, Russia had been viewed as a failed nation. Its people had been humbled. Kalugin had restored Russia's pride. He'd reminded the Russian people that their country still was a world player, if for no other reason than it controlled large numbers of nuclear missiles. Kalugin was loved by the Russian people—not because of what he did—but because of his carefully crafted image as a strongman willing to thumb his nose at a seemingly all-powerful America.

The United States had foolishly underestimated Kalugin. Pavel had not. The seasoned diplomat had recognized that Kalugin posed a threat, not only to the West, but to the entire world. The president's ultimate goal was the reunification of the old Soviet empire—and then, perhaps a bit more. Crimea had been his tiptoe into international waters. No one had stopped him.

A student of history, Pavel had seen a troubling similarity reemerging from the past. After World War I, Germany had been hit with punitive territorial, military, and economic penalties outlined in the 1919 Treaty of Versailles. It had been stripped of 13 percent of its land, including territories with names that few today would recognize. France had reclaimed Alsace-Lorraine, Belgium had taken control of Eupen and Malmedy, Denmark had gobbled up Northern Schleswig, Poland had taken parts of West Prussia and Silesia, Czechoslovakia won the Hultschin District, and Lithuania had been awarded Memel, a small strip in East Prussia along the Baltic Sea. In total, one-tenth of Germany's population, nearly seven million Germans living in 27,000 square miles, suddenly found themselves under what they considered foreign rule and reduced to second-class citizenship.

That land grabbing had left deep-rooted bitterness. Years later, when Adolf Hitler launched his first Nazi military attacks, he'd assured the West that he was only reacquiring what had been unfairly stripped from Germany after the first war. Many Germans in those forfeited regions welcomed the Third Reich's arrival.

In Pavel's eyes, Kalugin was adopting that same playbook. The old Communist Party loyalists were still alive in the former Soviet republics—waiting for reunification.

While the Americans had been preoccupied with Islamic terrorism and endless, unwinnable wars in Afghanistan and Iraq, Russia had quietly reasserted its international power. Ukraine, Crimea, Syria. Iran. Chechnya. Even Turkey.

Russian president Kalugin understood that the trick to defeating America was not a suicidal nuclear war—but a strategy to destroy the United States from within. Undermine its core democratic principles. Destroy its moral bedrock. Divide its people. Fuel hatred and distrust. Spread fear. Cause enough havoc and its own citizens would eat themselves.

A car from the Foreign Ministry was waiting for Pavel on the airport's tarmac. As he descended the portable stairs from the jet, he spotted his grandson, Peter, in the rear seat. Before Pavel's shoes touched the ground, three vehicles suddenly appeared.

General Gromyko. The cars blocked Pavel's ride. One of Gromyko's goons directed Pavel to the general's Mercedes-Benz, where Gromyko was smoking a Belomorkanal, an odd choice of cigarette given the general's preference for Western products. However, Belomorkanal cigarettes didn't have filters. Instead, each had a *papirosa*—a hollow cardboard tube at its base that served as a disposable cigarette holder—a sign of aristocracy and Russian pride in Gromyko's eyes.

"Yakov Prokofyevich," Gromyko said. "I'm ready to hear your report about the funeral."

"It was an American funeral like all other American funerals," Pavel replied. "I will be submitting my written account tomorrow when I return to my office."

"Deputy Minister, I am here now."

"Morale at our embassy is good. All details will be in my report tomorrow."

"Was there mention of Kiev? Do the Americans suspect us?"

"The Americans always suspect us. There was nothing to concern you."

"Do not presume to know what concerns me," Gromyko replied, slightly raising his voice.

Pavel nodded toward the Tu-134 aircraft. "I was under the impression these airplanes had been discontinued, but it was quite capable and very comfortable. Thank you for arranging it for me." A sarcastic comment slightly masked as a compliment.

Gromyko took a long drag. "Yakov Prokofyevich, what was said between you and the United States president after the funeral service? Your exact words."

For a moment, Pavel wondered if the general knew about the flash drive and password. In those same seconds, he concluded it was impossible. He'd been too careful. Gromyko was fishing.

"Ah, yes, the funeral reception," Pavel said. "I extended the appropriate regrets to the American president as instructed by our foreign minister."

"Did he ask you about Kiev?"

"No. I mentioned it to him."

"You mentioned it?" Gromyko repeated, clearly surprised.

"Yes, of course. I was instructed by the foreign minister to mention it. A slight provocation to help us learn the Americans' thinking. Certainly, you were aware of the foreign minister's order."

Clearly, he wasn't, which greatly pleased Pavel. He decided to taunt the general. "I presumed you had approved the script that I was instructed to say to the Americans."

Gromyko quietly smashed out what was left of his cigarette in an armrest ashtray.

Pavel continued: "Since it appears you were not aware, General, let me elaborate. I was told to inform President Fitzgerald that I had been in attendance at the Kiev news conference when the shooting began. I was instructed to say that I had escaped unharmed.

I was further told to listen carefully to the American president's reaction."

"And what was his reaction?"

"The American president's exact words, which I will be putting in my report tomorrow for the foreign minister, were 'Clearly you weren't a target.'"

"Are you certain that was all the American president said?"

Pavel raised a bushy eyebrow and turned his head to the side in a gesture meant to express bewilderment. "General Gromyko, you asked what I said to the president and how he responded. I have reported exactly what he said."

"Nothing more to your exchange when you were observed leaning in close to him shaking hands. Whispering."

So, Gromyko's spies had been watching. Pavel had anticipated it. Five junior diplomats had accompanied him to Washington. Which one had been the informant? Most likely, all of them.

"That whispering was when I said the words that the foreign minister had instructed me to say. I'm certain the foreign minister will provide you with the exact script that I was given to whisper. Now, if you do not have any other questions, I am tired and would like to return to my home."

Gromyko studied the diplomat's face, searching for some indication that he was holding back information. Pavel proved impossible to read. Lying was a well-regarded diplomatic skill, but all Russians raised during the Soviet period had become skilled at it. If there had been no bread in the stores, it was not because of failed crops; it was because of the Americans or the Jews, or some other explanation, even though everyone knew the truth. They simply were afraid to say it. Lies became like breathing, done effortlessly without thought. Telling the truth was what had been difficult.

Gromyko lit another Belomorkanal. "You don't smoke, do you Yakov Prokofyevich?"

"I tried it as a child and didn't prefer it."

"Yakov Prokofyevich, have you given any more thought to our discussion about your retirement?"

"I prefer to continue serving our country. Those who retire become easily bored."

"You are currently responsible for relations with European countries, European cooperation, interaction with the EU, NATO, and the Council of Europe," Gromyko said. "It is the president's wish that these tasks now be overseen by a different deputy minister who can better represent Russian interests abroad."

"If this is what the president wishes—"

"I have just told you it is."

"May I ask what my new responsibilities will be?"

"Still to be determined. Report to your office tomorrow, file a detailed report about your trip, and arrange to transfer your files to your replacement."

"As you wish."

Gromyko nodded toward Peter, whom the general could see waiting for Pavel. "Your grandson is deaf and dumb, is he not?"

"His diagnosis is selective mutism."

"Selective mutism?"

"I'm not certain how my grandson's medical condition is of concern to your duties."

"Would you prefer I ask him?"

"It is a disorder in which a person who is normally capable of speech cannot speak in specific situations or to specific people. It usually coexists with shyness and social anxiety."

"He can hear, and he can speak, but chooses not to," Gromyko summarized. "What has he told you about his parents' work and their deaths?"

"My grandson has not spoken to anyone for several years, including his own parents."

"You cannot be certain of this, can you? Many teenagers are talkative, yet you wish for me to believe your grandson has said nothing about his parents' laboratory work. Not a single question, nor has he shown the slightest curiosity about the accident that killed them. His parents worked in an important laboratory."

"My grandson knows nothing," Pavel said firmly. "He is under the care of our best doctors. You could speak to them about him. They believe the best course is to not pressure him, driving him deeper into his illness."

"Yakov Prokofyevich," Gromyko said, suddenly grinning. "You think me cruel when, in fact, my actions are done for the protection of Russia." He retrieved a white box with a red ribbon tied around it. A small sticker: Крупской, one of Russia's most famous chocolatiers. "I brought you candies for your grandson. You see, I am not as much a villain as you make me."

"Thank you, General. This is most thoughtful."

Gromyko playfully wagged a finger at Pavel. "There are only six candies in this box. They are of superior quality. I take no responsibility if you yourself become tempted, but they are for the child."

Pavel watched Gromyko and his entourage depart. He kissed his grandson's cheeks. The teen was lanky, rail thin, much like his father. His brown eyes reminded Pavel the most of his only daughter. "Dancing eyes" is what Pavel had called them when she was young. Always darting back and forth, absorbing every sight, wide when happy, narrow when cross, much more revealing than words.

"Chocolates," Pavel said, holding up the white box.

Peter took the box.

"A gift from General Gromyko."

The teen handed the box back to his grandfather.

Pavel nodded approvingly. "You know about him then. You know he was in charge of the laboratory where your parents died. Your parents talked about him, didn't they? His cruelty."

He looked into the boy's eyes and tousled the teen's hair.

"Yes, with your dancing eyes, you see more than most of us, don't you? Good."

Reaching forward, he dropped the box over the front seat next to the driver.

Twelve

Brett Garrett tugged the brim of his Washington Nationals baseball cap downward as he entered the Church of the Resurrection about two miles from his condo. Five steps down into a basement meeting room illuminated by rows of old fluorescent bulbs. Jacket collar turned up. Sunglasses even though it was evening. His attempt to conceal his face was nothing new to the two dozen gathered there. Most first-timers did it. A bearded man with a watermelon belly and dyed, thinning black hair said loudly, "My turn's tonight. Let's get started." The few still pouring coffee at a side table settled into the metal folding chairs. Garrett slipped into one closest to the exit.

"My name is Ray and I am an addict," the man said.

"Hello, Ray," everyone but Garrett replied.

"My addiction cost me a good job, my friends, my wife, my kids, and caused me to do things I'd never thought I'd do. If you're here tonight, you know what I'm saying."

Ray began reading from a worn handbook. "Best to pray. Spiritual strength is usually accompanied by a sense of calm. More than most people, we need to remind ourselves that God is the real worker of miracles here. At best, we are but instruments of our Higher Power."

Garrett thought about leaving, and thought about not leaving.

Ray continued: "Narcotics Anonymous is the spiritual moment that an addict discovers within themselves—the strength to stay clean one more day. When we share this with even one other addict, we activate the spirit of Narcotics Anonymous. This moment is what we share together in recovery and it is the heart of our program."

Closing the text, Ray said: "Jail, yep been there. More than once. I think they kept a cell reserved just for me."

A few knowing chuckles.

"Homeless, damn right. Waking up in my own vomit and waste. Yep. I've been spit on, called a bum. Lost all respect. But now, now I'm doing great. Five years clean. Every day's a new challenge but also a new opportunity. You got to take them one day at a time, it helps. God is my North Star. I've even started dating a good woman."

Spontaneous applause. Turning, he picked up a government pamphlet. "According to this, more than sixty thousand Americans are dying each year taking opioids." He paused and scanned their faces. "The cravings crawl up inside you like that monster in that movie *Alien*. You need more and more to feel normal and then you need more to prevent withdrawal, and then the real kick in the ass happens. No matter how much you take, the depression is still there."

Ray's eyes began to glisten. "Look at us. We're all good, decent Americans. None of us woke up one morning and said, 'I want to become an addict.' All of us have hated ourselves because of our own manipulative behaviors, lying, our irresponsibility. How can we allow a little chemical pill to ruin our lives? That's why you are here. One day at a time. Helping each other. Seeking God's help."

During the next hour, others volunteered to speak. One discussed how she was struggling. She'd relapsed. Taken drugs. Blamed stress at home. The attendees sympathized and encouraged her. Another announced he was two years clean. Applause. Garrett slipped out just as the meeting was wrapping up. He wanted to avoid the closing circle that he'd seen on a YouTube video about NA—when everyone held hands and chanted "One More Day!" like football players pumping themselves up before a big game.

Rather than Uber, he walked. Medical-assisted treatment. His primary doctor had told him, "It's your best shot to get off opioids. Buprenorphine and naloxone sublingual film tabs." Had that doctor ever taken them? First came the vomiting, then constipation, inability to sleep, irritability. Even worse, he still felt the cravings.

The walk helped. He emptied his mind but when he reached the door of his condo, he snapped to attention. A real estate sales pamphlet that he'd tucked between the door and its frame was now lying on the hallway floor. A one-cent coin near it. He drew his SIG Sauer from under his jacket and tested the doorknob. Unlocked. Whoever had entered or whoever was still inside didn't care that Garrett knew. He entered barrel first.

"An evening stroll?" a voice said.

"I should shoot you," Garrett replied.

CIA director Harold Harris nodded at the gun still pointing at him. "If you're not going to shoot, point that somewhere else." He was sitting on Garrett's gravel-gray, midcentury-modern sofa with honey walnut legs. It had been left behind by the former condo's owner as part of an "all furniture included" sale.

"I'm trying to decide."

"So much drama," Harris said.

Garrett lowered his pistol.

"The penny trick," Harris said, "a bit old-school isn't it?"

He was referring to the leaflet and one-cent coin lying in the hallway. When Garrett had left his apartment, he'd inserted a penny inside the ten-page pamphlet before inserting it between the door and its frame. To a passerby, it looked like an ad left by a Realtor seeking business. It was actually a warning device. An intruder would need to remove the leaflet and then replace it to cover his tracks. But as soon as he tugged loose the pamphlet, gravity would cause the penny to slip from its pages. Even if the intruder noticed the penny drop, he would not know which pages it had been hidden between, tipping off Garrett.

"Jack unlocked the door," Harris said. "You remember him."

Jack Moore was Director Harris's personal bodyguard and a former field operative who'd cut his teeth in Berlin back when there was still a wall there.

"He's ancient."

"He's outside in the car. There was a time when you would have spotted him."

Garrett sat down facing Harris. "Five minutes. I wouldn't want to keep you and your artifact babysitter from your next B-and-E."

Harris gazed at Garrett. "Still playing the victim."

"Playing? I am a victim—your victim. You lied to Congress about Cameroon."

"Have anything to drink around here?" Harris asked.

"Absolutely. You want a plate of sugar cookies, too?"

"Macallan neat."

"I got Old Crow. Naw, since you appreciate the truth, I've got nothing but water."

Harris let out a sigh.

"You got maybe two minutes left," Garrett said.

"The president asked me to thank you for delivering the flash drive from Kiev."

"He should have come himself. I would have served him Macallan."

Harris seemed much older to Garrett than the last time they'd been together. A Senate hearing. The sixty-some-year-old director probably had makeup on, knowing the cameras would be there. Now he looked spent. Too many late nights working. Too much stress. Being the keeper of the nation's secrets took a physical toll. Garrett tried to feel empathy but couldn't.

There had always been uneasiness between them long before Cameroon. Garrett suspected Harris wanted it that way. They had little in common. Harold Harris was a lawyer by training and a Washington bureaucrat by choice. He'd never been out in the cold.

When Langley had first wooed Garrett, he'd been intimidated by Harris. The director had reminded him of an old Navajo woman operating a loom he'd seen in Window Rock as a teen on a rare family vacation. She'd expertly twisted multiple strains, creating a design only she knew. People were Harris's threads. Expertly manipulated for the country's good. Or so Garrett had thought. Not until he had been betrayed had he seen the Machiavellian pattern.

"I need you to go to Moscow for me," Harris said.

For a moment, Garrett wondered if he was hallucinating. The medication. Some Freudian delusion.

"You what?"

"You in or out?"

"Just like that?" Garrett grunted. "The last time you asked, I lost my career, my reputation, and, oh yeah, nearly my life."

Harris waved his hand. "Crying doesn't become you."

Garrett reconsidered shooting him.

"I'm offering you an opportunity to get back in the game," Harris said. "Senator Stone's hearing was inconvenient, but you aren't homeless. Your buddy T. J. Kim hired you."

"Inconvenient?" Garrett said slowly, letting the word linger. "You lied to Congress about me and you lied to me. You betrayed me. Because of you, I went to prison. Because of you, I have a dishonorable discharge. And his name is Thomas Jefferson Kim, not T.J."

Harris shrugged. "Tell me, Garrett, how many Americans died in the bloodiest battle ever fought during a war?"

Garrett watched him, brows furrowed.

"Most people answer Gettysburg—when Americans on both sides died fighting each other. But it's not the battle that claimed the most American lives. Nor was it the Battle of the Bulge in World War Two or D-Day, when our boys were slaughtered on the beaches."

"I don't need a history lesson from you," Garrett said.

"The most Americans to die in a single battle was at Argonne Forest. World War One. More than twenty-six thousand Americans killed in that monthlong confrontation, another hundred thousand Americans wounded. Horrific carnage. But necessary."

"Expendable?"

"Sometimes a leader makes choices that require people to die. Do you believe for a moment any one of those men wanted to die? They were sacrificed for a greater good. Just like you were."

"What greater good? What did we get in return for sticking a knife in my back?"

"Senator Stone is a powerful man who's been trying to restrict the agency's powers for decades. Sometimes you feed an attacking dog. Besides, you weren't worth the fight. You ultimately made a choice, a wrong one."

"You promised to support my choice, to have my back. Get out."

Harris stood to leave. "I misjudged you, Garrett. I believed you really cared about our country."

"Guilt? You're trying to shame me into working for you? Okay, what's in Moscow that's so important to our country?"

"I need you to bring out two packages."

"Who?"

"Does it matter?"

"To me, yes."

"A potential asset and a teenager. The most important Russian asset to ever come over. You're his best chance of getting out alive with the kid. I'm putting together a team."

"What do I get out of all this?"

"Redemption. Isn't that what you want, Garrett?"

"You're the one in need of redemption."

Harris half-smiled. "I've given up on that years ago. Look in the mirror. Who are you trying to fool, Garrett? Suboxone. Yes, I know. I know everything. The midnight runs on your rebuilt British motorcycle. The faces of those who died in Cameroon. They died because of you, not me. I'm offering you a chance."

Garrett offered him an obscene gesture.

"The last refuge for someone who has no intelligent reply," Harris said, mocking him. He took an envelope from his jacket pocket and tossed it at Garrett's feet. "You want to hear more? Come tomorrow. Get back in the game. If not, sit here and feel sorry for yourself. Blame everyone. Everyone but yourself."

Thirteen

Valerie Mayberry wasn't certain what was happening. She was being loaned to the CIA for an indefinite period. Her boss, Sally North, had informed her when she arrived at work. FBI director Archibald Davidson had personally approved the detail. Moments later, Mayberry had received a telephone call. A woman's voice. An address in rural Virginia. A time. "Don't be late."

Mayberry had worked with her CIA counterintelligence counterparts before and never once enjoyed it. There was a long history of bad blood between the agency and bureau. Some dated to when the FBI director had grabbed headlines bragging about how the bureau had caught CIA traitor Aldrich Ames. Seven years later, the agency had caught FBI Agent Robert Hanssen spying. A publicity punch here, a jab there.

A voice coming from her Jaguar's GPS warned of an upcoming left turn as she drove northeast on Virginia Route 15. She spotted two black SUVs parked near a gravel road ahead before the GPS told her to turn.

"Driver's license and FBI credentials please, Ms. Mayberry," the CIA Protective Service officer said. Another used a mirror to sweep under her Jaguar. "Nice ride." She pulled away in second gear to avoid spitting gravel back at them. A half mile later, she topped a slight rise and saw the main house. Mayberry was used to great wealth, but this countryside estate startled her.

From the darker color of its graying stone, Mayberry guessed the two-story Georgian Revival was the original before matching stone additions had been added on each side. Most likely the 1770s. The locals called them "telescope houses" because of the added wings. Off to the house's right wing was a swimming pool as big as the community pools found in most suburbs. Off to its left was an equestrian arena with a grandstand and stables. The house, pool, and riding ring created a huge U from above with an ornate fountain anchored in its circular driveway.

Mayberry counted six vehicles parked there. Four matched the SUVs at the entrance. Obviously CIA. The next was an extended Cadillac sedan. Government issued. Armored. Someone important. Finally, a Mercedes-Benz SUV with a personalized tag: IEC BOSS.

Two officers were stationed outside the front door. They checked her ID again before letting her pass. An older man welcomed her inside.

"My name is Jack. May I please have your cell phone and any other electronic devices that you brought with you? Also, your personal weapon." Another guard appeared and took them.

"Thank you," Jack said. "Please, this way."

The modest entryway had aged wood-plank flooring typical of the period, but when Jack slid open two walnut pocket doors to Mayberry's right, she found herself entering an ornate ballroom with gold fixtures, a massive stone fireplace, and a highly polished black-and-white marble floor. The room was empty except for four chairs arranged in a circle. Thomas Jefferson Kim and Brett Garrett were seated in two of them.

"You're the last to arrive," Jack said.

Kim stood and chirped, "Good to see you again."

Garrett nodded from his chair.

Mayberry sat next to Kim.

"Can I offer anyone water, coffee, tea?" Jack asked.

"Unfortunately, the director is on a call and might be a while."

"I'll take a coffee," Kim said. Garrett shook his head. "Oolong tea—black dragon—if you have it," Mayberry said.

Jack fetched their drinks and left them. No small talk. Kim and Mayberry sipped from china cups. Garrett, arms folded across his chest, stared straight ahead. Fifteen minutes later, CIA director Harris entered along with Jack, offering neither an apology nor explanation.

"You will each need to sign the document Jack is distributing," Harris said.

"Excuse me," Kim said, "I generally don't sign anything without running it by my lawyer."

"Then you have a decision to make, don't you? Sign it or leave knowing that your departure could impact IEC's current and future government contracts."

Jack said, "It's a standard federal nondisclosure agreement. Pretty much boilerplate, with one exception that you will find on page seven, paragraph three."

Garrett was the first to find it. Stripped of legalese, it stated the signatory would be charged with espionage, not treason, if he or she violated the NDA.

"Espionage is punishable by death," Jack elaborated. "Treason isn't."

Mayberry signed. Kim grimaced and signed. Garrett glared at Harris and, with obvious reluctance, scribbled his name.

"Good," Harris said, as Jack collected the paperwork and left the ballroom. "The flash drive that Mr. Garrett brought from Kiev contained a videotaped message from Yakov Prokofyevich Pavel, the current number three in charge at the Russian Ministry of Foreign Affairs. He's willing to defect along with his grandson if we meet his conditions."

"Has anyone that high up ever defected?" Kim asked.

"No," Harris said.

"What conditions?" Mayberry asked.

"First, we have to get him and his grandson out of Russia alive, which will not be easy. That will be your job, Mr. Garrett." The three of them looked at Garrett, who didn't react.

"Because of who he is, Pavel can't simply go to an airport and purchase two tickets," the director continued. "He and his grandson would need permission and only would be allowed to travel outside Russia with a security detail. The Kremlin also maintains an old Soviet custom—making high government officials leave one family member behind when they go overseas."

Turning to Kim, Harris said, "We'll need your company to transfer Mr. Garrett to the U.S. embassy in Moscow as an IEC employee—a security guard—to make this work."

"No problem," Kim said. "That is, if Garrett wants to go."

"Why bother getting Pavel out?" Garrett asked. "If you have a flash drive of him offering to betray his country, just blackmail him in place, squeeze him dry. That's more your style, isn't it?"

"A bit shortsighted," Harris replied. "Pavel isn't stupid. He's holding back—including information about a national threat that he says is imminent."

"What kind of national threat?" Garrett asked.

"I'll get to that."

"How do you know this isn't a Russian provocation?" Mayberry asked.

"First, it's unlikely the Kremlin would risk sending us someone so high up as a dangle. He knows too many secrets. Second, Pavel's told us the name of an American government official recruited by Russian intelligence two years ago. A mole—to prove his bona fides."

"Pavel wants us to kill the rat before the rat can squeal on him in Moscow," Garrett said.

"Who's the mole?" Mayberry asked.

"Until he is arrested, that's not a question I should be answering."

"We just signed an NDA that says you will execute us if we repeat anything that's said here," Garrett replied sarcastically. "And you still don't trust us? How do we know this mole won't tell the Russians about the three of us?"

"He works at the NSA," Harris said. "He's not a threat to any of you. However, Pavel claims there is a second mole. Someone who can hurt you. There's a breach. A traitor who appears able to read all of our message traffic between Langley and Moscow."

Garrett grunted, unhappy.

"That's why we're meeting here," said Kim.

"Exactly," Harris replied. "It's also why I've invited you to be part of the team. Your company, IEC, operates its own communication satellites."

"Yes, three of them, and better, I might add, than the ones the government uses."

Leapfrogging ahead, Mayberry said, "You want Kim to keep in contact with Garrett while he's in Russia."

"Yes," Harris said. "No cable traffic. Also, only the four of us in this room and one additional person in Moscow will know about Pavel."

"Wait," Garrett said. "Who in Moscow?"

"Marcus Austin."

Garrett knew him. They'd worked together in Morocco before Austin became Moscow chief of station.

"Did he sign an NDA?" Garrett asked. "And aren't you forgetting your security team outside and Jack?"

"You, Mr. Kim, Agent Mayberry, Marcus Austin, and me," Harris said firmly, "are the only ones besides President Fitzgerald who know about Pavel's plea. I have not even told the president about how I intend to get Pavel out—about me bringing the three of you together. Despite your cynicism, this operation is being highly compartmentalized."

"What about this imminent threat?" Mayberry said.

"Yes, it's why you're part of this team, Agent Mayberry. I assume you are familiar with Kamera?"

Of course she was. In 1921, Vladimir Lenin ordered scientists to create poisons that would be completely undetected for use in political assassinations. Their secret lab was called "Kamera," which means "the Chamber" in Russian. Stalin tested poisons on Soviet prisoners, frequently dissidents, often causing excruciatingly painful deaths. The Kremlin assured the West in 1953 that the Chamber had been closed, but twenty-five years later, a Bulgarian defector named Georgi Markov was assassinated waiting at a London bus stop. A pellet containing the poison ricin was jabbed into Markov's leg through a KGB designed umbrella tip. It was quite ingenious. The killer poked him while he was waiting for a bus. The ricin was inside a tiny steel pellet coated with wax. When Markov's natural body temperature heated the wax, the poison entered his system. It took him days to die.

Twenty-eight years after Markov's death, another Kremlin critic, Alexander Litvinenko, was poisoned in London with radioactive-laced tea. Russia only got a slap on the hand and that emboldened the Kremlin. Six years after Litvinenko, Russian whistle-blower Alexander Perepilichny was poisoned in London with a toxic substance made from a little-known Chinese flower, gelsemium.

"In March 2018, former Russian army officer Sergei Skripal, who'd been spying for the British, and his daughter Yulia were poisoned in England," Harris reminded them. "They used Novichok, the deadliest nerve agent ever created—to date."

Harris leaned forward in his seat, resting his elbows on his knees while clasping his hands together. "By our count, more than thirty-eight prominent Russians have died under suspicious circumstances in recent years, many caused by exotic poisons."

"Let me guess," Garrett said. "Pavel told you Stalin's so-called Kamera operations were never really shut down and now Kalugin is using them to kill his enemies."

"It's exactly what he said," Harris acknowledged.

"Why has Pavel suddenly become so chatty? Why's he suddenly so eager to jump ship?" Garrett asked.

"His grandson, Peter. The teenager's parents were killed in Svetogorsk, Russia. Both were chemists working at a Kamera lab under the direct supervision of General Gromyko." He paused and glanced at each of them separately before continuing. "Pavel said Gromyko has developed a poison that he plans to use here in the U.S. That's the imminent threat."

"He wouldn't dare, would he?" Mayberry said.

"The Russians are growing more and more bold," Harris said. "Using social media to sow discord and interfere in elections both here and in Europe. Poisoning defectors. And we suspect they were behind the terrorist attack in Kiev. They use shills, straw men, to protect themselves."

"Who are they planning on poisoning in the U.S. and when?" Kim asked.

"Pavel knows but won't say. We need to get him out within two weeks, he said, or it will be too late."

"Russian defectors always hold their best card back," Mayberry added. "Use it as leverage."

"He could be bluffing," Garrett said.

"It's a risk we can't take," Harris answered. "The attack in Kiev was orchestrated by the Kremlin but was carried out by a European-based Antifa cell. We suspect they'll do the same here."

"Antifa?" Kim said. "Aren't they the good guys—the ones who protest against white supremacists? Hate Nazis. Why would they be shills for the Kremlin?"

"I can answer that," Mayberry said. "Radical Antifa members are predominantly far left and militant left. That's a wide swath. Self-described anarchists, socialists, and communists—lots of communists. There have been efforts in Congress to label Antifa as domestic terrorists but they've failed because a majority of Antifa members are naïve college kids recruited under the guise that their members fight racism, sexism, and Nazis. They use hashtags like #PunchANazi. The political left sees Antifa members as vigilante heroes, but the movement is deeply rooted in anticapitalism and socialist/communist teachings."

"You're correct," Harris said approvingly. "Its most radical members want to destroy our democratic and capitalistic system. During the 2017 presidential inauguration, anarchists dressed in black and wearing masks torched a limousine and vandalized four businesses in Washington, D.C. When a right-leaning commentator was scheduled to speak at UC Berkeley, Antifa protestors hurled Molotov cocktails into a campus building and attempted to light the student union on fire with people in it."

"I'm not certain how we run an intelligence operation on the right part of Antifa," Mayberry continued. "They're pretty unstructured—just showing up at rallies mostly to attack the alt-right. It's not like they hold weekly meetings."

"We have evidence that Moscow financially supports several Antifa organizers who are paid to stir up dissent," Harris said. "That's not information generally known by the gullible students whom they enlist for rallies. Gerald de Depardieu was an Antifa recruiter in Paris before he turned terrorist gunman in Kiev. He recruited Asyan Rivera. She's your in."

An *aha* look washed across Mayberry's face. "I get it. You need an FBI agent to do this because it's illegal for the CIA to carry out covert actions on U.S. soil. And you know I've already been asked to befriend her. But this is more than getting close enough to answer a few questions. You want me to join Antifa, don't you?"

"The bureau has done this sort of infiltration before," Harris replied.

"COINTELPRO," Mayberry replied, "and the bureau was heavily criticized. It infiltrated the Black

Panthers, anti–Vietnam War protestors, and the American Indian Movement. Agents lost their jobs."

"Be cautious, Agent Mayberry; the director here is good at having others take a fall for him." Garrett's voice said he was kidding, but his eyes were not.

Harris said, "COINTELPRO happened before Timothy McVeigh drove a truck bomb into Oklahoma City murdering a hundred and sixty-eight Americans in an act of domestic terrorism. Before he slaughtered fifteen children. The bureau monitors hate groups. Infiltrating radical leftists who believe in destroying capitalism and our government is no different from infiltrating a radical Islamic cell."

"Asyan Rivera wasn't in Europe when Kiev was attacked," Mayberry noted. "She could be just another naïve recruit."

"She came home six months before Ambassador Thorpe was murdered," Harris said. "We aren't sure why. Maybe De Depardieu actually loved her and wanted to protect her. Or maybe he sent her home to prepare for an attack here using Kamera-produced poison. If Garrett gets Pavel out, he'll tell us who, where, and when. If not, you have less than two weeks to find out."

Harris glanced at his watch. "If you need to get in touch with me, you can do it through Jack, but only tell him that we need to meet." Harris stood but decided to give a rah-rah closing speech. "Each of you has a specific assignment. Your country is depending on you. I can't stress that enough. We can't have Russians using poisons to kill Americans on our soil."

Harris exited. Jack reappeared to return the items that they had surrendered earlier.

"It would be best if you waited five minutes, until the director departs. Please stay in this room. This house is currently for sale. Better to not touch anything."

The moment Kim saw Director Harris's motorcade pulling away, he did a Google search to check the house's price.

Garrett's mind was elsewhere. "Left wing, right wing, chicken wing—it's all the same thing to the bureau, isn't that right, Mayberry?"

PART II

Escape from Moscow

Nobody ever did, or ever will, escape the consequences of his choices.
—ALFRED A. MONTAPERT

Fourteen

Two Years Earlier

A simple plan. Enter the Boko Haram camp before dawn where Elsa Eriksson was being held captive for ransom while the terrorists were sleeping. Counting Brett Garrett, fourteen SEALs. Intel put the number of jihadists at twenty. The Americans were better trained, better armed. Grab and go. Minimum engagement. Garrett felt confident.

The eight huts formed a C from a bird's view. No electricity. In the C's center a fire pit. Primitive. A half-dozen motorbikes leaning next to the mud-walled, thatched-roof dwellings. Patched together with so many spare parts their original manufacturers were unidentifiable. Two vehicles. Most menacing: a Toyota Tacoma pickup with a Soviet-made Z KPVT heavy *machine gun mounted on its bed—parked near the fire. A World War II–vintage deuce-and-a-half cargo truck steps outside the camp.*

From the darkness, Garrett took stock. No dogs, chickens, or ducks to sound an alarm. Team's sniper, Big Mac, and spotter, Curly, found high ground. A rock-covered hill on the camp's western edge. The others spread out strategically. Eyes on every entrance. Capable of killing anyone who emerged. They were ready.

Garrett, Senator, Sweet Tooth, and Bear moved forward. Silent. Two sentries outside the hostage hut—designated Alpha-1. Both unaware. Their Kalashnikov assault rifles leaning against the hut's walls. Teenagers chewing khat, a local leaf stimulant.

Garrett and Bear were the most skilled with knives. Garrett insisted his men carry two fixed blades. No folding ones. Right-side blade with a forward grip on the vest. Left side with a reverse grip. Immediate to unsheathe.

Garrett, Bear, Sweet Tooth, and Senator paired up when they reached the back of Alpha-1; each pair moved simultaneously in the opposite direction around it. A startled look on each target's face. Open mouths but no time to yell. Death. Sweet Tooth and Senator grabbed the bodies while Garrett and Bear slipped around the heavy blanket covering the hut's entrance.

Garrett's knife had been replaced by his *SIG Sauer P226*. Gunfire noise comes from gases popping from behind a bullet, similar to a car backfiring or opening a bottle of bubbly. Garrett's pistol was fitted with a suppressor that gave those gases a quieter place to go.

The guard inside was half-asleep, his back propped against the interior wall. His assault rifle on his lap. A lone candle burning next to him illuminated the interior. Garrett fired. A muffled thud. Another thud. Two rounds directly into the guard's chest. Known as a double tap. Another to the head if the target was wearing body armor. This dead jihadist wasn't.

Bear held the blanket open so the Senator and Sweet Tooth could drag the two dead sentries inside. They dropped them next to their freshly executed buddy.

The hooded figure curled up on the floor was trembling. Garrett had a passport photo for positive ID. He dropped to his knees. Checked her hands. They were white. "Elsa Eriksson," he whispered. "Don't scream. Don't speak. Navy SEALs. Nod if you understand."

The hood moved.

"I'm removing your hood. Don't freak on me."

He slipped it from her head and compared it to the photo. A match.

Garrett's ballistic helmet, outfitted with a flashlight, infrared strobe (used when signaling helicopters), and four tubes that allowed better peripheral vision than the standard two-lens night-vision goggles, seemed to confuse her. He lifted his helmet. Smiled.

"Relax. Nod if you can walk. Don't speak."

Senator cut the bindings holding her wrists. Garrett and Senator helped her stand. She was wobbly. Dehydration. Weak. Most likely unsure whether this was real or her dream.

"Thank you, Jesus," she muttered.

Garrett couldn't resist. "Not Jesus, ma'am. Navy SEALs."

In the candlelight she saw the three dead terrorists sprawled on the dirt floor and gasped.

Garrett covered her mouth, afraid she might squeal. "Ma'am, you must be quiet. Do you understand? They're still out there."

She had not fully understood that the other Boko Haram kidnappers were alive. Still outside the hut. Senator slipped behind her. Bear and Sweet Tooth on each side. Garrett took the lead. He peered outside. Through his headset: "Ready to move the package. We clear?"

"It's a go," Curly said. Everyone was in place.

"The C-4," Garrett asked.

"In place." A precaution. C-4 placed on the Boko Haram vehicles.

All they needed to do was to exit the hut, disappear into the darkness, rendezvous with the helicopters. Mission accomplished.

"Let's move!" Garrett said, drawing back the blanket covering. Eriksson touched his shoulder.

"Abidemi," she muttered in a hoarse whisper. "Do you have her?"

Garrett released the blanket, sealing them back inside the hut.

"Who?"

"My friend. They kidnapped us. I heard her screaming a few hours ago. She's in a different hut."

"American? Swedish? NGO?" he asked, although he suspected he knew the answer.

"Nigerian."

"Ma'am, we have to go."

"No," Eriksson said. "She's a Christian. She's only fourteen!"

"Ma'am, we must go. No time."

"No!" she repeated, this time more insistent. "They'll kill her."

"Ma'am, calm down. I'll ask."

All conversations between Garrett and his SEAL team were being monitored in Langley and at the Pentagon. Tactically designed military helmet cameras broadcast visuals. CIA director Harris was overseeing the rescue operation and already had overheard Eriksson's demand.

"We have an issue," Garrett said.

While those in Washington could hear all chatter between the SEALs, only Garrett could hear Director Harris. The other SEALs couldn't hear Harris, either.

"Yes, sir," Garrett replied. "I understand."

Eriksson was staring at him with hope-filled eyes.

"Ma'am, my orders are to get you and my men out of this camp immediately." He lowered his night-vision goggles.

"I won't leave without her," she said.

"Ma'am," Garrett replied, "come with us and once you're safe we'll determine which hut your friend is in."

Eriksson hesitated. "I don't believe you."

From outside the camp's perimeter, Curly interrupted. "Chief, you got company."

"Talk to me."

"On your left."

Peering out, Garrett spotted him. "You got eyes on target, Big Mac?"

"Affirmative," the sniper replied. "He's taking a piss."

Against the side of his hut. A slim thirty-something terrorist now twisting his head side to side. Stretching his neck.

The fire in the camp's center glowed red, creating minimal lighting but enough for the urinating terrorist to notice the sentries were not at their posts outside Alpha-1—if he looked.

"Orders?" Big Mac asked.

"Only if necessary."

Big Mac's sniper's rifle had a suppressor but the sound of the bullet's wake, like a miniature sonic boom, would be loud enough for others to hear.

Sweat beaded through Garrett's camouflage makeup. How long could one man pee?

"He's done," Big Mac reported.

Garrett checked. The terrorist was walking toward a different hut from the one that he'd exited. He'd not noticed the missing sentries.

"Where the hell's he going?" Garrett asked.

Big Mac tracked him across the camp, watched him lift a hut flap and go inside.

"You're clear," Curly reported.

"Ma'am," Garrett said, "you're putting yourself, my men, and me at great risk. People will die, including your friend if we don't leave right now. Do you understand?"

"We can't leave her. She's just a child."

A scream. The cries of a child.

"Abidemi!" Eriksson gasped. "He's hurting her!"

Fifteen

Current Day

The day after Yakov Prokofyevich Pavel returned to Moscow, he awoke a traitor. He'd always loved Mother Russia, having been taught from childbirth about collective patriotism, loyalty, sacrifice, and honor. How could Pavel live with himself now?

His decision to contact the Americans had not been impulsive. As a deputy foreign minister, Pavel never made life-changing decisions on a whim. The deaths of his daughter and son-in-law had been the tipping point, but his unhappiness already had been deeply rooted. The seeds had germinated with each power-grabbing move by President Kalugin. He'd discredited, arrested, imprisoned, or killed his opponents. He'd gleefully deconstructed a classless Marxist society, spinning it into a corrupt autocracy. A short, middle-aged narcissist, Kalugin lived in a world of moral weightlessness.

Pavel had rationalized his choice by convincing himself that he was not betraying Mother Russia. Its corrupt president had betrayed him and all Russians. Kalugin was the actual traitor.

Pavel needed to stick to his daily routine and wait for a signal from his newly chosen friends. He dressed and ate a light breakfast while sitting across the table from his mute grandson. He noticed the time and glanced outside expecting to see Dmitri Fedorovich Dusko, his driver, and his ministry-provided car.

Dusko hadn't yet arrived.

Pavel kissed Peter on the top of his head and stood at the window. Five, ten, fifteen minutes. Pavel telephoned the Foreign Ministry.

"I apologize, Deputy Minister," the head of motor cars said. "Your driver fell ill last night. He's been taken to the hospital. Whoever failed to send a substitute driver this morning will be punished."

"What hospital?" Pavel replied angrily.

"City Clinical Hospital number sixty-four on Vavilova."

Pavel called its chief medical officer and was immediately put through. His diplomatic rank mattered.

"Dmitri Fedorovich Dusko and his wife entered our facility suffering from debilitating diarrhea and vomiting," the medical officer reported. "Neither could walk without support and both were hallucinating."

"Are they better now?"

"Unfortunately, Deputy Minister, they are not. Both are unconscious and on life support. May I ask a few inquiries that might help us better understand what caused their illness? Did you see either of them last night?"

"Of course I saw my driver. You should already know this. Dusko picked me up at the airport near ten o'clock and drove me home. He appeared to be in excellent health when he unloaded my bags and left. How can this possibly be helpful?"

"Were you ill this morning?"

"Would I be speaking to you on the telephone if I were?"

"Yes, Deputy Minister. Only a few more questions. Do you know if Dmitri Dusko and his wife are heavy drinkers or did he happen to mention what he might be having, say, for dinner or a treat, later that night, shellfish, possibly?"

"I'm not in the habit of discussing my driver's drinking habits with him or his choice of cuisine or at what time he and his wife eat," Pavel snapped.

"Certainly, Deputy Minister. I asked only because their sudden illness is most likely related to gastrointestinal disturbances that typically result in excessive vomiting and diarrhea. I suspect your driver and his wife might be having an allergic reaction to some bacterial agent, perhaps ingested while eating contaminated shellfish."

Pavel hesitated, his mind remembering the ride home. "When were they admitted to your hospital?" he asked.

"Shortly before one a.m.," the doctor said, "about two hours after you observed Dusko in good health unloading your car."

"Unless you have further questions," Pavel said, "I have been as helpful as I can and have business to attend to."

"Thank you, Deputy Minister, for your time."

Pavel put down the phone receiver. He pictured General Gromyko.

"I brought you candies as a welcoming home gift . . . your grandson."

The general playfully wagging a pointed finger.

"Only six candies . . . superior quality. I take no responsibility if you yourself become tempted, but they are for the child."

Pavel had dropped the box of chocolates into the limousine's front seat for his driver.

A car from the ministry arrived. Pavel hurried outside from his five-room apartment on Leontyevski in the center of Moscow's historic houses. Pavel had inherited his apartment from his well-connected father, a high-ranking member of the Communist Party. It occupied the entire floor of what had been a late-nineteenth-century aristocrat's mansion. That was before the October Revolution ended the czarist reign and gave birth to the Soviet Union. His flat was only a five-minute walk from the Arbat Tverskaya metro stop, but Pavel had not used Moscow's famed underground since childhood. He'd depended completely on his government driver.

In his video flash drive, Pavel had left instructions. Paint a red X on the shell of an already graffiti-covered sidewalk public telephone on New Arbat Avenue. Pavel's morning commute to Smolenskaya Sennaya Square passed by the phone.

"Have you heard?" his substitute driver asked Pavel as they rode. Without waiting for an answer, he said, "The Americans arrested a spy. They claim he worked for us. NSA."

Pavel's eyes narrowed. He clenched his jaw.

"Is it your job to inform me of such news?" he rudely replied.

Russian counterintelligence officers would be on the hunt. How had the Americans caught him? Had their mole drawn suspicion on himself? Spent large sums of money? Been caught photographing documents? Or was it the most likely explanation. A Russian traitor had exposed an American one? It had been less than forty-eight hours since he'd given President Fitzgerald the password. Even someone as dull as Gromyko would eventually wonder about the timing of the spy's arrest and Pavel's trip to Washington.

Pavel's car was approaching the public telephone. Nothing. No red painted X on the shell covering it.

Gromyko already had tried poisoning him and Peter. He felt certain of it. The light of hope was dimming within him.

Sixteen

Valerie Mayberry slipped off her wedding ring. She had shadowed Asyan Rivera from her pricy Baltimore inner harbor condo to a picturesque western Pennsylvania town. Home to Smithmyer College.

Tailing Rivera had been simple. An FBI technician had planted a tracking device on her BMW. Mayberry had arrived at the school's parking lot a few moments after Rivera. Finding her on campus also had been easy. She was sipping a salted caramel mocha while sending a text at a table in the student center's food court, and did not look anything like a typical Smithmyer student.

Mayberry calculated the cost of Rivera's outfit. A Miu Miu cropped black denim jacket. Worn over a Dolce & Gabbana denim bralette. Skintight Prada black chopped tailored trousers. At least three grand on those three pieces. Valentino Garavani Rockstud combat boots, Italian made: $1,700? Panthère de Cartier sunglasses with gray gradient lenses: at least $900. Another $200 to have her initials engraved on the corner of one lens. Total cost of her rock girl chic outfit, easily $6,000.

In contrast, Mayberry's costume consisted of a Walmart fluted-sleeve floral-print blouse, Old Navy denim jeans with knee holes, and black Nike Flex running shoes. Around $200.

It was Rivera's handbag that most caught Mayberry's attention. A Louis Vuitton Sac Plat Fusion Fire Led Elvim 19 black leather satchel. Did any of the college boys ogling her realize it alone retailed for $54,000?

Rivera stood, having finished her drink and text. She disappeared into a nearby women's restroom. Mayberry entered the food court and out of habit carried the crumpled cup and soiled napkins that Rivera had left behind to a receptacle before sitting in a chair where she could watch the women's room.

She almost missed seeing Rivera exit. Gone was the designer outfit, replaced by an oversize black sweatshirt worn over black denim jeans. High-top sneakers. Her hair tucked under a black stocking cap. Mayberry assumed Rivera had packed her earlier outfit in the Under Armour gym bag slung over shoulder.

Mayberry followed her outside. Watched her deposit the gym bag into the BMW's trunk. Kept her distance as Rivera climbed a slight hill making her way to the school's auditorium where a crowd had gathered. Mayberry lost track of her in the swarm.

"Concert tonight?" Mayberry asked a nearby student.

"You're kidding, right?"

The jostling began. By the time Mayberry got inside, every seat was filled. She found room along a back wall.

Seconds later, protestors entered. Eight of them paraded down the center aisle to the front of the auditorium. Their leader was dressed in a brightly colored orange-and-black dashiki. The rest wore all black and masks. Three rubberized former presidents: Reagan, Carter, Clinton. A Zorro. A pink pussy-cat protest hat with scarf pulled up. Guy Fawkes—the flamboyantly anarchic terrorist in the comic book series *V for Vendetta*. Mayberry easily spotted Rivera hiding behind a glittery Mardi Gras jester's face.

The dashiki-clad leader, who wasn't wearing a disguise, raised a bullhorn and began to chant: "Hey, ho, racist professors need to go! Hey, ho, sexist professors need to go!"

Although the voices of her fellow protestors were

somewhat muted, they repeated her call. Others in the auditorium joined in.

"Hey, ho, racist professors need to go! Hey, ho, sexist professors need to go!"

Three campus security guards watched from the auditorium's aisles. Arms folded across their chests.

"We ain't lettin' no racist speak here tonight," the woman announced. "We ain't listenin' to any of his white-privilege bullshit!"

A student in a Smithmyer sweatshirt three rows from center stage yelled back: "He's not a racist. Let him speak."

"You ain't black," the woman declared. "You got no say in who be racist. You ain't a woman, either, you got no say in who be a misogynist."

Mayberry raised her cell phone, joining dozens of others videoing the protest. "Excuse me," she whispered to a coed scrunched against the auditorium wall beside her. "This is my first day here. What's going on?"

"The off-campus fight," she replied.

"What fight?"

The student quickly explained. Each year, Smith-myer held a Day of Nonattendance/Day of Reuniting event. Minority students left the campus to discuss diversity issues. They returned the next day to reunite with nonminority students. This year, its organizers turned tables. Everyone who wasn't a minority was told to stay off campus. Dr. Francis Williams, an English professor, had written an editorial challenging the switch.

The student pulled a folded campus newspaper article from the back pocket of her jeans. "Here's what he wrote. I'm saving it. Nothing like this ever happens at Smithmyer."

Mayberry scanned the clipping. "There's a difference between a group deciding to voluntarily vacate the campus," Dr. Williams had written, "and that same group telling others they have to go away. Leaving campus to raise consciousness about minority issues is a much-valued tradition at Smithmyer that all of us should respect. But demanding all whites leave the campus is a *show of force*, an act of oppression against nonminority faculty and students, and this is wrong."

She handed back the clipping. Mayberry had read about protests on college campuses about free speech but had never attended one.

"He's not a Nazi!" a supporter yelled. "He's got a First Amendment right to speak."

"Not when it's hate speech," the woman with the bullhorn replied. "That be verbal violence. Ain't protected by the First Amendment."

The protestor in the pussycat hat yelled, "You can't yell 'fire' in a crowded movie theater."

"She's right!" someone in the audience responded. "If what you say marginalizes people, you have no right to say it."

"What Dr. Williams wrote wasn't hate speech," one of his student supporters argued.

"Was too hate speech," the bullhorn leader answered. "Defending white supremacy always be hate speech. If you a Nazi, we gonna punch your face."

Cheers. Boos. Applause. Taunts. An argument now being waged in slogans.

"Hey, ho, he needs to go!"

"No, no, he's got to speak!"

An older, bearded white man appeared onstage, prompting the bullhorn protestor to yell: "Shut him up! Shut him up!"

Mayberry noticed the three security guards quietly leaving.

"Smithmyer students, please, please listen to me," Dr. Francis Williams said, raising his hands for silence. "Let's have a civil discussion here. A teachable moment."

For someone with such a genteel appearance, he had a surprisingly strong voice, no doubt honed by years of teaching. Even so, the auditorium's control booth personnel had to maximize the volume of Williams's handheld microphone for him to be heard above the crowd.

"Tonight is not about who should or shouldn't leave campus," Dr. Williams said. "It's about free and open discussion. We can't have free and open discussion of important ideas if we say that ideas are only valid if made by a person of the appropriate race or sexual identity. And we definitely can't have a discussion if we start calling opinions we disagree with 'verbal violence.' Confusing speech with violence guarantees someone will get hurt—because people will feel it appropriate to respond to something that offends them with actual violence!"

"Racist! Racist! Racist!" came through the bullhorn.

"Listen to me!" he continued. "I have stood up against racism my entire life. I was active in the civil rights movement. I have always proudly called myself a liberal. But I no longer recognize what passes for liberal these days. It used to be about being color-blind—about treating people as individuals with God-given rights. About freedom, about tolerance. Listening to others."

Beads of sweat glistened on Williams's forehead. "Now being a liberal is all about identity politics. It's about focusing on our differences instead of what makes us the same. Being color-blind is considered racist now! It's all been flipped upside down, and it's tearing us apart. Just look at us!" He paused to catch his breath. Then continued. "Today's argument is that if you're an LGBTQ black woman, your view of American society is automatically more valid than that of a straight white male. That is wrong. Logic and reason matter. Not victimization."

He raised his free hand hoping to quiet the crowd. Seeing it, the protest's leader screamed: "A Nazi salute. He's making a Nazi salute."

Williams immediately dropped his arm, making him seem guilty.

The bullhorn protestor seized the moment. Placing her open left palm on the stage, which was about four feet higher than the auditorium floor, she catapulted herself onto the platform with surprising dexterity. She ran toward Williams. In that instant, the room became eerily quiet.

The woman stopped an inch from him and screamed vulgarities into his face. Someone in the auditorium threw a punch. Within seconds, mayhem.

Mayberry joined others fleeing from the auditorium. Once outside, she hurried downhill to the visitors' lot where Rivera's BMW was parked. She waited several rows away from the car. Rivera appeared moments later, having ditched her Mardi Gras mask. The woman with her was the protest leader, minus her bullhorn. She was talking on a cell phone.

A Cadillac Escalade entered the lot and drove directly to the two women. Rivera opened its front passenger door for the protest leader to enter. Mayberry raised her cell but only captured a fuzzy photo of the Escalade. It had Washington, D.C., plates.

Rivera got into her BMW and drove in the opposite direction to the Escalade. Before Mayberry pursued her, she glanced at the Smithmyer College auditorium. The police had arrived, along with an ambulance. Two EMTs were helping a limping Dr. Williams outside to be examined. He was holding a handkerchief to his nose to stop the bleeding.

Seventeen

"Can this be hacked?" Brett Garrett asked, holding a satellite phone bearing the IEC label.

"It's the finest fully encrypted phone ever made," Thomas Jefferson Kim bragged.

"I'll grant you that, but can it be hacked? It's my ass hanging out in Moscow."

"The GMR-2 encryption algorithm is the most commonly used in SAT phones. The Chinese recently launched an attack using a reverse encryption procedure to decode the encryption key from the output key stream by hitting a 3.3 GHz satellite stream thousands of times with an inversion attack, which eventually produced a 64-bit encryption key enabling them to read and hear message traffic."

"In English, please, Dr. Mensa."

"The system that I specifically developed for the phone you are holding uses multiple encryption layers before it reaches our satellite where your voice will be further scrambled before being forwarded to a twin phone, the only one that has the necessary key code to unscramble your encrypted voice, although there will be a short delay when we speak. This specific phone's transmissions will bleed into the stream of other messages being sent to our satellite in random bursts, which means a hacker would have to identify the right burst. Like finding a needle in a—"

"I got it," Garrett said. "This phone can't be hacked."

"No, of course it can be hacked."

"You just told me—"

"Garrett, every secret code that's ever been written can be broken. The only question is how quickly."

"How long did it take the Chinese to hack into the most-used SAT-phone system—the one you mentioned? What's it called?"

"GMR-2."

"How long?"

"I was hoping you wouldn't ask."

"I'm asking."

"Two seconds. But this phone will take them longer and I'll be notified and begin throwing up barriers to stop them."

"Two seconds?" Garrett repeated, shaking his head. He tucked the phone into his backpack. "That's really disappointing."

"Sorry I can't drive you to the airport," Kim said. "You know, it's my niece's birthday."

"I'm not sorry at all."

"Remember, once you use this phone, the Russians or their mole will begin trying to hack it."

"Kim, I'm not calling you unless it is an extreme emergency."

The shortest flight from Dulles International to Moscow took under ten hours but it was on an Aeroflot flight and IEU employees only traveled on American-based airlines and their European partners. With a stopover in Brussels, that meant fourteen hours had passed before Garrett landed at Moscow's Domodedova Airport. Gilbert Hardin, a fellow IEC security employee, was holding a clipboard with IEC written on it under the misspelled name *Garrit*.

"Marcus Austin says he needs to see you," Hardin said, as soon as they were inside the Ford Expedition. "What's makes you so special?"

Garrett shrugged. He was tired and not interested in conversation.

"Austin never talked to any of us when we got here," Hardin continued. "Twenty-seven months I've been here, and he's never said a word to me."

Garrett sat back in the SUV's front passenger seat and closed his eyes.

"I'm thinking Kiev," Hardin said. "You were there. Everyone's heard."

"I got no idea," Garrett said, his eyes still shut. "IEC told me to come to Moscow, just like it did you."

"But you're not like me or the other boys, are you? You got an in with Kim, the owner. You're special."

Garrett opened his eyes. Hardin was a big man. About 280 pounds hanging on a six-two frame. A thick black beard and short ponytail held with a rubber band. Tip of a tattoo visible on his neck. Garrett checked the passenger-side mirror for a Russian tail. It was easy to spot. He assumed Hardin knew they were being shadowed but didn't care. A simple airport pickup along A-105 heading north into Moscow.

"You were a big hero in Kiev. Me and the boys will grant you that, Garrett. It's not what's got us concerned. You feel me? Or do I have to spell it out?"

Garrett stared straight ahead. Traffic was light.

"Just to be crystal clear," Hardin said, "me and the

boys have been talking about Cameroon, and we want you to know there ain't one of us who's going to take a bullet because you go soft—"

Garrett jammed his left elbow up, smashing it into Hardin's jaw. Turning in the passenger's seat, he took control of the steering wheel with his right hand to keep the Ford from swerving into the adjacent lane. Caught completely off guard, Hardin discovered his next sensation to be Garrett's left hand gripping his windpipe.

Hardin released his hold on the wheel and grabbed Garrett's fingers, trying to pry them free from his neck. Garrett tightened his hold, locking them. Hardin gasped, unable to breathe.

"You and the boys," Garrett said through gritted teeth, "don't need to concern yourself with me. You got that?"

Panicked, Hardin nodded.

Garrett released both of his hands, shifted back in his seat. Hardin grabbed the steering wheel. "You sucker-punched me!"

Garrett checked the rearview mirror for the Russians, who were still following, and leaned his head back, closing his eyes.

"This isn't over between us," Hardin said, spitting blood from his cracked lip that was swelling.

"Just tell me the time and place," Garrett said.

"Oh, I will. You and I will deal with this. I guarantee you that."

Hardin reached back between the seats for a box of tissues that was kept for passengers but couldn't grab it.

Garrett undid his seat belt, grabbed a handful, and tossed them onto Hardin's lap.

Neither spoke during the hour that it took them to reach the U.S. embassy compound in the Presnensky District. A redbrick wall, further protected by concrete crash barriers to prevent cars from penetrating the perimeter, encircled the American compound. The gates were steel. It was Garrett's first glimpse, and the main building did not impress him. It was a rectangular box that faced westward over Konyushkovskaya Street, a major thoroughfare. The monolithic structure had two exterior surfaces. One half of the façade was composed of light brownstone, the other multiple layers of glass and steel. The windows permitted natural light inside while reflecting different colors based on weather conditions.

As the Ford entered the complex, Hardin said, "I'm required to tell you. Blue badges for Americans. Yellow for foreign nationals and there's a bunch working here. Cooks. Cleaning crews. A hard line between the lower and upper floors. The top ones secured. At least they claim they are. I think the bastards got them bugged, too."

Garrett was already aware. On his flight to Moscow, he'd read a file Kim had prepared about the U.S. embassy's past. It was a big file. Between 1953 and 1976, the Soviets had irradiated the original embassy with microwaves. In 1964, covert Russian listening devices had been discovered planted inside the U.S. Seal attached to a podium. When a fire broke out on the old embassy's eighth floor during 1977, the KGB had sent agents dressed as firefighters inside to pilfer documents. Two years later, both sides had agreed to allow the other to construct new, larger embassies, which is when the current one was built. During construction, Soviet workers were caught riddling it with listening devices. A sophisticated interconnecting system, much like a spiderweb, with bugs concealed in the steel and concrete columns, precast floor slabs, and interior walls. Besides bugs, resonating devices that allowed the Russians to monitor precisely both electronic and verbal communications. Even fake bugs to throw off detectors. So many embedded in the structure that Congress discussed demolishing the entire building and starting over. U.S. intelligence agencies insisted they could make it secure, so work had continued. After the demise of the Soviet Union, the director of Russian foreign intelligence (the SVR) gave his counterparts at Langley blueprints that reportedly showed where every bug had been planted. It was hailed as a gesture of goodwill, but a study by U.S. inspectors later determined all of the devices that he'd revealed already had been located.

"Here's where you get out," Hardin said.

Grabbing his gear, Garrett considered goading him, saying thanks for the ride. But decided against it. Hardin was just the first. He knew there were others itching to get a piece of him. Some with yellow badges, others with green.

Eighteen

Through a FISA-authorized wiretap, Agent Valerie Mayberry overheard Aysan Rivera arranging to meet a friend, Basak Kaya. Drinks. The Fogo de Chao Brazilian Steak House. Shopping afterward at the Galleria at Tysons II in Northern Virginia. Mayberry knew the mall. The Galleria was recognized worldwide for selling luxury brands at cheaper prices than could be found in London, Paris, or Dubai. A Washington, D.C., newspaper claimed the ultrarich would fly into nearby Dulles Airport in their private jets, take limos to the mall, and return home after staying only long enough to shop. Gucci, Ferragamo, Louis Vuitton, Prada, Saint Laurent, Cartier. Even billionaires liked bargains.

Rivera's friend had dozens of unpaid parking tickets.

The Fairfax County police were happy to help. Basak Kaya was intercepted on Virginia Route 7 after leaving her parents' Great Falls mansion. A guaranteed three-hour delay. Three hours without her cell phone.

Mayberry arrived at the steakhouse bar ten minutes after Basak Kaya was supposed to be there. As before, Rivera was easy to spot. A jet-black Versace fringe cowboy silk blouse with Swarovski crystals. High-waisted, skinny-fit Versace leather-insert jeans. Christian Louboutin black velvet Italian-made pumps decorated with a rainbow of crystals.

Mayberry had chosen equally expensive wear. A black silk georgette slip dress by Gucci with an Ivory Lace stripe and trim under a black Gucci wool coat. Like Rivera's, Mayberry's suede shoes were Louboutin—ankle boots that might have appeared clunky with such a clinging dress, except the combination looked quirky-cool on her slim figure. It was Mayberry's choice of a clutch purse that she knew would guarantee Rivera's attention. Mayberry entered the restaurant shouldering a Hermès Grey Ostrich Leather Silver Hardware Birkin 35 bag that retailed at $63,000.

As Mayberry made her way to the bar, she felt a sense of joy for the first time in a long while. A false persona. An escape from the shroud of Noah's death. Easier to be someone else than herself.

In the old days, creating a legend had been rather simple. Not now. The Internet had changed everything. The bureau had been forced to adapt. Instead of erasing the past, Mayberry had chosen to conceal her lie under layers and layers of truth. A risky move. She was using her maiden name. She'd made no attempt to keep her privileged upbringing secret. The silver spoon. The elitist private schools. No need to hide her short marriage to her do-gooder, dead-journalist husband. The only lie was her employment. FBI. Her name on government records was her married name. She was fortunate. Having worked undercover previously there already was a thin veil. Minor tweaking. An instant Internet background check would reveal Mayberry was a high-end real estate agent, finding luxurious homes for 1 percent of the world's 1 percent. A job that required no advertising because of the natural desire for privacy among her elite clientele.

Mayberry sat two bar stools away from her target and considered how best to approach Rivera, who was texting on her phone, no doubt trying to reach her missing lunch guest. A man approached Rivera—close enough for Mayberry to overhear. Rivera was blunt: "Get lost!"

For a moment, Mayberry considered an approach. Moving closer to her. Saying something clever about how it might be easier for them to avoid the men in the bar if they sat together. They both were wearing Louboutins—another possible icebreaking line. Or she could bring up the Smithmyer protest, mention that she had been there. But none of those approaches felt entirely right.

Rivera walked into the ladies' room.

Mayberry heard a booming voice and men laughing. Her eyes followed the ruckus. A man, most likely in his fifties, moving from table to table, shaking hands, chatting with customers. A twenty-something younger man trailing him and handing out what appeared to be political campaign brochures. It took a moment for Mayberry to recognize him. One of Virginia's most conservative Republican congressmen. She spotted Rivera exiting the restroom, returning to the bar. This was Mayberry's chance.

"Good afternoon, young lady," Representative Keith Bennett said, flashing a row of perfectly capped teeth at Mayberry. "A beautiful rose among the thorns in this fine establishment."

"How dare you objectify me!" Mayberry exclaimed, slipping from her bar stool and confronting him.

"Ma'am, I was just paying you a compliment."

"You were patronizing me," she complained loudly, purposely drawing attention. "You're exactly what's wrong with Republicans and our government."

"What specifically have I done in Congress that has made you so upset?" he asked calmly, foolishly opening the door. He seemed confident that he could win her over. "Reasonable people can disagree."

"Not when it comes to issues that really matter. You're xenophobic, wanting to build a wall, close our borders."

"I'm the son of immigrants, but we can't let people come here illegally. There's a process." He was speaking louder, assuming that those listening around him would agree with his explanation. A man at a nearby table clapped.

"That's code for keeping everyone but white Europeans out," she snapped back. "You bigot."

"I'm certainly not," he answered, clearly surprised by her anger.

"That's what all racists say."

"I'm not a racist because I want to stop pregnant Chinese women from flying into California so their babies can automatically become U.S. citizens and go on welfare. It's called 'birth tourism.'"

"Where'd you hear about that? Fox fake News?"

"I'm just trying to have a logical debate," he said, smirking.

"The idea that there is an objective truth is what men say to women to shut them up," Mayberry shouted.

"Ma'am, I grew up poor in southwest Virginia, and from the looks of it, a lot poorer than you've ever been. My parents owned a small tobacco farm. I planted it, pulled suckers, topped plants, and harvested it. I started working at age twelve. No one ever gave me anything that I didn't work hard to earn."

"Stop calling me ma'am and stop objectifying me by my appearance. Your sappy story has nothing to do with white privilege and if you had half a brain you'd realize how stupid you sound. You got an invisible package of unearned assets and privileges the moment you dropped out of your mother's womb because you are white and you have a penis. If you can't own up to that, you're aiding the oppression of women and minorities. If you really cared about equality you would step aside and let a woman or someone of color take your job."

He began to step away, but he feared it might be perceived as defeat. A man at the bar was recording them with his phone from a stool in the corner behind Mayberry.

"No one ever gave me anything," he said, trying to keep his voice even-tempered. "I paid my way through college, joined the military to serve our country, fought in the Gulf War, worked two jobs and attended night school to earn my law degree and decided to enter politics because I wanted to serve others—how dare you tell me I'm privileged simply because I have white skin. You're the bigot, judging me by my skin color."

"Oh my God," Mayberry shrieked. "Your ignorance is exactly why we need a revolution! We need to tear down the elite. We need to end capitalism and Wall Street exploitation of the poor! Free college, free medicine, birth-to-grave benefits and protections. That's what government should be."

Bennett's aide stepped from behind them. "The congressman has spent more than enough time listening to your rude comments," he said in a low voice. His move was meant as a buffer. Instead, he'd played right into her plan.

"Don't threaten me," she screeched as she pulled a canister of pepper spray from her bag.

Bennett stepped backward so suddenly he bumped into a table. Unsteady, he reached for its edge, missed it, and fell onto the floor. A look of horror appeared on his aide's face when Mayberry aimed the canister at him.

She didn't shoot. Instead she dashed from the bar, shielding her face.

Her outburst worked. Aysan Rivera caught up with her in the parking lot.

"That was frickin' awesome," Rivera gushed. "You almost pepper-sprayed a congressman."

"I'm just lucky there were no cops around. They would have shot me."

Rivera glanced nervously at the restaurant's entrance. "You need to get going. Hey, I was supposed to meet a friend, but she never showed. You want to go to Georgetown and grab a drink?"

Fifty minutes later they were sitting inside the Rye Bar at the swanky Rosewood Hotel.

"Where'd you get the courage to do that?" Rivera asked.

"It's in my blood. I'm related to the Astors."

"Sorry, I'm not from here. I'm Turkish."

"America went through a period called the 'gilded age' when robber barons ran America—you know, the Rockefellers, Mellons, Carnegies, J. P. Morgans, Vanderbilts."

The blank look on Rivera's face showed she didn't recognize the names so she added, "They were the Bill Gates, Warren Buffetts, and Mark Zuckerbergs of today. Superrich and powerful. Mrs. William B. Astor drew up a list of four hundred New Yorkers—it was everyone who she said mattered in society."

"Talk about elitism," Rivera said.

"I know, right? And they were all white, of course. Get this, she chose four hundred because that's how many could fit in her Manhattan ballroom. The list was based on the husbands' wealth because women didn't work when the family had money. They were all rich, white Manhattan snobs."

Rivera covered her mouth. She'd taken a sip of her cocktail and started to laugh, nearly spitting it.

"What's so funny?" Mayberry asked.

"We're drinking Manhattans!"

"What's really funny is Mrs. Astor used her list, wealth, and connections to quietly undermine the men on it. She pushed the suffragette movement to get women the right to vote. I think she would have been proud of me today fighting the system."

"And you're related to her?"

"A distant relative, but my family was on that four hundred list and I can tell you, my relatives are all rich and a bunch of white oppressors. They're blind to the signs of late-stage capitalism. I sometimes think I was born in the wrong generation. I would have loved the nineteen sixties." She laughed. "America is so far gone—you can't trust the police because they're part of the problem—revolution is the only solution."

Mayberry decided to make a risky move. "Have

you ever heard of Antifa? Its motto is 'we go where the right-wingers go.' In Berkeley, they threw Molotov cocktails and smashed windows when an alt-right speaker appeared on campus. In New York, they forced a local community to cancel a local rose parade because Republicans were participating. When I saw that pompous Republican creep soliciting votes today, I decided I had to get into his face. I had to go where the right-wingers go."

For a moment, Mayberry wondered if she had tipped her hand. Rivera was clearly distracted. She stood from their table—and waved her hand.

"It's my friend," Rivera explained. "I finally reached her by text—but let's not talk politics. I've known her since we were kids and she won't understand."

Twelve hours later, Mayberry crawled into bed and gazed at the spinning ceiling above her. It had been a long time since she'd had so much to drink and been such a flirt.

She was still hungover in the morning when she met Director Harris in the backseat of his Cadillac near her condo.

"There's a video going viral showing a deranged woman running out of a restaurant after threatening a Virginia congressman," he said. "You're damn lucky it doesn't show your face."

Mayberry handed him a wad of receipts. "You'll have to cover these. The bureau's bean-counters would go into shock."

Harris put on half-glasses. "What the hell!" he exclaimed.

"It's only thirty thousand dollars," she said. "You don't get out much with this wealthy, younger set, do you? A single Cristal worth drinking is eighteen grand."

"And what do I get for your wild evening at tax-payers' expense?"

Her cell rang. She checked the caller ID and raised her right index finger to her lips to hush Harris, whose face turned flush with anger.

"That was Aysan," Mayberry said, putting down her phone. "Pay the bill. I'm in."

Nineteen

CIA station chief Marcus Austin didn't fit the mold of a State Department cultural attaché—his diplomatic cover. Early forties. Broad shoulders, thick neck. Someone who hit the free weights each morning and most likely at night, too. Wearing a too-snug short-sleeve dress shirt that accented his muscles on muscles. Shaved head. Loose necktie. Intimidating stare. There was a time in U.S. intelligence when station chiefs modeled themselves after George Smiley, the urbane intellectual who thought ten moves ahead. That was before the CIA became the tip of the spear in combating terrorism, when outmatching wits became less important than being capable of dropping alone into the mountains of Afghanistan to deliver bags of cash to a local warlord as an incentive to kill his Taliban kinsman. A man of Austin's physique was most likely ex-military—and ex-military at the State Department generally meant CIA.

"Brother, here's the skinny," Austin said from behind his desk inside the embassy. "One of my guys will go black tonight and spray-paint a signal on a telephone booth."

"Moscow still has phone booths?" Garrett replied.

"Pavel is old-school," Austin said, "which explains why he's using the same commo we used forty years ago. My guy paints a signal. Pavel sees it tomorrow morning while he's being driven to work. He knows we're ready to play. Tomorrow night, one of my guys takes his wife to the Bolshoi." He paused. "You like the ballet?"

"Sure, I go all the time," Garrett replied dryly.

Austin laughed too loudly. "Pavel will leave ballet tickets for my guy under the name Fred Thomas. On the back of the tickets are a series of numbers. One is a pickup time, but the actual time is four hours earlier than what's written. The other numbers are the coordinates, but they're reversed. Old-school, brother. We're talking Cold War. No electronics, no computers. No wireless bursts. Coded numbers on the back of a ballet ticket."

"If it works, why change, right?"

"More than that, brother. Russians fear change, especially the older types. How much do you know about this country?"

Austin didn't wait for Garrett to answer. "Brother," he said, "I've studied the Russians all my life and they may look like us, but they're not. A Russian who expects the absolute worst is an optimist. They were brought up being told to keep their heads down. Question authority and you were sent to Siberia or worse. Now that Kalugin is in charge, it's worse. A beating or a bullet."

"Or poison."

"You understand, brother. Let me tell you the truth about why the Soviet empire failed. There was no free enterprise. Everyone got paid by the state. Fifty rubles a month. Didn't matter if you were a brain surgeon or a ditch digger. That was socialism, brother. All one giant classless collective. Everyone equal. But it was total bullshit. There was no incentive. Taxi drivers got paid whether they picked up passengers or not. Why bother? Here's the crème de la crème. The biggest glass factory in the entire empire was just outside Moscow. You got no profit-or-loss statement because that's capitalism—so how do you know if the plant is doing good?"

Garrett hated being asked questions like this, trying to guess what the speaker expected as an answer. He stayed silent and looked at Austin.

"I'll tell you. You measured production. How many meters of glass is the plant turning out. Sounds right, huh? Until the geniuses running the plant realized they could turn out more meters if they dialed down the machines, making the glass thinner and thinner. Productivity increased, the Kremlin was happy, but the glass was so razor thin it broke as soon as it came off the assembly line. Completely worthless. But, hey, that didn't bother the plant manager because he ordered the broken pieces melted down and put back on the production line, causing productivity to increase even more. Everyone was as happy as a pig in mud and the plant never had a single truck make a delivery. That's communism, brother."

Austin chuckled.

"Here's the deal though, Garrett," he continued. "The system was stupid, but not its people. Only a fool underestimates bastards like Kalugin and Gromyko. Stone-cold killers just like Papa Stalin. Got another quick story for you, brother. A history lesson. Stalin's advisors tell him a certain percentage of Russians will turn against him. Traitors. For illustration purposes, let's say five percent. Stalin tells all the Communist Party chiefs in every village to identify those five percent and execute them. So what did they do?"

Austin hesitated, but Garrett again didn't bite.

"The secret police chief in each village," Austin continued, "tried to better each other to impress Stalin. 'Oh, Comrade Stalin, we found ten percent of our village so we killed them.' 'Papa Stalin, we found fifteen percent.' Do you think Stalin cared? He let them kill as many as they wanted. My point, brother, is that killing means nothing to people like Kalugin and Gromyko."

"Back to Yakov Pavel," Garrett said. "Your guy leaves the signal tonight. Pavel leaves Bolshoi tickets for your guy tomorrow night with the pickup location and time."

"That's right, brother, and you get him the very next. Then it's up to you to smuggle him out of Russia alive. Him and the kid. If everything goes right, you won't be here in Moscow long enough to take a satisfying crap."

Austin stood, opened a safe near his desk, and removed a red envelope, which he tossed to Garrett.

"Your extraction plan, brother. The name Gordievsky ring a bell?"

"Colonel Oleg Antonovich Gordievsky, former KGB now living in England."

"MI-6 was working him when someone ratted him out. Told Moscow. But the KGB needed evidence, so it ordered him home. Interrogated him for five hours. Drugged him. The works. But Gordievsky didn't crack. They released him but kept watching, hoping he'd panic and screw up. Instead, he goes out for a morning jog. Loses his KGB tail, hops on a train to the Finnish border, where he meets a British embassy car. Crawls into a hiding spot between the backseat and trunk and the Brits get him across the border into Finland. Langley wants you to do the same. Only you aren't going via train or Finland."

"Where and how?"

"A Zil 5301 Bychok—a small commercial truck built during the Soviet era before Zil stopped making vehicles because they were pieces of junk."

"That's hardly reassuring."

Austin chuckled. He was enjoying himself. "Got you one from 1996—and I've made modifications. Thick metal plates inside the doors and engine compartment. Should stop most rounds if they start shooting."

"The windows?"

"Sorry, brother, couldn't get bullet-resistant glass on short notice. You wouldn't want it too easy, right?"

"How fast does this Zil go?"

"With the added armor, possibly sixty."

"Where do I delivery Pavel and the kid?"

"Ukraine border."

"What? Ukraine? Ambassador Thorpe was just assassinated there."

"Last place they'll think you'll drive." Austin eyed the envelope he'd tossed Garrett. "Fake passports, visas, documents about the vehicle you'll be taking, rubles, and maps of Russian roadways."

"You get this in the dip pouch?" Garrett asked suspiciously.

"No, brother, Harris didn't want to risk it since someone's reading our communications with Langley. Hand delivered to me."

"Whose hands?"

For the first time since they'd begun talking, Austin frowned and let out a sigh. "Ambassador Edward Todd Duncan. He and his wife brought the packet back after Thorpe's D.C. funeral. They'd stayed behind in Washington for a few days of R-and-R so Harris used Duncan as his courier."

Garrett noticed that the seal on the red envelope was broken.

Austin came from behind his desk and leaned his butt against it, so he was now standing directly in front of Garrett. "The answer is Ambassador Duncan opened it before delivering it to me."

"Why?"

"He wasn't supposed to, brother. Director Harris screwed up trusting him, but nobody is going to say anything."

Garrett didn't like it. Not a bit. Now another possible breach—if Ambassador Duncan blabbed something about its contents.

"So why'd Duncan open a top secret, hand-delivered packet that Director Harris gave him? He must've told the ambassador not to open it."

"Because Harris and I believe Duncan's wife is cheating on him with a Russian. Full name is Ivan Yovovich Sokolov. I'm assuming Duncan opened it to make certain Harris and I weren't going behind his back, talking about his wife."

"Huh? You want to repeat that for me?"

"Life's full of twists, brother. Duncan gets himself appointed because he's a billionaire donor. Ran an international conglomerate before deciding he wanted to become an ambassador."

"Don't most donors choose Paris or London?" Garrett asked. "Who wants to come to Moscow?"

"Duncan's grandmother's family had some Russian ties. His wife, Heidi, she's half his age and still very attractive. Was a Vegas showgirl when they met. Do I need to fill in the blanks about this marriage?"

"And you think she's cheating with a Russian."

"Not any Russian, brother. Ivan Sokolov. Son of a Russian oligarch with close ties to Kalugin. I see Kalugin's fingers all over this."

"You got proof?"

"Of Kalugin sending Sokolov to get in her pants?" Austin asked.

"No, of this alleged affair."

"One of my people spotted him chatting her up at reception a few months back. Good-looking guy, super-rich. Next we know, she's trying to lose her protective detail. Insisting she go out shopping unaccompanied by security to Russian stores. You tell me, what billion-aire's wife goes shopping in Moscow? We let her go but tailed her. Met Sokolov at a hotel. We got photos and some juicy recordings."

"What did her husband say—assuming you told him?"

"I did. He got huffy, denied it, complained to the president, and blamed me. Said his wife doesn't know anything. No foul, no harm. I was told to back off."

"What are the chances Duncan told her about me?" Garrett asked. "Worse, that she tipped off Ivan Sokolov?"

Austin let out a sigh. "Wish I knew, brother. Wish I knew." He walked back around his desk to his safe and removed a second package. This one was still sealed.

"A friend of yours," Austin said, handing it to him.

It contained Garrett's SIG Sauer P226 pistol with extra ammo.

"Glad to have it."

"I gotta believe Duncan didn't tell his wife," Austin continued. "I gotta believe he was just checking to see if we were communicating about her."

"Yeah, but I'm sure he read it. Curiosity and all."

Austin nodded. "I agree, but reading and telling someone are two different things. Look, brother, we got a good plan. You pick up Pavel and the kid two days from now. You spend maybe ten, twelve hours driving to Ukraine. Then you're done. Besides, if it goes bad and you get snatched, Harris will get you out."

Garrett wished he believed that. "I don't have diplomatic immunity like you do—brother," he said.

"Go grab a shower," Austin said. "Duncan's throwing a birthday party for his daughter tonight. I want you there."

"For a kids' birthday inside the embassy?"

"I invited two or three other IEC security guards to make it look legit. The Russians need to see you working as a guard and two guests will be of special interest to you. Ivan Sokolov and General Gromyko. Besides, it's a birthday party. Cake, ice cream."

"Do I have to sing?"

Twenty

"You bring your pepper spray?" Aysan Rivera asked.

Valerie Mayberry plucked a red spray canister from the right pocket of her J.Crew military-inspired wax-cotton jacket to show Rivera.

"Never leave home without it," Mayberry said, smiling. "Where we heading?"

They had parked their cars earlier at the Tysons Galleria and were now riding in a rented Ford Fusion hybrid traveling south on the Capitol Beltway, a sixty-four-mile major thoroughfare encircling Washington, D.C.

"Guinea Station," Rivera said, momentarily taking her eyes off the always-jammed expressway to smile at her passenger. "They're honoring a Confederate general there today."

Mayberry typed the words "Guinea Station" into her smartphone. She wanted to double-check what she remembered from books she'd read about Virginia history and the Civil War.

"We alone or is someone else meeting us there?" Mayberry asked.

"A half dozen of us, including Makayla."

"Makayla?"

"Do you remember how you mentioned Antifa when we were having drinks? She's an Antifa organizer. She calls us when there's a rally or protest or what we're going to today. A ceremony honoring a racist slaveholder."

"Where's she from?"

"Some friendly advice. Don't ask too many questions," Rivera said. "I vouched for you, but you'll have to prove yourself today. All of us had to. Ask too many questions and everyone will think you're a cop."

"Me, a cop? How many cops you know who wear Christian Louboutins? What sort of proof?"

"Makayla will tell you."

Mayberry focused on her phone. Guinea Station was the location of the Thomas Jonathan "Stonewall" Jackson Shrine, a national military park. The railway house

there had been a critical supply hub for the Confederacy. Nearly all of General Robert E. Lee's troops had
passed through it for supplies during the war. In April
1863, Union general Joseph "Fighting Joe" Hooker had
launched a campaign to capture the Confederacy's capital city—Richmond. To do that, Hooker needed to first
seize the rail station, cutting off rebel supply lines. The
Battle of Chancellorsville became one of the bloodiest
in the Civil War. Historians would later call it "General
Lee's perfect battle." Hugely outnumbered, General Lee
divided his troops in half, a highly risky move, and used
them to outflank the larger Union forces being led by
a more timid General Hooker. Some 24,000 soldiers on
both sides died during that battle. The South's biggest
loss was Stonewall Jackson, arguably Lee's best general.
He was mistakenly shot by his own men at night and
transported with thousands of other wounded soldiers
to a plantation near Guinea Station. He survived his
wound, but died eight days later from pneumonia.

Mayberry pulled up pictures of Stonewall Jackson's
Shrine.

A plain, one-story rectangular house painted white
where Jackson had succumbed.

She started to explain what she had read, but Rivera
dismissed her after the first few sentences.

"I don't care about historical stuff," Rivera said.

"Germans don't put up shrines honoring Nazis. The U.S. shouldn't be honoring racists."

"Who's honoring Jackson today?" Mayberry asked.

"Like I said, Makayla will tell you. And remember, not so many questions. Just go with it."

Mayberry didn't respond and Rivera intentionally changed subjects. "Have you ever heard of Ovelia Transtoto? Her latest line is dazzling."

The two women talked couture until they reached the Interstate 95 exit to the Jackson Shrine. About four miles from the park's entrance, Rivera turned onto the road's shoulder, where a windowless black van and two other rented cars were waiting.

"Let's go," Rivera said, leading the way.

Mayberry counted eight crowded inside the van around a woman whom Mayberry immediately recognized. She had led the Smithmyer College protest. She'd been the one yelling through a bullhorn.

"This is Makayla," Rivera said proudly after closing the van's door behind them.

"I'm Valerie," Mayberry said, extending her hand.

Makayla looked at it but didn't shake it. "You're here because Aysan vouched for you and showed me the Internet video of you confronting that Republican bigot, but you get no respect from me until I see you doing business."

"Fair enough," Mayberry said.

Makayla turned her face away and began issuing instructions to the Antifa members, who were affixing shin guards and shoulder pads over their street clothes. Finally, Makayla spoke to Mayberry.

"We'll learn today what you're made of," she said.

"Short of murder," Mayberry replied, "I'm in."

"Oh, we'd never kill anyone," Rivera interjected. "We're here to fight the Nazis and fascists and protect peaceful protestors."

Mayberry noticed that Makayla didn't comment. Instead the Antifa leader handed a photo to Mayberry. A thirty-something man with red hair, white shirt, light blue tie. "This is your target. I want you to pepper-spray him when we get there," Makayla said. She studied Mayberry's face for some betraying glance, a hesitation.

"Who is he?" Mayberry asked.

"Does that matter to you?" Makayla asked.

Rivera said, "He's the principal at a local high school."

"Stonewall Jackson High School," a man near Makayla volunteered.

"All she needs to know is he's a racist," Makayla said.

"We tried to reason with him," the man said, undeterred, "and the local school board. Emails, letters demanding the school's name be changed. They shouldn't be honoring a slave owner and American traitor by naming a school after him. But they refused."

"They were warned," Rivera added.

The man continued: "The principal's response was predictable. The same old crap about how Stonewall Jackson is part of Virginia's history."

"Rednecks," another Antifa member in the van interjected.

"This wreath-laying ceremony is an annual tradition at the high school," the first man who'd spoken explained. "They claim it's history but it's all about reminding people of color to stay in their place. Honoring Jackson is meant to intimidate. It's an act of aggression and violence."

"How do black students at the school feel?" Mayberry asked.

"They've been oppressed so long, they don't even know it," he replied.

"We'll wake them up today," Makayla added, retaking control of the conversation. "As for you, Valerie Mayberry, all you need to do is get close enough to smell this principal's stink and gas him. Aim for his eyes. Now, you just said, anything short of murder. You got a problem with actually using that Mace you brought or is it just for appearances?"

"Nobody calls it Mace anymore," Mayberry said, correcting her. She noticed Makayla's eyes narrow.

"Answer my question?" Makayla said.

"Right in his face," Mayberry replied.

Rivera and the others grinned.

"The rest of us will create a diversion for you," Makayla said. "After you gas him, look for this black van. If you miss it, we're not waiting."

"Yeah, you'll have to call an Uber," the man next to her said, laughing.

"Local television will be there," Makayla said. "And a newspaper reporter too. I tipped them off. So you need to hide your faces, otherwise the cops will come after us."

The man offered Mayberry a hockey goalie's mask. But Makayla pushed his hand aside.

"She can't get close to him wearing that," Makayla said. She thrust out her hand. She was holding a blue scarf. "Pull this up around your mouth moments before you spray him." Next she offered Mayberry a Washington Redskins cap. "They will assume you are one of them if you wear this. Remember, when the black van comes, we go. And I'll be watching you. All of us will. You don't come with us if you don't spray him good."

Rivera slid open the parked van's side door. Everyone but its driver exited. Back inside the Ford rental,

Rivera slipped a black stocking cap onto her head and drove the car onto the roadway.

"Makayla doesn't like me," Mayberry said.

"She treats everyone like that. She doesn't like to get close to people."

"Where's she from? I picked up a bit of a foreign accent."

"No questions, remember?"

About a mile from the shrine, Rivera said, "Makayla has one of our people already there. He's live-streaming so we'll know exactly when to hit 'em."

Rivera handed her phone to Mayberry. The principal was speaking in front of the shrine's white building where Jackson had died. Next to him was a wreath made of gray and white carnations designed to resemble Stonewall Jackson's bearded face.

"There's been much in the news lately about Confederate monuments," the principal could be heard saying over the phone's live stream. "Let me be clear. As Americans, we all condemn neo-Nazis, the KKK, and racism and bigotry in all of its forms. It is wrong. Period. There is no debate. The question that you students need to ask yourselves is this: 'Is acknowledging and honoring our southern history and our heritage offensive? Or is it part of our history and do we need to learn and understand it?'"

The principal was using the wreath-laying ceremony as a teachable moment. "In the eyes of the political far left, anyone who opposes the removal of a statue commemorating Confederate soldiers automatically is classified as a bigot, anti-Semitic, and any other harsh emotional condemnation that they can throw on you. However, Condoleezza Rice, the first African American woman to serve as secretary of state, held a somewhat different view than this. When asked about removing Confederate statues, she said, 'When you start wiping out your history, sanitizing your history to make you feel better, it's a bad thing.'"

Continuing: "You students need to think seriously about what would happen if we begin sanitizing Virginia's past and discrediting every one of our forefathers by judging them by today's standards and attitudes rather than those that existed during their own time periods. If we remove statues to Confederate soldiers, should we also tear down monuments to George Washington and Thomas Jefferson in our nation's capital because both owned slaves? Where do you draw a sensible line? Is it reasonable to keep such monuments and explain their context with informational placards, or must they be destroyed?"

"Let's have a show of hands," he said. "How many of you have visited Mount Rushmore?"

About two dozen hands shot into the air.

"What should we do about Teddy Roosevelt? He referred to the white race, and I will quote him here, as the 'forward race,' whose responsibility it was to raise the status of minorities through training the 'backward race[s] in industrial efficiency, political capacity and domestic morality.' He declared that whites were responsible for preserving the 'high civilization wrought out by (our nation's) forefathers.' Does that mean we'll need to sandblast his face from Mount Rushmore for words that he was speaking that he believed would be helpful to minorities? Which brings us to Abraham Lincoln. Surely, he deserves to stay on Mount Rushmore. After all, Lincoln issued a declaration emancipating all slaves. But did you know that as a lawyer, Lincoln represented a slaveholder in court who was seeking to remand his slave, Jane Bryant, and her four children back to slavery?"

He paused and then said, "My point is that racism is and has been an ugly stain on our history, but should it be the single and only ethical standard we use in judging our forebears? Before you answer, ask yourself, do you want to be judged by the standards of today? Or by the standards that will be acceptable, whatever they might be, in two hundred years by people looking backward at you? As students, you should form your own opinions. As for me, when I read about a historical figure such as Stonewall Jackson, I see him as a whole person—a dynamic figure during his age, a product of the South who played a significant role at a pivotal time in our nation's history. We cannot and should not obliterate his name and banish him from our history books. This is why we have come together today to educate ourselves about the Civil War, the bloody Battle of Chancellorsville, his crucial role in it, and the pivotal role Jackson played in Virginia history. Like him or not, he is a historical figure of importance."

Mayberry handed back Rivera's cell phone. Rivera said, "Remember, you need to stay in this car when the caravan gets there. Scrunch down, and let us draw attention away from you."

Within moments, the three rental cars entered the shrine's parking lot. Everyone but Mayberry bolted from them. They hollered and waved handmade signs—END BIGOTRY. FIGHT RACISM.

The masked protestors formed a wedge, driving themselves into the center of the crowd from its right edge. As instructed, Mayberry hung back before slipping from the car and walking calmly around the crowd's left edge. More than two hundred were attending the ceremony. Nearly all were white, except for several dozen black, Latino, and Asian students.

Among the adults were teachers and a handful of gray-haired grandmothers. Daughters of the Confederacy. A few elderly men, one with a walker. Many of the students were wearing sports clothing imprinted with the Stonewall Jackson High School mascot—a horse on its hind legs with a Stars and Bars flag behind it. The horse was Little Sorrel. Stonewall Jackson's favorite mount. So beloved in Dixie that when the animal died, a taxidermist mounted it. Now on permanent display at the Virginia Military Institute Museum in Lexington, the oldest state-funded military school in the nation.

The school principal had been in the midst of explaining how Jackson had received his nickname "Stonewall" at the First Battle of Bull Run when the protestors appeared.

"Everyone stay calm!" he exclaimed into the microphone he was holding.

"Racists! Racists!" protesters chanted. The Antifa members began shoving students, teachers—anyone in their path. Tempers flared. An elderly Daughters of the Confederacy onlooker refused to move, was pushed and fell backward onto the grass, crying out in pain. A protester lowered his shoulder and thrust himself into a male teacher who happened to be the school's football coach. Several of his players ran to his side. One threw a punch and the melee began.

Mayberry continued unnoticed along the crowd's outer perimeter, reaching the white clapboard house, now ten feet away from the principal, who was looking in the opposite direction from her, desperately trying to get his students to return to three yellow school buses parked in the lot.

"Don't fight!" he hollered.

Mayberry spotted the television cameraman filming the disruption happening in the center of the crowd. A woman with a Nikon—a local reporter, no doubt—also was snapping shots. No one was watching Mayberry. That's when Mayberry noticed Makayla. Standing away from the others, watching her. Their eyes locked. Mayberry raised the scarf that Makayla had given her, lowered her cap's lid, and drew the pepper-spray canister from her jacket pocket.

Her first thought was to intentionally miss the principal. She could claim bad aim. But would Makayla believe her? Out of the corner of his eye, the principal noticed her, saw her arm raised, turned, and faced her. She pressed the spray's trigger. He tried to protect his face but the oleoresin capsaicin pepper extraction, tinted with red dye, splashed onto his cheeks and mouth. The dye made it appear as if he were bleeding. He screamed from the burning sensation now stinging his skin and began spitting.

The cameraman noticed, spun around, and began filming the temporarily blinded principal. Makayla had disappeared from Mayberry's sight. She turned her head and retreated. Hoping to avoid being filmed.

The black van raced into the parking lot. Its horn blaring, causing students to scamper out of its way. Mayberry reached the lot just as the van came to a stop.

She was less than ten yards from it. That is when it happened.

A deafening explosion. The wooden walls of the Jackson Shrine blew in all directions. Splintered wooden planks hewed before the Civil War became deadly projectiles. One struck Mayberry in the back of her head, knocking her onto the blacktop. Confused, she reached backward, feeling the rear of her skull. Blood. She could hear others moaning, screaming for help. She tried to stand but fell.

Glancing forward, she saw Rivera and her fellow demonstrators about to shut the van's sliding door and flee. They were leaving her behind.

Mayberry felt a hand grab her jacket and jerk her onto her feet.

"I'm not leaving anyone behind this time," Makayla declared, dragging her into the van.

Twenty-One

Brett Garrett searched his backpack. Where was it? Panic. Each pocket unzipped. Bag shaken. Held upside down. Contents tumbling out, scattering onto the floor of his IEC quarters. Dropping to his knees, Garrett combed through each item. The packet wasn't there. The Russians. Airport. They must have taken it when they searched his bag. One had distracted him asking a series of robotic questions. Typical harassment, he'd assumed. He'd surprised them answering in Russian. Still, he had missed their theft.

Suboxone. How easy it must have been to palm. Garrett's doctor had warned him against going cold turkey. His body needed it. It was chemically dependent on it. Otherwise, withdrawal would kick in. The first seventy-two hours would be the worst. Garrett had read about how dangerous it was to just stop. Nausea. Vomiting. Insomnia. Indigestion. Anxiety. Irritability. Cravings. Fever. Chills. Sweating. Most frightening, difficulty concentrating. Lack of focus at a time when he would need it the most. After seventy-two hours would come feelings of despair, depression, and intense cravings for the drug.

He returned his possessions to his backpack and immediately realized that he was sweating. Was withdrawal beginning or was it psychological?

He showered, dressed in a navy-blue polo shirt, gray slacks, and gray blazer—the formal dress for an IEC security guard—and took a deep breath. He'd never known of an IEC employee being invited to a kid's birthday party. Their job was to remain out of sight, only seen when diplomats and their families needed protection and only then when they traveled outside the compound.

Only recently had the State Department hired private guards in Russia. Before President Kalugin and General Gromyko there had been no need. The harassment had begun with embassy employees being detained at airports. Next, stopped by police when driving. The wife of a senior diplomat had been assaulted in front of her two young children while on a stroll in Gorky Park. Hooligans, the Moscow police had declared. But

CIA chief of station Austin knew better. Two American teenagers beaten when they emerged from a Moscow ice cream shop. Both hospitalized, one with a broken leg, the other a fractured nose. Austin had wanted to strike back. Director Harris had said no.

Instead, State had hired Thomas Jefferson Kim's IEC company to provide private security. At first, the Russians refused to let them be armed, arguing the embassy should hire Russian bodyguards. There were plenty. After the collapse of the Soviet Union, kidnapping and killing had become cheaper than negotiating a business deal or settling a squabble in court. Nearly 2 percent of Russia's working population were licensed as security guards. That was 1.5 million Russians. It only took the equivalent of $200 to buy a license. Pay another $200 and you could carry a concealed weapon.

Garrett tried to steady his nerves as he stepped out of his room.

"You," a voice hollered.

Gilbert Hardin had come ready to fight. Revenge for the sucker punch during the airport ride. He'd brought two buddies.

"Stand down," Garrett said. "I got somewhere to be."

"Oh, I forgot. You're special. Off to a little kiddies' birthday party," Hardin taunted. "The business between us won't take long."

"Later, I said."

Hardin and his buddies blocked the hallway.

"Say please," Hardin said.

"Really?" Garrett said. "Are we in third grade or had you already dropped out by then?"

"Smart mouth, Garrett. But this is more than just that sucker punch you landed. Cameroon. Some of us knew your men there. We don't trust you."

Garrett let out a loud sigh. "You had that punch coming. Even more. But I'll play your game. Now *please* let me pass," he said.

Hardin clenched his fists. Eager to throw a punch. "Say 'please with sugar on top.'"

Garrett shook his head in disgust. He didn't have time for this.

"After the party," he said. "You, me, and your pals. We can settle this. But for now, get out of my way."

"No. Say 'pretty please.' I want to hear it," Hardin repeated.

Garrett fought his urge to engage. It wasn't the right time. "Pretty please may I pass."

Hardin grinned at his pals. "Okay, boys, let's let Mr. Tough Guy go to his kiddie party."

Neither the U.S. Marines stationed at the door nor the State Department security detail asked for an ID when Garrett entered the embassy. An older woman wearing an equally old blue wool business suit greeted him from behind a table positioned in the center hallway where she was directing traffic. Adults to her left, children to her right.

"Mr. Garrett," she said, "my name is Miss Gloria Whitworth, personal assistant to the ambassador's wife, Mrs. Heidi Duncan." Her formality and stature reminded him of his fifth-grade teacher. That teacher had not liked him. Nor had he liked her.

"No name tags tonight," she said, "but you can wear one of these." She glanced down to the table at a display of cheap-jeweled tiaras, pink-and-blue paper cones with elastic neckbands, and bright red top hats with HAPPY BIRTHDAY inscribed on their brims.

"I'm not much for hats," Garrett said.

"The ambassador and his wife are wearing them."

So was Miss Whitworth—a cardboard gold crown.

Garrett glanced to his left into the open doorway of the children's party. A disco ball. Painted-face clown with giant orange feet. A magician in a cape. A gaggle of squealing tweens in sequin-embellished, multilayered tulle party skirts and boys uncomfortable in suits and ties, awkwardly waiting at a self-serve ice cream machine.

Garrett shifted his glance to the adult room. Cocktails. Chamber music. Lots of evening wear. Adults in party hats chitchatting.

"The kid's party looks more fun," he said dryly, "and I don't like kids."

"Which hat would you prefer?" she asked.

"I'll pass."

Ambassador Duncan and Heidi Duncan were situated near the entrance. Garrett moved to skip by them but a hand grabbed his upper arm, guiding him back into the receiving line.

"I'm your date tonight," the woman holding him said.

Midforties. Black hair worn short. Black glasses. A pleasing face, but not someone who would draw stares when entering a room. Dressed professionally. Physically fit. He'd never seen her before but assumed she worked for Austin and was, therefore, CIA.

"Mr. Ambassador and Ms. Duncan," she announced, "let me introduce our newest arrival, Mr. Brett Garrett with IEC."

"Ah, the man from Kiev," the ambassador said, extending his hand. Forced smile. "Nasty place, Ukraine. I didn't really know Ambassador Thorpe—he was career, unlike me. But I heard great things about him after he was murdered. Went to his funeral, of course. Just returned."

Ambassador Duncan was in his early seventies. Silver, slicked-back hair. Thin. Tall. A gold wedding band on his left, silver Harvard signet ring on his right. Tailored Italian suit. Standing beside him, his wife. Heidi looked like a woman fighting middle age. Cosmetic surgery. Birdlike diet. Carefully coiffed brunette. Glistening white teeth. Soft, dainty hand. Multiple-carat diamond wedding ring.

"I remember you from television," she said. "The congressional hearings. What was the name of that country where that senator's son died?"

Garrett suspected she already knew. What he didn't know was if she also had been told about the reason he had come to Moscow.

"Thanks for inviting me to your party," he replied.

"Don't thank me, thank my husband. I don't really believe we need a security guard here, especially you."

Garrett had met her type before. He'd always found it curious that women born of privilege felt little need to prove themselves, but those who had climbed the social ladder nearly always were blatant snobs, eager to belittle those whom they saw as beneath them.

"Let's get a drink," the woman still clutching his arm said, guiding him toward a corner bar.

"How's Marcus Austin as a boss," he asked her.

"I don't work for Austin. I'm on Mrs. Duncan's personal staff. You met my boss in the hallway."

"The ice queen wearing the gold crown?"

"Miss Whitworth tends to be a bit stuffy," the woman said, smiling. "But she's old-fashioned in her ways. What are you drinking?"

"Miss Whitworth," he said, puckering his lips and raising his voice, mocking her, "would not approve. I'm on duty."

"No, you're on display."

She ordered him a Klinskoye Svetloe. "It's Russian, similar to Yuengling," she explained. "You're a curiosity because of your reputation. On display, so smile."

He didn't but he did follow her eyes as they both surveyed the ballroom. About a hundred guests. He spotted a familiar face and grimaced. A network news reporter who'd covered the Cameroon congressional hearings apparently now working in Moscow.

"I thought it was you," the correspondent said as he approached.

Without warning, the woman next to Garrett stumbled forward, splashing her pinot noir against the reporter's chest.

"I'm so, so sorry," she said loudly. "New heels."

She dabbed her napkin on his now-stained shirt. "A men's room is just down the hall. Remember to blot; don't rub or you'll never get it out."

Garrett saw a flash of anger as the reporter hurried away.

"You sure you don't work for Austin?" he asked.

She gave him a sly grin. "Let me get a real drink now. The truth is I don't care much for red wine." She ordered a scotch neat and led him to an open space next to a large photograph of President Ronald Reagan and General Secretary Mikhail Gorbachev.

"This was taken at their first meeting in 1985," she explained. "The Geneva Summit. Sadly, most of his countrymen today consider Gorbachev a traitor."

She nudged him. "You're about to be replaced as the object of everyone's curiosity." She nodded toward a tall, athletic man in his late twenties who'd entered. He was wearing bright red cowboy boots. "That's Ivan Yovovich Sokolov."

Garrett watched as Heidi Duncan smiled flirtatiously when shaking his hand. No reaction from her ambassador husband. Masks in a pageant.

"He wears those god-awful boots because he bought a Texas franchise—something with a red mascot," she said.

"What sort of team?"

"Do I look like I read the sports page?"

Another nudge to his side. "Ah, now the real star of the party has arrived."

Garrett recognized him from photos. Edged by two bodyguards, General Andre Gromyko strutted into the room, parading directly to the ambassador and his wife, forcing the others in line to stand aside.

In cinema, villains wear their villainy. Black cowboy hat. Scarred face. Permanent sneer. An outer ugliness that reflects an inner ruthlessness. Not so in real life. General Andre Gromyko was a pudgy Russian in his late fifties. Salt-and-pepper full beard. Thinning hair. Round pie face. Completely ordinary. The banality of evil.

"No general's uniform tonight," she said. "Probably didn't want to be confused for one of the clowns at the kids' party with all the medals and ribbons he's awarded himself." She chuckled at her own joke and when Gromyko looked their way, she raised her drink in salute, a gesture that he ignored.

Instead, Gromyko was studying Garrett. The look of a predator assessing a foe. Neither man blinked. Mano a mano. A hateful stare. Gromyko slowly looked away. What exactly the general knew about Garrett was unclear. What was clear is that both understood what sort of men they were and that if they met, how each would react. Natural-born enemies.

Garrett felt nauseous and it wasn't from his Russian beer.

The woman noticed. "You starting withdrawal? Austin said the Russians confiscated your Suboxone at the airport."

"I thought you didn't work for Austin. And does anyone keep anything secret around here?"

She chuckled. "I can help."

"You can get my meds back?"

"No, they're long gone. How about lorcaserin?"

"Never heard of it."

"A weight-loss drug but some claim it works better than Suboxone. You'll need something to stay focused."

"You the residential Dr. FeelGood?"

"There's a prescription bottle of lorcaserin in Heidi Duncan's office desk upstairs."

Garrett looked across the room. Heidi Duncan was still chatting with her husband and Solokov. She noticed Garrett's glance and glared at him.

"Why would she need an obesity drug? And I'm sure she isn't going to just hand over her pills."

"Preventive maintenance. Sticking your finger down your throat gets tiresome after a while. How good are you at sneaking into an office?"

"I'm more a kick-down-the-front-door type."

She took a sip of her scotch. "Somehow, that doesn't surprise me. First, we have to get you by Miss Whitworth in the hallway to access the staircase. Next, there are cameras upstairs in the hallway but not in her private office where the pills are kept. Top right drawer of her desk. It's the bottle marked Belviq."

"Can't you ask her or get them for me? You work for her."

"No, she keeps the drawer locked because she doesn't want anyone to know she takes them, especially me. And I'm not the person who needs them. You are. Your problem. You do the B-and-E."

She checked her watch. "The power is about to go off thanks to Austin. When it does, the emergency lighting will come on, but it takes about four minutes for the hallway cameras outside her office upstairs to reboot. It's an antiquated system. That gives you four minutes to climb two flights of stairs, get into her office, take enough pills to last while you're in Russia, and come back to the birthday party."

"I'm not David Blaine."

"You don't need to be." She took his hand and he felt the outline of a key in her palm. "Master key," she said. "You'll have to return it."

"How do we get by Miss Whitworth?"

"I will help with that."

Garrett realized he was trusting a complete stranger.

"You haven't told me your name," he said.

"You haven't asked?"

"I should know the name of a fellow burglar."

"Giorgia Capello but everyone calls me Ginger and, no, I'm not and never have been a redhead. It's just a nickname."

As they started toward the hallway, Capello stopped at the bar and asked for a Perrier. She delivered it to Miss Whitworth, who was still at the table with party hats. The stairway was directly behind her.

"I'm here to relieve you," Capello said cheerfully.

Whitworth looked suspiciously at Garrett.

Capello said, "I've managed to convince Mr. Garrett to change his mind. He'd like a hat."

Garrett chose a red top hat that was much too large for his head. He felt ridiculous.

Capello said, "Miss Whitworth, you did all of the planning for this party and you're so good at these events, it's time for you to join it and let me watch the table. Most everyone we invited already has arrived."

A disapproving look swept across the older woman's face. "I was asked to welcome guests. Not be one."

"Now, Gloria, really, you should—"

The lights went out. Loud shrieks from the children's room. The emergency lights popped on. A girl burst into the hallway and darted into the adult room. "Mommy! Daddy!" she squealed.

"Oh my," Miss Whitworth said. "Ginger, maybe you should take over for a few minutes while I sort this out." She looked at Garrett. "Are you coming or leaving?"

"I'm still reviewing my hat options."

Miss Whitworth hurried inside the ballroom.

"Remember cameras in the hallway and outer office," Capello said. "Four minutes."

He darted behind the table and up the stairs.

Capello checked the adult room to see if anyone had seen him. It didn't appear so. Everyone was focused on Ambassador Duncan, who had dropped to his knees to be eye level with his upset daughter, who seemed panicked.

"The music's stopped," she declared through tears.

"Probably because the lights went out," Duncan said.

"No, Liam broke it," she replied. "He started punching buttons on the computer. He thinks he's so smart."

Reaching out to straighten her daughter's jeweled birthday tiara, Heidi Duncan said, "Don't you worry, princess."

"Would you like me to summon Mr. Duwar?" Miss Whitworth asked, having suddenly appeared behind the birthday girl.

"Yes," Heidi Duncan replied. Speaking to her

daughter, she added, "Now you go back into the other room with Miss Whitworth and she'll get the music working."

In the hallway heading toward the children's party, Miss Whitworth noticed Garrett was nowhere to be seen. "Mr. Garrett?" she asked.

Capello replied, "Little boys' room."

Upstairs, Garrett inserted the master key into Heidi Duncan's office suite. He tried the top drawer. Locked. Grabbing a letter opener, he jammed its tip between the drawer and desktop, and pressed on the side of the bolt, prying it down.

Tick-tock, tick-tock. He needed to hurry.

Inside were a dozen prescription bottles. He was taking too much time. There were a dozen brown pill bottles. Lorcaserin. He couldn't find it. Then remembered. Capello had called it a different name. Seconds passed. He cursed his growing inability to concentrate. Belville? Belust? No—Belviq? He rechecked each bottle. Thankfully, only one began with a B.

He stole five pills. Returned the bottles. Forced the drawer shut and hurried to the doorway. Peeking into the hallway, he saw a blinking red light directly under the camera lens. He had run out of time. Pulling the paper top hat as far as possible over his head, he lowered his chin and dashed for the stairway.

Capello was waiting anxiously in the hallway. He reached her at the same time a man dressed in a tan shalwar kameez—long shirt and baggy trousers favored by men in the Indian subcontinent—was approaching her from the building's entrance. He was slender with long curly hair knotted in a bun and a beard. He and Garrett reached Capello at the same time from opposite sides.

"Krishma," Capello said warmly, greeting him. "Miss Whitworth and the children are waiting for you. A computer issue." She nodded toward the kids' room.

The man gave Garrett a curious stare. "We haven't met," he said, extending his hand. "Krishma Duwar."

Garrett shook his hand but didn't offer his name. "Nice to meet you."

Capello interrupted: "Miss Whitworth hates to wait. You best go inside."

Duwar looked a few more moments at Garrett. Then at the stairs that he had seen him descending. "Perhaps we will meet again later," he said.

When Duwar was gone, Garrett said, "He saw me coming down the stairs. Who is he? Will he tell?"

"He's the embassy IT expert. Global Intelligence Technologies," she replied. "I don't know if he'll mention it."

"It might not matter. The camera's red light was blinking. I took more than four minutes. I tried to hide my face with this stupid hat." He tossed it on the hallway table.

"I wouldn't worry about the cameras," she said. "You actually had eight to ten minutes. I wanted to keep you on your toes."

Miss Whitworth emerged from the children's party accompanied by Duwar.

"Crisis averted," she said. "As always, Mr. Duwar worked his magic. I'm certain both the ambassador and Mrs. Duncan will want to personally thank you for saving their daughter's birthday party. You should join them in the ballroom."

"You're very kind," Duwar replied, picking up a birthday hat and putting it on his head.

"Will you be joining the party, too?" Duwar asked Garrett.

"No, I've had enough excitement for the night."

"Miss Whitworth told me that you're the infamous Brett Garrett who now works for my company's competitor, IEC."

"Guilty as charged on both counts," Garrett replied. Speaking to Capello, he added, "Would you mind walking me outside. I'm still trying to find my way around here."

Outside, he said, "That IT man—Duwar—does he help the ambassador with his computer?"

"Yes, all of the time. And also Heidi. She's the worst with her computer."

He stopped. "Good night, Ms. Capello. I trust you'll tell Austin about our little operation tonight— even though you claim to be on the ambassador's wife's staff."

"The IEC housing quarters are to your left," she replied. "It should take you about four minutes to get there." She laughed before reentering the building.

Twenty-Two

"I have to tell the FBI," Valerie Mayberry declared. She was huddled with CIA director Harris in his government-issued Cadillac. This time on a service road behind a Walmart at the Fair Lakes Shopping Center off Interstate 66. His driver was standing watch outside.

"You work for me," Harris declared. "I'll decide when and if the FBI needs to know about yesterday's shrine bombing."

"I'm temporarily detailed to you but I'm still an FBI employee and I witnessed a crime. People were murdered. Others wounded. I have to file a report."

"No, you don't. You reported everything to me, that's sufficient."

"But I know who was responsible. Makayla did it.

The bureau needs to know about her Antifa cell. She's a murderer."

"Did you see her detonate that bomb?" he asked. "You don't have any evidence. On the other hand, you shot pepper spray into a high school principal's eyes during a fatal domestic terrorist attack."

"I had to. I was undercover."

He grunted. "Don't be naïve. The media will exploit the hell out of this—especially after reporters identify you as the crazed woman in a viral video threatening a Virginia congressman with pepper spray. Your career will be finished. Worse, you will go to jail."

"You could explain it to Sally North and Director Davison."

"Explain what? I never instructed you to threaten a United States congressman with pepper spray or assault a high school principal during a terrorist attack. You acted on your own. Let me remind you that there's also an NDA. Any disclosure about our operation or admission that you were undercover would violate that."

"You can't use that against me. NDAs are invalid if something illegal happens and one party knows about it."

Harris chuckled. "Oh my dear, do you really think you're smarter? In civil cases that might be true. But not in a covert operation classified top secret. The entire reason why we have top secret operations is to keep the public from knowing what you did. If you tell anyone what happened at that shrine, I will personally see to it that you'll go to prison for life. You're dispensable."

She couldn't tell if he was bluffing. His tone and angry voice suggested he wasn't. She also suspected Harris could be vengeful. If anyone were to be blamed for not stopping the shrine bombing, he would make certain it was her, not him.

Changing tactics, Harris tempered his voice. "Valerie, when you came to work for me, you entered the world of realpolitik. The bureau doesn't need your help solving that bombing. You need to stay focused on the bigger prize, and that's Pavel. The clock is ticking. Yes, it's horrific that two innocent people were murdered yesterday during the shrine bombing. But Antifa would have exploded that bomb whether you had been there or not. We needed you there because—based on the boldness of that bombing—Makayla is our best lead and most likely candidate to be the one helping General Gromyko."

The CIA director rested his arm on the top of the back car seat above her shoulders. He leaned in so close she could smell the stench of his morning coffee. "Remember the attack in Kiev? The first terrorist out the door? The one that you theorized might have been a woman?"

"Makayla?"

"It's another reason why you need to keep your mouth shut about the shrine and keep embedding yourself inside her Antifa cell. It's more important to stop her from killing again with poison than to identify her now and possibly have her go underground. Now tell me again exactly what Makayla said when she grabbed your jacket and pulled you into that van."

"I think she said, 'I'm not leaving anyone behind this time.'"

"Think isn't good enough, Mayberry. Did she or did she not say 'this time'? Because that clearly suggests she was one of the terrorists at Kiev who left Gabriel de Depardieu behind. Think, damn it!"

"I'd just been struck with a board on the back of the skull."

"What you don't know is we're comparing your Smithmyer College video to the security taped footage of the masked terrorists in Kiev."

"If it's Makayla," she said, "you're eventually going to have to tell the bureau because the CIA can't arrest her. You'll have to tell my bosses about the shrine bombing and disclose that I was there. When that happens, they're going to be furious that I didn't tell them now."

She glanced out the tinted window. She was trapped in a catch-22.

"What if Pavel is lying?" she asked. "What if he's fabricating this entire Kamera poisoning scenario about Gromyko murdering Americans to make himself so indispensable that you'll do anything to get him and his grandson out alive?"

"Not believing him puts us at greater risk than believing."

She grunted, unconvinced.

He said, "The Russians are pushing the edges—look at the poison murders in London. President Kalugin is out to undermine and destroy us. You've grown up being told that all people, regardless of their nationality, are basically good and decent and want peace. But that's the stuff of fairy tales. Kalugin wants you and me and every American who he can kill dead. That's realpolitik. You can't make friends with a crocodile. Now, when is your next meeting with Rivera? Has she told you how to contact Makayla?"

"I'm meeting Rivera this afternoon for drinks and shopping. And, no, I have no idea how to contact Makayla."

"Squeeze her. Find out how to contact Makayla."

He handed her a business card. "When you have something, call this number and ask for Mr. Smith.

He'll get information to me. We're done meeting face-to-face."

"You're distancing yourself from me, aren't you? Setting me up. Just like you did Brett Garrett in Cameroon."

The veins in his neck bulged, his eyes narrowed, and she saw hate in them. Harris reached over her lap and opened the passenger door for her to exit.

"Go!" he snapped.

Later that day, Mayberry left her Reston condo to meet Rivera as planned. Rivera had suggested Nostos, one of the finest and pricier Greek restaurants in the Tysons Corner area. Mayberry had just parked outside the eatery when her phone dinged. Text message. New meeting spot. Yelp reviews gave Petit le Diner a half star. Odd, given Rivera's five-diamond preferences.

Mayberry arrived at the French restaurant and immediately checked its nearly empty bar. No Rivera. She scanned the largely vacant dining room. She wasn't there. At least, Mayberry didn't immediately spot her. It took a second and then a third look. Rivera was nearly unrecognizable at a table for two in a dark far corner. She was wearing no bling. Skinny jeans with holes. A gray lace-paneled, roll-tab sleeve blouse. Nice, but department store goods. Cheap sneakers. An oversize floppy hat. Hiding behind no-brand sunglasses that were so huge they covered half her face.

"What's up with the new look?" Mayberry asked jokingly, pulling out a chair with a worn seat cushion at Rivera's table.

"Those two—the ones who got—you know—who died yesterday," Rivera whispered, nervously glancing around the room at a half-dozen patrons. "I'm leaving for Turkey tonight."

Reaching across the table, Mayberry placed her hands on top of Rivera's. "This is ridiculous. You weren't responsible and neither am I."

"You're wrong, Valerie. We can be charged as accessories to murder—even as domestic terrorists."

"Who told you that?"

"My father. He could tell I was upset. He began asking—I told him everything and he called our family attorney. They told me not to meet you, but I needed to warn you. We're friends and you have money. You need to disappear, too. Tonight."

"Where would I go?"

"Come to Turkey with me."

"No. You don't have to run. We can go to the FBI and explain," Mayberry said. "We could turn ourselves in."

Rivera jerked back her hands from under Mayberry's. "I'm Muslim. My mother is from Turkey. How can you—of all people—say I should go to the corrupt FBI?"

"Okay, okay," Mayberry replied, hoping to calm her. "It was a stupid idea."

Rivera began to cry. "You got to believe me. I didn't know they were going to kill old people, children."

Mayberry noticed a waiter approaching. She waved him off.

"So, you didn't know about the bomb?" Mayberry asked.

Rivera looked frightened. "Why are you asking me that?"

"I just wondered if I was the only one who didn't—"

Rivera interrupted. "Are you saying you are innocent and I am not?"

"No, of course not."

"Demonstrating at a college, yes. Pepper-spraying racists, yes. Calling for a revolution, ending capitalism, yes. But murdering people at some stupid Civil War memorial, no, no, no. I swear I didn't know."

Without warning, Rivera reached out and grabbed Mayberry's hands, still resting on the table between. She squeezed tightly. "You have to run. It's not just the FBI. It's Makayla."

Rivera's eyes flitted across the restaurant. "That man sitting over there." She nodded toward a table close to the restaurant's front door. A hulking figure was watching them.

"He works for my father. A bodyguard. It's not safe. Makayla has powerful friends everywhere, including Washington."

"Who? What friends?"

"The bomb. On the news, they said it was C-4 explosive—like what you see in movies. No ordinary person can walk into a store and buy it."

"Someone in the military is helping her?"

"Why are you asking me these questions?" Rivera said, clearly frightened. And then she flip-flopped and volunteered more information. She was a Dr. Jekyll and Mr. Hyde in her moods. "There's something I never told you. Something about me. When I was in Paris at school I took a French lover, Gabriel, and he's the one who introduced me to Antifa. She was there, too."

"Makayla in Paris?"

"The three of us became friends. But he's dead now."

"How?"

Rivera paused, took a long drink of water that she'd been brought earlier. "He was killed, and it was her fault."

Rivera began to cry. "He told me things—things he wasn't supposed to tell me. He sent me away from Paris months before he died. He didn't want me implicated. I begged him to come here with me, but he was a true believer, just like her. He truly loved me, but she came here after he died. I was afraid to tell her no. She's . . . she's . . . killed people before."

"How and when?" Mayberry asked quietly.

"A shooting. One of her plans. Don't you see? If the FBI discovered I knew she had already been involved in a terrorist act, they would not believe anything I said about yesterday's bombing. I'm in too deep and now, so are you."

Rivera looked around the restaurant again to ensure no one could hear them. None of the customers appeared to be watching them. Four women by a window chatting. Two men in suits talking loudly out of earshot. The bodyguard.

"It's okay," Mayberry said reassuringly. "No one can hear us. You said your lover introduced you to Makayla?"

"Yes, he told me that she knew many important people, including people in the States. I went to a protest at a college. Smithmyer. This was before I met you. This person—a white man—picked her up in the parking lot after that demonstration. He was her D.C. contact, I think."

"What's his name? Do you know where he works?"

Again, Rivera's mood swung between paranoia and a need to confess. "You are asking too many questions. Stop asking."

For several moments, they sat in silence and then Rivera said, "I believe he works at the U.S. Capitol." Quickly followed by "You're interrogating me!"

Rivera began breathing rapidly. "My father's lawyer warned me. He said others at the shrine—they would turn against me, testify against everyone else. Is that why you're asking me all these questions? I thought we were friends. I came to warn you!"

"I'm not going to betray you," Mayberry replied, trying to steady her. "I'm asking about Makayla because I can't flee the country. The best way for me to protect both of *us* is to learn everything I can about Makayla. I will never, ever mention you, I swear, Aysan. But your father's lawyer is right. If I get arrested, I'll give them her name. She's the one who did this to us. She's the one who should be punished. But I don't know if Makayla is even her real name. I need to know how to contact her. Please, if you know her phone number, tell me. Tell me and if something happens to either of us, I will tell the FBI about her, but never you. I swear it."

Rivera didn't speak. More water. More fidgeting. More scanning the room with her eyes.

"Aysan, we're friends," Mayberry said. "You can trust me."

"Can I? If I tell you her number, you might warn her that I'm leaving Antifa. Running away."

"I wouldn't do that. You're my friend."

Without warning, Rivera pushed out her chair and stood to go.

"My father's attorney said no one is my friend. He says everyone will turn against everyone."

"Makayla's number, please," Mayberry pleaded. Real emotion crept into her voice. "I need it to protect myself and you."

Rivera hesitated. She looked down at Mayberry, looked into her eyes. "I do trust you," she said. "You didn't know about the bomb." She pulled an ink pen from her purse. Grabbed Mayberry's palm and scribbled three numbers on it, but stopped suddenly and jerked back her hand.

"No, no, no! I can't do this!" She jammed the pen back into her purse and spun around.

"Wait, wait," Mayberry said, rising from her seat.

But Rivera was already darting toward her bodyguard and the restaurant's exit.

Mayberry sat back down at the table. She read the digits: 2-0-2. The original long-distance area code for Washington, D.C. She needed to think. Consider her options. If she called "Mr. Smith" and reported everything to Director Harris, the CIA would intercept Rivera after she fled the United States. They'd wait for her to get overseas. Otherwise, the FBI would need to get involved. Harris wouldn't want that. He wouldn't want Rivera talking about her good Antifa pal Valerie Mayberry and recounting how she was at the shrine bombing.

Her second option would be to tip off the FBI. Director Harris would be furious, and it would get her into trouble, but it would be better for Rivera. The FBI would treat Rivera better than the agency overseas. Mayberry felt genuinely sorry for Rivera. A gullible student, easily recruited by the oldest method ever. A lover.

A third option. Play dumb. Let whatever fate awaited Rivera play out. Tell no one. Not Director Harris and not the FBI. Sit tight. Forget their meeting here ever happened. She'd promised not to hurt Rivera.

Mayberry reviewed her options. A waiter came. She ordered and continued to ponder as she ate. After she'd paid the bill and walked outside, Mayberry dialed a number on her cell.

"Mr. Smith," she said. "I have information for Director Harris."

Twenty-Three

Deputy Foreign Minister Yakov Prokofyevich Pavel saw the CIA's signal at 7:33 a.m. Moscow time. A black circle spray-painted the previous night on the public phone shell. The Americans' signal that they were ready to pick him and Peter up later that day.

Pavel betrayed no emotion—not even a smile—as he rode along New Arbat Avenue in his chauffeured government car toward the Russian Foreign Ministry.

Getting instructions to the Americans via Bolshoi tickets had proven simple and easy—all thanks, ironically, to General Gromyko. The general had stripped Pavel of nearly all diplomatic duties. To further humiliate him, he'd put Pavel in charge of arranging tours for visiting dignitaries—a menial task normally assigned to a junior diplomat. Whenever the Bolshoi was scheduled to perform, a ballet employee would deliver a packet of tickets for Pavel to disperse. Last night's production had corresponded with the arrival of an American oil company delegation in Moscow to cut a deal for offshore drilling rights in the Chaivo Field, located in the Sea of Okhotsk. It had been effortless for Pavel to write coded instructions on the backside of a pair of Bolshoi tickets and leave them at the will-call window for the fictional "Fred Thomas."

The fact that Pavel had accomplished this under Gromyko's nose greatly pleased him. Now he was ready for the next stage in his well-planned escape. As soon as his grandson had arrived in Moscow, Pavel had enrolled him in Moscow State School #57, which had been the city's most elite school during the Soviet period. After the collapse, most wealthy Russians had begun sending their children to the private Humanitarian Classical Gymnasium in the exclusive Moscow suburb of Zhukovka. Pavel's choice had pleased the school's headmaster, who had been completely unaware of the actual reason for it. The school was near the intersection of Komsomolskiy Prospekt and the Third Ring Road, major roads, along with numerous museums and other sites, including the Donskoy Monastery and Gorky Park.

Pavel had called the headmaster nearly every afternoon and requested that Peter be dismissed early. The pretense was that Pavel wanted to familiarize the teenager with Moscow's many cultural treasures that he'd missed growing up in rural areas. By doing so, he was establishing a pattern, so his request today would not appear out of place.

Pavel knew General Gromyko was watching his every move, especially after the Americans had stupidly arrested an NSA employee so quickly after Pavel's return from Ambassador Thorpe's funeral.

When Pavel arrived in his office, he telephoned the school's headmaster, knowing one of Gromyko's goons would be listening in. Pavel said he needed Peter dismissed at three o'clock.

"Where will you be taking your grandson today?" the headmaster asked.

"The Museum of Art Deco."

"An excellent choice," the headmaster replied. "And close to our school."

Pavel had lied. After picking up his grandson, he would tell his driver to take them to another close site—the Public Museum of the Moscow Metro. It was a relatively unknown gallery with displays that chronicled the construction of what arguably was the most beautiful city transit system in the world. Launched during Stalin's reign, Moscow's first underground stations were works of public art, with magnificent marble columns, ceiling murals painted by Russia's finest masters, and gold-plated light fixtures. They were meant to impress the Soviet masses—visible proof that communism had a glorious future. The fact that only top party members could afford cars and everyone else had to depend on mass transit was largely ignored.

Pavel had selected the metro museum because it was housed above the Sportivnaya metro station, so-named because it served the nearby Luzhniki Olympic Complex. Although he had not been trained in evasion techniques, Pavel was clever enough to know his chances of disappearing in a crowd would be better inside a bustling metro station crammed with Muscovites boarding and exiting a constant stream of subway cars.

After notifying the headmaster, Pavel took a moment to simply sit and breathe. It was much too late for him to change his mind, nor did he wish to, yet he felt a genuine sadness as he glanced around his office, finally settling his eyes on the worn briefcase on his desk. To avoid suspicion, Pavel had not packed anything unusual in it with the exception of a single envelope. It contained two photographs. His daughter, her husband, and Peter as a child, and a much older one of Pavel's deceased parents. As true believers, they would have been horrified about what he was about to do. Everything else that he owned that connected him to his past, his decades of service to Mother Russia, and his family roots would be left behind for Gromyko to pick over like the vulture that he was. All Pavel would possess would be his memories.

8:30 a.m., Moscow, U.S. Embassy

Marcus Austin summoned Brett Garrett.

"It's a go," Austin announced the moment Garrett arrived. "You'll meet Pavel and his grandson between three ten and three thirty this afternoon. That's a twenty-minute window to get him and Peter into the van."

"That's a long window," Garrett replied. "Where's the pickup?"

"The address that Pavel wrote on the Bolshoi tickets is for a Billa market near the Sportivnaya metro. It was the first foreign-owned grocery chain permitted after the Soviet Union collapsed."

Austin unfolded a map of Moscow on his office desk and stabbed his index finger onto the store's location. "I had Ginger—your escort at last night's birthday party—drive by there early this morning to check things out."

"So, she does work for you. Was she followed?" Garrett asked.

"Ginger is deep cover. Smart and tough. She knows how to avoid tails. I'd trust her with my life."

"That's your life. Not mine."

"Stop being a bitch, brother," Austin cajoled. "I know Director Harris bent you over when he testified before Senator Cormac Stone about Cameroon. He screwed up, but you know me, brother. We've worked together and I'm telling you straight up my girl is solid. No one has a clue she's part of my team. That's how deep-cover she is. Helping you today can possibly blow years and years of her insinuating herself into State. You should respect that."

Garrett didn't reply so Austin continued: "Now, there's not going to be any street parking outside that store, but you'll be driving a delivery truck. You can park on the street or jump its wheels on the curb."

"Twenty minutes is a long time to block traffic," Garrett noted.

"Not in Moscow. Drivers are used to having streets blocked and your Russian is passable enough if a cop shows up. Besides, like I just said, Billa is foreign owned. Even if someone identifies you as an American, which they probably will, there's a fabricated work permit in the document packet I gave you yesterday."

"Any idea how Pavel and the kid are planning on getting to the store without Gromyko and his FSB thugs tailing them?"

"None," Austin said.

Garrett cursed. "You're trusting this guy to not be followed? If he is, Gromyko will arrest me."

"He and his grandson will be shot if caught," Austin replied. "That's a pretty good incentive to be careful. Now let's move on. After you pick them up, you will exit the city here." He shifted his finger to Moscow's Third Ring. "Pavel's clever. You'll already be on the southwestern outer end of Moscow, with lots of possible escape routes."

"And exactly where am I delivering them in Ukraine?"

"Novhorod-Siverskyi," Austin replied. He spread out another map, laying it over the first. It was of southwest Russia. "A village in the northeast corner of Ukraine, far away from the fighting in the southeast. About seventeen thousand residents. Director Harris chose it personally because it's less than thirty miles from the Russian border and most of the people who live there hate the Russians and Ukrainians. You should fit right in." He chuckled at his own joke.

"Is there anyone they do love?"

"Not really, including Americans, but they're dirt poor and are descended from a long line of mercenaries."

"I trust the agency was the highest bidder."

"Faith, brother, you got to have it. A little background for you. Novhorod-Siverskyi has a long history of turmoil, dating back to when princes used to fight over it back in 1044. The Mongols ransacked it in the 1200s. Next up, the Lithuanians, the Poles, the Germans, and finally Russia."

"The agency provide you with all that historical data?"

"I read it on Wikipedia, brother." Austin chuckled. "Despite who's in charge, the people are Cossacks, which means they're loyal only to their own blood and money."

Austin continued, "The city is off the beaten path, although a few tourists come to visit its churches, a monastery, or a couple statues of princes and princesses who've been maggot food for centuries."

"Let's cut to the chase, shall we?"

"It's roughly three hundred and sixty-six miles from Moscow. At seventy miles an hour on a nice blacktop that's only a five-hour drive. The truck's top speed is probably sixty and the roads are full of potholes so you won't be able to drive even that fast. I'm guessing ten to twelve hours."

"Wikipedia?"

Austin grinned. "Mapquest."

"Border-crossing station?"

Austin produced several satellite photographs of the Russian–Ukraine border near Novhorod-Siverskyi. He spread them out over the maps. "If you stay on this main road, there's a crossing station when you exit Russia. Basically, a tollbooth with two officers. They'll go home around midnight. But to be safe, you turn off the main road about five miles before you reach them." He pointed to a close-up image of the terrain. "There's a dirt road that cuts across a field. Follow it and you'll end up in Ukraine. Rejoin the main road and you've just avoided the checkpoint. The only person you may meet would be an angry farmer."

"A Cossack. Riding a horse armed with a sword."

"Garrett, you and I both know Harris isn't going to allow anything bad to happen to Pavel once you cross into Ukraine. You might be expendable, but not a deputy foreign minister. Wouldn't be surprised if Director Harris is going to be there personally to greet Pavel and interrogate him on the flight home. He's intent on finding out how Gromyko is reading our mail here."

Garrett shuffled through the aerial shots. "How old?"

"Taken within the past five days. They're accurate. Plus, if you run into a problem, use your SAT phone connection to Thomas Jefferson Kim at IEC. He can guide you using it as a GPS locator. He's been briefed. In fact, this border crossing was devised by Harris before you touched down in Moscow. The only missing piece is how Pavel intends to get himself and grandson to the Billa store."

"Was all this in the packet Ambassador Duncan delivered? The one he read through."

Austin nodded. "Faith, brother. You got to trust someone." He reached under the photos and southwestern map of Russia to retrieve the city map.

"This is where the Zil is waiting for you." He checked his watch. "Go grab your gear and meet me in thirty outside."

"What's the truck carrying, in case I'm asked?"

"Boxes of Nestlé-Russia breakfast cereals," Austin said. "Russians love cornflakes. Fresh clothing for you, Pavel, and Peter, their fake travel documents and fake passports. There's a carve out between the cab and the boxes in the cargo area where the old man and his grandson can hide, if necessary. You enter it through an opening behind the passenger seat."

Garrett nodded.

Austin handed him a set of truck keys.

Ten Minutes Later, U.S. Embassy, IEC Living Quarters

Brett Garrett tucked his IEC documentation papers, U.S. passport, and Russian work visa and concealed weapon permit into a gym bag. Next was the SAT phone and SIG Sauer pistol with extra ammo. He splashed water on his face and gulped down one of the pills he'd stolen the night before from Heidi Duncan's private weight-loss stash. He held up his right hand to see if any tremors had set in. Not so far.

The pills hadn't given him as much relief as Suboxone, but it had stopped most of the sweating and curbed his urge to vomit. Garrett stepped from his room—and came face-to-face again with Gilbert Hardin and two of his IEC buddies waiting in the hallway.

"You didn't show last night after the birthday party," Hardin said. "Time to play."

"Sorry, pal, I'm in a rush."

"You've already used that lame excuse," one of Hardin's pals sneered.

"Listen, Garrett, I checked the duty roster and you aren't on it," Hardin said. "You're ducking me."

Garrett lowered the gym bag on the tile floor. "In the interest of saving time, let's say I let you sucker-punch me and we'll call it square."

Hardin glanced at his buddies, shrugged, and said, "Fair enough." Hardin was a big man, with softball-size fists and thick biceps. Garrett braced himself.

Hardin lowered his right shoulder and let fly a thunder-packed blow against the left side of Garrett's head, causing his mouth to flood with blood and nearly knocking him unconscious.

Garrett staggered back, spit, and felt one of his teeth to determine if it was cracked. "That was a hell of a wallop. I'll give that to you, Hardin. Now we're even." He leaned forward to retrieve his gym bag. Hardin stepped forward and caught Garrett in his abdomen by surprise, knocking the wind out of him and causing him to fall on his knees, clutching his gut.

"No, Garrett, *now* we're even," Hardin declared triumphantly. He turned his head to smile at his buddies.

He never saw it coming. By the time he realized Garrett was springing upward onto his feet, it was too late. He might have spotted Garrett's left, but he certainly didn't have time to react to his right. Garrett was too quick. His left busted Hardin's nose, his right landed under Hardin's jaw knocking his head backward with tremendous force. A loud cracking noise.

Most men would have been knocked out, but then the same could have been said about the blow that Hardin had first landed on Garrett. Instead Hardin came at

Garrett with both of his huge fists, ready for blood. Garrett feigned surprise and ducked, causing Hardin to follow his fist. Garrett delivered two hard punches to Hardin's middle but the big man still did not fall. Because of his size and strength, Hardin was used to defeating his opponents with a few mighty blows and was not a well-practiced pugilist. Although smaller, Garrett sidestepped and quick-punched Hardin, hitting his face three times without taking any shots in return. His fourth hit caused Hardin's eyes to tilt upward, a fifth and Hardin was done. He collapsed onto the hallway floor.

"Get out of my way," Garrett said to the other two.

"It was a fair fight," one said. Both stepped clear.

**Five Minutes Later,
Outside the U.S. Embassy**

"What kept you—" Marcus Austin started to ask but stopped when he saw the swelling around Garrett's eye, his bloody swollen lips, and nasty red bruises on his cheeks. He'd beaten Hardin but not without first taking several licks.

"You look like hell," Austin said. "We don't have much time. Get in the third car and keep down."

Austin usually required his people to take a minimum of ten hours to go black in Moscow. Even longer during daylight. Moscow was a city of snitches. Its older residents had been groomed during the Soviet days. Back then, every Russian had been required to meet weekly with block captains to be questioned about their friends, neighbors, or strangers. Everyone was suspect. Everyone was a rat. The best got rewarded. It was a custom that had been passed on to the younger generation.

Garrett was riding with a State Department protective detail that was escorting Ambassador Duncan and Heidi to Vnukovo International Airport, south of Moscow, for a flight to Geneva. An international financial summit. Everyone knew the FSB would be trailing the embassy's four-vehicle convoy. Garrett's escape would be on the return ride. He would leap from the passenger side of the third SUV as it turned at a tight V intersection. The fourth SUV guarding the rear of the convoy would slow, giving Garrett a maximum of ten seconds before the FSB following them could make the turn. Ten seconds. Just enough time for him to disappear down the stairs of a nearby metro station and hope the Muscovites on the street minded their own business and didn't wave down the FSB cars.

Inside the tinted-glass third vehicle, Garrett slipped on a pair of worn deliveryman coveralls. Through his swollen eyes, he checked his gym bag a second time. Everything was there, including his SIG Sauer.

Three Minutes before 2:00 p.m., Russian Foreign Ministry

Deputy Foreign Minister Pavel tucked a thick file of papers into his briefcase to give the appearance that he was taking work home. He checked his reflection in the mirror hanging near his door, straightened his burgundy tie, and surveyed the room's interior for a final time. The past.

"I'm leaving to take my grandson to a museum," he declared as he passed his longtime secretary.

"Excuse me, Deputy Minister, but there's a meeting at three today that you are scheduled to attend. Should I warn them you might be a few minutes late?" she asked.

He glared down at her. "You have fulfilled your duties by informing me of the meeting. If I wished for you to tell them, I would have asked."

She was used to his ill temper and sharp tone and quickly lowered her eyes. "Yes, Deputy Minister."

For a moment, he considered apologizing. They had worked together nearly three decades. She had followed him up the chain of command and, after he fled, he knew Gromyko would interrogate her and, most likely, punish her for not realizing that Pavel planned to defect.

He realized that he knew little about her personal life. She was widowed and had grandchildren but lived alone. He'd never bothered to inquire where. She, on the other hand, knew a great deal about him. After his wife had died, she'd taken on the task of keeping tabs on his housekeeper, ordering his clothing, and handling all the dozens of forms when his daughter's ashes and those of her husband had been returned to Moscow. She'd also dealt with the paperwork required to enroll Peter in Moscow State School #57.

Yet even she could not be trusted. If he suddenly changed character and offered her a warm parting word, she might report him. He kept walking and rode the elevator downstairs to where his driver was waiting.

They arrived at 3:05 p.m. outside Peter's school, where the headmaster was patiently waiting at its front entrance. Pavel offered no apology for being tardy, extended no appreciation for the headmaster's personal attention to Peter. There was no need. Pavel knew that the headmaster was treating him with the upmost respect because someday that same headmaster intended to seek a favor—at least the headmaster thought that he would be able to do that. A joke on him now that Pavel was going to defect. Tit-for-tat was how the old Soviet system worked. Everyone knelt to the *nomenklatura* to keep the Rube Goldberg country limping along. It was still the way Russia operated.

"Drop us at the Public Museum of the Moscow Metro," Pavel instructed his driver.

"Not the Museum of Art Deco?" he replied.

He'd not mentioned the art deco museum. Clearly, that information had been relayed to the driver either by one of Gromyko's goons listening to Pavel's earlier call or the headmaster.

"When does a driver control a deputy minister's schedule?" Pavel asked indignantly. "You will wait outside the Public Museum of the Moscow Metro until we are finished."

Pavel rode with Peter in silence. He remembered a time when his grandson had spoken. Peter had stopped unexpectedly at age five. No one could explain why. Pavel suddenly felt an urge. He reached over and tousled Peter's dark brown hair that the teen wore too unkempt for Pavel's tastes. Peter smiled at him and then shifted his head to avoid Pavel's hand. He looked outside. He'd always been a curious boy.

Students at School #57 were not required to wear uniforms but Pavel had demanded that his grandson dress appropriate to his grandfather's status. Nothing with U.S. or British sports logos. No baseball caps. No denim jeans, despite their popularity, or fancy athletic shoes. This afternoon Peter was wearing a red wool sweater over a dark blue button-collared shirt and black leather shoes. Pavel noticed sideburn hairs beginning to appear on the thirteen-year-old's baby-soft skin. Although Peter didn't speak, he paid attention. Answered with nods and facial expressions. He was lanky, an awkward teen when he moved.

Pavel removed the envelope with the two family photos from his briefcase and handed them to Peter to see. His grandson's sparkling blue eyes lit up. Pavel took them back and slipped them in his suit coat pocket. He was taking them from his briefcase because it would have appeared odd for Pavel to tote his briefcase into the museum.

"Come, Peter," Pavel said, taking the teen's hand when they arrived outside the three-story museum. As they exited the car, Pavel saw three men in dark suits step from a vehicle behind them. There was no parking on the busy street and the fact that both his driver and their driver remained parked there was a clear signal that they were either Gromyko's men or FSB officers.

Pavel checked the time and realized he was running late. Ten after three. No time to waste. He guided Peter inside the building, but rather than going upstairs to the museum, he led his grandson down a flight of stairs to the entrance of the underground train station.

Opened in 1957, the stop was not nearly as ornate as Stalin's original creations. Still, it was ornate. Dark gray and black floor tiles. Brown marble-covered walls. Gold-plated sconces illuminating a wide corridor packed with travelers.

Pavel heard the sound of a train entering and quickened their pace, still holding his grandson's hand while glancing over his shoulder at the three men who were now pushing their way through the throngs of riders that separated them from Pavel. Down a flight of stairs to the platform, still a good forty feet or so ahead of them.

Pavel went immediately to the first car of the train, ignoring those on the platform packing its cars. He tapped on the train engineer's window but was ignored until he flashed his ministry credentials. Behind him, the three pursuers were being stalled trying to descend the stairs. Too many riders blocked their way but they were closing in.

"What's your name?" Pavel demanded when the engineer slid open the car's window.

"Yuri Kuznetsov," the startled driver replied.

"I am Deputy Foreign Minister Yakov Prokofyevich Pavel and I need you to follow my exact instructions. Do you understand?"

"Yes, Deputy Minister."

Pavel looked over his shoulder again. His three pursuers were still midway down the stairs, still being blocked.

Pavel barked out his orders.

"Deputy Minister, may I ask—"

"Not if you wish to continue being employed, Yuri Kuznetsov."

Still holding Peter's hand, Pavel lifted his red Foreign Ministry passport, waving it for all riders to see.

"Make room!" he shouted. Those on the platform parted. Two women, who'd already boarded the first car, obediently exited so Pavel and Peter could enter.

Pavel watched from inside the car as the three FSB officers shoved their way through the mob and forced themselves onto the third car—the one closest to the subway steps—just as the train's doors were closing.

The engineer drove the train forward but suddenly stopped after traveling less than five feet and opened the doors. But only to the first car. He had done exactly as Pavel had instructed him.

Pavel pulled Peter outside onto the platform. The engineer immediately closed the first car's doors and drove the train forward, trapping the three men following Pavel in the third car.

"We must hurry!" Pavel exclaimed, tugging his grandson through the curious crowd waiting for the next train. They headed upstairs and outside. The Billa market was less than a block away.

Brett Garrett stepped from the Zil delivery truck outside the store's entrance when he spotted Pavel and Peter approaching.

He moved quickly, opening the passenger door. Peter first. Pavel next. In under thirty seconds, Garrett was popping the Zil into first gear.

The Billa market was located on a rectangular block. Its entrance faced Khamovnicheskiy, an east-westbound street. At the western end of the block was Usacheva, which ran north-south. The eastern end connected to Dovatora. The street at the top of the rectangle—that ran parallel to Khamovnicheskiy— was Savelyeva, completing the rectangle.

As Garrett headed east, two GAZ-2330 Tigr armored military vehicles suddenly appeared, nose-to-nose, blocking the Dovatora intersection. Ten tons of armored vehicles now blocked their escape route. Garrett could see General Andre Gromyko stepping from them. Ten armed men, five on either side of him. Weapons pointed at the Zil delivery truck.

"It's a trap!" Pavel exclaimed. "Gromyko knew!"

Garrett didn't have time to agree or calculate who had betrayed their escape plan. He threw the truck into reverse and began speeding backward west against one-way traffic toward Usacheva. Cars behind him honked, drivers swerved, but before they could reach the north-south intersection, two more Tigr military vehicles appeared, closing off their route.

Panicked, Pavel reached for the door handle, ready to flee on foot, but Garrett grabbed his shoulder.

"If you want the kid to survive, stay put," he ordered. "Crawl onto the floor. It's armored. Both of you." The old man and his grandson slid together from their seats into the narrow footwell that had been reinforced with heavy steel plates.

Garrett pressed down on the Zil's accelerator, catapulting east once again, heading directly at the two Tigrs and General Gromyko.

The sight of the speeding Zil caused Gromyko to run for cover. Shouting, "The engine! The tires! The American driver stays alive!"

His men fired their Vityaz-SN submachine guns; 9x19 mm slugs peppered the front of the approaching truck. Several pierced the radiator. Steam shot from the holes, but the truck kept speeding forward. Other slugs punctured the Zil's tires but didn't flatten them. The truck's regular tires had been replaced by Marcus Austin with Hutchinson Composite RunFlat tires, as bulletproof as possible. Despite Gromyko's warnings to aim low, the Zil's windshield became a spiderweb of cracks and bullet holes. Working in Garrett's favor was the ammunition. The shooters were firing hollow points designed to mushroom on impact for maximum damage to human flesh. Good for killing people, but not effective at piercing armor.

It looked as if the Zil was on a kamikaze path, about to crash headfirst into the two military vehicles blockading its route. But when it reached the entrance to the metro station, Garrett swerved hard to his left, jumping the vehicle onto the sidewalk, causing watching people to dive out of its path. There wasn't a street here but there was a pedestrian walkway. It ran along the western edge of the Sportivnaya metro station. Just wide enough for the Zil.

But Garrett wasn't free yet. Midway up the pedestrian walkway that connected Khamovnicheskiy to Savelyeva, its northern border, were six concrete steps.

In those split seconds, Garrett tried to calculate if what remained of the Zil's front tires would hit the bottom step and mount it, lifting the truck up to the subsequent steps. Or would the front-heavy Zil's nose slam into the upper steps first before its front tires made contact, stopping the vehicle cold. He had no choice.

Garrett braced for a collision as he pushed the Zil's engine to its limits. The first sound he heard was the truck's front bumper scraping the bottom of the first step, sending sparks flying on each side. But before its front bumper collided with the second step, the front wheels hit and bounced up, lifting the vehicle, enabling it to awkwardly climb the staircase.

Garrett's risky move caught Gromyko completely off guard. He'd not stationed any vehicles or men on Savelyeva. Garrett turned left when he reached it, driving toward Usacheva, the north-south avenue to his west. As he entered that intersection, the two Tigr vehicles that had been blocking Khamovnicheskiy backed up from their nose-to-nose position. Both drove north on Usacheva in pursuit.

Garrett's encrypted SAT phone rang. From the footwell, Pavel opened the gym bag and handed Garrett his phone.

"Heard your driving is worse than mine," Thomas Jefferson Kim chirped. He was watching Garrett from one of his satellites.

"Funny, but I'm a bit busy right now."

"Drive toward the Novodevichy Convent," Kim said. "I got Marcus Austin on another line to help us get you free. I'll pass his instructions to you."

"Where the hell is Novo—this convent?" Garrett asked, checking the truck's rear side mirrors. The two Tigrs were closing in. Even more worrisome, one of Gromyko's men in the lead Tigr was standing in the gun portal, readying a 7.62 PKP "Pecheneg" machine gun. Unlike the weapons fired by Gromyko's ground troops, that machine gun's rounds were capable of penetrating the Zil's cargo area and cab when fired from behind.

Kim said, "Get ready to take the first left turn, running west."

General Gromyko's Mercedes was more agile and quicker than the Tigrs, but he was starting from the farthest distance. Playing catch-up. Still, from Kim's office in Tysons Corner, he could see the general joining his troops in pursuit.

"Oh," Kim said, "I forgot to mention that that left will take you on a one-way street, going against oncoming traffic."

Garrett didn't have time to reply. He swerved left at the same moment the machine gunner behind him unleashed a barrage of rounds. Because Garrett was turning in front of a southbound truck, that vehicle took the brunt of the rounds. Bullets blew into the vehicle's cab, instantly killing its driver and causing the truck to smash into a storefront.

Garrett tossed the SAT phone to Peter. "I need both hands." The teen immediately slipped up onto the seat next to him, buckled his seat belt, and held the phone near enough so Garrett could hear over its speaker.

Garrett downshifted and began swerving left and then right to avoid the one-way traffic coming at him. The GAZ Tigr turned left, too. Its gunner was about to unleash another round of bullets when one of the on-coming cars swerved onto the sidewalk to avoid the Zil and then jerked back onto the street, its driver unaware that the Tigr was about to hit him. The more powerful military vehicle smashed into his car, knocking it onto its side, sending a cascade of golden sparks in all di-rections. That collision caused two more cars that had dodged the Zil to hit the car in front of the Tigr. The second Tigr rear-ended the first, completely jamming the street, making it impassable. The first Tigr's driver pushed down hard on the accelerator, hoping to climb over the stopped vehicles. Instead the Tigr got stuck on the roof of the first car. A furious Gromyko, who was following them, ordered his driver to reverse and find a parallel street.

Through the Zil's cracked windshield, Garrett spot-ted turban-shaped spires in front of him as he turned off the one-way street onto a north-south thoroughfare. Four gold-plated domes.

"I see the convent!" he hollered at the SAT phone.

The seventeenth-century monastery had been built as a fortress to defend the city at the elbow of the Moscow River.

"It's got castle walls around it!" Garrett yelled. "How am I supposed to get inside them?"

"You're not," Kim said. "Austin says there's a cemetery south of it. I can see it on my screen. Head south."

"A what? Did you say graveyard?"

"Novodevichy Cemetery. Get to its front gate."

Garrett swerved, sideswiping a slow-moving car. The screech of metal on metal echoed throughout the cab. The jolt caused the SAT phone to fly from Peter's hand. It smacked against the inside of the windshield. Peter scrambled to grab it but missed. It fell under Garrett's feet. Pavel reached over, grabbed it, and then crawled up onto the truck seat, buckling himself in next to his grandson.

Garrett was now speeding down Luznetskiy Proyezd along the edge of the convent. From his right-side mirror, Garrett spotted General Gromyko's Mercedes coming behind him on the busy boulevard. Garrett had to do something to slow him.

He swerved the Zil again, this time sideswiping a Lada sedan, which spun out of control. A perfect 360. It was hit from behind by another vehicle. The Lada toppled over onto its side. Drivers slammed on their brakes to avoid a pileup. It would be enough to delay but not to stop Gromyko.

The cemetery's entrance appeared just as the Zil began to sputter and slow down, thanks to its now-empty radiator. Garrett turned the limping Zil into its entrance and stopped.

"Now what!" he demanded over the SAT.

That's when he spotted Ginger Capello exiting a BMW X5 luxury sedan with its engine running.

"Gromyko's coming!" she screamed.

Garrett, Peter, and Pavel leapt from Zil's cab and hurried into the waiting BMW. There was no time to thank Capello or ask how she planned to avoid being arrested.

Garrett sped back onto the southbound lane.

Through the sedan's back mirror, he watched Capello toss a packet into the truck's cab before she darted into the cemetery, lowering a black veil from her hat.

Gromyko reached the abandoned Zil just when the truck's cab exploded.

Garrett turned onto the entrance of the Third Ring. Peter was still holding the SAT phone.

"Gromyko didn't see your vehicle," Kim announced. "He's stopped at the cemetery."

"What about Capello?" Garrett asked.

"Who?"

Before Garrett could explain, Kim said in a panicked voice, "They're hacking our call. Toss the SAT phone now before they can identify you."

Garrett lowered the BMW's window.

"Get rid of it!" Kim exclaimed.

"Gordievsky," Garrett said, as he tossed the SAT out onto the highway.

Unharmed but fuming, General Gromyko exited his Mercedes and studied the burning Zil wreckage. His eyes scanned the cemetery. A veiled woman was walking toward an older car some two hundred yards away near a side exit.

He ducked back inside his car. "Follow that woman," he ordered.

"General, I can't," his driver said. He pointed toward the front of the Mercedes.

Gromyko stepped out and walked forward to examine his much-prized car. A shaft of metal from the exploding Zil had penetrated the car's front with such explosive force that it had punched through the engine's protective barrier. His car was useless.

PART III

A Killer Cometh

Death is the solution to all problems.
No man—no problem.

—Joseph Stalin

Twenty Four

Two years earlier

"Abidemi!" Elsa Eriksson cried. "They're raping her!"

"Chief, she's not our mission," Senator cautioned.

Senator was right. Garrett's orders were to rescue Eriksson from her Boko Haram kidnappers in this eight-hut Cameroon village. Not her fourteen-year-old friend who was being assaulted.

Another scream pierced the early-morning stillness.

"She's gonna wake everyone up," Sweet Tooth said.

"That dude got up early to be first in line. No sloppy seconds," Senator replied.

Eriksson gasped.

Through his headset, Garrett heard CIA director Harris ask: "What's the holdup?"

"Sir," he said, "we believe a fourteen-year-old Nigerian who was captured is being raped in a hut near us."

"Not your problem, Chief," Harris replied.

Only Garrett could hear their conversation.

"Sir, she's nearby."

"This isn't the Peace Corps."

"We can hear her screaming, sir."

"Then cover your ears."

"Sir, she's fourteen. How old is your granddaughter?"

Silence.

"How do you know about my granddaughter?" Harris asked.

"Newspaper. When you were appointed. What if it were her?"

"Listen, Garrett," Harris said, "you're on the ground and I'm not. So, here's the deal. You evaluate and decide. If you believe you can complete your mission, rescue that kid, and get out okay, then do it and I'll have your back. But your mission and your men come first. Granddaughter or not. Are we clear, Chief?"

"Yes, sir," Garrett said.

Bear had overheard Garrett's side of the conversation. "What'd Washington say?" he asked.

"My call."

"What was that stuff about having a granddaughter."

Garrett looked at Bear. "Harris didn't want to bother until I mentioned his granddaughter. Then he promised to back me up."

Garrett spoke to Eriksson. "We can't rescue her as long as you're in danger. You're our primary objective. You must leave now if you want us to save your friend. Nod if you understand."

Eriksson nodded.

Speaking to Bear, Garrett said, "You and Sweet Tooth get her to the others. Have the second team escort her immediately to the helos. The first team stays put until Senator and I snatch the other girl."

Garrett felt closest to his first team. Big Mac—the sniper. His spotter, aka Curly. Bear, Sweet Tooth, and a SEAL called Spider. The only unknown was Senator, who'd joined them late and was untested.

Bear peeked outside the hut's entrance. There was no movement.

Through his microphone, Garrett spoke to his sniper. "Big Mac?"

"All clear, Chief."

Garrett tapped Bear's shoulder. Bear pushed aside the heavy blanket covering the hut's doorway.

"God will protect," Eriksson whispered as she passed Garrett.

"Let's hope he protects all of us," he replied.

She followed Bear outside. Sweet Tooth fell in behind as they disappeared around the circular hut.

Abidemi's screams had turned into sobs. They reminded Garrett of the whimpering he'd heard in Arkansas when he'd once struck a stray dog with his truck, knocking it into a roadside ditch. Garrett peered outside, taking stock of the C-shaped camp illuminated by the embers of a dying fire. Abidemi's cries were coming from a hut near Alpha-1 where he and Senator were positioned.

"Need confirmation," Garrett told Big Mac. "Where's the girl?"

"Second hut to your right. You facing out your door."

"Wait," Senator said. "You're really serious about rescuing her? I thought you were just putting on an act to get the package to cooperate."

"We're getting the girl," Garrett replied. "There was one guard inside this hut. They'll have at least one in the girl's hut, plus the rapist."

"What if there's more?" Senator asked. "We got no idea who could be in that hut and there's only two of us."

Garrett regretted not sending Senator back with Eriksson and having a more veteran SEAL stay.

Senator said, "I need to know if Washington okayed this."

"You need to know what I tell you," Garrett answered, not hiding the anger in his voice.

"But if this isn't part of our mission—"

Garrett cut him short. "Listen to me and listen good. We're going to rescue that little girl. You got that? Or do we need to take this a step higher than words?"

For a moment, the two men stared at each other. Garrett sensed fear.

"Senator, we can do this," he said, reassuringly. "Just fall back on your training. We'll grab the girl and be on a helo heading home in the blink of an eye."

"Yes, sir," Senator said. Now he seemed embarrassed. "I'm fine, sir. Let's do it."

Garrett was holding his SIG Sauer. He had a Heckler & Koch MP7 assault rifle with a suppressor strapped to his back. Senator was holding a Heckler & Koch 416 assault rifle with a ten-inch barrel and suppressor.

"Pistol," Garrett ordered. Senator shouldered his rifle. Drew his M-9.

"You follow my lead," Garrett said, "and this will turn out just fine. You'll be a hero. Maybe get a medal. Are you ready?"

"Yes, Chief."

Garrett stepped into the morning air and slipped silently across the hard-packed earth to the hut where Big Mac had said the girl was being held. Outside its blanket door covering, he could hear Abidemi's pitiful sobs.

Using hand signals, Garrett positioned Senator to the right side of the opening while he stationed himself on its left. They entered the hut simultaneously.

Three terrorists. One on top of Abidemi, who was lying on the floor. Two Boko Haram watching, one on each side of her. Garrett double-tapped the one on the left. Senator shot the one directly in front of him. The rapist rose to his knees just as two of Garrett's SIG Sauer rounds punched into his chest. He fell forward onto Abidemi, who began shoving his corpse, trying to free herself from his heavy body. Hysterical.

Senator grabbed the dead man's shirt and jerked him away from the girl.

"Elsa sent us," Garrett said in a calming voice. "We're taking you home."

Her face was covered with sweat and wet with tears. She grabbed her one-piece dress, which had been ripped from her earlier. Began scooting backward. Away from them.

Senator dropped to his knees. He spoke quietly to her. "You're scared. So am I. But we've come to take you home. Just calm down and do what we say."

Garrett surveyed the hut's candle-lighted interior.

A second blanket was hanging from the ceiling. Dividing the hut in half. He nodded toward Senator, who noticed the blanket and moved into position. One, two, three. They drew back the barrier.

"Oh my God!" Senator gasped, lowering his pistol.

At least ten girls. Huddled together. Terrified. Garrett guessed their ages were seven to twelve. Two completely naked. Spinning around, Garrett said, "Abidemi." He wasn't certain if any of the other girls understood English. "Can you speak to them?"

It took her a moment to comprehend.

"Tell them to keep absolutely quiet," he said. "No talking. No crying. We're friends."

He reached out to Abidemi. Reluctantly, she took his hand. Moved in slow unsteady steps. She spoke in Hausa, the most common language spoken by Muslims in the region.

"Sweet Jesus," Senator said. "Now what, Chief?"

Garrett's mind was running the numbers. Two Black Hawk UH-60 Sikorsky helicopters en route to extricate two SEAL teams and the package. Each could carry eleven combat soldiers. Total capacity: 22. He was overseeing two seven-man teams—14 men. That left 8 open spaces. Eriksson—number 15 of 22. Abidemi—number 16. Six more openings, maybe seven because these kids were scrawny. *Six openings for ten girls. Four would be left behind. Which four? An alternative came to him. He could simply take Abidemi, leave the others behind. Sophie's Choice. He hadn't anticipated this.*

Through his head microphone, Garrett informed Harris about the additional girls. The CIA director cut loose with a string of expletives.

"We'll need a third helo," Garrett said.

"No way," Harris said. "I'm not putting more Americans at risk. I shouldn't have backed you. You made the wrong choice. Now man up, leave 'em, and complete your mission. These kids are expendable. Leave them. That's an order. . . ."

Garrett looked into the children's terrified faces. *Three klicks to the helo rendezvous point—3.1 miles. They would slow down everyone. Make everyone vulnerable. The smart move was to leave them, as Director Harris had ordered him. The children were collateral damage, the victims of a senseless war. They were not his problem. They were not worth Americans dying to save them.*

"Chief, sunlight's gonna be here soon," Big Mac said through Garrett's headset. "Remember these pricks pray before dawn."

"Status, main package?" Garrett responded.

"Second team is hoofing her to rendezvous. ETA probably thirty minutes."

"Chief," Big Mac said, "we got to move, otherwise there's going to be a shit show."

Garrett took a deep breath. Switched off communication with Director Harris. He'd decided to talk to the entire first team, every man.

"There're more girls than one."

"How many more?" Big Mac asked.

"Ten more. Little kids. Washington won't send a third helo. Says to leave them. Says they're expendable. We all know what that means. So, I'm going to ask each of you. Speak freely. Do we leave or take them?"

The Senator spoke first. "I knew this was wrong. They aren't our mission. I say we leave them."

"What we have here is a pending O.K. Corral scenario," Sweet Tooth said, sounding philosophical. "Blood and guts, but hell, I've always been a sucker for westerns. I say we take 'em. Every last one of them."

"Bear?" Garrett asked.

"I go with you, Chief. Your decision is mine. I kill when you tell me and hold my trigger when you tell me. Your call."

"I say every day is a good day to kill Ali Babas," Big Mac volunteered. "Let's save the girls and kill every one of these jihadist bastards."

"Curly?" Garrett asked the sniper spotter.

"I go where Big Mac goes," he replied. "I'm down with saving them."

"Spider, that leaves you? Speak freely."

"I got a baby girl at home. Enough said."

The Senator was the only one who'd objected.

"Looks like you're outvoted."

"I'll do it, but when we get back, I'm filing a report."

"Write what you want," Garrett said. "Just lift your load."

Garrett ran a different set of numbers. Bad guys. They'd already killed the two sentries guarding the Alpha-1 hut. Plus, the one inside the hut guarding Eriksson. The rapist and his two buddies were dead. That totaled six. Fourteen tangos remaining according to intel. Twice the number of Garrett and his team. Still, Garrett had faith in his men, including Senator.

"We're coming out," Garrett told Big Mac via the headset. He resumed communications with Director Harris in Washington.

"What the hell is happening?" Harris demanded. "Why'd you go off air?"

"We're bringing the girls with us," Garrett said.

"Like hell you are."

"We'll need another helo." Garrett switched off his connection with the director.

"Get these girls together," Garrett told Senator and

Abidemi. She didn't react. "You want to live?" he asked sternly. "You get these girls into a line, tell them to keep quiet, not panic, otherwise we all end up dead. You understand that? Dead."

She nodded. He and Senator stripped shirts from two dead terrorists at their feet. Handed them to Abidemi for the two naked children. She spoke to the girls in a hushed voice.

"Only eight are coming," Abidemi announced.

"What?" Garrett replied.

"One's already dead and her sister won't leave her."

"Try to convince her. If she stays, she dies," Garrett said. "Tell her that."

The tiny girl began sobbing.

"Line them up."

Garrett holstered his pistol. Unstrapped his assault rifle. Senator followed his example.

"Big Mac?" Garrett said. "We're moving. I'll need two supports behind this hut. Helping us herd. Sweet Tooth, you know the way. Bring Spider."

"Always wanted to be a shepherd," Sweet Tooth joked. "Be there in three."

Waiting made it seem twice that. Garrett pushed the questions nagging at him out of his head. He was disobeying a direct order. There'd be hell to pay. He looked again at the girls. Stay focused.

"We're in position," Sweet Tooth announced. "Send them out."

"Let's go!" Garrett told Abidemi. He held open the blanket door cover. Senator came next to lead the girls behind the hut to Sweet Tooth and Spider. Abidemi remained with Garrett to assist getting the girls out.

Garrett counted eight, not nine.

"We're short one," he said.

"The dead girl's sister. I told you. Let me try—"

"Hurry, we're exposed," he said.

The last girl stuck out her head from behind the blanket in the center of the hut.

Abidemi took her hand and helped her outside. They followed Garrett to where Sweet Tooth and Spider were waiting with the others behind the hut. They moved as a covey to where Big Mac, Curly, and Bear were positioned—about a hundred yards from the huts' perimeter.

"Let's get to the helos," Garrett said.

"Chief!" Big Mac said. He'd been keeping an eye on the camp. Two terrorists were emerging from their huts. Holding prayer cloths. Assault rifles. They greeted each other and then one noticed that the two sentries outside Alpha-1 hut were not at their posts. One dropped his prayer cloth, grasped his Kalashnikov with both hands, and was about to shout an alarm.

"Take 'em," Garrett said.

Big Mac was good at what he did. One shot. One dead terrorist. The second fell before he had a chance to comprehend what had happened to his buddy. But the sound of the sniper's rounds, even suppressed, were like claps of thunder in the quiet morning air.

"Senator and Spider, get these kids moving to the helos. Now!" Garrett commanded. With Abidemi's help, Senator led the way. Spider took the rear guard. They began running with the girls, leaving the other five SEALs behind to cover them.

Big Mac and Curly were on high ground—a slight rise from the flat earth protected by several large rocks. Sweet Tooth, Bear, and Garrett dug in beside them. Five against the twelve remaining jihadists in the huts.

Three Boko Haram fighters came running out, unsure what was happening.

"Wait," Garrett said through his headset. He wanted as many of them exposed as possible. He was counting. Nine still in the huts. The three jihadists outside the dwellings examined their two dead comrades. One began yelling. They scanned the darkness around the camp, searching for some sign. The SEALs remained hidden. A fourth terrorist emerged and bolted toward the Tacoma truck with its Soviet-made ZKPUT heavy machine gun, unaware it had been booby-trapped when the SEALs first arrived.

Big Mac aimed his MK-12 sniper rifle—a variation of the standard M-16 created to be more compact and lighter than larger sniper weapons.

"Wait, use the C-4," Garrett said. "Let's keep them guessing where we are."

Bear held off until the jihadist had climbed onto the truck's bed. The deafening blast blew the truck upward. It came crashing down as a fireball. The other jihadists started to seek cover in their huts.

"Now," Garrett said. Big Mac fired. Methodical. The other SEALs joined him. Within moments, the remaining three jihadists were eliminated.

Another fighter ran outside, firing his Kalashnikov in all directions. Big Mac martyred him. It was obvious now where the SEAL team was positioned. Rifles poked from behind the hut's heavy cloth coverings. Return fire. The jihadists' barrage continued for several minutes before the Boko Haram fighters stopped. A moment passed and then intense Kalashnikov gunfire. Garrett understood. This second exchange was cover fire.

A single terrorist suddenly appeared at the bottom of the slight rise below their position. He'd managed to escape from the camp without being seen, perhaps by knocking a hole in the back of his hut. He was less than fifteen yards away, close enough for Garrett to hear him hollering, "Allahu akbar! Allahu akbar!"

"Suicide vest!" Garrett yelled.

The attacker's finger slipped off the dead-man switch as he ran forward. Hundreds of lethal metal pellets blew in all directions. The explosion was deafening. A shock wave.

Bear was struck in his face. A single metal ball passed directly through his fleshly cheek, exiting out the other side, splintering several teeth. Curly got it the worst. His left shoulder was covered with bleeding holes, making his arm inoperable.

The explosion rallied the remaining jihadists. Six Boko Haram fighters scrambled from their hiding places.

Garrett, Sweet Tooth, Big Mac, and a wounded Bear took aim. Killing two. The four others ducked for cover behind the huts. They would try to outflank the SEALs.

"Blow the deuce," Garrett ordered. Despite his mouth wound, Bear trigged the C-4 planted earlier. The explosion illuminated the entire encampment. One terrorist near the truck was engulfed by flames. Screamed and dropped to the ground. He didn't move.

The others were easy to spot. Approaching the SEALs from their left, two fighters began scampering up the rocks. Sweet Tooth grabbed a modified M-79. The single-shot, shoulder-fired grenade launcher was loaded with a twenty-seven-pellet round. Buckshot. Fatal at such close range. One jihadist was killed instantly, the other seriously wounded. He fell, crying in pain. Garrett finished him.

"There's one more out there," Garrett said.

"Boss, I counted twenty," Big Mac said.

"Nineteen," Garrett said. "We're missing one, unless intel was off. I'm certain of it."

They waited for a long minute, with Big Mac and Garrett keeping watch while Sweet Tooth, their medic, attended to Curly and Bear.

"We need to get Curly out to save his arm," Sweet Tooth advised. "Bear can't speak but looks like a clear pass-through. Jaw appears broken. But we gotta get moving before both go into shock."

"Let's move," Garrett said, his eyes still darting across the camp, searching for that twentieth fighter, silently praying that he'd miscounted.

Sweet Tooth put his arm around Curly's waist, lifting him to his feet. Once he was steady, Curly slapped away Sweet Tooth's arm. "My feet are fine, it's my damn arm that's falling off."

In twenty-five minutes they had caught up with the slower-moving girls being escorted to the rendezvous spot by Senator and Spider.

"Oh, my God!" Senator said when he spotted Curly's arm. "I knew this was going bad."

"If you faint, Senator, we leave you," Curly replied, grimacing.

Garrett kept staring back. No sign through his night-vision that they were being tracked.

No one spoke as the entourage continued. Garrett heard the sounds of a helicopter flying above them. Elsa Eriksson and the second SEAL team were en route to Nigeria. The other bird would be waiting— but only with space for eleven. Someone would have to wait behind.

Garrett clicked on his communication with Langley, hoping that a third helo was en route.

"Two wounded, no dead, all terrorists terminated," he said.

Again, Harris cursed. "This is your fault, Garrett. You got one helo waiting," Harris said. "I'll send back the other one. But when you are out of there, you'll pay for this."

It took them nearly thirty more minutes to reach the extraction point and second waiting helo. Curly and Bear boarded. Sweet Tooth continued doctoring them as he climbed on board. He was trying to keep shock from setting in. *The Golden Hour.* Garrett noticed Big Mac limping. He'd not said a word. There were bloodstains on his right thigh. The suicide vest. Garrett ordered him to get on board. That left Spider, Garrett, and Senator, along with Abidemi and nine girls to fill seven spots. Garrett helped Abidemi onto the aircraft.

"Spider," Garrett said. "Sweet Tooth is busy taking care of Curly, you get on board and nursemaid the girls."

Abidemi climbed off the helicopter. "You'll need me to talk to the ones left behind. They're frightened and will panic."

Senator started to board. "Let's go, Chief. The next helo can get the girls."

"No," Garrett said. He knew there would be no helo unless at least one SEAL stayed behind.

A pilot spoke to Garrett. "These little girls are so light, I can get one more on board."

Senator looked at the girls and then at Garrett. He reluctantly stepped off the helo so that more girls could board. The final count—everyone on board except for two girls, Abidemi, Senator, and Garrett.

"Your ride should be back in thirty," the pilot said.

They watched the helicopter lift off. Disappear into the horizon. It was starting to get light. Dawn. Garrett and Senator kept watch. Abidemi and the two girls huddled together, cowering, terrified.

"Status report," Harris demanded from Langley.

"No tangos in sight. We got three girls and the two of us still waiting."

"Was it worth it, Garrett?" Harris asked. "Worth two Americans injured? Worth your career?" He didn't hide the anger in his voice.

Garrett looked at Abidemi comforting the girls.

"Yes, sir," he replied. He switched off his microphone.

Senator said, "The girl, Abidemi, she's brave."

"You got to be to survive in this hellhole," Garrett replied.

"What kind of men are these?" Senator said. "Kidnapping and raping children and then praying?"

Garrett shook his head. "You did okay for your first mission," he said. "Be sure to put that in your report."

Senator gave him a sheepish look. "What report is that? I don't know of any report."

The sun was peeking over the terrain.

Garrett heard the rescue helicopter approaching. Senator set off a smoke flare. Red. The helo landed.

Still no sign of terrorists. Senator helped Abidemi and the two girls aboard. Climbed on.

"Thanks for not forgetting us," Senator joked to its pilot.

Garrett was the last in, still checking the surrounding area. Still looking for that twentieth fighter. The helicopter began lifting from the ground.

"We made it!" the Senator beamed. He nodded at Abidemi.

Garrett felt a sense of relief. They had made it. He looked out.

That's when he saw the twentieth jihadist. That's when he saw the RPG lifted to his shoulder.

Twenty-Five

Current Day

"You should have put a bullet in Pavel's head when he returned from Washington," an enraged Russian president Kalugin declared. It was the morning after. "You should have shot him like the others."

General Andre Borsovich Gromyko didn't have to ask who the "others" were.

Russian journalist Anna Stepanovna Politkovskaya had been the toe first dipped into the water. Arrested by Russian military forces for her reporting in Chechnya, Politkovskaya had been fatally shot in her own building's elevator. Back then, the Kremlin had felt an obligation to the West to conduct a mock trial. Five men sentenced. Scapegoats.

After that, the pretending had ended.

Kremlin critic Boris Yefimovich Nemtsov. Four bullets. Fired from behind him while crossing the Bolshoy Moskvoretsky Bridge near the Kremlin. The reason: he'd revealed the true wealth that the Russian president had stolen. Twenty palaces and villas, fifteen helicopters, forty-three private aircraft, two yachts—one with a waterfall—and a multimillion-ruble palatial estate under construction. How had a Russian president become a billionaire many times over while supposedly living on a $100,000 annual salary?

"A bullet to the head of a deputy minister would have complicated things," Gromyko said, quietly hoping to justify his actions.

President Kalugin scoffed. "And what would the West do?"

"Not only the West. Pavel still has influential friends here, around us in Moscow."

Kalugin's face became flushed. "And what?" he repeated, his anger intensifying. "They are nothing but frightened field mice."

"We can't murder everyone," Gromyko replied.

"Have you learned nothing from history? From Stalin? You only have to kill enough. The others will cower."

"We agreed that poisoning Pavel with candy was the best way to cast suspicion on the Americans."

"Yes, that was the argument you made," Kalugin said. "The West accuses us of using poison in England. We accuse the Americans of poisoning Pavel. But your poison only killed his driver and wife."

Kalugin was quiet while he pondered yesterday's escape. Gunfire on Moscow's streets. Car crashes. A truck explosion. Cell phone videos on social media had chronicled the carnage. Gromyko had arranged for the state-controlled television to announce Pavel and his grandson had been kidnapped. Chechen rebels. Radical Islamists. No mention of any American involvement. Within hours, photos of Pavel and Peter had been distributed everywhere. A reward offered. Roadblocks erected. Security tightened at all border crossings, airports, train stations, and harbors. *Help rescue Pavel and Peter!* Not since the peak of the Cold War had such an impenetrable Iron Curtain been raised at the borders. Or such a huge lie been told.

"Has he told the Americans?" asked Kalugin.

"Pavel never would have disclosed all of our plans until he was safely in America. To do otherwise was to risk the Americans simply leaving him here."

"An assumption."

"No traitor gives away the crown jewel until he is safe. The Americans might suspect, but they cannot possibly know who we have targeted with our poison.

Or who is helping us. Our tracks are covered. We can still move forward with our plan."

Kalugin nodded toward official reports on his desk. "Tell me the truth, not what these official versions say. How did Pavel make contact with the Americans?"

"I suspect he spoke directly to the American president at the Washington funeral for their dead Ukrainian ambassador."

Kalugin slapped his open palm down on his wooden desk. "You were warned the Americans had sent this man—Brett Garrett—to help him escape. You knew he was waiting yesterday for Pavel and his grandson. You had men watching the Billa. You could have arrested him."

"We needed to wait until he and Pavel were together."

"Yes, yes, yes, this is what you said," Kalugin grunted, "and now? You let them escape like smoke through your fingers."

"We know where the American was told to go. Ukraine. At the border near the city of Novhorod-Siverskyi. We will catch them there."

Kalugin sneered. "Do you assume this American is as big a fool as you are showing yourself to be?"

Gromyko shrugged, hoping to minimize the president's anger. "It will not matter. He cannot escape. If Garrett contacts the American embassy, we will know from our friend there. If he uses any public phone in Russia, we will know. If he attempts to communicate with America by a satellite phone, as he did when we were pursuing him, we will know. He is only one man and he is alone without help. He and Pavel will never cross our borders. I swear to you that I will bring Pavel, his grandson, and the American to you on their knees within the next forty-eight hours."

"General Gromyko," Kalugin said in a solemn voice, "your elbow is close, yet you still cannot bite it."

Gromyko's face turned red upon hearing the familiar Russian proverb.

"We have been comrades a long, long time, so I will speak plainly to you," Kalugin said. "If Pavel lives and the Americans discover our Kamera plan, it is you who will receive the next bullet to the head."

Twenty-Six

Thomas Jefferson Kim was exuberant when he entered the CIA safe house in Ashburn, Virginia, shortly before 8:00 a.m. and was immediately disappointed when he found only Valerie Mayberry waiting inside. They sat in awkward silence in the second-level living room of the town house that was identical to hundreds of others in the massive suburban development.

Ten minutes later, the grinding sound beneath them of the ground-floor garage door signaled CIA director Harris's arrival.

Kim couldn't wait for formalities. He rose from his seat on a beige sofa and blurted out: "I know how General Gromyko knew where to ambush Garrett and Pavel. Ambassador Duncan told them!"

"What?" Mayberry said, clearly shocked. "The ambassador is a Russian mole?"

"No," Kim said. "I mean, he didn't do it intentionally, but he's to blame."

Harris sat down on an overstuffed beige chair and motioned to Kim and Mayberry to return to their seats on the sofa.

"You've just made a serious accusation," Harris said, calmly.

"When Garrett was escaping yesterday," Kim began, "I called him on his SAT phone and a hacker immediately began trying to intercept our conversation."

"Yes, we already know that," Harris said.

"Ever since that SAT call, this same Russian hacker has been trying to break into my IEC network. A nonstop assault and I've been firing back, trying to penetrate his system."

"Cyber combat," Mayberry said.

"Exactly," Kim declared, excitedly. "Without getting technical, early this morning I succeeded in breaking into his system, but only long enough to copy several hundred megabytes of data before he blocked me. What I discovered is your network has been breached."

Kim removed a stack of printed-out messages from his briefcase. "At first, I thought the hacker used an advanced version of Pawn Storm—a cyberattack the

Russians launched a few years back aimed at NATO, the White House, the German parliament, and a slew of Eastern European governments. It used at least six zero-days, including a critical Java vulnerability, to conduct advanced credential phishing."

"They got it from phishing?" Mayberry said.

"Russian hackers sent emails to government officials that appeared to come from a legitimate server—let's say Yahoo. The emails warned there had been a 'server failure' and that all emails that were supposed to have been delivered a day or two earlier had been 'undeliverable.' To fix the failure, the user was told to hit a 'start service' button."

"And someone fell for it," Director Harris said.

"Absolutely," Kim replied, grinning. "These phishing warnings were so well done that even a Yahoo service technician would've had trouble identifying them as fakes. All it took was for a couple of government Yahoo users to click and the Russians were inside their targets. Their spyware began spreading and collecting personal information and messages."

"And that's how they figured out where Garrett would be?" Mayberry asked.

"No. I mean, that was my first theory. That's what the hacker wanted me to think. It was a red herring. The hacker in Moscow was invited inside."

"What? Who invited this hacker in?" Harris asked.

"Ambassador Duncan. My guess is he had a computer problem and whoever fixed his machine created a carefully hidden mirror account," Kim replied. "What makes this so ingenious is the hacker not only can read message traffic, including the ambassador's secure emails, he also can block them or, if he chooses, he can answer them posing as someone else. This hacker is really brilliant. Not like me, but still brilliant."

Kim handed out several printouts from his briefcase.

"If what you are saying is correct, it explains the communications breach," Harris said, "but not how General Gromyko knew about yesterday's ambush. My instructions to Garrett were hand-delivered and none of us knew about the rendezvous site at the Billa grocery until the morning of the extraction."

"That's right, Director Harris," Kim replied, "but these printouts show that Ambassador Duncan was sending emails while he was flying to Geneva for an economic summit."

"Who was he sending them to?" Mayberry asked.

"The secretary of state's personal account. They were intercepted and blocked by the hacker."

Harris and Mayberry scanned the printouts while Kim continued. "The first intercepted emails were about the summit, but then Ambassador Duncan reported that a female embassy employee threw red wine on a network television correspondent at a birthday party for his daughter. This correspondent had written several complimentary stories about the ambassador's wife, Heidi. They were friends. The reporter suspected the female employee was shielding Brett Garrett, protecting him. So the reporter asked Heidi Duncan after the party if the employee was a covert CIA officer posing as a member of her staff."

"You can't reveal if someone is a CIA operative," Mayberry said.

"Heidi didn't, but she did mention it to her husband. She told him that she might have a deep-cover CIA agent on her staff and that prompted the ambassador to go on an email tirade."

Kim leaned forward from his sofa seat. Elbows resting on his knees. Eyes looking directly at Harris. "This is where the ambassador screws the pooch."

Harris looked sullen. "Please continue."

"Ambassador Duncan tells the secretary that the CIA apparently is spying on Heidi and he wants the agency to back off. What the ambassador doesn't realize is the hacker is intercepting his emails and it's at this point where the hacker begins writing back to Duncan on the aircraft."

"Are you telling me this hacker began interrogating him?" Harris asked.

"Exactly, the hacker asks why Brett Garrett is in Moscow and Duncan—thinking he is communicating with the secretary—tells him everything, including how Garrett was in the midst of smuggling a high-ranking Russian asset out of the country. He was like water gushing from a garden hose."

"Why would he do something so careless?" Mayberry asked.

"Because he thought he was talking to the secretary and because he was venting. He was furious the CIA was spying on his wife."

Harris put down the printouts that Kim had handed him. "This is why the president shouldn't have doled out the Russian ambassadorship as a political plum. A few hours of security protocol training apparently wasn't enough for him."

"In his defense," Kim said, "there's no way Ambassador Duncan realized he was exchanging emails with a Russian hacker."

"Have you identified this hacker?" Mayberry asked.

"Only by his nom de plume—*Magician*. Because of his computer skills, I suspect he works for GIT inside the Moscow Station."

"Your rival when it comes to government computer contracts," Harris noted.

"Perhaps it's time for State to switch IT support," Kim replied.

Harris said, "I'll deal with this. Now, has Garrett tried to contact you?"

"No," Kim said. "Our last communication was on the SAT phone twenty-four hours ago during the Moscow chase."

"Do you know what's happened to him and the others?" Mayberry asked Harris.

Director Harris shook his head. "The last word Garrett spoke before destroying the SAT phone was 'Gordievsky,'" Harris said.

"Like the KGB defector who MI-6 got out of Russia?" Mayberry asked. "It must be a message. The Brits wrote emergency instructions on how to flee Russia in invisible ink in a collection of Shakespeare sonnets and gave it to Gordievsky. When he got into trouble, he soaked the book in water and they appeared. That's how he knew to take the train to the Finnish border," Mayberry recalled.

Harris agreed. "He's not going to Ukraine. We assume he's going to follow Gordievsky's escape route."

"Where did Gordievsky cross over?" Kim asked.

"Just outside Vyborg," Mayberry answered. "About twenty-four miles from the Finnish border. Before Stalin seized it, Vyborg belonged to Finland."

"How far is Vyborg from Moscow?" Kim asked.

"If you're driving, eleven or twelve hours," Harris replied.

"If he drove all night, he could already be there waiting," Mayberry said.

Harris disagreed. "The main highway between Moscow and St. Petersburg would be too risky. Even if General Gromyko assumes Garrett is heading to Ukraine, he will have roadblocks along all major routes east."

Addressing Kim, Harris said, "I need you in Langley working with my people to positively identify this Magician. We need to nail him. But before you go, answer me this. Can you tell me if this Magician intercepted the call in time to hear the word *Gordevisky*?"

"I'm not sure," Kim said. "I'd put the odds at fifty-fifty."

"Thank you, Mr. Kim," Harris said. "You can go now." He waited until Kim had exited the safe house.

"There's a high probability that General Gromyko is going to catch Garrett and Pavel," Harris said. "If they do, Gromyko will, more than likely, kill them and move forward with his poison attack here. That means you're our best option for learning where the Antifa attack will happen and when."

"Aysan Rivera," Mayberry said. "Have your people intercepted her from wherever she fled?"

"No, she never boarded her plane at Dulles."

"Where is she?" Mayberry said, genuinely concerned.

"I was hoping you could answer that question."

Twenty-Seven

Deputy Foreign Minister Pavel began complaining twenty minutes after they exited Moscow. "We should be in a Range Rover. The mafia drives them and the police won't trouble them. In this BMW, they will think we're rich and can pay a large bribe."

The State Inspection of Safety of Road Traffic officers (GIBDD) were known to find any excuse to pull over drivers and threatened them with jail unless they were paid bribes.

Another gripe seconds later. This time about the two major highways connecting Moscow to St. Petersburg. "The M-11 is where a wealthy Russian would drive. Fewer holes. Not the M-10. You selected the wrong road."

Next came a direct order. "Drive faster. You're calling attention to us by traveling so slowly."

Garrett eyeballed the BMW's speedometer. The national speed limit was 100 kilometers (about 62 mph). He was driving 144 kilometers (90 mph) and still being pressured.

Garrett ignored Pavel.

By this point they'd been on the M-10 motorway long enough for General Gromyko to have ordered roadblocks. Garrett could see a line of cars slowing in front of them. He had counterfeit documents, passports, and travel papers in his gym bag, but Gromyko would have distributed photos of Pavel and Peter, and the two of them would be recognized even though they were traveling under fake names. Would a lucrative bribe be enough for a GIBDD or FSB officer to look the other way? Risky. Another alternative: Garrett's SIG Sauer. Kill anyone who stopped them. Even more risky.

"We need to get off this highway now," Garrett announced. "We should find someplace to hide—at least until night."

"You didn't plan for this?" Pavel asked. "The SVR would have."

"I wasn't planning on being ambushed in Moscow."

"There was a leak obviously by your people," Pavel lectured. "Americans talk too much. Involve too many. Now turn off the motorway and I will direct you to a dacha where we will be safe from Gromyko."

"Whose dacha? Nothing you own, nothing your family owns, nothing your relatives own, nothing your friends own."

"Don't waste my time telling me the obvious. Gromyko will not look for us where I am taking you."

Slowing the car, Garrett said, "I don't like it."

"Gromyko will not think of this dacha because it belonged to a family whose daughter he raped and murdered."

"They'll take you in?" Garrett asked.

"What I told you is sufficient."

"No, it isn't."

Pavel didn't reply. He was sulking. He was not used to anyone giving him orders.

Garrett pulled to the side of the road, parked, and turned off the engine.

Pavel wet his lips. "Gromyko was not the first to abuse this woman," he explained. "A Soviet foreign minister violated her when she was a child. The father protested to the Foreign Ministry, and I was put in charge of paying restitution. That's how it was done in the Soviet days. We didn't murder people. I was a junior diplomat and part of the restitution was building the family a dacha. I found the girl a good job after she finished school."

"I thought you said Gromyko raped and murdered her?"

"Yes, he did. It happened several years later. The girl's boss took her to a party. She was an adult and quite beautiful. Gromyko was there and when she rejected his advances, he raped her. When her father demanded justice this time, there was no restitution. Gromyko killed him, her, the entire family. He will not think to look for us there. He isn't aware of my earlier connection to the family."

"How can you be sure no one is living there now?"

"Tell me, Mr. Garrett," Pavel replied, "all of the residents know what Gromyko did. Would you risk moving into that dacha?"

Unlike the highway, Pavel directed Garrett onto ruts, washed-out sections of road, and potholes in what road was not yet washed away. Moscow was modern, but this countryside reminded Garrett of developing countries he'd seen. "All the young have left the county," Pavel volunteered. "The collectives provided work. There is nothing here now except the old, decay, and the stench of death."

Ten minutes after they passed through a village, Pavel ordered Garrett to turn onto what had been a dirt road but now was a barely visible path overgrown with weeds.

Several limbs had fallen onto the entrance to the heavily treed property. With Peter's help, Garrett moved them aside while Pavel waited. Eventually they entered a meadow with a creek and no visible neighbors. "This is the price the state puts on child molestation," Garrett said. "How old was the girl?"

"That is of no importance to you."

A log cabin made from hand-hewed timber had been built by the creek more than a century before. A newer building had been added to it, but it was now several decades old. Long ago faded were its yellow walls with green trim. The panes in two windows were cracked. So many weeds had overtaken the front door that it would have been impossible to pull outward. A single wooden T from a clothesline stubbornly stood erect. Its mate had fallen. A waist-high, fenced-in area enclosed what Garrett assumed had been a vegetable garden. Fireplace wood was neatly stacked near an outdoor toilet. Easily missed was an ax protruding from a chopping block. Both had been overtaken by an indigenous vine that had curled itself around the stump and up the tool.

Garrett maneuvered the BMW to the back side of the original log cabin and discovered that one wall had been removed from it as a conversion project, turning it into a garage. A 1980s-era Lada was parked inside.

Despite dry rot, the tires were still inflated even though the box-shaped Lada's bright red paint was layered with dirt and bird dung.

Pavel was the first to enter, swatting his hand in front of his face to clear cobwebs. This back door opened inward and he pushed hard against the door, forcing it across the planked floor.

"Fetch firewood," Pavel ordered his grandson.

"No," Garrett said. "Smoke will get attention."

Peter looked at his grandfather, who shrugged and relented.

Garrett was surprised when he stepped inside. The dacha's interior had remained untouched by human hands. A single, large room, with a curtain closing off a sleeping area. The bed still carefully made. No electricity. Glass jars of canned fruits filled the kitchen cabinets. Contents black now, impossible to identify. Everything store-bought in paper boxes had been ravaged by mice. A musty smell. Two framed watercolors mounted near chairs. A single framed photograph. Parents. Two boys. A girl, maybe five at the time.

A piano.

"The father insisted," Pavel said without emotion, "for his daughter to take playing lessons."

Peter walked to it and pushed a dusty white key. Out of tune but it worked.

"Play something for us," Pavel said. He glanced at Garrett, adding, "Peter is a prodigy. You can play any piece of music to him one time, and he can duplicate it."

The teenager sat and began to play.

Pavel closed his eyes and hummed along. "Tchaikovsky," he said. "This is from *The Seasons.* November."

He continued to hum along and then said:

In your loneliness do not look at the road,
And do not rush out after the troika.
Suppress at once and forever the fear of longing in
your heart.

Peter struck a wrong key.

"You half-wit!" his grandfather snapped, opening his eyes. "If you can't play Tchaikovsky correctly, you shouldn't try."

The teen stopped. Ashamed.

"I thought he did a pretty damn good job," Garrett said.

"Every child in America does a damn good job even when they don't," Pavel retorted. "It is why you are weak."

Pavel walked across the room to a decorative wooden cabinet. "We are saved," he declared, removing two bottles of unopened vodka, which he placed on the dacha's only table.

"Peter, fetch us three glasses," he said. "Vodka. Our gift to the world."

He opened the first bottle and filled three cups. "There are many false stereotypes about Russians, but drinking vodka is not one of them." He examined the bottle. "*Russki Standard,* one of our most popular. Every educated Russian knows the history of vodka. Why? Because the outside world always asks us, 'Why do Russians drink so much vodka?' Do you know the history, Mr. Garrett?"

"No," he replied, happy that Pavel was now talking so freely.

"Pyotr Arsenjevitch Smirnov introduced vodka to the czars but, like all the rich, he fled Russia after the October Revolution. Where did he go? Where else but America? A joke. His vodka wasn't accepted there until some American advertising man called it 'white whiskey.' Pearls before swine."

Pavel raised his glass. "Let's have a toast. You must toast. Let's toast to us following in the footsteps of Smirnov to America!"

Pavel downed his in one swallow. The teen pushed his away. Garrett sniffed the vodka.

"Vodka doesn't go bad," Pavel declared. He reached

across the table and reclaimed his grandson's still full glass, which he also drank in a single gulp. He refilled both glasses for himself.

"Do you think I am trying to poison you?" he asked Garrett.

"Isn't that how Tchaikovsky died?"

Pavel's face lit up. "Ah, so now you are trying to impress me. Tchaikovsky died from cholera caused by drinking unboiled water." He dropped his voice to a whisper and added, "There are others who say he committed suicide from depression brought on by living in Russia." He laughed and drank one of the glasses before him, his third shot.

Garrett took his first sip. "How is Gromyko planning on attacking the U.S.?"

Pavel's toothy smile became a frown. "Mr. Garrett, I prefer being kissed before I am—" He stopped short, censoring his language for the sake of his grandson. "You want to learn what I know, first get us to America alive. No more talk about this. We drink and discuss happy things."

He emptied the fourth glass and nodded at Garrett's still nearly full one. "Mr. Garrett, let me further disabuse you of any diabolical thoughts. It is physically impossible for an American, any American, including you, to outdrink a Russian when it comes to vodka. If you are hoping to get me drunk to loosen my tongue, you will be deeply disappointed."

Garrett finished his glass and turned it over so Pavel couldn't refill it.

"My father was an alcoholic," he said.

"Every Russian's father is an alcoholic," Pavel said, laughing.

"Mine killed himself and my mother in a car crash."

"And what?" said Pavel. "You are telling us this sad story to win my sympathy? You hope to establish some personal bond, some intimacy? You forget that you are seated at a table with a Soviet-trained diplomat who has survived a poison attack. You are seated with a Russian father whose only daughter and his son-in-law are dead, leaving my grandson here without a parent. Do you think you have suffered because your parents died? You Americans know nothing about suffering."

Pavel downed the glass before him. "My country lost thirty-one million people during World War Two. Three hundred thousand soldiers were killed during the Siege of Leningrad. Another million killed, wounded, missing, or captured at Stalingrad along with forty thousand civilians. We remember this because every family in Russia lost someone. You are like spoiled children compared to us. We know death. We accept death. We expect death."

Despite Pavel's earlier bragging, the vodka was taking root. His eyes were becoming glassy.

"You hoped to impress me because you knew about Tchaikovsky's death. Tell me about Vasily Semyonovich Grossman if you are so well educated about my country."

"You win. I have no idea who that is," Garrett replied.

"This is because Americans only study American history. They are ignorant about the rest of the world. Grossman was a journalist for the Red Army newspaper *Krasnaya Zvezda*. He wrote firsthand accounts of the battles of Moscow, Stalingrad, Kursk, and Berlin. He was the first to tell us about the Nazi extermination camp at Treblinka."

Pavel licked his lips. Perspiration was forming on his forehead.

"Did I tell you he was a Jew?" Pavel asked. "This is why Stalin eventually banned his writings and books. This Jew—this Grossman—he saw more human suffering than other men."

Pavel closed his eyes, leaned his head back as if he were reaching into the back of his mind to retrieve information. "Grossman wrote this: 'There are people whose souls have just withered. People who are willing to go along with anything evil—anything so as not to be suspected of disagreeing with whoever is in power.'"

His head fell forward, his eyes open. "This Jew was writing about the Germans. The Nazis. But he could be talking about my people today. Gromyko. Kalugin. Everyone lives in fear of them. My daughter and her husband are dead but they did not have withered souls."

The first bottle was now empty. Pavel opened the second.

"You Americans suffer but it is from infantile stupidity. You think I am a drunkard uttering nonsense, but these cretins—Gromyko and Kalugin—they are your creations. Your Alice in Wonderland view of the world gave them birth."

Pavel stared at the glass before him, as if it had become a crystal ball.

"Tonight's lecture will be about American foreign policy," he loudly declared in his well-lubricated voice. "After our great Soviet Union became ashes, your leaders called for a 'new world order.' The mighty United States and its like-minded Western countries would forever solve all problems with diplomacy instead of brute force."

"You're a diplomat," Garrett said, daring to interrupt. "You must believe in diplomacy."

"I'm a realist. You Americans believe all people are good and decent. You believe if you can only teach your Jeffersonian democracy and your Statue of Liberty ideals, why then, everyone will become like you, embrace your ideals, and the world's problems will end."

His words were being spat out like tiny spears tipped in sarcasm. "What happened to this magnificent new world order of your creation? Your Alice in Wonderland adventure?"

Leaning forward, he wagged a forefinger in Garrett's face. "Your naïve Alice met radical Islamists who want to kill everyone who doesn't accept their beliefs. They don't give a damn about your democratic principles. Your Alice met Hamas and Hezbollah, who have pledged to destroy Israel and kill all Jews. They don't give a damn about your Judeo-Christian morals. Your Alice met North Korea and Iran and politely asked them to stop building nuclear weapons. Ha. Shall I go on? The Taliban in Afghanistan. China with its arms buildup, and most of all, your stupid Alice was seduced and is being played the fool by Mother Russia."

His sarcasm had become contempt. "Your new world order has made the world worse because you have shown weakness, and the scent of weakness is like a bleeding animal to vultures such as Vyachesian Leninovich Kalugin. Do you not understand that a man like him will do whatever is necessary to stay in power? Do you not understand that the billions he has stolen and the oligarchs who have helped him will never peacefully relinquish their power? He and his comrades are men who eat and eat and eat and instead of filling their stomachs, they demand for themselves more and more and more."

With a shaking hand, he poured, splashing most onto the tabletop.

"I will now share with you Kalugin's new world order. Destroy NATO. Cause chaos in Europe. Undercut U.S. democracy. Crimea was his first nibble. This man is conducting hybrid warfare and you don't even understand the term."

"Hybrid warfare?" Garrett said. "You are correct. I don't understand that term."

Pavel paused, collecting his thoughts. "Think of a series of dials for various levels of aggression. He can spin them up and down as needed. You think I'm drunk, but I am telling you a truth." He took a deep breath, focused, and said, in a quick cadence as if he were afraid to speak it slowly and forget it, "Kalugin is creating a multilayered, nonlinear system of strife that is nearly impossible for traditional defense and foreign policy doctrines to analyze and counter." He smiled at himself, clearly delighted that he could utter such a sentence in his inebriated condition.

His eyelids drooped. His voice became a mumble. His grandson slid back from the table and took the old man's left arm, helping him stand.

"My history lesson must end," Pavel declared. "Death is not found behind the mountains but behind our shoulders. Ready to pounce."

Peter led his grandfather to the bed and removed the old man's coat and shoes. He lay down next to him. Within seconds the old man was snoring. Still seated at the table, Garrett noticed the teen wiping his eyes. He was crying. Garrett stepped outside. It was cold. He took one of the stolen pills that he'd kept in his pants pocket.

The next morning, Garrett examined the Lada. The old car would draw less attention than a BMW. Squirrels had nested under its hood, so he removed the debris. Chewed through wires. But the split rubber fuel line to the carburetor was the biggest problem. He was searching for some sort of tape when Pavel and Peter appeared.

"Squirrels ate through the rubber fuel line," he said. "This car's in horrible shape."

"These cars were in horrible shape when brand new," Pavel replied. "Peter, fetch me a knife."

The boy did as told and watched as Pavel reached down and cut the Lada's rubber brake line, removing enough of it to replace the fuel line.

"Problem solved," he declared.

"You just ruined the brakes."

"We need to drive forward. Not stop. Do you not know how to downshift?"

Garrett already had siphoned enough gas from the BMW to see if the engine would turn over. Swapped batteries. The tired old engine coughed, spit, died. A second try. Smoke blew from its exhaust. Incredibly, it was running, but without brakes.

"Here is what we shall do," Pavel announced, clearly feeling empowered. "We wait until nightfall. By then Gromyko will be under intense pressure to end the roadblocks on all major roads. Traffic will be so bottle-necked, he will face a riot if he doesn't. The police will not bother us for bribes, because in this car, it's obvious we have no money to pay them. We drive to Klin and take the train to St. Petersburg to cross into Finland."

Garrett didn't reply. He'd never told Pavel the escape route. Pavel noticed the curious look on the American's face. He said, "Mr. Garrett, are you not following the same escape route as Oleg Gordievsky?"

"How did you know that?"

Pavel laughed. "Everyone knows the story. Every-one will assume, including General Gromyko."

Twenty-Eight

"**I** need to see you!"

Aysan Rivera's voice sounded panicked.

"Are you okay?" Valerie Mayberry asked. "Where are you?"

"Meet me tonight. Eight o'clock. James Joyce Irish Pub near my condo. One of my bodyguards—he's named Eric—will be there."

Rivera ended the call.

Mayberry texted a follow-up. Waited. No reply.

She called Mr. Smith, the go-between between Director Harris and her.

"I need to speak to him. It's important."

"He's in meetings."

"Tell him Aysan resurfaced and wants to meet me. Now."

Ten minutes later, her phone rang.

"I'll send backup," Director Harris said.

"If she sees anyone but me, she'll run."

"No one will see them, including you, unless they need to be seen."

The pub was crowded, and Mayberry was afraid that her contact, Eric, might not be able to find her, so she sat outside at a patio table. It was chilly and the only others near her were two men smoking. She was wearing a leather bomber jacket. It helped conceal her Glock 19. She hadn't planned on eating but suspected it might look strange if she didn't order. A Guinness and homemade Irish brown bread—the pub's specialty. She nursed both and wondered: What did Rivera want? Had she changed her mind about surrendering to the bureau? If so, Mayberry would have to come clean to her FBI bosses about the unsuspecting role that she'd played at the Stonewall Jackson Shrine bombing. Or did Rivera want to meet because she'd decided to reveal the final digits to Makayla's phone number? Either way, Mayberry had no reason to believe her cover had been blown. If she could continue to worm her way deeper into Makayla's Antifa cell, she could discover where the pending Russian attack would happen. All thoughts while waiting.

Eight p.m. Nothing. Eight fifteen still no contact. Eight thirty the bread and beer were consumed. Eight forty-five—a thirty-something white man wearing a cap stepped out from inside the pub, casually lit a cigarette, looked at Mayberry, finished his smoke, and walked to her table.

"I'm Eric," he said. He offered her a navy-blue raincoat and matching cap. They were identical to what he was wearing. "It's not haute couture, but please. A disguise of sorts."

She put the raincoat over her bomber jacket and pulled the cap down tightly on her head, shielding her face.

"Button the jacket, please," he said.

She hesitated, knowing if she buttoned it, she would lose immediate access to her Glock.

"I apologize for making you wait so long out here," he continued. "A security precaution for everyone's safety."

She put him at six foot two, guessed he was about 240 pounds. Blue eyes behind wire glasses. A bit of unshaven scruff. A disarming smile.

"I wasn't followed," she said. She still hadn't buttoned the raincoat.

He raised his right cuff and spoke into a hidden microphone. A couple emerged from the pub. They were wearing raincoats and caps that were identical to the ones he and Mayberry had on. Four identically dressed figures.

"We've buttoned our raincoats," he said.

Mayberry buttoned hers.

They exited the pub's patio as a single unit with the couple moving between them to confuse anyone watching from a distance. When they'd gone about a block, the couple broke away, taking a side street while Eric and Mayberry continued to the nearby National Katyn Memorial Fountain.

The monument, which commemorated the mass executions by the Soviet secret police of some 22,000 Polish intellectuals in 1940, was in the center of a traffic circle. Mayberry stuck next to Eric, neither of them speaking, moving counterclockwise around the monument. Without warning, he stopped, spun around, and walked clockwise, retracing the steps they'd just taken.

She understood. He was checking to see if anyone was trailing them. It was an elementary but effective detection technique. He led her onto Aliceanna Street, one of four avenues that fed into the circle. After walking east for four blocks, he reversed course, returning to the circle. Next he entered Lancaster Street, where they performed the same ritual. Mayberry assumed another one of Aysan's bodyguards was positioned somewhere near the circle at a vantage point that allowed him or her to see if someone was going up and down the same side streets as them, always returning to the circle. It would be a dead giveaway. She began to worry. What if they spotted the CIA surveillance team Harris had sent to shadow her? She casually checked their surroundings. No sign of anyone following them. Harris said they would be ghosts.

They had just entered the fourth side street emanating from the circle when a windowless white van slowed next to them. This was an especially dark avenue. The van's sliding door opened and a man leapt out. He was aiming his handgun at Mayberry. She glanced at Eric. She'd not seen him draw a Ruger LCP subcompact pistol from his raincoat.

"Get in the van," Eric ordered.

Mayberry was outmatched. Two armed men with their guns drawn and no way for her to draw her Glock.

Where was her backup?

From the van's front passenger seat, she heard a familiar voice.

"Get in or we kill you here," Makayla Jones said.

Eric shoved her toward the van.

No one was coming to rescue her. She stepped inside, followed by both men.

"Makayla, why are you doing this to me?" she asked in her most innocent-sounding voice.

The driver turned up the volume on the radio, making it impossible for anyone to hear any conversation, and checked the side mirrors while accelerating.

They exited Baltimore, traveling south on Interstate 95 toward Washington, but after several miles, the driver exited and reversed his route, heading back into the city toward the Port of Baltimore. For an hour, they rode through side streets, doubling back, turning onto alleys, traveling on one-way streets. When they reached a warehouse near its docks, the driver stopped, then Eric opened the side door and stepped outside. Makayla joined him.

"You two stay in the van," she ordered the driver and the other armed man. "In case uninvited guests show up."

With Eric nudging her forward, Mayberry followed Makayla toward the warehouse. She glanced around. Still no backup. Makayla shut the door behind them and said, "Give me your pepper spray."

"I didn't bring it. I thought I was meeting friends."

Eric handed Makayla his Ruger LCP so he could frisk Mayberry. He unbuttoned her raincoat, reached inside, and confiscated her Glock 19.

"This is how you greet your friends?" he grunted. He tucked the pistol into the waistband of his pants and continued frisking her.

"Where is Aysan?" Mayberry asked.

Eric discovered Mayberry's cell phone in her jacket pocket. He handed it to Makayla and reclaimed his Ruger LCP from her, which he pointed at Mayberry.

"That's everything," he announced.

"We should have frisked her in the van." Makayla peeled apart Mayberry's cell phone, plucking the SID card from it. She threw the card away, dropped the phone onto the concrete floor, and stomped it several times with her heel.

Nodding at Mayberry, she said, "Get undressed."

"What? Why?"

"Do it!" Eric snapped.

Mayberry let the raincoat fall onto the floor.

"Is this really necessary?" she protested.

"Want Eric to help you?" Makayla asked.

He smirked.

"Let's all calm down," Mayberry said as she removed her bomber jacket, which she tossed onto the floor. She bent down to untie her shoes and remove her socks. Rising, she unhooked her belt and shimmied, causing her denim jeans to slide down around her feet. Stepping from them, she unbuttoned and removed her blouse.

"Happy now?" she asked sarcastically, wearing only a bra and underwear. "I'm not wearing a wire."

"Turn around," Makayla ordered, carefully inspecting her. Satisfied, she said, "Get your pants and blouse back on. Leave the shoes, socks, and jacket on the floor."

Mayberry did as told.

"Follow me," Makayla ordered. They walked through a maze of bright red cargo containers until they reached a lighted corner of the warehouse.

Aysan Rivera. No glitz, no glamour, no designer clothing. She had been stripped to her underwear and was bound to a heavy wooden chair with gray duct tape wrapped around her wrists and ankles. No makeup, hair tangled, puffed red face from being repeatedly struck. Eyes closed. Badly swollen. Chin leaning down against her chest. Drool from her mouth. Next to her a table. A syringe. Prescription bottles. A tablespoon and cigarette lighter.

Mayberry noticed another item on the table. Rivera's cell phone. She recognized its diamond-encrusted case. Rivera must have been beaten and drugged after she had called Mayberry, luring her into this trap.

"Wake up, Aysan!" Makayla ordered.

No response. Makayla slapped Rivera against her left cheek. Rivera stirred. Another harsh slap. This one caused her to squint. She managed to raise her chin. Her drug-induced fog was lifting.

Makayla addressed Mayberry, who was standing about ten feet away from her. "This little bird has been singing about you."

Eric, who was standing next to Mayberry, turned so that he could watch Makayla and Rivera, but also keep his Ruger LCP leveled at Mayberry's chest.

"She's told us," Makayla continued, "you wanted her to go to the FBI. To snitch me out."

Mayberry said nothing. Consciously not reacting.

Makayla said, "Aysan was trying to run away, leave the country."

She glanced at Rivera. "Such a disappointment." Reaching down, she clasped Rivera's chin between her thumb and forefinger, wagging it back and forth, as if her captive were a puppet. "Did you hear me? Are you listening?"

Rivera appeared to gradually become more aware of her surroundings.

"Antifa is everywhere," Makayla said. "I knew about your plan the moment you bought your airplane ticket online. I knew you intended to fly away."

Makayla released her hold on Rivera's chin, which dropped back onto her chest.

Addressing Mayberry, Makayla said, "Your charade is over, Special Agent Valerie Mayberry."

Mayberry's eyes narrowed. "Someone has been telling you lies."

"So you know nothing about Brett Garrett and the CIA's plans to smuggle Deputy Minister Pavel out of Moscow? You know nothing about IEC and Kim helping him?"

In spite of her stoic appearance, Mayberry was stunned.

Makayla said, "I told you we are everywhere. After I dispose of this little bird, I will enjoy putting you in this chair. Hearing what you can tell me. You will tell me everything I ask. I promise you that."

Makayla reached over to the table near the chair where Aysan was restrained. Percocet. 10/650. Maximum prescribed dose. She crushed several pills and put the powder onto a tablespoon. A touch of water. Bit of vitamin C pack as an acidic solution. Heated by a lighter to a bubble.

The threat of another dose seemed to jar Rivera awake. She began squirming

"No, pleeasse," Rivera pleaded.

Through her swollen eyes, Rivera fully comprehended that Mayberry was there. "You did this to me!" she cried.

"That's right, little bird. She was supposed to be your friend," Makayla said.

Both looked at Mayberry, but she didn't react. Her

thoughts were elsewhere. Where was her promised backup?

"This is the price you pay, little bird," Makayla continued, "for introducing an FBI agent into our cell. You vouched for her based on what—her taste in clothes designers?"

"Don't!" Rivera gasped.

Makayla opened two packets of condoms and tied them together, making an addict's tourniquet on Rivera's upper left arm.

"You'll soon be just another opioid overdose," Makayla said.

"My father will pay. I'll disappear."

Makayla found a vein on Rivera's left forearm. Closest to the wrist was best in case the vein collapsed. You could always move up the arm. Bevel needle hole pointed up. Increased the flow into the view from the syringe. She lowered the injection. Mesmerizing to watch. Too mesmerizing.

Mayberry slipped her right hand from her side to the front of her pants. Makayla and her driver had overlooked a concealed weapon. Their mistake had been allowing Mayberry to unfasten her belt, drop her denim jeans to the warehouse's concrete floor, and step free of them. What neither of her captors had noticed was the stainless-steel woven belt around Mayberry's waist—held together by a pair of matching three-inch-long powerful magnets. The belt was pencil thin, so it wouldn't snag on pant loops.

Mayberry gripped the belt's clasp, separating the magnets.

Now!

She whipped the belt free at the exact moment Makayla inserted the needle into Rivera's arm. Eric was watching Makayla flag the needle—pulling back on the syringe plunger to draw blood into the hotshot, checking to ensure the needle had hit its intended target.

Mayberry snapped the belt's magnet tip like a bullwhip, catching him completely off guard. Its silver tip struck with such force that it broke the metal frame of his glasses at the hinge and drove a piece of the frame into his eye, impaling his iris, instantly blinding his left eye. He yelped and instinctively reached for his face to remove the jagged frame, dropping the Ruger LCP at his feet so he could use both hands.

Makayla heard him cry out and looked at Mayberry just as the undercover agent was diving to the floor, scooping up Eric's discarded Ruger. Now on her back, she fired upward into Eric's torso. The impact of three rounds sent him stumbling backward. A well-placed fourth caused him to collapse.

Mayberry turned. Makayla, who'd been unarmed, was gone.

Rivera groaned. The half-filled syringe was still dangling from her arm.

Mayberry checked Rivera's pulse. Weak. Her lips were beginning to turn blue. Her skin felt cold. Mayberry grabbed Rivera's diamond-encrusted cell phone from the table. Dialed 911.

"I need Narcan! Hurry!"

"What's your address?"

"A warehouse near the docks."

"Who has overdosed?"

Mayberry didn't have time to answer. Most 911 dispatchers can get an approximate location of a cell phone call, but not always.

Makayla and the two men, who had been waiting outside in the van, could return at any moment, only this time Makayla would be armed.

Mayberry glanced left, right. A fire alarm. She pulled it. The electronic drone of the alarm echoed through the warehouse. Emergency lights flashed on. She retrieved her Glock 19 from the waistband of Eric's corpse. Armed now with a pistol in each hand, she hid between cargo containers and waited for an attack. Nothing.

"Aysan," she called. "Nod if you can hear me."

No response.

She emerged and checked Rivera's pulse again. Barely noticeable. She hurriedly wiped her fingerprints from the Ruger LCP, placed it on the table, grabbed Rivera's cell phone, and dashed through the cargo containers to where her jacket, socks, and shoes were lying. Dressing quickly, she inched her way to the doorway. She had to be certain Makayla and the other two were gone before she could go back, untie Rivera, and possibly begin CPR. The warehouse door was open. She looked outside but didn't see the van. She exited the warehouse, searching for the van. She heard sirens. The flashing lights of an approaching ambulance, fire trucks.

No time to go back inside. Instead, she hurried from the warehouse and found a place to disappear in its shadows.

She watched first responders entering the warehouse. No one noticed her. Using Rivera's phone, Mayberry called Mr. Smith.

"This is Special Agent Valerie Mayberry. I need to see him. My cover has been blown and where in the hell was my backup!"

Twenty-Nine

Yakov Prokofyevich Pavel gazed through the Lada's dirty passenger window at the darkening evening sky outside the Klin railway station.

"Mr. Garrett," Pavel said wistfully. "The Russian poet, Fyodor Tyutchev, wrote:

Russia cannot be understood with the mind alone,
No ordinary yardstick can span her greatness:
She stands alone, unique—
In Russia, one can only believe.

It was a pensive moment for the fleeing deputy foreign minister.

"Your beloved Russia is trying to kill you and your grandson," Garrett reminded him.

"Not Russia," Pavel bristled. "Gromyko and Kalugin. You may take me to America, but I will always be a Russian."

They had driven from their dacha hideaway to the Klin railway station without attracting notice. Peter had been sent inside to purchase three tickets to Vyborg via St. Petersburg. Garrett had cut his hair short, military style—a thin disguise. Their plan: purchase the tickets and board a train scheduled to arrive within the next ten minutes.

Garrett's eyes darted back and forth between the station's main entrance and his watch.

"What's taking so long?" he asked. "Do they always demand to see passports?"

"And I should know this, why?" Pavel scoffed. His underlings at the Foreign Ministry had always made his travel arrangements.

A loud whistle. A locomotive pulling into the station. Garrett opened the driver's door. He and Pavel walked in hurried steps toward the tracks. Passengers were exiting the train cars. Others began boarding. No sign of Peter with their tickets.

Garrett scanned for police.

Peter burst from the station door frantically waving their tickets. They entered a railcar just as its *provodnitsa* was shutting its door.

"Next time, you will be left," the stout, older woman attendant scolded. They followed her down a narrow corridor as the train slowly pulled from the station. She stopped at a four berth *kupe*—a cramped compartment with two bunk beds facing one another. A middle-aged man inside looked up from the *Moskovskiy Komsomolets* newspaper.

Pavel stopped at the berth's doorway. Garrett braced himself for a scene. He suspected Pavel was about to complain about the dingy quarters. He was accustomed to high-speed Sapsan trains that raced between St. Petersburg and Moscow at speeds of 150 mph. *Grand Express* railcars, lavishly decorated, each with its own television, private toilet, and shower. This was a *passazhirsky* train, which smelled of human sweat and urine. The blue padding on the berth's bench seats, which doubled as mattresses, was worn flat. The floor badly stained. A lone bright yellow crocus in a cheap glass vase placed on a steel table under the window was the berth's only nicety.

"My grandson—he is being treated for tuberculosis," Pavel said quietly to the woman. "Although a doctor has cleared him for travel, one never knows how contagious he still might be."

As he spoke, Pavel slipped a five-hundred-ruble note, roughly ten U.S. dollars, into the woman's pudgy hand.

Peter coughed convincingly.

The *provodnitsa* gave Pavel a cold look. Another five-hundred-ruble note changed hands. She entered the berth and ordered the lone rider to gather his belongings. He protested, but when she threatened to eject him from her railcar, he threw the newspaper onto the floor and angrily grabbed his bag to follow her to a different berth. As he slipped by Pavel, he cursed him.

"A clever lie and a bribe," Garrett said approvingly when they were alone.

Pavel sat on the bunk opposite him facing the rear of the train. Peter would sleep in the top bunk above, but plopped down next to Garrett to get settled.

"Isn't it the same in every country—a threat or a bribe?" Pavel asked. Without waiting for a reply, he said, "Peter, what happened in the station?"

Reaching into his jacket, the teen produced the three CIA doctored passports and returned them to Garrett. He spread his hands apart and rapidly opened and closed his fingers.

"He's saying there was a long line, many ticket buyers," Pavel interpreted.

"Ask him if he had to show the passports?" Garrett said.

"You ask him. His hearing is not impaired."

From his jacket pocket, Peter removed a slip of paper that Pavel had given him. The words: *Three tickets. Vyborg. I don't speak* were written on the sheet. Someone had scribbled in pencil. *Show me your passports.*

"They wrote because they assumed he couldn't hear," Pavel said. "Just like you." Pavel laughed. Peter grinned.

"Did you show them?" Garrett asked again, impatiently.

The teen glanced at his grandfather and flashed a mischievous grin.

"I've taught my grandson how to get things done," Pavel said. "Without complications."

Peter took a wad of thousand-ruble notes from his pocket and handed them to his grandfather, who counted them. "I gave him ten thousand, and there are only eight remaining. This means he had to pay two thousand to purchase our tickets—without producing passports."

"Why doesn't he talk?" Garrett asked.

"He must not have anything he wants to say," Pavel said dismissively.

Garrett picked up the discarded newspaper from the floor. Photos of Pavel and Peter were printed above the front-page fold. *Kidnapped after touring the Metro*

Museum in Moscow. Call local police or the FSB if seen. A knock. Garrett flipped over the newspaper, hiding its pictures. The *provodnitsa* entered with a tray. A bottle of vodka, two beers. Soda for the teen. Some cut fruit. Crackers. Glasses.

"Come, drink with us," Pavel told her, turning on the charm. "There is nothing better than Russia vodka and a good Russian woman to pass the time on a train ride!"

"I have nine compartments on my car and I'm past the age when I wished to party with passengers." Still, she returned his flirtatious glance.

"Such a pity," he said.

Pavel noticed the beer. "Ah, excellent, beer without vodka is throwing away your money. It is a common Russian saying. And to drink without a woman at your side is truly tragic. But my comrades and I will somehow manage." He handed the woman another five-hundred-ruble note.

"You need to look at the newspaper," Garrett said, as soon as she left them.

"What will I learn that I already don't know? Nothing. Today's news is written with a pitchfork on flowing water."

The teen eagerly ate the snacks and downed his soda. Pavel focused on the beer and vodka.

Two hours later, the attendant returned, this time with three plastic sealed packages. Each contained two sheets, a pillowcase, and one towel. She retrieved the food tray, leaving the unfinished vodka on the table, and extended her hand for payment. Pavel glanced at Garrett, implying it was his turn to pay. Garrett handed her a one-hundred-ruble note. Even though it was more than what the average passenger was charged for bedding, she continued to hold out her hand. Pavel chuckled and fetched another five-hundred note from his pocket. Again she smiled at the old man.

Garrett flipped shut a loosely attached interior latch on the door after she was gone. It was supposed to keep the berth secure, but every enterprising thief would know how to slip a coat hanger between the jam and lift it. He took the vodka bottle and placed it against the door so it would be knocked over if opened, sounding an alarm.

Peter obediently made his grandfather's bed and helped him remove his shirt, shoes, and pants. Within minutes the intoxicated diplomat was snoring loudly. Peter climbed onto the upper bunk above him. Garrett took a blue pill from his gym bag and swallowed it. Ginger Capello had assured him lorcaserin would lessen his cravings, delay withdrawal, but his head was throbbing, and he was wide awake. Jittery.

From his bag, he removed a map of Russia. He noticed his right hand was shaking.

MI-6 had smuggled Oleg Gordievsky into Finland near Vyborg. It was where Garrett assumed the agency would expect him to cross with Pavel and Peter. It was likely that General Gromyko would have extra men waiting there as a precaution. The train ride was seventy-six miles from St. Petersburg to Vyborg, a fishing village. Escaping by boat would be less risky than overland travel, he decided. Once safely in Finland, he could contact Thomas Jefferson Kim.

Garrett traced his forefinger across Vyborg Bay, estimating the shortest course. He suddenly realized Peter was watching him. The teen hopped down from the top berth and shook awake his sleeping grandfather.

"What! What!" the old man grumbled. The teen shook him harder and motioned toward the map. He pointed at the bay.

"My grandson is trying to warn you," Pavel muttered, "that the islands and shores of Vyborg Bay are strictly guarded by border control. Heavily patrolled. Anyone entering a three-mile zone will be captured."

The teen slid his finger down the map from Vyborg Bay along the train route toward St. Petersburg, stopping midway at Roshchino Leningrad Oblast. A much smaller village. From there he moved his hand to the Gulf of Finland.

"I get it," Garrett said. "We'll get off the train at Roshchino, not Vyborg."

Satisfied, Peter returned to the top berth. Garrett turned off the light, removed his SIG Sauer. Tucked it next to him under a top sheet and listened to Pavel snoring again.

The berth had no curtains on its window. Garrett rested the back of his head on his raised hands as a pillow, slightly propping up his head. He was watching the berth's door. Lights and shadows from outside the car danced across it. Only the stars and moon penetrated the darkness when the railcar moved through rural areas, but when the train slowed, the lights from whatever village they'd entered would illuminate the entire berth. He listened to the sounds of passengers boarding and leaving the train. He became familiar with the *provodnitsa*'s lumbering footsteps as she passed their berth trudging along the corridor. There was only one toilet at the end of the car, three berths away, and either those using it didn't shut its door tightly, or its latch was broken. Garrett could hear the door banging against the side of the train until either the attendant or the next occupant secured it.

He thought about Russians and Americans and official lies and broken promises. He thought about betrayal and obstacles they still faced. Had Heidi Duncan noticed the missing weight-loss pills that he'd stolen from her embassy desk? Had General Gromyko recognized Capello when she'd exploded the Zil delivery truck they'd used to escape? There hadn't been any mention of him or possible U.S. involvement in the newspaper's account.

Unable to sleep, he took another blue pill to calm his nerves and closed his eyes. Twilight sleep. In German: *Dammerschlaf.* Partial narcosis. Awake enough to be conscious but not fully awake. Was it the pill? Was he high or was it caution that was keeping him half-awake?

There. He saw it. Or was it a dream? A trick of light and shadows. The interior latch rising. The door beginning to open. The quick sound of the vodka bottle being knocked across the berth's floor.

By the time Garrett realized what was happening it was too late. Hooded men were already inside. One pushed his knee against Garrett's chest making it difficult for him to breath, pinning him helpless on the lower bunk. He felt hands grabbing his limbs. One man per arm, one per leg. Within seconds, they'd tossed him on the floor, his hands cuffed, legs secured with a plastic cord. Stripped the SIG Sauer from him.

He locked his teeth when one of the attackers tried to stuff an object into his mouth. A hard slap against his head. Mouth forced open. Pavel was blissfully snoring during the attack. Peter was also asleep. Dragged out into the corridor, Garrett found himself looking up at a pleased General Gromyko. Behind him, the *provodnitsa*. Her body had been placed in a sitting position on the floor, her back against the railcar's side, her neck broken. Lifeless eyes staring forward. Standing nearby was the passenger who'd been in the berth when they'd arrived. The front-page newspaper photographs. Him stopping to stare into Pavel's face and curse him when he was ejected. It all made sense.

With the toe of his polished boot, Gromyko kicked Garrett along the side of his skull.

PART IV

The Devil's Breath

Those who serve us with poison will
eventually swallow it and poison themselves.
—VLADIMIR VLADIMIROVICH PUTIN

Thirty

Two Years Ago

Senator Cormac Stone was one of the most liberal members of the U.S. Congress and, even before his son's death in Cameroon, he'd despised the CIA. The senior senator from California claimed it had done more harm than good and he could easily cite its failures.

The Bay of Pigs—a flubbed agency plot to overthrow Fidel Castro. The Cuban Missile Crisis—the agency had declared a month before that the Soviets would never attempt to put a nuclear weapon on the island. The Iranian Revolution—the agency had reported six months before it that the Shah's reign was secure. The collapse of the USSR—it had never seen it coming.

The impetus for creating the CIA in 1947 had been the Japanese bombing at Pearl Harbor. Yet the agency had not stopped the September 11, 2001, terrorist attacks, even though it knew that two of the hijackers were members of al-Qaeda and held valid U.S. visas.

More recently, there was the "weapons of mass destruction" fiasco and finally the CIA-informed Obama administration's insistence that the Arab Spring would undercut al-Qaeda when, in fact, it had led to the rise of the Islamic State and upheaval in Egypt and Libya.

Now Senator Stone's only son, Petty Officer 3rd Class Richard Stone, aka "Senator" to his fellow SEALs, had been killed in action during his first CIA-directed operation.

Senator Stone wanted vengeance, and as the ranking minority member of the U.S. Senate Select Committee on Intelligence, he had enough clout to demand a public hearing.

CIA director Harold Harris was his first witness inside the Hart Senate Office Building. In his written statement, he quickly outlined the nonclassified basics. Mission's purpose: rescue kidnapped NGO worker Elsa Eriksson. Location: terrorists' camp in Cameroon. Overall success: Eriksson freed, an estimated twenty terrorists killed. Casualties: four Navy SEALs injured. Fatalities: three Nigerian locals, two Navy pilots, and

Petty Officer 3rd Class Richard Stone. Cause of deaths: RPG striking rescue helicopter. Survivors of that attack: only one, Chief Petty Officer Brett Garrett.

"You sent these SEALs in for one reason and one reason only, to rescue Ms. Elsa Eriksson, is that correct?" Senator Stone asked Harris.

"Yes, that is correct, Senator."

"But the objective of that mission changed, did it not?"

"No, Senator, the primary objective was always the same—to rescue Ms. Eriksson. However, upon entering the Boko Haram camp, the SEAL team discovered a second hostage."

"Hold on," Senator Stone said. "Did this second hostage—was she a U.S. citizen?"

"No, sir, she was a Nigerian aid worker."

"What specific order did you give Chief Garrett when he informed you of this second hostage?"

Harris looked directly at the panel of eight senators from the majority party and seven from the minority who were seated behind an elevated platform much like courtroom judges. He moved from one face to another, seeking sympathy, trying to convey with his eyes that he bore no culpability for what had happened.

"I specifically told Chief Garrett not to put his men in harm's way by attempting to rescue that second local worker," Harris answered.

It was a lie, but Harris said it with confidence that only he and Garrett knew the truth about their communications that night.

Without prompting, Harris elaborated. "This rescue mission depended on complete surprise. A quick entrance and extraction. The agency had done its due diligence, and while I felt tremendous sympathy for this second hostage, I understood that any attempt to rescue her would threaten our objective and certainly put American lives in grave danger."

"Director Harris," Senator Stone asked, reading from questions prepared by his staff, "did Chief Brett Garrett obey your direct order to exit the camp immediately with Ms. Eriksson and leave the second hostage behind?"

"No, Senator, he did not."

"Did he, in fact, separate his men into two teams, sending a seven-man team back with Ms. Eriksson to a waiting rescue helicopter?"

"Yes, Senator, he separated his men into two different ones."

"How many Boko Haram fighters were in this camp?"

"As many as twenty, Senator."

"And how many SEALs remained there after Chief Garrett divided his men?"

"Only seven."

"Director Harris, were you aware that Chief Garrett was disobeying your direct order?"

"No, sir. Chief Garrett had switched off his headset, temporarily ending all communication with me."

"Why would someone under your command turn off his headset?"

"I believe it was because Chief Garrett had decided to ignore my direct order, which he did. He had decided before asking me to rescue the Nigerian worker."

"When did you next hear from Chief Garrett?"

"When he informed me his team required a third rescue helicopter because he had discovered—while rescuing the second hostage—that there were more Nigerian locals being held hostage in the camp."

"These were not U.S. citizens—is that correct?"

"Yes, they were Nigerian locals. I reiterated that we only had two rescue helicopters waiting at the rendezvous site and there was not sufficient room for an additional ten non-U.S. personnel. I told Chief Garrett that he should not have separated his men into two groups. He should have left the camp with his complete team immediately after he had freed Ms. Eriksson."

More lies. A twisting of the knife that Harris already had inserted into Garrett's back.

Harris continued: "I again ordered him to leave the camp immediately—without the additional hostages—because we simply were not prepared to assist non-U.S. personnel and doing so would put his men in even graver danger."

Harris paused and sadly shook his head. "Senator, if I may, a personal note. All of us involved in this operation would have preferred saving as many hostages as possible from these terrorists, but that was not Brett Garrett's decision to make. It was mine, and sometimes being in charge demands making difficult choices—as you know, Senator. I could not legitimately put the lives of American soldiers at risk at that moment and jeopardize the success of our mission. I was perfectly willing to send men back to that camp to rescue the hostages, but only after we had developed a feasible and workable plan. Not a half-cocked, emotionally driven one."

"Did Chief Garrett obey these orders from you?" Senator Stone said, continuing with his scripted questions.

"He did not. He took it upon himself to escort additional non-U.S. personnel from the camp, knowing there was no room for them at the rendezvous site."

"Did the SEALs whom he dispatched to escort Ms. Eriksson to the rendezvous site—did that first team *safely complete its mission without engaging any enemy combatants?"*

"Yes, Senator, they were able to extract Ms. Eriksson without incident."

"Would it be safe to assume, Director Harris, that if Chief Garrett had not divided his team and had he escorted Ms. Eriksson to the two waiting helicopters— this mission would have been a success and no Americans would have been wounded or killed?"

Harris didn't hesitate.

"Yes, Senator, I believe that is a correct assumption."

"Director Harris," Senator Stone said, glancing up from his list of questions, "it's clear to me, and I'm sure to my fellow committee members, that you are attempting to shift all blame and responsibility for what happened in Cameroon onto Chief Garrett, but what does this incident say about your ability to lead the CIA? You were in charge, not Chief Garrett."

"Nothing," Harris replied in a calm voice. "The agency is not to blame, and neither am I. Mr. Garrett bears complete responsibility."

"Why am I not surprised by your answer?" Senator Stone said sarcastically. "Are you telling this committee that you are not responsible for the actions of the people under your command? What sort of leader makes such a statement?"

"An honest one," Harris replied defiantly. "My mistake was trusting Chief Garrett, but in my business, you have to trust others to accomplish your goals. Fault me for that, Senator, but don't fault me for the death of your son. His death lies on Chief Garrett's shoulders."

"No, Director, it is on both of yours. You chose Chief Garrett—a man who didn't respect you—to run this mission. Earning your people's respect is part of leadership and, based on what has happened, leadership is severely lacking at your agency. My son's blood is on your hands, too."

Harris took his licks, but he was confident that he'd put enough blame on Garrett to satisfy the White House and keep his job as director secure.

Witnesses often sat inside the committee room listening to testimony and waiting for their turn, but Brett Garrett was under military guard awaiting a court-martial. The hearing was being broadcast live on national television. He watched Harris testify from an adjoining room and he felt both betrayed and frustrated.

Director Harris had classified key details about the mission, hiding information from Congress. There had been no disclosure that the Nigerian locals were children or that Abidemi was being raped when Garrett decided to save her. Harris only told Senator Stone, the committee, and the media what he wanted them to hear.

Still recovering and being heavily medicated for burns, Garrett was escorted into the Senate chamber by guards and two military-assigned defense counsels, who'd been appointed to represent him at his upcoming court-martial. His hands were cuffed.

"Chief Brett Garrett," Senator Stone began, "I have been told that upon advice of your legal counsel, you will choose to cite the Fifth Amendment and not answer a single question posed by this investigative committee. Is that correct, sir?"

Garrett nodded.

"I asked you a direct question, and this committee requires a verbal reply from you, even if you are, in my opinion, taking a coward's way out of acknowledging your role and responsibility in the wounding of your men and the death of my son."

Senator Stone spat his words. Filled with hatred. He glared at Garrett.

One of the defense lawyers whispered into Garrett's ear. Except for cameras clicking, the room was silent. Garrett leaned forward and spoke into the microphone. "I have been advised by my attorneys to cite my Fifth Amendment right."

Stone shouted: "To not incriminate yourself."

Garrett had wanted to testify. He'd wanted to expose Harris as a liar. After all, the director had given him permission that night to rescue Abidemi. Garrett had wanted to tell the American public that his fellow SEALs, except for Senator, had agreed that they should save the other children. But before the hearing, his attorneys had come to him with a deal—a deal that had been engineered behind the scenes by Harris. If Garrett agreed to plead the Fifth at the hearing, a military tribunal would go easy on him. He'd only do eighteen months at the U.S. Disciplinary Barracks in Fort Leavenworth, Kansas. If he rejected their offer, he would be sentenced to a minimum of fifteen years, probably longer, possibly his entire life.

Garrett sat mum for the next ten minutes while Senator Stone pelted him with questions that he refused to answer, all crafted to verbally castrate him. Even after that dressing-down, Stone wanted more. His staff rolled a large television into the hearing room. The lights dimmed and Richard Stone appeared as an infant. Home movies chronicling his life. A toddler jumping in and out of a plastic baby pool. A ten-year-old performing in an elementary school concert. Trombone. Richard Stone driving his first car. Now posing with his proud parents in a naval uniform. The images on the screen turned ugly. Photos of Bear's wounded

*face taken in a Nigerian first-aid tent. Curly's blood-
ied arm. Big Mac's bleeding thigh. The burned corpses
of helicopter pilots being loaded for transport, and the
finale—a television news clip showing Petty Officer 3rd
Class Richard Stone's funeral procession at Arlington
National Cemetery with his mother and Senator Stone
in mourning. Stone's aged and wrinkled face wet with
tears as a folded American flag was passed to them.*

*There had never been as emotional a hearing as this
one before the committee. Several in attendance were
sobbing. When the lights came on, Senator Stone's
voice cracked with emotion. "Get this witness out of
our sight."*

*By law, courts-martial are public—if the public is
told where they are held and permitted to enter military property. A month later, Garrett's court-martial
was conducted aboard a Nimitz-class U.S. aircraft
carrier on maneuvers near the Indian Ocean. No reporters attended. Eighteen months after that, Garrett
was dishonorably discharged and released.*

Thirty-One

Current Day

Title: **Fallen Angel**
Originator Classification: SECRET NOFORM
Levy date: 12-12
Discipline: HUMINT

Subject Heidi Duncan, wife of Ambassador Edward Todd Duncan, observed entering Sovietsky Hotel at 1400 hours unescorted. Russian national, Ivan Sokolov, observed at 1415 hours entering Sovietsky Hotel. Subject Heidi Duncan was known to possess a personal Samsung Galaxy model cell phone. Registration number 375867. At 1430 hours, authorization was given by COS Moscow to utilize OVERHEARD protocol on subject Duncan's Galaxy phone enabling recording of sounds being heard through aforementioned Samsung Galaxy device. Intercept included muffled conversations (unintelligible) and noises commensurate with sexual activity. Moaning. Pleasurable groans. Subject Duncan observed leaving Sovietsky Hotel at 1623 hours, followed at 1641 hours by aforementioned Sokolov.

C lassified CIA cables describing what appeared to be a sexual affair between Heidi Duncan and the playboy son of a Russian oligarch went viral within minutes after being posted on Maxi-Leaks, a Europe-based website. The three hundred messages were communications between Moscow COS Marcus Austin, his CIA underlings responsible for surveilling Heidi Duncan, and Langley headquarters.

In several, Austin speculated that the ambassador's wife had been successfully recruited as what Russian intelligence called a "SPECIAL UNOFFICIAL CONTACT"—a top-level source with high social or political status who may or may not recognize he or she is being milked for information.

The most salacious cables were riddled with inappropriate sexual comments written by male CIA officers describing acts they would willingly perform on Heidi Duncan. These smutty locker room jokes, mostly questioning Ambassador Duncan's ability to satisfy his much younger wife, logged the most hits.

The ambassador and Heidi were finishing breakfast in the President Wilson Hotel's Royal Penthouse suite in Geneva, Switzerland, when an aide informed them about the Maxi-Leaks disclosures. It was the final day of the high-profile three-day European economic summit that Duncan was attending.

Duncan immediately shooed away his staff and began reading.

"They followed me like I was a criminal!" Heidi whined as she also scanned the leaked cables.

"They have recordings of you with him," Duncan stammered. "My god Heidi. 'Moaning.' 'Pleasurable groans.'"

"I met Ivan for lunch several times, but we never had sex. This is a smear campaign. It's all lies. You know the CIA has never liked you."

Edward Todd Duncan studied his wife's flushed face. Listened to the frightened tone in her voice. When the president had nominated him, the opposition party had viciously attacked his character during a four-day Senate confirmation hearing. Fired ex-employees had been traipsed before cameras. His wife's lavish spending and younger age had prompted tabloid fodder. A Marie Antoinette gold digger. The State Department's careerists had collaborated with Senate staffers to draft complicated questions about international affairs to trip him up. He'd been a Washington outsider, and Washington had dug deep into his past, finding every dirty tidbit about him—and her. After a second day of being in the national media spotlight's harsh glare, Heidi had urged him to withdraw. They could retreat in comfort to the Hamptons. They didn't need such harsh public scrutiny. He'd refused because he'd wanted to serve his country, to give back something for all that America had given him, and a two-vote margin had been enough for confirmation. After that, he'd thought the sniping would end.

As he listened to Heidi, his visceral reaction was not because of her suspected infidelity. After all, he'd dragged her unwillingly to Moscow, where she'd quickly become bored. It was anger at the CIA. How dare its officers spend months dogging his wife behind his back! How dare lesser men litter their cables with cruel sexual puns at his expense! Even more outrageous, someone inside the agency had chosen to release those cables!

Duncan had a strong prenuptial agreement and could have easily cast Heidi aside. But he loved her—even if she had betrayed him.

"I'm calling the president," he announced.

It was a few minutes after 9:00 a.m. in Geneva, which meant it was 3:00 a.m. in Washington, D.C. The president's chief of staff resisted waking his boss. He suggested the ambassador go through proper channels. Call the secretary of state. Duncan refused. After a fifteen-minute hold, a sleepy President Fitzgerald came on a secure line.

"Heidi is terribly hurt and I'm spitting mad," Duncan began.

"Todd," which is how the president addressed Duncan, "let's have Geoffrey Baker—you know him, he heads up White House communications—look into this and formulate a plan with you and State."

"Plan? Here's a plan. Director Harris apologizes to Heidi and me, takes full responsibility for his agency leaks, and announces the cables either were fabricated or edited by whoever gave them to Maxi-Leaks. Then he resigns. I want Marcus Austin and every one of those sons of bitches in Moscow who wrote about my wife fired, too."

"Todd, remind me, who is Marcus Austin?"

"The agency's chief of station in Moscow."

"Does he have some personal animus toward you?"

"They all do. I'm a political appointee. An outsider."

"I've not read these cables. Did Heidi meet with this Russian?"

"Harris and Austin warned me months ago that Sokolov was trying to recruit Heidi. I told them it was utter nonsense. I've never told her anything classified, and she's never asked. They met for a few innocent lunches. That's all."

"Todd, Heidi should not have been meeting with this fellow without an escort from the embassy accompanying her. That's just common sense." The president sounded testy.

Their conversation was not sounding the way Duncan had imagined. Continuing, the president said, "If Director Harris or this Austin fellow overstepped their authority, I'll deal with them. For now, wait for Geoffrey to call. I'm going back to bed."

"Waiting isn't a viable option," Duncan protested. "You owe me this. I raised a lot of money for you, and I want them fired."

Silence. President Fitzgerald had ended their call.

A visibly upset Duncan returned to the penthouse suite's living room, where Heidi was pacing.

"What'd he'd say?" she asked nervously. "How's he going to fix this?"

Ambassador Duncan poured himself a scotch from the well-stocked bar and plopped down in a chair. "The president blames you."

She burst into tears and darted into the bedroom, slamming its door.

Duncan sipped his scotch slowly, waited, and stewed. Another scotch before the White House communications director called. His advice was straightforward. Under no circumstances make any comment. Return to Moscow. Keep a low profile until media interest dies down. Most important of all, Heidi Duncan was to end all social contact with Ivan Sokolov.

Heidi reemerged from the bedroom to ask about the call.

"We're to act as if none of this is happening," Duncan said. "You are never, ever to see Sokolov again. Is that clear?"

"What about Austin and Harris and those terrible comments about me, about us?" she asked in a timid voice.

"I've been told to ignore everything."

"That's it? You're not allowed to defend my reputation?"

He scowled at her.

An aide knocked and handed him a paper.

"What's happening?" Heidi asked. "What's it say?"

Her husband read it aloud. "The Associated Press. Moscow dateline. Ivan Sokolov told reporters outside his apartment in Moscow today that any implication that he and his family were involved in a Russian intelligence-gathering operation to recruit Heidi Duncan as an American spy was a complete fabrication. 'Cables posted by Maxi-Leaks are a CIA provocation,' Sokolov said, 'intended to embarrass Russian president Vyachesian Kalugin.' Sokolov acknowledged that he and Mrs. Duncan had had an 'intimate relationship' but said they never discussed matters of national importance to the United States or Russia."

"He's exaggerating. Flattering himself," Heidi said. "I'm not an idiot. I wouldn't cheat on you."

"You *are* an idiot," Duncan said angrily, rising from his seat. "You met him alone in a hotel."

She hurried to where he was standing, threw her arms around his waist, laid her wet cheek against his chest, and quietly sobbed. He did not return her hug.

Another knock on the suite door.

"What the hell is it!" Duncan said.

His top aide entered. Whispered to Duncan. After he had gone, Duncan said, "Heidi, clean yourself up. We're leaving. I've been told to resign. We've been told to stay in seclusion until this blows over."

"Where will we go?"

"I'm going to our home in Grand Cayman."

Her hands were trembling. She was hoping for comfort, support. Instead he walked toward the study. "You can come too if you haven't made other plans. I've got a call to make. I'm not letting those bastards in Langley and Moscow get away with this."

Ambassador Duncan's call to California senator Cormac Stone was unexpected. Stone had been one of Duncan's harshest critics at his confirmation hearing.

"Senator," Duncan said, getting right to the point, "Director Harris and his chief of station in Moscow have humiliated my wife and me."

"I've been told about the cables," Stone replied with no detectible sympathy.

"Tip O'Neill said, 'All politics is local,'" Duncan said. "My brief sojourn has taught me that all politics is *personal*. Director Harris is hiding information from your Senate committee."

"Mr. Ambassador," Senator Stone replied, "you're making a serious allegation."

"Harris is running a covert operation in Moscow outside regular channels—intentionally to keep you from knowing about it."

"Why? What sort of operation?"

"He's using Brett Garrett."

The line went quiet, and for several moments Duncan thought they'd been disconnected.

Finally, Stone said, "I'm listening."

Thirty-Two

CIA director Harold Harris reviewed a staff-prepared summary of the Maxi-Leaks cables while being driven to Capitol Hill. He'd been summoned by the chairman of the Senate Select Committee on Intelligence. Harris viewed most members of Congress with contempt. They were meddlers. Outsiders. He'd spent his entire career in the intelligence world. The politicians peering over his shoulders had never recruited an asset, never ran a covert operation, never stolen secrets from a rival nation or lost an operative in the field. Even worse, politicians were notorious leakers—when it served their purpose.

As he rode east on Constitution Avenue, Harris looked at the looming United States Capitol Building on the eastern end of the National Mall. Neoclassical architecture inspired by ancient Greece and Rome to evoke the ideals that guided the nation's founders. Its final design chosen by President George Washington himself. Built, burnt, rebuilt, extended, and restored. Nearly six hundred rooms now on five levels. North-side: the U.S. Senate chamber. South side: the House of Representatives. Joined together by a rotunda topped by nearly nine million pounds of a cast-iron dome. The bronze statue of Freedom, often mistaken by tourists as a Native American statue, poised on the Capitol's peak.

Director Harris had been awestruck when he'd walked through the building as a teenager, brought by his parents on a family vacation. Majesty. The best and the brightest. Living gods. No longer. He knew its occupants too well.

He was not being summoned before the full Senate committee today at the Hart Senate Office Building, where he had testified two years earlier about the bungled Cameroon operation and Brett Garrett. This time Harris was reporting in a much more intimate setting. He exited his car and went through a private entrance into the Capitol Visitor Center, an underground labyrinth below the East Capitol grounds. Nearly 700,000 square feet on three basement levels tucked beneath well-tended grass and shady old trees. He doubted if any of the three million visitors who annually toured it were aware it contained the intelligence committee's SCIF tucked deep within its bowels. Pronounced "skiff," the acronym stood for Sensitive Compartmented Information Facility—a secure vault whose thick walls were lined with acoustic attenuation technology to prevent audio penetration. It was protected around the clock by U. S. Capitol Police and routinely swept for listening devices.

By law, Congress was entitled to know the country's most carefully held secrets. Simply by getting elected, any member could request intelligence reports. What was distributed to them, however, was deliberately parceled out and Harris had become adept at keeping information hidden.

Harris had been warned that the only attendees today would be the committee's chairman, the Senate majority and minority leaders, and the committee's vice chair—Senator Cormac Stone—the same senator who had chastised him about his handling of the Cameroon rescue, the man who detested the CIA, the one whose son had been killed.

Together these four senators ruled their chamber and Director Harris expected all of them to be outraged by the Maxi-Leaks disclosures.

To the average voter, a senator was a senator, a House member, a House member. In the halls of Congress, few were equal. The bottom-feeders were House freshmen. Two-year terms blew by quickly. Some were voted out of office without ever learning the deliberative body's unspoken rules. Every member of Congress could introduce a bill. Brag about that legislation to the hometown media. But legislation went nowhere unless the leadership in both chambers willed it. The Senate and House majority and minority leaders, along with their whips, controlled the ship. They kept their power by politicking. Rewards. Punishment. Nothing moved without a favor, a promise, a handshake. To survive, you had to play by the rules, be part of the team. On the campaign trail, every wannabe railed against the Washington establishment. Once under the Capitol dome, those who didn't join its chorus perished. *Mr. Smith Goes to Washington?* A Hollywood fantasy. Everyone collected favors. Everyone bartered. Everyone took a knee.

Of the four senators waiting for Harris, none had played the game better than California's Senator Stone. He'd walked the halls for forty years, ranking him ninth historically in Senate longevity. An untouchable. A left-wing liberal from a previous generation who'd happily discovered a new wave of young voters to support his "progressive" agenda—that was the new buzzword. *Progressive!*

California had sent Ronald Reagan to Washington in the 1980s. The conservatives' ultimate superhero. That was then. Today nearly 45 percent of California voters were registered Democrats, compared to only 25 percent Republicans. Of the remaining independents, a majority voted for "progressive" candidates. More important, California voters had money. Silicon Valley and Hollywood. More billionaires than any other state.

Senator Stone had amassed a war chest richer than any potential challenger by preaching that socialism wasn't a dirty word. It was the perfection of a benevolent federal government.

The disdain that Director Harris felt toward Congress was mirrored by the contempt that Senator Stone felt for him and the entire intelligence community. In Stone's view, the government had created a bloated, unwieldy, monstrous, top-secret underworld after the 9/11 attacks. Some 1,271 different government organizations and 1,931 private companies collected data at more than ten thousand locations under contracts with U.S. intelligence agencies. Senator Stone had been horrified by President George W. Bush's infamous Patriot Act. Unidentified roving wiretaps. Lone-wolf warrants for electronic surveillance. Big Brother had taken control. Senator Stone viewed himself as the final guardian at the gate, fighting to keep the beast from entering.

Harris left his cell phones outside the spy-proof chamber. Entered and found the senators waiting. He was told to sit at the witness table facing the four Lords of the Senate. They peered down at him from cushioned chairs arranged much like a small amphitheater.

The committee's chair asked the first round of questions. Were the CIA cables leaked on Maxi-Leaks authentic? Yes, they were. Did the director know who had leaked them? No, but a diligent investigation was under way and COS Marcus Austin had been recalled to Langley for disciplinary action. Why had the CIA not informed Congress about Heidi Duncan's liaisons with the son of a Russian oligarch? The agency lacked sufficient evidence of any wrongdoing. It operated on evidence, not gossip.

And so it went for twenty minutes.

Harris felt satisfied by his responses when the chairman finished interrogating him.

Now it was Senator Stone's turn. He held up a newspaper. Harris had assumed it was going to be the *New York Times* or *Washington Post*. It was not.

Moskovskiy Komsomolets.

Large photos of Russian deputy foreign minister Yakov Prokofyevich Pavel and his grandson Peter. Kidnapped. A shoot-out on Moscow's streets.

"Is this your handiwork?" Stone asked.

Harris had prepared for questions about Maxi-Leaks. Not this. He quickly deduced that Ambassador Edward Todd Duncan had tipped off Stone. He had to assume that Duncan had regurgitated everything that he'd known about Pavel before leaving for the Geneva summit.

"I am aware of the newspaper article," Harris said nonchalantly.

"I didn't ask if you were aware of the article. I asked if you are responsible for the events it describes."

Harris was venturing into dangerous territory. By law, President Randle Fitzgerald and his cabinet were required to "fully and currently" inform both the Senate and the House intelligence committees about every covert action. No exceptions. Even if a president felt it was necessary to limit the most sensitive information, he still was required to notify the top congressional leadership. Smuggling Pavel out of Russia was undoubtedly a covert operation that the president should have informed Congress about, but Harris knew Fitzgerald hadn't. Harris knew because he hadn't kept the president informed after their initial discussion and viewing of Pavel's video offer to defect. Instead, he'd chosen to go off the grid. His actions made both Fitzgerald and, more important, him guilty of breaking the law—but only if caught.

Although Harris was not under oath, whatever he said would come back to haunt him. He girded himself.

"I am not responsible for the events described in that newspaper article," Harris said.

"I know you weren't personally in Moscow. I'm asking if your agency was involved in this car chase carnage?"

The lawyer in Harris sought loopholes, and he immediately recognized one. Brett Garrett was not a CIA employee.

"Senator, no one from the CIA was responsible for the car chase described in that article."

Senator Stone had questioned hundreds of federal bureaucrats during congressional hearings, and he recognized when a witness was playing verbal dodgeball.

"Let's cut to the quick, shall we?" Senator Stone said. "Is a covert CIA operation currently under way to extricate Deputy Russian Foreign Minister Yakov Pavel from Russia?"

"As the senator already knows, the agency is always open to recruiting high-level sources who we believe can help us."

"That's not what I asked. I asked if a covert operation is currently under way to smuggle Pavel out of

Russia—an operation, about which neither you nor the president has informed us?"

"I do not believe the newspaper article states there was any U.S. involvement in the car chase incident," Harris replied.

"I don't give a damn what this article claims," Senator Stone said, clearly becoming angry. "Are you and the agency currently engaged in a covert operation to smuggle Pavel out of Russia? It's a direct question. Yes or no?"

"Senator, as I just explained, I would be derelict in not pursuing all possible and probable means to recruit human assets, especially someone as important as Deputy Minister Pavel. We are constantly testing the waters with dozens of potential sources, but that doesn't mean we get involved in car chases and shoot-outs on Moscow's streets."

"You're trying to avoid giving me a direct answer. Let me simplify my question. Is the president aware of a covert operation to smuggle Pavel out of Russia?"

"I cannot say what the president may or may not be aware of, only what communications I have engaged in with him."

Stone's eyes narrowed. He'd heard enough evasion. "Have you told President Fitzgerald about a CIA covert operation to extricate Deputy Minister Pavel out of Russia?" he demanded, adding, "This is the fourth time I have asked you this same question, sir. I expect you to answer it."

But it wasn't the *same* question.

Director Harris had been forcing Senator Stone to repeat his question for a clever reason. He'd hoped Stone's rephrasing would give him a lawyerly out and, this time, it had. *"Have you told President Fitzgerald about a CIA covert operation . . ."*

While Harris and the president had discussed Pavel's possible defection, Harris had not finalized that operation until *after* their initial talk. Because of that, Harris had never actually told the White House about a covert operation. It was hair-splitting, but hair-splitting mattered when you had something to hide—a lesson well established when then president Bill Clinton and his attorneys argued about the definition of what constituted "sexual relations."

Harris said, "Senator Stone, I have not informed President Fitzgerald about any such covert operation."

"Isn't it true, Director Harris," Stone asked, "that you sent Brett Garrett, a dishonorably discharged former Navy SEAL and the man responsible for my son's murder, to get Pavel and his grandson out of Russia? And neither you nor the president informed this committee—as required by law?"

"With all due respect, Senator, Brett Garrett is not a CIA employee."

"Did you or did you not arrange for Brett Garrett, as a civilian, to go to Moscow to escort Pavel and his grandson out of Russia?" Senator Stone shouted, finally losing his temper.

"Again, Garrett is not under my employ or direction."

Stone leaned forward and glared at Harris.

"Do you recognize the name Jack Strong?" he asked.

"I do not."

"Perhaps you knew him by his SEAL nickname, Bear?" Stone continued.

"Senator, I do not remember the individual to whom you are referring."

"Bear—Jack Strong—was on the Cameroon rescue mission two years ago with my son. You may be interested to know he now works here at the Capitol and he recently came to see me."

Harris remained Sphinx-like.

"Do you recall your sworn testimony before our committee two years ago when you testified that you had ordered Brett Garrett not to rescue other hostages? If your memory fails you, I will read it because I have a transcript."

Without waiting, Senator Stone read from a paper:

Question asked by Senator Stone: "What specific order did you give Chief Garrett when he informed you of this second hostage?"

Answer: Director Harris: "I specifically told Chief Garrett not to put his men in harm's way by attempting to rescue that second worker."

"Director Harris, is that still your answer—that Garrett disobeyed a direct order from you?"

"I'd have to review my notes."

"Stop this charade, Director Harris!" Stone snapped. "Jack Strong claims you gave Garrett permission to rescue that second hostage—that Garrett persuaded you by mentioning the hostage was a young girl and the same age as your granddaughter—that you told Garrett you'd—quote—'have his back'—if things went bad."

Harris hadn't seen this coming.

Senator Stone continued: "Director Harris, I believe you committed perjury when you testified two years ago about the events in Cameroon. You hid information and lied to protect yourself just as, I suspect, you are lying again right now. Your actions and conduct are a clear display of the utter disregard that you have for us and the United States Congress. Sir, I'm putting you on notice. I intend to seek your removal as director."

Harris accidentally bit the side of his cheek while clenching his teeth.

"Now I have one final question," Senator Stone said sternly. "Where is Brett Garrett right now? Is he with Deputy Minister Pavel and his grandson? Is he attempting to smuggle them out of Russia?"

"Senator," Harris replied, looking defiantly into Stone's eyes, "I honestly do not know where Garrett, Pavel, and his grandson may be."

Thirty-Three

Brett Garrett regained consciousness on the cargo floor of an Mi-26 Russian air force helicopter. Handcuffed, legs bound. The hovering aircraft's interior was massive. Capable of transporting ninety Russian troops. Garrett counted fourteen other passengers, including Pavel, Peter, and General Gromyko. The rest were Gromyko's men, some of whom had helped subdue him on the train before Gromyko's boot toe had knocked him out.

The helicopter landed with a jolt. Four guards carried the manacled Garrett outside. He didn't resist. Pointless. Instead, he took note of their destination. They'd landed in a clearing edged by forest some twenty meters from a windowless, one-story bunker. Pavel and Peter, who were not restrained, were escorted from the aircraft.

Through a heavy steel door they entered. Down a brightly lit corridor they went. Stopping finally at a metal door at the end of the hallway. An electronic keypad. Beep. Ding. Each a slightly different tone. An electronic bolt slid open. Garrett was carried inside. He lifted his head just in time to keep it from smacking the concrete floor when he was dropped. Pavel and Peter followed him inside. One of Gromyko's men tossed a pail into the room. "To pee," he said.

"Deputy Minister," General Gromyko said mockingly, joining them with two of his guards, "these accommodations are not what you are accustomed to, but your stay here will be extremely brief."

"I have rights under our constitution," Pavel protested.

Gromyko scoffed. "Arrogance. Even now. You are a traitor, Yakov Prokofyevich, and have only one right. The right to die."

Gromyko glanced at Peter.

Pavel said, "General, my grandson is innocent. Harmless."

"Was your grandson not traveling with a traitor?"

The teenager lowered his eyes.

Gromyko looked at Garrett, prone and helpless on the floor, wrists handcuffed, and ankles tied by a plastic band.

"You have big balls, Brett Garrett, believing you could transport a deputy minister out of Russia during my watch."

"The game isn't over," Garrett said.

"Like all Americans, you overestimate your skills. You SEALs are nothing," Gromyko retorted. "It would take four of you to defeat a single fighter under my direct command. Russians are strong. Our president has a black belt in judo, and I train regularly with him. Your president is weak."

"I've watched the YouTube videos of your president with his 'supersecret' Russian fighting technique."

"SAMBO," Gromyko said proudly, impressed that Garrett had referenced the videos. "It's purely Russian. 'Self-defense without arms'—a skill your military has been trying to steal from us. I have personally witnessed President Kalugin use it to defeat all challengers."

"What I saw was not SAMBO, it was *ukemi*."

"I myself am an expert in martial arts," Gromyko replied. "There is no such thing as *ukemi* judo."

"A Japanese term. It means having your opponent fake a fall because he doesn't want to embarrass his boss by kicking his ass."

Gromyko raised his boot and Garrett quickly turned his head, expecting a kick. The general laughed and returned his boot to the floor.

"Is this your Hollywood movie plan? Taunt me? Do you believe I will order you freed so that you can then defeat me in hand-to-hand combat and somehow escape?"

"I would take satisfaction in kicking your ass."

"I have watched your movies with their cheap stunts. Americans always win, but in truth, you sit in theaters with buckets of greasy popcorn and diet sodas. You teach your children to be weaklings."

Raising his voice in mock falsetto, Gromyko mimicked: "Mommy, Mommy, a bully called me a bad name at school. Please call our lawyer!"

Garrett responded, "The question is not how tough most Americans are. It's how tough are you?"

Gromyko lifted his boot but stopped himself. "Who is lying on the floor and who is standing above him with a boot?" He spat on Garrett's face and started to leave, only to quickly spin around and kick an unprepared Garrett in his abdomen.

"Does that feel like *ukemi*?" he demanded.

A guard shut the door. The sound of the six-button code, the dead bolt sliding back into place.

Pavel sank to one knee and used a handkerchief to wipe Garrett's face. Peter began waving his hands. A flurry of gestures. Pavel interpreted. "Peter knows this building. It's where his parents worked. Near Svetogorsk, about thirty miles north of Vyborg. This is a Kamera—a poison factory."

"How close are we to the Finnish border?"

The old man touched Garrett's ribs, causing him to flinch in pain.

"It is too late for that, my friend," he said.

"Prop me up against a wall," Garrett said.

"Better for you to lie flat if your ribs are broken."

"The wall, please."

Pavel took one arm. Peter the other, pulling the handcuffed and leg-bound Garrett up against the wall. From there he examined their surroundings. A twin pair of fluorescent tubes mounted in the ceiling illuminated the room, which was as large as a one-car garage. Walls: a drab gray. Faded white ceiling. Peeling paint. Directly across from him were rows of wooden six-by-six-inch boxes with names scrawled on paper tabs above each cubby. Dozens and dozens of them attached to the wall. All appeared empty. The wall that Garrett was now leaning against held only one item. An old poster. World War II propaganda. A silk-screen Stalin, red flag behind him, tiny Russian airplanes dropping bombs hovering around his head. At his midsection, a huge battleship. In the foreground, rows of marching soldiers. A Russian tank. The inscription: "*Long live the Red Army of workers and peasants—the true guard of the Soviet borders."*

Garrett looked at the back of the room. Two tiers of fifty-gallon drums on wooden pallets. Each marked with a bright yellow sticker. A black skull and crossbones. Hazardous waste.

He looked at the doorway. A mail slot. No windows. No obvious ways to escape.

"This must have been a mailroom," Garrett concluded, "before they began storing toxic waste in it."

Pavel sat down next to Garrett and spoke to Peter, who was still standing in front of both men. "You must be a man now. General Gromyko will return us to Moscow, where I will be tried and executed. I still have friends there. They will find a way to protect you. They have no reason to harm you. I have a sister in Belarus. Go there."

Garrett fought the urge to vomit. His head was throbbing. His ribs hurt. He was wet with perspiration even though the room was chilly. The opioid cravings were kicking in.

He inspected the ceiling. Peter was skinny. There was no air vent.

Peter took a seat next to his grandfather. Leaned against the old man's shoulder. They heard the electronic lock beep six times. The bolt opening. General Gromyko reappeared with his guards.

"Free the American's ankles and get him onto his feet," the general ordered.

Addressing Pavel, who had stood, Gromyko said, "I'm putting on a special demonstration in your honor." Two guards moved forward to escort him out into the hallway. Peter leapt to his feet to accompany him but was stopped by guards.

"Your grandfather has told me you can speak but choose not to. Is that true?" Gromyko asked.

Peter shrugged, still looking out the door at his grandfather, who was being taken away.

Gromyko slapped the teen. Hard.

"When I ask a question, you will answer. Now speak."

Peter nodded.

Gromyko slapped him again.

"Picking on kids a turn-on for you?" Garrett asked.

Gromyko turned his attention to Garrett. "Bring them both," he told his men. "They might enjoy our little show."

The entourage walked along a maze of corridors. Some rooms they passed had windows. Garrett could see men and women in white lab coats, masks, caps, and latex gloves working in them. In other rooms, scientists were outfitted in hazmat suits with face masks fed by air tanks as if they were underwater divers. A few laboratories were fully outfitted but empty. One lab they passed was completely burnt inside. Black scorched walls.

Gromyko stopped when they reached double doors. His men opened them. The large meeting room inside had chairs arranged in front of a black curtain. Garrett counted three women and six men. All but one were wearing lab smocks and had plastic-coated name tags. Kamera scientists, Garrett presumed. The other: Ivan Sokolov in his red cowboy boots.

Gromyko had his men direct Peter to the front of the room while Garrett was guarded at the back. The general positioned Peter so that the teen was facing the curtain. The black covering fell, exposing a thick glass that reached from the floor to the ceiling. On the opposite side, Deputy Foreign Minister Yakov Prokofyevich Pavel. Stripped naked.

"You son of a bitch, Gromyko," Pavel yelled, his voice coming through an overhead speaker. "I'll rip your ass and poke out your eyes!"

The other three walls, floor, and ceiling of the enclosed chamber were covered with white tiles. The bright lights and the whiteness of the interior seemed to rob Pavel of his pigmentation. He was overweight, had little muscle tone and saggy skin.

Gromyko addressed his guests. "The perfect poison must be odorless. Colorless. Without taste when ingested and impossible to detect after it kills. Ricin. Polonium-210. Each a progressive step forward, but each failing to meet all of those requirements for perfection."

His eyes darted between the scientists. "You are supposed to be Russia's best, but even with Novichok, you failed to kill two traitors in England."

Turning, he rapped on the glass much like a petulant child taunting a caged zoo animal. He nudged Peter nearer so the teen was only inches from it. Pavel immediately placed his palm against the barrier.

"Go ahead," Gromyko urged Peter. The teen raised his palm so that it and the old man's palm were symbolically touching with the glass separating them.

"This boy's parents—the daughter and son-in-law of the deputy minister—were close to creating a perfect poison. I personally named their concoction Devil's Breath—a rather theatrical description but better than referring to it by its chemical compound."

He spoke directly to Ivan Sokolov. "Don't you agree that Devil's Breath is a good brand name?"

"Branding is important," Sokolov chuckled, "even for a poison, I suspect."

Gromyko laughed, and everyone but Garrett and Peter joined in.

"I was so looking forward to them finally giving it to me, but—"

Sokolov interrupted. "General, with such a terrifying name, how safe is your Devil's Breath to transport?"

A clearly irked Gromyko replied, "Are you calling me a fool?"

The grin on Sokolov's face vanished.

"It will be in canisters aboard your airplane, and I will be accompanying it to America. Would I poison myself?"

"I apologize, it's just that I've heard rumors and saw the burned laboratory down the hall."

"Yes, the traitors who betrayed me and their colleagues in this laboratory. I believe they had created my perfect poison but rather than delivering it to me, they destroyed it. Burned their laboratory. Erased all notes."

He paused and then suddenly grinned. "An irony, is it not? While trying to obliterate Devil's Breath, some variant of it escaped and killed them both. Perhaps I should call it the Son of Devil's Breath." He chuckled.

Peter quietly began to cry. From behind the glass, Pavel mouthed, "Be strong. Be a man."

Gromyko continued: "No one in this room has been able to re-create what they achieved. Instead, the best they can do is reproduce this variant killer. It is better than what we have but still flawed. A demonstration is in order." He turned to watch Pavel.

Anticipating what was about to happen, Pavel raised both hands and jabbed his extended middle fingers like knives at Gromyko.

A single *pop* came from above Pavel. The old man looked up. A puff of red mist appeared from a tiny hole in the ceiling. It was visible only for an instant, no longer than a mere blink. Blood began trickling from Pavel's nose as he stared at his grandson in horror. Desperate, the old man pressed his hands against his face. He collapsed.

"No!" Peter shrieked.

"Ah, so the child can speak with the right prompting," Gromyko said triumphantly.

Peter started toward Gromyko with raised fists but was immediately stopped by guards.

Gazing at Pavel's naked corpse behind the glass, Gromyko slowly began to clap. One by one, the others watching did the same, except for the sobbing teenager and Garrett.

"The puff of red. The bloody nose," Gromyko said in a disappointed voice. "These are the flaws that my brilliant scientists here have yet to resolve. The flaws in my unperfected poison." He cast his eyes on the scientists before him.

"General Gromyko," one of the scientists said, "we

are close. We should have your Devil's Breath within a few months."

"But I need it now!" he said sternly. "Perhaps if one of you joined Yakov Prokofyevich in this chamber, your colleagues would work more diligently."

The scientist lowered his eyes.

Gromyko called to the back of the room. "A tiny puff killed Yakov Prokofyevich, but he was an old man and old men are easier to kill. How much is necessary to dispose of a healthy American Navy SEAL?"

Shifting his glance to Peter, he added, "Or a Russian teenager?"

Gromyko again looked at Pavel's corpse. "I've been told it takes a full twelve hours to guarantee the poison completely dissipates from this testing chamber. Is that correct?"

The scientist with the downed eyes said, "Yes, General. We need twelve hours to clear it."

"Unfortunately," Gromyko continued, shifting his gaze to Garrett, "I must leave with Mr. Sokolov for America, so I will not be here to watch you die, but I have set aside enough time to amuse myself by breaking every bone in your body."

"General," the scientist said sheepishly, "we need the American to be in good health if we want the best results tomorrow."

Gromyko opened his palms before him, as if he were holding a scale, judging his two options.

"Breaking every bone in your body," he said to Garrett, "or providing my scientists with a healthy specimen."

"I've beaten men," Garrett said, "but only a deranged sadist enjoys it."

"Ah, you see, everyone, what he delivers to me as an insult, I take as a compliment. There is no deranged sadism necessary when it comes to beating and killing Americans. I take great joy in it and will take equal joy in using this variant of Devil's Breath to kill dozens and dozens of your countrymen. Now, Mr. Garrett, is that your final insult before I make my decision? Answer wisely."

"I think Deputy Minister Pavel's final gesture summed up my thoughts about you."

Gromyko smirked. "You have hubris, but not much creativity."

He lowered his palms and addressed the scientists. "You will have your healthy specimen. I have a flight to take."

Turning his attention back to Garrett, he added, "We will not meet again. You have failed to save Pavel, and you will die knowing that you did not stop me from using this imperfect poison to kill Americans. I will offer you a parting thought—a Russian saying. 'He is brave when fighting against sheep, and when fighting against a brave man, he's a sheep himself.' Would you like to *baa* now for us, Mr. Garrett?"

Everyone but Garrett and Peter laughed.

Thirty-Four

CIA director Harold Harris was in the middle of a late-night meeting discussing his personal crisis when he was told Valerie Mayberry had called. He felt relieved. The CIA backup team that he'd sent to Baltimore had watched Mayberry being forced into a van at gunpoint, but he'd ordered it to stand down, to not intervene. He wanted to learn where that van was going.

It had been a risk but one that Harris had been willing to take. And then his ghost team had lost track of the van in Baltimore and, with it, Mayberry.

After that, he'd assumed the worst.

Mayberry had told Mr. Smith that she was heading home. She'd given him the number of a backup cell phone that she kept in her condo. As soon as she got there, she retrieved it. An email response from Director Harris.

"Contact no one until we can discuss face to face. That's an order. Glad you are safe."

Adrenaline was still pumping through her. Too anxious to sleep. She waited.

A watched pot never boils. Six a.m. and still no call. Mayberry switched on the early-morning news.

Aysan Rivera, the daughter of a prominent Baltimore family, had been found dead in a Port of Baltimore warehouse, the newscaster announced. Police were withholding information, but sources said Rivera had been restrained with duct tape and was wearing only her underwear when found. Detectives suspected a predator, possibly a serial killer.

Mayberry fought the urge to vomit. Instant guilt. If she had immediately freed Aysan Rivera from her restraints and administered CPR instead of chasing after Makayla, maybe she could have saved Rivera. Another disturbing thought. One that had been nagging at her ever since she'd fled the Baltimore warehouse. She had witnessed Rivera's murder and had not told anyone. She had called Mr. Smith instead of staying and telling the Baltimore police what she knew. She needed to contact Sally North and tell her FBI boss. But if she did, she would be disobeying Director Harris, who was technically her boss.

Mayberry followed rules. She felt safe within parameters. She began pacing in her condo. Couldn't think of anything else. The FBI didn't know that she'd participated in the Antifa bombing at the Stonewall Jackson Shrine. Now she'd witnessed Rivera being given a fatal opioid dose. She was getting deeper and deeper. Even more culpable.

She stared at her cell phone.

Why hadn't Harris responded? He was torturing her. Every moment put her in more legal jeopardy. Plus, Makayla Jones was still roaming free.

Going into her bathroom, she found a bottle of Xanax that had been prescribed after Noah had died. She swallowed two without water.

At 7:00 a.m., when the local newscast gave way to the national news, Mayberry got her first plausible explanation for why Harris had not yet contacted her. He was on his way to make the rounds on Capitol Hill. Lobbying to save his job.

California senator Stone had been so outraged by the Maxi-Leaks disclosures that he was introducing legislation to "censure" the director. Harris was a presidential appointee, which meant the Senate couldn't outright fire him, but it could apply political pressure on President Fitzgerald to replace him. The Senate had never censured a CIA director, only presidents and its own members. Most famously, Alexander Hamilton, the newscaster said.

At least three times, Mayberry picked up her cell and started to call Sally North's private number at the bureau. Each time she stopped. She was an accomplice to murder. She hurried into the bathroom and threw up.

Morning became afternoon. Still waiting. No return call from Harris. Late afternoon found Mayberry still frozen. She began heating leftover chicken noodle soup to take her mind off everything. It didn't work. She gave herself a mental deadline. If Director Harris didn't contact her by the time she finished eating her soup, she would come clean to Sally North and the bureau. Ask for mercy.

She had just downed her first spoonful when her phone dinged, signaling an email. It was from Harris.

8 Ellanor C. Lawrence Park off 28. Behind Walney Visitor Center. Small amphitheater. Turn left, take trail heading Southeast toward Cabell's Mill.

She checked her watch: 7:38 p.m. She'd have to hurry. Abandoning her soup, she grabbed her jacket

and Glock 19. As she rode the elevator to the condo's underground garage, she wondered why Harris
had chosen a local park. They'd always met in his
government-provided Cadillac or at a safe house. Was
he taking extra steps to ensure no one saw them meeting? Another explanation came to her. She had just
been drawn into a trap in Baltimore. Could this be one,
too? Paranoia or perception? She checked the email
on her phone. Compared the most recent to the first
that she'd received after notifying Mr. Smith. The two
emails matched. Still, just to be certain, she forwarded
Harris's email to Thomas Jefferson Kim at IEC. He was
a computer expert. He would know if she had reason to
worry.

"It's from Harris. Safe to meet," Kim replied.

Mayberry frequently jogged in Ellanor C. Lawrence
Park, 650 acres of forested hills south of Reston off State
Highway 28. She arrived at the park's visitor center, an
eighteenth-century farmhouse called Walney, so named
because of the walnut trees encircling it. Twilight was
bleeding into night. She fetched a flashlight from her
glove box and smiled at a couple loading a cooler and
two toddlers into their car. The park was closing and
once that couple departed, Mayberry's Jaguar would be
the only vehicle in the lot. She hurried down the hill
from the stone farmhouse to rows of wooden benches

facing an outdoor stage. As directed, she turned left on a hardened earth path.

Although it was growing darker, she was reluctant to switch on her flashlight. Doing so would make her easy to spot, and she still was uneasy about meeting Harris in such a remote area.

Ten minutes down the path, she stopped. An emerging half-moon illuminated the trail, but she had entered a section under a thick canopy of trees. It was filled with shadows. She was now walking along the bottom of a ravine, with a creek flowing next to her and rising hills on either side. Something darted across the path, startling her. Two squirrels. The park was overrun with them. She moved cautiously in the darkness, watching each step to avoid stumbling on the uneven terrain. Suddenly something felt squishy under her left running shoe and she smelled a horrible odor. A pet owner had cleaned up after his dog but had discarded the plastic bag on the path, leaving it for her to step on.

The trail that she was following connected the Walney farmhouse to a pond and Cabell's Mill, another building that had been an operating mill until 1916. Ellanor Lawrence and her husband David, the founder of *U.S. News & World Report*, had purchased the mill in the 1930s, converting it into a guesthouse. Lots of notables had picnicked in this sanctuary, including Franklin and Eleanor Roosevelt. Historical trivia— Mayberry's OCD compulsion. Back then, this had been farmland. Today a lone sliver of greenery tucked between endless suburbs.

Because hers had been the only car parked at the Walney visitor center, Mayberry assumed Director Harris had arrived at the park's more southern Cabell's Mill entrance. It was closest to a major highway. If so, he'd be walking north toward her on the path.

Mayberry took several more steps and nearly slipped because of a wet spot caused by water splashing from the creek next to her. She caught herself. It would be impossible for her to continue safely without using her flashlight. She put her finger on its switch but stopped before turning it on.

A sound. To her immediate right across the creek. Squirrels? Not this time. A man's cough. He'd chosen higher ground, looking down into the ravine. An old black pine tree, at least two feet in circumference, was a step ahead. Another black pine had fallen at its base along the creek. She quietly stepped from the path, transferring her unlit flashlight into her left hand while drawing her Glock 19 with her right.

Another muffled cough. The snapping of a dry branch. Whoever was on the hill was moving down toward her. Mayberry dropped on her haunches and pressed her back against the upright pine, positioning herself between it and its fallen twin. She was now hiding behind a wedge created by the two trees.

A flashlight beam. Someone was approaching on the trail from the direction of Cabell's Mill. At this distance, she couldn't identify who it might be. The approaching figure crossed a wooden bridge over the creek some thirty yards south from where she was hiding.

A loud splash. Several expletives. The unknown cougher to her right apparently had slipped while coming down the ravine. Fallen into the ankle-deep creek next to the path.

"Valerie?" the man on the footpath called out, after hearing the sound of thrashing and cursing. The voice was not Director Harris's. It was Thomas Jefferson Kim.

Phew, phew, phew, phew. The four sounds mimicked those of a storm door slapping shut, but Mayberry recognized them as gunshots. Most likely .22-caliber rounds fired from a pistol with a suppressor. They had been shot by the unknown man on her right.

She heard Kim holler. He dropped his flashlight.

Phew. Phew.

Mayberry rose from her hiding spot behind the trees, flipping on her flashlight and aiming her Glock 19 in one coordinated move. The flashlight beam exposed the gunman's face. Standing only a few yards from her. She recognized him. He was an Antifa member. From inside the van in Baltimore when she had been abducted. One of the men who'd been ordered by Makayla to wait outside the warehouse.

She and Kim had walked into an ambush.

Mayberry fired two rounds. Her Glock 19's bark was deafening compared to the Walther P22 pistol in the ambusher's hand. He was dead by the time his head hit the creek water.

A slug whizzed by Mayberry and smacked into the tall black pine next to her. She doused her flashlight and ducked behind the fallen tree into her hiding spot. Someone else was in the woods—a second shooter.

Blam, blam, blam, blam. The shots being fired at her were not suppressed and appeared to be coming from a heavier-caliber pistol. Fired on her left, but she couldn't be certain of the shooter's exact location.

Mayberry lay down flat on the damp ground as the slugs continued to hit the trees protecting her. Raising her Glock above the barrier, she fired wildly. Five rounds squeezed off as quickly as she could pull the Glock's trigger. She stopped, listened. Nothing. Raising her handgun again, she emptied its clip into the blackness. Reloaded.

"Mayberry!" Kim yelled from the trail.

His cry was greeted by a fresh round of gunshots from the unknown attacker—this time aimed at Kim.

Mayberry knew why Kim had called out. He was drawing fire, pulling attention away from her. She peeked over the log, and this time, when the shooter fired at Kim, Mayberry saw the muzzle flashes.

Mayberry rose up and fired four shots from her Glock 19 in two-round bursts.

Ducking down, she waited. Nothing. Rising to her knees, she switched on her flashlight, aiming it to her left up the ravine. She caught a fleeing Antifa shooter in the light.

Makayla Jones was disappearing over the rise.

Mayberry fired, but Makayla was gone.

She hurried back onto the path and ran to where Kim was lying on his back. Her flashlight showed him clutching his bloody right bicep. His jacket had three noticeable holes.

"Both of those bastards shot me," he said, gulping for air.

"Tell me you're wearing a vest!"

He nodded affirmatively. "I was suspicious after I got an email from Harris telling me to come to a park. . . ."

"Wait, I sent you emails that Harris had written me," she replied. "I asked if they were legitimate and you emailed back that they were. It was safe for me to come here."

"How many emails did you get from Harris?" Kim asked.

"I got one immediately after I had called asking for a meeting. I got a second one much later telling me to come to the park. I forwarded both to you."

"I never received them," Kim said. He thought for a moment. "My guess is the first email was legitimate. It came from Harris. But the Magician—the mole—sent the second one to you and also one to me pretending he was Harris."

"Helping Makayla ambush us."

"Right, the Magician has tapped into all of our email accounts. Mine, yours, and Harris's. He's manipulating us."

"Who is he?"

"I'm still not sure, but I'm going to catch him."

She helped Kim stand. He was wobbly but regained his breath.

"Let me see your wound."

She helped him remove his shirt, the bullet-resistant vest, and the T-shirt under it. Three rounds were smashed into the vest's fabric, leaving him bruised and with a possible broken rib, but none of the higher-caliber slugs had penetrated it. Another round, much smaller and most likely from a .22-caliber pistol, was embedded in his upper arm.

"It hurts like hell," Kim said.

"I'm contacting Harris," she replied, "by phone, not email!"

She dialed "Mr. Smith" on her backup cell. Within minutes Harris called her. Their conversation was brief, one-sided. If the Magician was intercepting emails, he might also be monitoring their calls.

When finished, Mayberry briefed Kim. "Harris is sending people here to clean up this mess. I've been told to take you to a local emergency care. He and his people will meet us there. I'll drive."

"Really—you'll drive," Kim replied sarcastically, still clutching the bullet wound in his arm.

They found their way to the Cabell's Mill lot where Kim's Mercedes was parked, reaching it about the same time a van arrived. Four men stepped from it.

"Where's the package?" one asked.

"Follow the path heading north. You'll reach a footbridge, he'll be on the left of the trail, facedown in the creek," she replied.

Mayberry got behind the wheel.

"Where'd he tell us to go?" Kim asked.

"A strip mall. Only a couple miles away."

He cursed. "I fell for this ambush because I was so eager to meet with you and Harris. I let down my guard. I wanted to tell you that I've identified Makayla. It wasn't easy—in fact—it was damn hard, but I did it."

"Who is she?"

"Nataniela Kalanga. She is not and never has been an American citizen. She's an illegal."

"Kalanga, what sort of name is that?"

"Her parents are from Angola. Back when the superpowers cared about Africa, the Soviets made a move there. The CIA went in to stop them, which led to a bloody civil war. Makayla's grandfathers worked for the KGB. When the Soviets pulled out, the KGB resettled their families in Moscow, but neither liked it. Both families moved to Belarus. One son married the other family's daughter, and the result was Nataniela Kalanga."

Kim paused for a moment. He had worked diligently to identify Makayla Jones, aka Nataniela Kalanga, and he wasn't going to hurry his account.

"We went through thousands of records—passports, facial recognition images at airports—the agency, bureau, Interpol, people in Ukraine and France. It was tedious, difficult work," he recalled. "The agency and I had trouble getting a positive identification because she changed her name when she initially crossed from Belarus into France. She was posing there as Adalene Petit. That's also the name she used when she entered the United States on a student visa. She attended undergrad at Stanford before returning to France. By the time she met Gabriel de Depardieu and Aysan Rivera at the Ecole Normale Supérieure school in Paris, she'd changed her identity a third time. She had become Makayla Jones with a complete set of U.S. credentials."

Kim paused to catch his breath and added, "Getting shot really sucks."

Mayberry drove them into the strip mall where the emergent care was located.

"How'd she'd manage to obtain a U.S. passport?" Mayberry asked.

"While she was a student here, she obtained a copy of the real Makayla Jones's birth certificate and used it to get a Missouri driver's license with a St. Louis address."

"Missouri? St. Louis? Is that where the actual Makayla Jones lives?"

"It's where she's buried. Her parents in St. Louis told us they'd lost a baby girl from SIDS at nine months. They named her Makayla Jones. They had no idea Nataniela Kalanga, aka Adalene Petit, had assumed their dead child's identity. Because the real Makayla Jones was an infant, there was no Social Security number—until the fake Makayla obtained one. With a Social Security number, driver's license, and birth certificate, she got a U.S. passport."

Mayberry parked the SUV outside the emergent care, and a couple stepped from a nearby Ford Taurus.

"We'll handle it from here," the woman said. She led Kim into an urgent care that was tucked between a Baskin-Robbins and Zips dry cleaners.

Director Harris had told Mayberry to stay outside and wait. Ten minutes later, he arrived. Unlike the others, who had come from nearby buildings in Reston, he'd had farther to drive. She joined him in the backseat of his Cadillac.

Before either of them had a chance to speak, Director Harris's phone dinged. He'd received an unsolicited email from a Russian server. He opened it. A thirty-second video. Russian foreign minister Yakov Prokofyevich Pavel, naked, locked in a glass-fronted chamber. Him raising his hands in obscene gestures. A barely noticeable puff of red about his head. He glanced up. Collapsed. Dead.

The director's phone dinged a second time. Another emailed video. Brett Garrett handcuffed. Peter standing next to him, crying.

A two-word message: "I win."

Thirty-Five

Peter had stopped sobbing by the time he and Garrett were once again locked inside the Kamera's converted mailroom. Garrett's hands remained shackled in front of him. Twelve hours before he was fated to die. How many others had served as Russian lab rats?

"Peter," he said, "I think I see a ballpoint pen in one of those mailbox cubbyholes, can you get it? It's on the top row and I can't reach it."

Peter followed his eyes but didn't immediately see it.

"About fifth from left," Garrett said.

The teen removed a blue plastic ballpoint pen from the slot.

"Some of these older ink pens could be opened. See if there's a brass ink cartridge inside."

Peter unscrewed the pen and withdrew a round cartridge.

"Fantastic," Garrett said. "Now you need to begin bending that cartridge back and forth until it breaks in half."

The youth quickly snapped it into two pieces.

Garrett turned his palms upward so the teen could see the restraint's keyhole. Like most handcuffs, these were opened with a hollow key that turned around a permanent center stem.

"I need you to jam that cartridge into the keyhole onto its stem. The pen's circumference is slightly smaller, so it's going to split at its tip. If you do it right, we can pry that split open, turning the cartridge into a key."

Peter shoved the cartridge onto the stem. With his fingernail, he separated part of its split end, bending it outward. It took him several attempts, but he was able to open the lock.

"Great job!" Garrett said, freeing his hands. "Using a ballpoint pen is an old trick used by prisoners. Now we have to get that door open. Can you get your hand through its mail slot?"

Peter lifted the narrow cover, which opened inward. Peeking through it, he could see the electronic keypad. It was mounted to his right on the hallway's back wall. He forced his hand and wrist through the mail slot, but he couldn't reach the pad. It was simply too far away.

Garrett searched the room for some sort of extension. The plastic pail that had been tossed inside to serve as a toilet had a metal handle. He broke it free and straightened it. He guessed it was about twenty-six inches long.

"Try this," he said, handing it to Peter.

Peter slipped his hand through the slot and maneuvered the wire. It reached the telephone-like buttons.

"Can you push them?" Garrett asked.

He jabbed the wire against the pad. It struck a digit and they heard a beep.

"You're doing great," Garrett said. "I saw at least three numbers when the guards were unlocking it. It's a start but we're going to need all six. Did you see any of them?"

Peter shook his head no.

It seemed hopeless. Peter pulled the wire back inside, and both of them sat on the floor, thinking. There had to be a solution. They had to escape.

Garrett's mind flashed back to when he'd heard Peter playing Tchaikovsky for his grandfather on the piano at the dacha outside Moscow. Peter could play any tune once he heard it, Pavel had claimed.

"You heard the sounds when the guard pushed the keys, didn't you?" he asked.

The boy's face lit up. He grabbed the straightened wire and crammed his hand through the mail slot, reaching the keypad with its tip. He touched each digit to hear its unique sound.

"Can you replicate it?" Garrett asked.

Peter hit the first digit. Then he stopped and pulled back the wire. He looked at Garrett. He was scared.

"You can do this," Garrett said. "Your grandfather called you a child prodigy. Remember the sounds the pad made."

Peter stuck the wire through the slot. Six distinct tones. He began to tap on the keypad, and when he finished, Garrett heard the electronic bolt sliding open.

"You did it! Your grandfather would be proud!"

A beaming Peter took the wire and immediately looked for a place to hide it.

"No point in that," Garrett said. "If they catch us, they aren't going to bring us back here."

Garrett opened the door. It was now after midnight. The lab workers had gone for the day. The dimly lighted hallway was empty. Garrett led. When they reached the end of the hallway, he stopped.

A diagram of the Kamera building was posted on the wall in case of a fire. Four exits. Garrett knew each would be guarded. The one at the rear of the building was the closest. Garrett ripped the map from the wall for them to follow. The building was composed of east-west hallways that connected at each end with two north-west corridors. The corridors ran along the structures' walls and were how workers moved from one hallway to the next. Garrett and Peter stopped walking when they reached a corner at the back of the building. It was on Garrett's left. He dropped to his knees and looked around it. Two uniformed guards were protecting the exit. One sitting behind a desk. The other on a chair leaning back against the corridor's exterior wall. Neither noticed Garrett.

Garrett backed up and, with Peter, retraced their steps along the east-west hallway. They checked the knobs on each lab door. Three per side, facing each other. Two were unlocked. One lab was next to the north-south corridor that Garrett had peeked around. The other unlocked one was in the opposite direction at the farthest end of the hallway.

Garrett returned to the corner and opened the unlocked lab there. He led the teen inside. Like the other labs, it had huge windows from the waist up. "Hide under the window so you can't be seen if someone looks in," Garrett said. The lights in the lab were turned off. Peter crouched near the interior wall facing the hallway. Garrett intentionally left the door cracked open.

He hurried down the hallway to the other unlocked lab at the far end and entered it. The room contained four tables, each covered with a wide assortment of glass bottles, test tubes, and other equipment. Garrett slipped off his left shoe, removed his sock, replaced his shoe, and paused at a table that held brass weights used to calibrate scales. He dropped several into his sock, knotting its end. A crude weapon.

A chemistry chart was hanging nearby on the wall. As a student of Russian history, Garrett knew that Dimitri Bonavich Mendeleev, an eccentric Russian scientist, was the first to compose the periodic table of the elements. He also knew Mendeleev had moved to Germany in the 1860s to work with a scientist named Robert Bunsen, the inventor of the Bunsen burner. There were eight burners in the room, two per lab table. He disconnected all of the rubber hoses that connected them to gas pipes except for the burner nearest the door. He turned on the gas, lit the burner at the door, shut it behind him, and darted along the hallway to the lab where Peter was hiding. He crouched next to the teen.

Garrett had no idea how long it would take for the methane gas to fill the room and be ignited by the single flame. It didn't take long.

The explosion blew off the lab's closed door and busted its window. Flames shot into the hallway. One of the guards rounded the corner. He stopped as soon as he saw the fire and turned his head to yell back to his partner.

Garrett leapt into the hallway, swinging his weighted sock like a billy club. It hit the guard with such force that Garrett heard the man's skull crack. He dropped onto the floor. Garrett bent down, switched the weighted sock to his left hand, and used his right to retrieve the guard's Makarov 9 mm pistol. He was rising from the body when the second guard rounded the corner and saw him.

The Russian lunged at Garrett, grabbing his right wrist with both hands, forcing him to raise the pistol upward. Unable to hit the Russian in his face because of his raised arms, Garrett swung the weighed sock with his left hand as hard as he could and smacked it against the Russian's testicles. It took two more hits before the Russian loosen his grip on Garrett's hand. Lowering the Makarov, Garrett fired twice directly into the guard's face.

"Hurry!" Garrett hollered to Peter. "The others will come."

They darted around the corner and out the exit.

Garrett surveyed the forest encircling them. He had no idea which direction to go, only that they needed to hide.

Peter grabbed his arm and took the lead. He entered the trees with Garrett behind him. Twenty minutes later, Garrett realized Peter had led them to the edge of Svetogorsk.

"No," Garrett said. "Too risky. We need to avoid people."

Peter shook his head, disagreeing. He pointed at a five-story, badly weathered apartment complex.

"No!" Garrett said.

But Peter continued marching toward the building.

Garrett hesitated and then followed. No one was in the first-floor hallway. Peter knocked on a door.

Still holding the Makarov, Garrett nervously glanced to his left and right. This was insanity. Surely someone would wake up and see them.

The door opened a crack. A woman looked and then swung it open.

"Peter!" she said in a hushed voice, thrusting her arms around him.

Garrett followed Peter inside. The woman was kissing the teen on his cheeks and forehead. She began to cry.

"God has answered my prayer," she whispered to Peter. "I was there when your parents died in the snow. I prayed over them, but they took you before I could find you. They told me you were in Moscow with your grandfather. Now God has sent you here to me."

Peter smiled.

"We have to cross the border," Garrett said. "People are after us."

She removed a coat from her closet, slipping it over her nightclothes. "My car is outside. There's a place you can cross without being seen."

Thirty-Six

Thomas Jefferson Kim and Valerie Mayberry were waiting when Brett Garrett landed at Joint Base Andrews, south of Washington, D.C. Garrett had never felt so grateful to be home.

"What happened to your arm?" he asked when he saw Kim on the tarmac wearing a sling.

"I got shot. I can still use a keyboard, but I can't drive."

"Thank God," Garrett said, chuckling.

Kim's wife, Rose, was waiting next to the couple's Mercedes SUV.

"She's my new driver," Kim beamed. "I taught her."

Garrett noticed she was wearing a Glock 21 around her waist.

"She's my new bodyguard, too," Kim added. "I taught her to shoot."

"Swell," Garrett said skeptically.

He addressed Mayberry as the two of them slipped into the SUV's rear seats. "We meeting Harris?"

"Nope," she replied, "he's still on Capitol Hill trying to save his job."

"What's that about? I've been a bit preoccupied," Garrett replied.

From the front seat, Kim elaborated, "Senator Stone introduced a motion to officially censure Harris. Vote is tomorrow. Because of Maxi-Leaks—at least that's the official version. Apparently, Ambassador Duncan told Stone about you being in Moscow and Stone's furious at Harris for not informing the Senate about Pavel and you."

"What's Maxi-Leaks got to do with any of that?" Garrett asked.

Mayberry caught him up as Rose Kim wove through the evening rush hour toward IEC's Tysons Corner building.

"Marcus Austin was recalled from Moscow," Mayberry said. "He's supposed to be on leave pending a disciplinary hearing, but Harris has him handling the three of us—still off the grid—at least for now."

"That's a gutsy move, especially if Stone has my scent," Garrett noted.

"And a move that I'm not happy with," Mayberry added. "It's time to bring the FBI in on this."

"Until you called," Kim said, abruptly changing subjects, "we thought you were dead. Show him the emailed videos, Valerie."

Mayberry used her cell phone to play the recordings that the Magician had sent. Garrett relived watching Pavel being gassed and seeing Peter and himself being held as prisoners.

"I was planning your funeral," Rose Kim chirped, as she drove. "No expenses spared, right, husband?"

"Sorry to disappoint," Garrett said.

Kim turned his head so he could face Garrett in the rear seat. "I'm still trying to positively identify the Magician. I know he operates out of Moscow and I'm almost certain he works for GIT because of his computer skills and embassy access."

Rose Kim honked at a slow-moving car and darted around it, cursing in Korean. "I taught her to swear," Kim bragged, grinning.

"When Gromyko was at the poison factory, he said he was coming to America," Garrett said.

"Ivan Sokolov's private jet landed at Reagan National three days ago, before you surfaced alive,"

Mayberry said. "Sokolov only stayed long enough to drop off General Gromyko and a Russian named Boris Petrov, whom we've identified as Gromyko's bodyguard."

"Gromyko must have been carrying the poisonous gas—the variant of his perfect Devil's Breath," Garrett said. "He and Sokolov talked about it at the Kamera just before Gromyko murdered Pavel."

"Which brings me back to my earlier comment. We need to get the FBI involved if Gromyko brought gas in," Mayberry said. "Gromyko and Petrov used their diplomatic passports, so their luggage wasn't checked. Fortunately, the bureau routinely follows high-ranking Russians when they enter the country, especially someone such as General Gromyko."

"Where'd he go?" Garrett asked. "If he had the poison, he wouldn't want to hang on to it for long."

"Directly to the former Soviet embassy," Mayberry replied. "It's right down the street from—"

"The White House," Garrett said, completing her sentence.

"The Russian ambassador just happened to be throwing a party for a who's who of Russian bootlickers. Lots of cars entering and exiting at the same time. Lots of guests, including this one," Mayberry said.

She handed him a photo of a man wearing a long

jacket, hat, and sunglasses—even though it was night when the FBI surveillance photo was taken.

"No one had seen him there before," Mayberry continued, "so I asked Homeland Security for a background check. Turns out his name is Mirzo Rakhmon, and he entered the United States on the same morning as Gromyko—only in Philadelphia and using a Tajikistan passport. The FBI was able to ID everyone else attending the embassy party."

Garrett studied the photo. "There is no Mirzo Rakhmon from Tajikistan," he said. "He's shaved his beard and probably cut off his hair under the hat. I'm guessing he's also done something to his face—maybe a fake nose. But I recognize him from Moscow."

"Moscow? Who is he?" Mayberry asked.

"Krishma Duwar. I met him at the ambassador's daughter's birthday party and I'm guessing he's the Magician who's been intercepting messages."

"So they flew into different cities but met at the embassy party," Mayberry said. "That's where Gromyko must have passed the gas to him."

Rose Kim laughed loudly, causing Mayberry to pause. "I don't see what's funny about that."

Her husband said, "You said Gromyko passed gas."

Garrett smiled. Mayberry didn't. "Gromyko wouldn't have wanted anyone from Antifa coming to the Russian embassy to get the canister," Mayberry said. "He'd want to cover his tracks."

They arrived at the IEC headquarters underground parking garage. On the elevator ride to Kim's office, Mayberry said, "I don't think we have a choice now. I'm going to call Marcus Austin. He's got to alert my bosses at the FBI. If he doesn't, I will."

"Hold on," Garrett said. "Harris is still in charge, and he won't like it. Not when he's lobbying for his job. If Senator Stone finds out what is happening, Harris will be done."

"Since when do you care about Harris?" Mayberry asked.

"I wasn't thinking about Harris," Garrett replied. "I was thinking about the three of us. So far, Harris is the only one who knows what we've done. He's betrayed me before, remember? He'll do it again and blame us if it saves his own neck."

"You're worried he'll blame you for Pavel's death, aren't you?" Mayberry asked.

"Have you done anything for Harris that would best be kept secret?" he retorted.

Mayberry thought about the Stonewall Jackson Shrine bombing. Aysan Rivera's murder.

"How about this," Kim interjected. "We tell Austin about Duwar and insist the FBI is told, but make it clear that it's up to him and Harris to decide what and how much."

Kim glanced at Mayberry. "That makes sense," she said. "You in, Garrett?"

"Make the call," he responded. "Duwar entered the country using a fake passport. That's enough to get him arrested. No need to mention the poison gas and cause a panic."

"That's ridiculous," Mayberry said. "Austin and Harris have to tell the FBI about the gas. They'll have to know what they're facing when they catch him."

"The only reason you know about the gas is because I saw Gromyko use it and heard him talk about bringing it here. We can't even be certain Gromyko transported it here and passed it to him," Garrett said.

"I'm not going to put Americans' lives in danger, especially law enforcement," Mayberry said in a harsh voice. "You have no authority here, Garrett. You've completed the mission that Harris gave you. Your only role was to get Pavel and Peter out of Russia. You're done."

"You saying I failed?"

"I'm saying your job is over. Let me do mine."

"I don't think you have the power to fire me," he said. "I'll say when I'm done."

Hoping to end their argument, Kim asked, "What about Peter? What did you do with the teen?"

Garrett turned his gaze away from Mayberry. "The agency's put him in London for safekeeping."

When the elevator doors opened, all of them except Rose moved into Kim's office. Kim began a computer search for information about Duwar while Mayberry telephoned Marcus Austin. When she finished speaking to him, she said, "Austin will talk to Harris. He agrees that we have to inform the FBI, but he said Harris will only want to disclose that Duwar is a suspected terrorist possibly carrying poison gas. No background."

"Duwar is going to need help if he wants to inflict maximum damage releasing the gas," Garrett said.

"Makayla Jones," Mayberry replied. "We know the two of them are working together. Duwar helped her ambush us by sending fake emails.

"She won't hesitate to use that gas and, yes, she will want to kill as many Americans as she can."

"What's their target?" Kim asked. "It could be anywhere on the East Coast."

"Washington," Mayberry said. "Either here or Baltimore, another city Makayla apparently knows well."

"The Kamera scientists killed Pavel by releasing it in the air," Garrett said, thinking out loud.

"Airborne," Mayberry agreed. "The poison would be most effective in an enclosed area, not FedEx Field or on the National Mall."

"MGM's new casino would be packed with people," Kim volunteered. "Maybe a Smithsonian museum or maybe the Verizon Center downtown."

"The subway. Metro Center," Mayberry said. "A major hub would hold the gas longer and possibly spread it like blood through veins. Union Station would be a smart choice, too. Easy to access. Lots of people."

"What if Gromyko's priority is not killing numbers but killing prominent targets?" Garrett asked.

"The White House is too closely guarded," Mayberry replied.

"I just pulled up Duwar's records," Kim said. "His parents are both respected professors teaching in Islamabad. Duwar is the oldest of five children, all successful—doctors, lawyers, professors. He's the only one who didn't return home after getting educated here. He came over on a student visa, did his undergrad work at Stanford in computer science—"

"Wait," Mayberry said.

Kim and Garrett looked at her. "On the night when we were ambushed, you said Makayla Jones's real name was Nataniela Kalanga, but she'd changed it to Adalene

Petit after she slipped into France and then she came to the U.S. on a student visa to attend *Stanford*."

"That's got to be where they met," Garrett concluded.

"Leftist cells have been popular on California campuses for decades," Mayberry said.

A quick knock. Rose Kim entered the room. "A Delaware state trooper just gave a speeding ticket to a driver in a rental car whose passport identified him as Mirzo Rakhmon," she said.

"How'd you know?" Mayberry said. "I doubt if Austin or Harris has had time to tell the FBI to put out an APB."

"I added his name to the thousands of databases IEC routinely monitors," Rose Kim explained. "He was stopped minutes ago driving north."

Thomas Jefferson Kim said, "I can pull the car's license tag off that ticket. Rental cars have tracking devices."

"Delaware," Garrett repeated. "Maybe the target isn't Washington. Maybe it's Manhattan."

"I'm going after him," Mayberry said. "My car's downstairs."

Garrett didn't ask. He simply followed her.

Thirty-Seven

"What'd Rose Kim slip you as we were leaving her husband's office?" Mayberry asked.

She and Garrett were riding north on Interstate 95, having just passed through Baltimore. He didn't realize she'd noticed the handoff. The best way to avoid a question was to ask one, especially one that irks your inquisitor.

"Kim read your medical records," Garrett said. "Told me you have ADHD."

"So much for doctor-patient confidentiality," she said, clearly irritated.

"You're OCD, too," he said.

"I've never been diagnosed with OCD. That's not in my medical records."

"It's more of a personal observation."

Mayberry tightened her grasp on the Jaguar's leather-wrapped steering wheel.

"With those issues, how'd you get into the bureau?" he asked.

"With your issues, how'd you get into the Navy?" she shot back.

"Just making small talk."

"You must be really fun on first dates."

"Nobody wants to date SEALs," he said. "Not after they find out what the pay and schedules are like."

"Oh, and people hear FBI and can't wait to get to know you."

"Your late husband, what'd he think about you joining the bureau?"

"That wasn't in my file? I've asked fewer personal questions in a criminal interrogation. You want to share personal information? Why'd your fiancée dump you after Cameroon?"

He turned his head. Glanced out the passenger window.

"I was in Leavenworth. She couldn't see a future with a dishonorably discharged ex-con."

His voice was sad, and for a second, she wished she'd not asked. But only for a second.

He checked the F-type's center console navigation screen. They were approaching Delaware.

"Why'd you marry him? Your late husband," he asked.

"I loved him. Why else?"

"What was he like?"

"Nothing like you."

"Ha, I already guessed that. You're not my type, Mayberry. You'd be a challenge to live with."

"I'm sure your fiancée had lots of reasons besides you being an ex-con to leave."

He ignored the slight.

"My husband was a voyeur. They all are—reporters. I intrigued him. My job intrigued him. He was writing a story about the FBI when we first met. I refused to talk to him. That was like blood in the water for a shark."

"I'm guessing he married you for your money."

"Why do you have to be so insulting?" she asked. "But no, that wasn't a factor. Noah didn't care about money. What attracted him was crawling into other people's skins. The more complicated, the better. I used to say he was fascinated by others' lives because it kept him from having to examine his own. And he was much better than you at asking questions so he could dodge answering them. What did Rose Kim give you?"

"Every man wants a rich wife. Only rich people say money doesn't matter and the truth is, it usually matters most. Tell me, Mayberry, where does being rich, really rich, start nowadays—ten million, fifty million? Three hundred million?"

"The reason I find you irritating, Garrett, has nothing to do with your bank account."

"We're talking about your husband, not me. Or does asking questions about him make you uncomfortable?"

"Does me asking you about Rose Kim and what she gave you make you uncomfortable?"

She downshifted and pulled into the E-ZPass lane to enter the New Jersey Turnpike.

She said, "Noah made everyone feel as if they were the most fascinating person he'd ever met when he interviewed them, rather than verbally waterboarding them like you do. Are you going to answer my question or keep avoiding it?"

"I've never been accused of being a smooth talker," Garrett said. "I'll give you that."

"Since we're making comparisons, I used to wonder how he could get people to share their innermost secrets and then write a story using those secrets that totally eviscerated them."

"Cold. But that's what reporters do."

"Like I said, a voyeur. Not a stayer. He met people, heard their stories, and moved on."

"He married you, didn't he? Stayed on?"

"Yes."

But she didn't elaborate, and he'd expected a more definitive reply. Indignant even.

"You did love him, right?" Garrett pried.

"Yes, but that is none of your business."

For several moments, they watched the scenery in silence.

"When we got back to camp in Afghanistan," Garrett said, "reporters would run up, stick a microphone in our faces. 'What's it like?' I never commented."

"Noah would have gotten you to comment."

"No, he wouldn't have. I'm sure he was as good as you claimed, but that's not it. How do you describe what happens when you're in the suck? What we did? What we saw? War is not something you can understand unless you experience it. Ever play craps? It's the difference between watching someone gambling and being the guy who puts his entire paycheck on the line, knowing he's not going to eat for a week or maybe a month. Only in war, it's not money that's at risk. It's coming home in a body bag."

"Noah was blown to bits in a helicopter that he never should have boarded," she said angrily. "He understood war, even if he didn't carry a gun."

Her face was flush.

"With all your money, Mayberry," he said quietly,

"why aren't you sitting on some island drinking piña coladas working on your tan and painting your toenails? Did your husband figure you out? Crawl into your skin?"

"I don't drink piña coladas. I don't want skin cancer. I pay someone else to give me a pedicure. And your last question is none of your business."

Again, neither spoke. This time for several minutes and then she said quietly, "I'm not a rabbit."

"A rabbit?"

"That's how people the likes of Gromyko and Kalugin see our world. There are those who get eaten and those who eat them. And then there are those of us who protect the rabbits from being eaten. With all my money and flaws, that's who I am. That's what Noah finally understood when he got into my skin. I care about other people."

She continued staring straight ahead.

"I see that," he said. "Suboxone." The word came out so quickly, his admission seemed to surprise even him. "That's what Rose Kim gave me. I have an opioid addiction. Got hooked after being burned in Cameroon. The Navy, hell, it didn't care when I was recovering. Didn't care when I was in Leavenworth. Vicodin, OxyContin, Percocet, Opana. At first it was for physical pain."

"What about now?" she asked. "I have a right to know if we continue to work together."

Her cell rang. She pushed a button on her car's steering wheel answering it.

"Duwar's rental car is parked at the Thirtieth Street Station in Philly," Kim said over the Jaguar's speakers. "I hacked into the rail station's surveillance system. Footage of him boarding a northbound train."

"No one ever inspects bags on a train," Garrett said.

"Get the bureau to stop the train," Mayberry said.

"Not so simple. New Jersey Transit. The train he boarded already has made several local stops. Most of those stops don't have security cameras. I informed Marcus, and he relayed the information to Sally North, at the bureau. They're all over this. Austin said that Harris wants both of you to turn around and come back. He wants to minimize your involvement."

"I'm FBI," Mayberry replied. "Where are they setting up?"

"Penn Station," Kim said.

"They'll need someone who has seen Duwar's face to ID him," Garrett said.

"My car's GPS says we'll get to Penn Station by—"

Kim interrupted her. "I'm tracking you on my computer. Actually, I've been listening to your conservation since you left."

"What the—" Mayberry stammered.

"Intercepting conversations is an IEC specialty," Kim replied. "And your little tête-à-tête has been most entertaining." They heard a woman giggle. Rooe must have been with Kim.

"Penn Station is the busiest rail hub in the country," Mayberry said, ignoring his comments. Her memory bank of details was kicking in. "More than six hundred and fifty thousand passengers go through there every day. That's more than all three major airports combined. A needle in a haystack."

"What's this Jag do?" Garrett asked. "Aren't FBI agents immune to speeding tickets?"

Few trains were entering Penn Station when they arrived shortly before midnight. It was swarming with heavily armed law enforcement officers. Mayberry found Sally North at the bureau's makeshift command center.

"What's the latest on Duwar?" Mayberry asked.

"Who's Duwar?" North replied. "Do you mean Mirzo Rakhmon?"

Mayberry realized that neither Director Harris nor Marcus Austin had disclosed Rakhmon's actual name or past.

North said, "We didn't let the train Rakhmon boarded in Philly stop here. Kept it going north out of the city and then side-railed it. No sign of him when our teams boarded."

"Any luck with surveillance cameras along the route?" Mayberry asked.

"No, we don't know where or when he got off. Our people are walking the tracks right now in case he jumped when the train was pulling into this station. Twenty-one separate rail lines. Seven tunnels. It would help if the agency was sharing information. They won't say a damn thing except that Rakhmon is a suspected terrorist who entered the country illegally and could have a bomb or some kind of poisonous gas with him."

For the first time, North noticed Garrett standing a few steps behind Mayberry. "You're the last person we need here," North said, glaring at him.

Garrett didn't reply.

North said, "Get him out of here. You, too. We don't need the heat. Go back to Washington. I never saw either of you, and this conversation never happened."

An hour outside Manhattan traveling South on the New Jersey Turnpike, Mayberry received a text. She was no longer on loan to the CIA.

"It's over," she said. "Kim, you, and me. Marcus Austin has been escorted from agency headquarters, put on indefinite leave pending a criminal investigation. I've already been reassigned."

"What about Harris?"

"He's still hanging on. The Senate votes later this morning on whether to censure him."

She smacked the top of the steering wheel and cursed.

"We should stop in Baltimore for pancakes," Garrett said.

"What?"

"I know a place."

Thirty-Eight

Pancakes.

Brett Garrett lifted one and slid two sunny-side-up eggs between the top cake and the one underneath it, creating his own sandwich. He stabbed the center of the short stack with a fork, piercing the trapped yokes until yellow oozed out.

Mayberry watched. She'd separated her cheese omelet so no part of it was touching the mixed fruit that she'd ordered with it.

"It all ends up in the same place," he said, taking his first bite. "And it's better than MREs."

He'd realized during their return ride that he'd not eaten since his flight from Finland. There'd been no time. Besides being hungry, Garrett wanted time to think. Duwar. Gromyko. Makayla Jones. Devil's

Breath. Its deadly variant. Potential targets. New York's Penn Station. It was a lot to process, and for some reason, something didn't feel right.

Mayberry had followed his directions to a local eatery only because she was in no rush to report back to the FBI for debriefing. She'd turned off Interstate 95 and traveled down side streets until they'd reached a building with a weathered exterior and billboard that proclaimed it served Baltimore's best breakfast. A hand-printed sign inside read: "Cash Tip's Pleas."

"They misspelled *please* and don't need an apostrophe" Mayberry noted from her seat opposite him in a well-worn booth. "Someone should tell them."

"It's been that way since this place opened." He took another bite.

Mayberry's eyes took inventory. Tired 1970s décor. Every booth filled. Customers hurrying in to pick up takeout orders. A silver bell above the door that dinged each time it opened—something Garrett appeared to block out but that was irritating her.

"I don't like being reassigned," she said. "Duwar, Makayla—they are still out there. No one is going after Antifa."

A seventy-something, white-haired woman armed with a coffeepot appeared.

"How's life treating you, Della?" Garrett asked.

"You mean 'mistreating me,'" she answered. "My arthritis is killing me, and Joe is getting harder to live with, but we can't close this dump and move to Florida because people like you keep coming in. Hey, sweetie, you wanna run off to Daytona with me? I'm a pretty nice catch, you got to admit."

"Yes, you are, Della. Maybe tomorrow," he replied. "My colleague here says you misspelled *please* on your sign."

"Is that right?" She turned and hollered toward an opening where prepared food from the kitchen was placed under heat lamps until it was picked up. "Joe, got a gal here says we can't spell right."

"R-I-G-H-T," a man wearing a paper chef's hat yelled through the opening.

Mayberry heard chuckles from the regulars perched on the counter stools and seated in booths.

Refilling their cups, Della said to Mayberry, "This one with you, he's not too clever, but he is damn easy on the eyes." She winked at Garrett and sauntered off to another booth.

"How come you know so much about this place?" she asked.

"I like pancakes."

The television screen positioned above and behind his head caught her eye.

"You need to see this," she said in a quiet but alarmed voice, glancing upward. He turned and read the moving caption. *Deadly shootout. Suspected terrorist fatally shot by police.*

The volume was set too low for them to hear, but the video showed everything. A SWAT team approached a suspect in the early-morning darkness outside a tiny brick rail station in Morristown, New Jersey, west of New York City. A commuter line. The man pulled a pistol, fired, was shot dead on the train platform. Two men in hazmat suits carefully removed a briefcase from his grasp.

"That's Krishma Duwar!" she said. "Now I have a good reason to get to headquarters." She pushed her plate aside. "To hell with Harris. I'm telling them about Makayla Jones, Antifa, the bombing, and Rivera's murder. If I have to go down, then so be it."

"Why?" Garrett asked, returning to his pancakes. "If Duwar has the gas, it's over."

"How can you sit here and say that based on everything you know, everything I know?"

"Think about it. No one wants to hear what we got to say." He forked another piece of pancake and rubbed it on the bleeding egg yolk smeared on his plate.

"That's not true. You need to tell the bureau what happened in Russia."

He put down his fork. "No, I don't," he said sternly. "The CIA doesn't want anyone to know I failed to smuggle a diplomat out of Russia. That's hardly an inducement for others to defect and not something I'm proud of. The Russians will deny Kamera exists anyway, which is what they have been doing since Stalin. And the White House doesn't want to admit its CIA director went off the grid and hid information from the president and Congress. It's easier for everyone to think that Duwar was a lone Pakistani terrorist. It's over, Mayberry, and you shooting off your mouth is just going to make everything worse—for all of us."

"You saw Gromyko murder Pavel. You can prove the Russians are involved. I know about Antifa and Makayla Jones. I know she blew up the shrine, murdered Rivera."

"The entire reason Harris chose me was so if things went bad in Russia, he'd have a scapegoat. You talk, and he'll paint me as some crazed lone wolf. You talk, and he'll find a way to blame you, too. Listen to me. I know Harris, and he will crucify us both if you talk."

"Kim will back us up. He'll go against Harris. He'll tell the truth, and he's not done anything wrong."

"You don't know that. Listen, Kim is my best friend, actually my only real friend, but his entire company depends on government contracts, and you don't know what he might have done for Harris in the past. I'm not going to destroy what he's built by telling everyone about Kamera. The same is true about Peter; he's had enough misery in his life and mentioning him will only make him a target. President Kalugin will hunt him down and kill him. Do you want his blood on your hands?"

She slid from the booth. "We have to tell the truth even if the White House, Harris, and the Kremlin don't want us to—even if you don't want me to. Because it's the truth and Makayla Jones and Antifa are still out there."

She looked down at him. "I thought more of you, Garrett."

She was walking toward the door when her phone rang. She answered, listened, and spun around, hurrying to the booth. "Kim has found something we need to see. We need to go right now."

Neither spoke until Mayberry turned off the Capital Beltway and entered the District.

"I thought we were going to Kim's Tysons Corner office," Garrett said suspiciously. "This isn't some stupid scheme by you to take me to agency headquarters, is it?"

"No," she replied. "He's meeting us at the Capitol Visitor Center."

When they reached it, she said, "They won't let us inside with our guns. We'll have to leave them in the trunk."

Kim was waiting in the lower-level restaurant. His right knee bounced up and down nervously. He waved as soon as he spotted them entering Emancipation Hall.

Opening a file folder, he said, "While you two were chasing Duwar, I've been digging into his past. We already knew that he and Makayla Jones were at Stanford together—which I overlooked because she was enrolled as a French exchange student under the name Adalene Petit."

He put a photo from the *Stanford Daily*—the university's student-run newspaper—on the table. It showed an academic dean presenting an award to six students. Krishma Duwar was in the photograph, but Makayla Jones aka Adalene Petit wasn't.

"Duwar was a member of the college's honors fraternity," Kim said as he removed a second photo from his file. It was another university newspaper photograph, only it showed masked demonstrators vandalizing a campus police car.

Kim pointed at a masked man standing on the car's roof, waving an Antifa flag—a red, white, and black banner with the German words ANTIFASCHISTISCHE AKTION printed on it.

"What are you seeing that I'm not?" Mayberry asked. "Duwar isn't in this second photo."

"How can you be certain?" Garrett asked. "The protestors are all wearing masks."

"Because everyone has white hands. Duwar is Pakistani," she said.

"That's exactly right," Kim said, obviously pleased. "Now look at the fingers of the man waving the Antifa flag."

Mayberry and Garrett did, and still didn't understand Kim's point.

"His ring," Kim added. He produced a third photo—an enlargement of a gold ring visible on the demonstrator's little finger.

"Men wear pinkie rings?" Garrett asked.

"It's a signet ring," Mayberry said, correcting him. "Or, more precisely, a 'gentleman's ring' and, yes, they've been around since Old Testament days."

"Rich kids like them," Kim interjected. "They're a fad."

He rearranged his photos, placing the ski-masked protestor next to the honors award picture. The nexus—the gold signet ring.

"The student in the honors photo standing next to Duwar is the same student waving the Antifa flag," Kim said. "You can tell it's him because he's wearing the same ring in both photos. Do you see it?"

"Yes," Garrett said. "So who is he?"

Kim pulled a final photograph from his file. It showed the same man from the award photo—only now he was older and wearing a suit and tie while posing for an identification badge.

"This is a head shot from the U.S. Capitol Police database. The honor student and Antifa protestor wearing his signet ring is Terrance Collins. Currently employed by California senator Cormac Stone as his legislative director."

"Oh my God!" Mayberry gasped, making a connection. "I saw Makayla Jones leave the parking lot after the Smithmyer protest in a car with D.C. plates." She paused, remembering. "Aysan Rivera told me that Makayla had a connection high up on Capitol Hill. He's got to be Collins."

Suddenly all of the mismatched pieces came together in Garrett's mind. "We've been after the wrong man. Duwar is a red herring," he said. "They wanted us to follow him and assume he had the gas in his briefcase."

"I'll call the bureau and ask if they found the gas," Mayberry volunteered, reaching for her cell.

"Today's censure vote," Garrett said.

"Oh no," Mayberry cried.

"Senators are rarely in the chamber unless there's a critical vote," Kim said.

"They'll all be there," Mayberry said. She glanced at a wall clock in the restaurant. It was 9:48 a.m. "The Senate always convenes at ten a.m."

"I'm guessing the censure vote will be its first item," Kim said.

Mayberry started to dial Sally North's number at the bureau. Garrett reached over and pushed her hand away.

"No time for that," he said. "No one is going to believe you—especially Senator Stone. We don't have any real evidence. Just conjecture."

"He's right," Kim said. "You can't accuse one of Stone's top aides of being an Antifa terrorist based on the photos I've shown you."

"Makayla Jones," Mayberry said. "Terrance Collins would have Makayla get the nerve gas from Duwar. Collins wouldn't want to risk exposing himself by possibly being seen with Duwar. She'll take that risk and deliver it to him. But only at the last minute. She's got to be in the Capitol."

"You're right," Garrett said. "Makayla has to be here. She'd give it to him at the last possible moment."

Garrett started for the Senate chamber. Mayberry hurried to catch up.

Thirty-Nine

At one time, anyone who wished could walk onto the Senate floor. House members, foreign ambassadors, tycoons, as well as ordinary citizens. In 1859, the Senate stopped the free-for-all, limiting access to senators and their aides only.

Mayberry or Garrett knew they wouldn't get close to the second-floor chamber in the Capitol's north wing. So they talked their way past Capitol Hill officers to the third-floor visitors' gallery. It ringed the chamber, allowing spectators to peer down, as if in a coliseum.

"Sorry, all available visitor seats are occupied," a U.S. Capitol Police officer informed them at the balcony's entrance.

Mayberry flashed her badge. "FBI official business. It's urgent."

"If it's so urgent, why hasn't anyone told me about it?" the unimpressed guard replied. "You'll need a pass from a senator and, I already told you, it's full this morning."

"This badge is our pass," she persisted. "We don't have time for this."

"You got any idea how many federal employees try to use their badges to get by us when there's a historic vote?" he asked.

"Listen," she said sternly. "You need to call your supervisor. Senators' lives could be at stake."

He spoke into a microphone attached to his uniform near his neck. "Lieutenant, we need you to come to the entrance. I got an FBI agent who's demanding entry."

Mayberry whispered to Garrett. "I know of another way. You stay. Talk to this idiot's boss."

She walked around a corner and down a hallway to where a different U.S. Capitol Police officer was standing guard. As she neared him, she removed her wallet from her purse and opened it to the section where she kept credit cards. Good. It still was there.

Her husband had been an accredited member of the Senate and House press galleries. When Noah had left for Afghanistan, he'd left his credential on their bedroom bureau. After his death, she'd tucked it into her purse. Carrying that badge had been a reminder. A tiny piece of him. She placed her thumb over the ID's photo and quickened her step.

There was a time when the third-floor press gallery entrance had been unguarded. That was before the 9/11 terrorist attacks and the swelling of Internet bloggers and social media publications. Who was a legitimate journalist? A "standing committee of correspondents" made that call, composed mostly of reporters working for major newspapers. She approached the door holding the color-coded ID, stepping behind two harried *New York Times* reporters hurrying by the guard. He waved all three of them through.

The room contained rows of cubicles. As she navigated her way to the door that opened into the Senate press gallery, she caught the eye of the press room's director, who was responsible for overseeing the day-to-day operations. Unlike the officer at the gallery's entrance, he prided himself on recognizing every reporter who covered Capitol Hill. He began walking toward her as she ducked through a door into the chamber.

Mayberry found herself standing at the top of stadium-style seating on the third-floor balcony directly above the Senate dais where the presiding officer sat. From her vantage point, she could see all one hundred

Senate desks arranged in a semicircle. A wide center aisle divided the members of the two political parties. Republicans facing the dais were on her right, Democrats on her left. The most senior and powerful members sat closest to the dais. The president pro tempore—the ranking senator from the majority party—was running today's proceedings.

Senator Stone was sitting at his front-row desk patiently waiting for the morning's business to be called. The Senate chaplain already had given the opening prayer, and the Pledge of Allegiance had been recited. Stone was glancing over written remarks.

Mayberry didn't see his legislative aide, Terrance Collins. She eyeballed the visitors' gallery across from her.

Makayla Jones. A front-row seat. How had she gotten there? The answer was obvious. Collins had secured it for her. She would want to be present to ensure he delivered the case. Didn't lose his nerve.

Mayberry followed Makayla's eyes. She was looking down into the chamber. Terrance Collins had just entered at the back of the Senate floor.

Athletic, handsome, nearly forty, dressed like a successful Wall Street equity partner. Mayberry checked his fingers. The same signet ring. On his pinkie. He was carrying a briefcase, walking toward Senator Stone's desk.

He casually placed the briefcase next to Stone's feet, briefly chatted with his boss, and then turned to exit. He'd left the case behind!

"Madame." A stern voice behind Mayberry. The press gallery director. "Madame," he repeated louder. She felt his fingers take hold of her left bicep. "Please step back into the press gallery and show me your badge. We don't want a scene, do we?"

Mayberry checked for Brett Garrett across from her in the visitors' gallery. He still hadn't gotten into the balcony.

Outside the gallery, Garrett calculated the odds of getting by the four U.S. Capitol Police officers stationed between him and the gallery doorway. Smile. Rush them. Garrett clenched his fists.

A ding. The sound of the elevator behind him. Its doors opening. A man's voice. Sounded strangely familiar.

"Where's the FBI agent causing a ruckus?" the officer asked.

Garrett turned around. Faced him.

"Holy crap!" the lieutenant exclaimed. "Brett Garrett."

"Bear," Garrett said, his face becoming a huge

grin at the sight of his former SEAL buddy. "How'd you get in charge?"

"After Cameroon knocked me out of the Navy, I got hired here." He opened his mouth wide. "Like my fake choppers. Cost the government a fortune."

Garrett noticed the scar on Bear's cheeks where projectiles from a jihadist's suicide vest had penetrated his face.

"We never talked," Garrett said. "That night—"

"Chief, you made the right call, rescuing those little girls. We're solid. Now tell me, why are you trying to bulldoze your way into my gallery?"

"Chasing a terrorist," Garrett said, lowering his voice. "A woman. Thirties. Think she's inside. Goes by the name Makayla Jones."

The officer listening to them checked a list. "Sir," he said, "no one named Makayla Jones has a guest pass."

"She would have gotten it from Senator Cormac Stone's staff," Garrett said.

"Four passes from Senator Stone's office, but no one with that name."

Bear said, "Chief, you know if Stone looked up in the gallery and saw your face, there'd be hell to pay. I'd lose my job."

"We're brothers," Garrett said.

"Don't go there, Chief. It was different then."

"You trusted me with your life. If there's a terrorist inside and I believe there is, people—senators—are going to die."

Bear sucked in a deep breath. Took a moment to decide. "One quick look. You and me. Then we're out. You got it?"

Garrett followed Bear to the door.

That's when they both heard a woman scream.

A scene? That's exactly what Valerie Mayberry wanted.

She twisted her arm loose from the grasp of the press gallery director and hurried down the five steps to the balcony's lip. She threw herself over and screamed as she fell.

Mayberry hit the chamber floor hard and immediately fell forward onto the blue carpet in front of the dais. Pushing herself onto her knees, she thrust her FBI badge above her head and yelled, "FBI! Bomb! Run!"

For an instant, no one moved. The entire chamber was completely spellbound. Silent. Startled.

"Terrorist bomb!" she screamed.

A Senate page kneeling at the edge of the dais was the first to bolt up the center aisle. Senate clerks seated behind a long marble table at the dais abandoned their posts. The presiding senator rushed from his high-backed chair. Within seconds, a human stampede jammed the exits and blocked the U.S. Capitol Police officers stationed outside, keeping them from entering the chamber. Mayberry stood and hurried toward the briefcase.

At the visitors' gallery doorway, Bear yelled, "We got a jumper!"

Followed by his men, he rushed to a stairway that led down to the second floor.

Garrett shoved his way through the frightened spectators fleeing the gallery. Only one visitor made no attempt to escape.

Makayla Jones. She'd unbuttoned her blouse. Removed a clear plastic mask shaped to hide over a bra cup and a tiny plastic tube containing oxygen hidden in her ample cleavage. Several minutes of safe air. She saw Garrett coming.

Down below them, Valerie Mayberry had reached the briefcase. Lifted it from the floor. Placed it on Senator Stone's wooden desk. The clasps were locked. She ran her fingers over the case's top. Along the case's sides. There. She felt it! A dime-size hole on its upper left side. She pressed her forefinger against it. Pressed hard. Covering it.

Makayla had been forced to leave her phone and other personal items outside the gallery, but the officers had not taken her Apple Watch. She pressed an app and immediately covered her mouth with her home-made oxygen mask.

Mayberry felt pressure against her left forefinger. The poison. Trying to escape. She pressed harder on the hole, successfully keeping the gas from bursting out.

Makayla had expected the gas to be expelled. She saw Mayberry's finger over the hole. Lowering her gas mask, she straddled the balcony's barrier. Just like Mayberry, she was about to jump down onto the Senate floor.

Garrett reached her as she let loose of the railing. Reaching forward, he grabbed her left wrist. She was too heavy for him to pull back but he held on to her long enough to snatch the oxygen mask from her grasp before she fell.

Makayla landed on a Senate desk. A crack. Instant pain. A snapped bone. Compound fracture. She forced herself upright and moved from one desk to the next supporting herself, making her way toward Mayberry. Even though they both would be poisoned, she was intent on prying Mayberry's fingers off the case's escape hole, freeing the gas.

Garrett started to leap over the balcony but realized it was too late. Makayla would reach Mayberry first. A thought. A desperate move. He balled up the mask and tube that he'd taken from Makayla. Rocket arm. That's what his high school baseball teammates had called him. Deadly accurate. Capable of throwing a hardball at nearly a hundred miles per hour. Cocking back his arm, Garrett heaved the mask and its plastic tube of oxygen.

It smacked onto the top of Senator Stone's desk and slid off onto the carpet. Mayberry bent forward, scooped it up with her free right hand while carefully keeping her left finger pressed against the case's hole, preventing the gas from escaping.

Makayla was within a foot of her now. She jutted out her hands to slap away Mayberry's finger from the opening. Mayberry lifted the case so its hole was aimed directly at Makayla. She slid her finger off the hole and then immediately covered it. A puff of red mist. Shot into Makayla's eyes.

Behind the oxygen mask covering her nose and mouth, Mayberry stared at Makayla. A look of sheer terror.

The Antifa leader fell onto the carpet. Her body shook. Her face was frozen in anger. A bit of blood trickled from her nose—until her heart stopped pumping. She was dead.

Bear burst into the chamber.

"Poison gas!" Garrett hollered from the gallery. "Stop. Get out!"

Bear pulled back, raised his arms, signaling the officers behind him. "Get hazmat!" he hollered, closing the chamber doors. "Everyone stay back. Evacuate!"

Mayberry glanced up into the balcony at Garrett.

He smiled at her. They'd done it. And then he saw something red coming from the bottom of the gas mask pressed against her face.

Blood.

Forty

G arrett rushed from the visitors' gallery using the same staircase that Bear had taken earlier to reach the second floor. The scene outside the Senate chamber was mayhem. Scrambling senators, staff, and visitors. A hazmat team was threading between them toward the closed Senate chamber's doors.

Garrett spotted Terrance Collins. Senator Stone's legislative aide returned his stare. Collins shoved people from his path and hurried to escape toward the heart of the Capitol—its domed, circular rotunda, nearly a hundred feet in diameter, soaring 180 feet from its marble floor to its interior peak.

Garrett gave chase. Once free of the mob, Collins broke into a run, distancing himself from Garrett. But the legislative aide stopped when he reached the rotunda's perimeter. Rather than hurrying through it, he turned to his immediate left and opened a door that normally was guarded. It was a staircase, which he began ascending until he reached a landing. He stopped and listened to hear if he had fooled Garrett.

He heard the stairway door below him open, shut. A man's footsteps. Collins was trapped. He had no choice but to climb the gradually narrowing stairs to the building's roof. Suddenly he encountered a Capitol Police officer descending the staircase.

Collins raised his Senate staff ID attached to a lanyard around his neck. "A terrorist—behind me! Coming up the stairs!"

The officer drew his Glock 22 and let Collins slip by him.

Garrett appeared moments later.

"Stop!" the officer hollered, aiming his .40-caliber weapon at Garrett's chest.

Garrett froze beneath him, raised both hands. In a calm voice, he said, "The Senate staffer who you just let by you is an Antifa terrorist."

The officer kept his gun pointed at Garrett.

"Call Bear," Garrett said, still standing two steps beneath the officer.

"Bear? Who are you, Goldilocks?"

"Your lieutenant, Jack Strong. We called him Bear when he was a Navy SEAL. Just call him on your radio. Tell him that I'm Brett Garrett."

Switching his Glock to his left hand, he raised his right to use the radio microphone positioned on his shirt to the side of his chin.

"Lieutenant Strong," he said, lowering his head, "got a guy here claiming he's pursuing a terrorist up to the roof." Pausing, he asked, "What'd you say your name was?"

"Brett Garrett."

The officer repeated it, but there was no response. Either the signal was weak inside the enclosed stairwell or too many Capitol Police officers were trying to communicate on the same channel. He tried again, but got no response.

"I don't know you," the officer said, "but I know the staffer who went up on the roof. I've seen him with Senator Stone. Let's you and me go down these stairs and let the lieutenant sort this out."

"He'll escape," Garrett warned. "He's trapped now. Try your radio again."

The officer was now holding his Glock with both hands, but he freed his right one to use his radio microphone. Garrett flew upward, catching the policeman by surprise, grabbing the officer's left wrist with both hands and stepping in front of him. He shoved the Glock upward, forcing the officer to twist his torso on the narrow stairs. He lost his balance and started to fall forward. As he did, he instinctively released his hold on his weapon. The officer fell past Garrett, landing on his face below him. Disarmed, he looked helplessly at Garrett, who was aiming the Glock at him.

"Go get help!" Garrett ordered.

Afraid to avert his eyes, the officer backed down the stairs watching the gun barrel.

The roof exit opened at the base of the giant Capitol dome. To protect the building's roof from damage, the door led to a raised platform with guardrails. That platform led to a four-foot-wide walkway that extended out to the Capitol's western front. This walkway also was elevated above the roof. It ended at a flagpole aligned with the center of the dome.

Terrance Collins was standing next to the flagpole with his left arm wrapped around the chest of a woman. A box cutter was in his right hand, its blade pressed against her neck. Garrett assumed she was an employee of the Architect of the Capitol Office, which was responsible for raising and lowering flags—more than three hundred per day on three poles atop the roof—a tradition that dated back to 1937, when a constituent asked his congressman for a souvenir flag that had flown above the Capitol.

"Give me the gun!" Collins shouted. The two men were about thirty feet from each other.

Garrett slowly stepped toward him.

The woman—in her midforties, straight brown hair, about five foot four and chubby—was crying. Collins tightened his arm around her chest and pressed the blade against her cheek.

"You got kids?" Collins asked his hostage. His mouth close to her ear. "Tell him you got kids."

The hostage tried to speak, but Collins was now squeezing her so tightly that she was having trouble breathing.

"No one needs to get hurt," Garrett said. "You want the gun—I'll give you the gun. I'll let you go. I don't care. Eventually, you'll be caught—or maybe you won't."

Garrett's willingness to cooperate seemed to confuse Collins.

"You're not in charge here," Collins shouted.

"You're right. You have the box cutter. But think about this. It was Makayla who released the gas, not you. D.C. doesn't have a death penalty."

"You think I'm stupid? The feds can execute me. Now, give me the gun and get off the walkway. Climb down onto the roof and lay down."

"No problem but the gun might go flying off the walkway if I slide it from here. Let me walk a few feet closer. You can tell me when to stop." Garrett turned the gun sideways in his hand. "First, I'm going to switch on the safety so it doesn't accidentally fire when I slide it. The safety switch is just above the grip."

Garrett started stepping forward. When he was about fifteen feet away, Collins yelled, "Stop! You're close enough! Slide it to me now!"

"Okay, calm down. I'm no hero," Garrett said. He bent down, placed the Glock on the walkway, and shoved it with his hand much like a shuffleboard disc. It stopped about two feet in front of Collins.

Still crouched, Garrett looked upward at the hostage's face. Her eyes rolled back. Without realizing it, Collins was choking her. Her legs went out from under her, catching him off guard. Collins shoved her sideways and reached down to grab the Glock.

Garrett bolted upward from his crouched position like a runner shooting from starting blocks. If Collins had lifted and fired the gun the moment he first grabbed it, he couldn't have missed Garrett. But he'd heard Garrett talking about a safety switch, and he fumbled with the handgun trying to find it.

The Glock model 22's safety was not on the side of the pistol. It was part of its trigger. By the time Collins realized he'd been misled, Garrett was within inches of hitting him. Collins fired the half-raised handgun.

The round pierced Garrett's right leg at a downward angle, splintering his tibia. But his momentum kept him flying forward. His shoulder slammed into Collins's chest, knocking the Senate staffer upward off his feet.

While guardrails edged the elevated walkway, no barriers encircled the flagpole. It was a three-foot drop from the flagpole platform to the slanted Capitol roof.

Collins tumbled backward and struck the parapet beneath him. He hit the barrier that ringed the western front of the majestic building with the back of his thighs. Waving his arms wildly, Collins continued falling backward over the building's edge.

Garrett watched Collins disappear from the rooftop. Despite the intense pain in his leg, he forced himself to crawl forward and fell clumsily headfirst from the flagpole platform onto the roof. Determined, he continued and pulled himself up on the parapet so that he could spy over it. Collins's body was splayed on the Capitol's marble landing in the same spot where recent presidents had been sworn into office.

Collins was dead.

Forty-One

"We're dealing with an unfamiliar toxin," Dr. Sandra Peabody, a nationally renowned poison expert at George Washington University Hospital, said.

Valerie Mayberry had been rushed to an emergency isolation unit at the hospital located six blocks from the White House. FBI director Archibald Davidson and Sally North were being briefed in a private waiting room about her tenuous condition.

"We're dealing with some weaponized organophosphate derivative," Dr. Peabody explained. "The same chemical structure backbone as other organophosphate pesticides used in agriculture, only modified to make it more deadly. Ms. Mayberry absorbed it through her skin."

"Skin contact is how Kim Jong Nam, half brother of North Korean leader Kim Jong Un, was murdered," Director Davidson volunteered.

"Yes, I helped advise his medical team. His attackers smeared his face with poison," Dr. Peabody replied. "Until now, we thought Novichok was the deadliest of nerve agents, but this new variation appears to be even more lethal, although it works much the same way. It binds itself to a receptor site in the brain where it disrupts cholinesterase, a type of enzyme needed for proper functioning of the nervous system. I've given Ms. Mayberry oxime; it's a nitrogen-containing chemical compound that we use as an antidote. It's designed to clean the binding site so the cholinesterase is liberated and can begin working again."

"Then she'll recover?" North asked in a hopeful voice.

"I really can't say at this point.," Dr. Peabody replied sadly. "This new variant appears to have been engineered to prevent our antidote from working. That's part of what makes it different from what we have seen before. As in all poisoning cases, the first step is immediate symptom management. And that is the protocol that we are attempting here."

Continuing, she said, "People poisoned with these types of nerve toxins essentially die because of secretions—vomiting, diarrhea, and urinary incontinence occurring all at once—and since Ms. Mayberry has been here, we've seen secretions begin. Luckily, we've reacted quickly. To stop them, we have given her high doses of atropine, a medicine derived from the belladonna plant, sometimes called 'deadly nightshade.' It works in two ways. It dries out secretions and increases the heart rate, which slows after exposure to a nerve agent. It buys us time to see if the oxime antidote will work."

"How long before you will know if the antidote is doing its job?" Davidson asked.

"This patient had a blood vessel in her nose break," Peabody said, ignoring his question. "That's uncommon in nerve agent poisonings such as this. We expect to see runny eyes, drooling, rapid breathing, diarrhea, confusion, nausea, but even with extreme exposure to poisons such as sarin—which has been one of the most widely used chemical weapons in recent times, especially in Syria—we have not seen bleeding noses. Whoever is responsible for creating this poison has added a new molecule."

"Is there a tipping point?" Davidson asked, slightly modifying his initial question.

"I know you want me to predict the outcome of our protocol. Tell you when she will get better or if our protocol is working. All I can tell you is we are doing everything possible and the next twenty-eight hours are critical. If she survives during this window, her chances of recovery are much greater. But even then, there is a high chance of permanent damage. She could be paralyzed, unable to speak, lose her memory."

The doctor shifted her eyes from Davidson to North. "If you want to help and you are religious, I'd suggest you begin praying."

"One of my people will be staying here twenty-four/ seven," Davidson said. "Please keep him informed so he can relay messages to us."

"I've been told that her parents are flying in from Greenwich with their own specialist to assist you," North said. "I'll be dispatching my people to the air-port to bring them here."

"Always willing to consult," Dr. Peabody replied. "The more minds, the better. Now, I need to get back to my patient."

After she was gone, North said, "I'd like to speak to Valerie's parents when they arrive. We need to tell them about her bravery."

"Yes, I should speak to them, too," Davidson said. "Now, what about Brett Garrett?"

"The nurses said he's in surgery," North replied.

"Sally," Davidson said quietly, "this has the agen-cy's fingerprints all over it, and Director Harris has not been forthcoming about any of it. There will be dozens of investigations. When I got here, there were already reporters outside the hospital shouting questions. You need to find out what happened and assess the impact on the bureau. Do you have any idea what Agent Mayberry has been doing since she was detailed to Harris?"

"No, sir. I planned to debrief her this morning."

A knock. One of the director's aides. "Senator Stone is down the hall speaking to Dr. Peabody," he said. "The senator is asking where you are."

"Less said, the better," Davidson whispered to North, "until we get this sorted out."

Senator Stone joined them. "According to Dr. Peabody, the next twenty-eight hours are critical," he said. "I'm sorry. Please know I will be praying for her."

"Thank you," Davidson and North replied in unison.

Stone let out a loud sigh. "I've been told it was a staff member of mine who brought the poison into the Senate."

"Our people are already investigating," Davidson replied. "But, yes, that appears true."

"Terrance Collins. I don't understand. He never said or did a damn thing that hinted he was capable of this."

"We'll know more after Brett Garrett gets out of surgery," North said, "and we speak to him."

"Brett Garrett," Senator Stone repeated. "He and I seemed destined to encounter each other. I was told he was the one who chased Collins onto the roof." He shook his head. "For the life of me, I can't understand why a member of my office family would do something so horrific. I trusted him. I believed he was a good man and he tried to murder me and everyone else in the chamber."

"He would have succeeded except for Agent Mayberry and Garrett," Davidson said. "They're heroes."

"I know that!" Stone exclaimed. "What I don't know is how they came to be in the Senate this morning—and why they didn't warn anyone before then."

"Senator," Davidson said, "we're not sure. Perhaps Director Harris can answer those questions."

"Harris. He's up to his eyeballs in this disaster," the senator said bitterly. "It has his stench." The senator shook his head, pressed his lips together.

"What's our world coming to?" he continued. "An attack on the Senate floor. I just don't know anymore."

North thought she saw tears forming in the senator's eyes. He looked sad. Weary. Very much like a tired old man, not a proud Lord of the Senate.

"Please keep me informed about Agent Mayberry," he said softly, excusing himself.

———

As he left the private waiting room and walked toward the nurses' station and elevators, Senator Stone sought to regain his composure. He still had to face reporters waiting outside. They'd expect a statement. He was not yet ready. He asked the duty nurse where Brett Garrett was undergoing surgery.

The male nurse checked his computer and said, "I'll call you an escort, Senator. This building can be confusing." Looking up from his seat, the nurse noticed Senator Stone's sweat-covered face. "Sir, are you feeling okay?" he asked, rising from his chair. "Let me check your vitals."

"No, no, that will not be necessary," Stone replied. "Just get me that escort."

Garrett was still in surgery when Stone entered a private waiting room on a different hospital floor. "I'll get the chief surgeon to brief you as soon as the surgical team is finished," the escort said.

Pale green walls. Darker green carpet. Senator Stone noticed another man waiting. The stranger stood, approached him, but not with an outstretched hand.

"Why are you here?" Thomas Jefferson Kim demanded.

"And who are you?" Senator Stone replied. "A reporter?"

"I'm Brett Garrett's closest friend, and I've got something to tell you, Senator, that needs to be said."

His aggressive tone surprised Senator Stone.

"I fought side by side with Garrett," Kim said defensively. "I was critically wounded. He literally carried me out of a firefight. If it weren't for him, I wouldn't be here."

Stone started to interrupt, but Kim ignored him and kept talking.

"Some young people enlist because they want a way out of their hometowns, are looking for adventure, to travel, or want to learn a trade. Brett Garrett told me once why he joined, and it wasn't for any of those reasons. He made up his mind the day two commercial jets crashed into the twin towers. The day he watched Americans leaping to their deaths. He joined because he loves this country. He felt it was his duty. Laugh if you want. Call it blind patriotism. Call it naïve. But the America that he believes in and is willing to die for is not defined by ethnicity, heritage, or even birthright. His America is an ideal. That's what makes us different, isn't it? Freedom. Democracy. Equality. Our ideals? Those are not empty words to him and whenever his fellow Americans take their freedoms for granted, disparage America, disrespect its flag, anger wells inside him. That's because he genuinely believes we are living in that 'shining city upon a hill.' A city that has been bought with the blood of the thousands before him in that long gray line—the fallen on the Western Front, Omaha Beach, Imo Jima, the Yalu River, Khe Sanh, Khafji, and the Helmand Province.

"There's no ambiguity in him. He sees only white knights and black knights. Even after you stripped away his honor on national television, even after Director Harris lied about him and what happened in Cameroon, even after the Navy imprisoned him and dishonorably discharged him, Garrett's devotion to his country never waned because he believes America is not you or a bunch of Supreme Court judges or even the president. It is an ideal, and that's bigger than any of you. Blame him for your son's death if you want. Continue to hate him. But what happened today shows you who he is, and he's a hell of a better man than you or me."

Kim turned and marched back to his seat.

Senator Stone looked at Kim for several moments before leaving. As he rode the hospital's elevator to the lobby, his mind flashed back. Two years earlier. Hart Senate Office Building. Director Harris was testifying. Cameroon. Blaming Garrett. Refusing to take any responsibility for the deaths. His son. In his mind, Senator Stone saw himself leaning forward in his seat.

His voice rising. His temper flaring. He was scolding Director Harris.

"*Are you telling this committee that you are not responsible for the actions of the people under your command? What sort of leader makes such a statement?*"

The opening elevator doors snapped him back to reality. He walked slowly across the hospital lobby and through the glass doors to where security guards had corralled reporters and television crews. Questions were shouted. Nearly indistinguishable.

"Senator Stone! Senator Stone! Senator Stone!"

"Did your aide take gas into the Senate?"

"Why did Terrance Collins do it?"

"Was he trying to kill you or every senator?"

"Where'd he get it?

Senator Stone raised his hand to quiet them.

"I'm prepared to make a brief statement," he said. "I'll not be answering any questions."

He took a deep breath and felt tears welling in his eyes as he looked out at the camera lenses. Outstretched microphones. A sea of faces.

"After serving our great nation for forty-plus years," he said, "I've decided to retire."

Forty-Two

Russian president Vyachesian Kalugin entered the hash marks, skating at full speed directly toward the net, the puck dancing on the edge of his stick. The score was tied, which is what Kalugin preferred in the final moments of his weekly ice hockey matches—and what his rivals and teammates always delivered. Just as they made certain he would have the puck for a game-deciding shot.

The goalie wavered. Only seconds remaining. Would Kalugin shoot, pass, or drive around the net? Two opponents rushed him, but Kalugin glided through them.

He transferred his weight to his front skate nearest the puck and pulled back his stick. Firing.

His shot veered to the net's right. A sure miss. The goalie lunged at it. The puck smacked his leg pads. Deflected into the net.

A loud horn blast.

Kalugin raised his hands triumphantly at the victory as his teammates mobbed him celebrating.

He skated to the defeated goalie.

"I would have missed," Kalugin shouted, "if you'd been in the correct position."

"Bad luck for me," the goalie replied, "good luck for you."

"There was no luck," Kalugin declared. "I beat you." He turned his skates, so he was now standing next to the goalie in front of the net. "This is where you should have positioned your skates to protect the net," he said, demonstrating for all of the players. "Your mistake was jumping toward the puck instead of leaving it alone."

"Thank you," the goalie replied. There was no mention that he had once played on a Russian Olympic medal–winning team and knew exactly where he should have been positioned during a direct attack.

As Kalugin exited from the ice, he boasted to a teammate, "If I weren't president, I would have been a professional in this sport."

It was unclear to those who played each week if the president's narcissism kept him from seeing through the final shot ruses or if he fully understood that the games were always fixed to flatter him and simply didn't care. A benefit of his power.

Kalugin had just removed his skates when Nikolai Aleksandrovich Kazakov entered the plush presidential changing room at the ice rink built with public funds near Kalugin's private estate in Novo-Ogaryovo, twenty-five minutes west of Moscow.

"Mr. President," General Gromyko's deputy said, "I have the general on a secure line. It is an urgent matter."

"Help me with my shoulder pads," Kalugin replied. "And stay."

Kazakov only could hear Kalugin's end of the conversation, but with each second, he watched the president become more and more agitated.

"Diplomatic immunity will not protect you, not for this!" Kalugin shouted.

Followed by, "Brett Garrett. The same American who twice escaped from you?"

Kalugin slammed down the phone when he ended the call.

"Join me in a bath," he said, starting to strip. There was nothing sexual about the request. It was not unusual for the Russian president to discuss matters in a sauna. Being naked was how he could guarantee no secret recordings or eavesdropping. The self-contained cubicles that he'd ordered specially made were immune to foreign penetration. The sauna also gave him a psychological advantage. Kalugin was proud of his physique. He began each morning spending two hours swimming, another hour with his personal trainers. He felt superior when those around him were stripped naked with all of their physical faults exposed.

"A revolutionary group failed to release a poisonous gas in the United States Senate," Kalugin said when they were seated on a wooden bench in the heat. "No American politicians were killed, but the general suspects the Americans will blame us."

Kazakov already knew about Gromyko's Kamera laboratory and his delivery of the Devil's Breath variant to Antifa radicals. He knew President Kalugin had approved of the plan. But if the president now wished to distance himself, Kazakov would play along.

"You cannot be blamed," Kazakov said. "You are innocent. Russia is innocent. Nothing but lies."

"The Americans will have no choice but to retaliate. This was a direct attack on members of their government," Kalugin continued, clearly concerned. "Cyber warfare is inconsequential compared to an attempted mass murder."

"Yes, if they can find a connection with us," Kazakov said, "they will demand blood. They started a war because of the attack by jihadists in New York and at their Pentagon, but surely they would not risk a nuclear confrontation," Kazakov said. "We are not Iraq or Afghanistan."

For a moment neither spoke. Kalugin was thinking.

"If I may speak openly," Kazakov said, breaking the silence, "this is a problem of General Gromyko's creation."

"And so?" Kalugin replied.

"He should bear all responsibility. It is his doing, not yours. He should be the one who is punished."

Kalugin turned his head, looked at Kazakov. How quickly he had turned on his superior. The president smiled. These were the men whom he chose to advise him. A paradoxical situation. He'd needed the likes of Gromyko and Kazakov to crush his opponents when he was rising to power. He needed them to retain his power. Unscrupulous men to do his bidding without moral misgivings. They intimidated and murdered for him. Yet Kalugin was no fool. He understood these same men would turn on him if he ever became vulnerable. Primates eating their young. It had been no different in Stalin's day.

"Nikolai Aleksandrovich," Kalugin replied, "General Gromyko ate the dog but choked on its tail." He chuckled. It was an old Russian expression that Kalugin's mother had taught him—to laugh at someone who had performed a difficult feat but tripped up at the end and failed.

Continuing, he said, "I will immediately deny all Russian involvement if the Americans accuse us. In a matter as grave as this, the Americans will need evidence. This always has been their pattern. They cannot justify retaliation based on speculation, even when the culprits are obvious. Unfortunately, there is someone who is an eyewitness, someone who can directly tie this attempted poisoning to General Gromyko."

"I overheard his name in your conversation," Kazakov said.

"Brett Garrett—the American the CIA sent here to escort the traitor Yakov Pavel to the West. He has been to the Kamera laboratory in Svetogorsk."

Once again, this was information Kazakov already knew, but he remained quiet. Listening.

"General Gromyko just assured me that he will eliminate this witness," Kalugin said. "He is sending a man."

"Without Garrett, the Americans will have only hearsay," Kazakov said.

It was a comment, but it sounded more like a question.

Kalugin used a towel to wipe his sweat-covered face. He was again thinking through his thoughts, wanting to be certain of his plan.

"How many Zasion officers are currently in our embassy in Washington?" he asked. A reference to Russia's elite Zasion Special Operations Group, whose existence was officially denied by the Kremlin but whose soldiers were used to protect Russian diplomats.

"Five," Kazakov replied. "Under the command of Fedor Ivanovich Vasiliev."

"Tell him that he needs to escort General Gromyko back to Moscow immediately. Tell him we do not want to risk having the Americans detain the general for questioning."

"They wouldn't dare. Such a move would break all diplomatic protocols."

Kalugin scoffed. "I suspect that line already has been crossed." He again wiped the sweat from his face. "The general flew to America on a private plane, not a government aircraft," he said. "This is a good thing. It was not a government flight. It suggests that he was operating independently. It would be best if that same private airplane returned for the general. To bring him back home."

He twisted in his seat so that he was now looking directly at Kazakov. "It would be best if that aircraft encountered a mechanical malfunction while returning across the Atlantic."

"Survivors?"

"None."

Forty-Three

The slug fired into Brett Garrett's leg had been a hollow-point round, designed to mushroom upon impact to cause maximum damage. His tibia, the second-largest bone in the body, had been fractured and it had taken surgeons more than four hours to perform open reduction and internal fixation (ORIF), a procedure that involved placing a metal rod down the inner aspect of the bone to stabilize and repair the fracture.

He had awoken from anesthesia in recovery but had been given several high doses of morphine, despite his opioid addiction, as well as powerful sleep medication before being moved to a private hospital room. He immediately fell into a deep sleep.

Sally North had instructed an FBI agent to stick

close to Garrett and alert her when he was coherent enough to be interviewed. Thomas Jefferson Kim had taken it upon himself to have an IEC security guard stationed outside Garrett's door, primarily to keep reporters from intruding.

A few minutes after 3:00 a.m., while the FBI agent was flirting with the nurses at a workstation, a lone assassin peered out from an emergency stairway and, seeing no one, stepped onto the rectangular floor. He'd already familiarized himself with the layout: two hallways running north to south holding five rooms each, joined at their ends by matching east-west corridors. The end units housed three patient rooms apiece. The nurses' workstation was located in a cut-through in the center of the wing, allowing easy access to the longer hallways. Glass offices on each side of the nurses' station filled the rest of the unit. Normally, lights in these offices allowed the nurses to look directly through them. Because it was night, those lights were switched off, diminishing the view.

Garrett's room was on the southeast corner. Gromyko's hired assassin entered the floor at its northwest corner, as far away as possible from Garrett's room. The assassin ducked into a nearby patient's room where an elderly woman was sleeping peacefully, attached to monitors tracking her vital signs. He clutched the woman's throat with his right hand and began to squeeze while covering her mouth with his left palm. Her eyes shot open, and she struggled to grab hold of the stranger strangling her, but she was no match, and within moments, an alarm sounded inside the nurses' station.

Knowing they would respond via the west hallway running north, the assassin dashed into the east hallway and walked by the now-empty nurses' base. The FBI agent who'd been chatting there had followed the nurses.

Garrett's room was easy to identify because it was the only one with a security guard outside it. He was sitting scanning through Facebook on his cell phone.

As Gromyko's man neared the IEC guard, the killer slipped his right hand up under his light blue jacket.

The guard glanced up and saw him approaching. The killer smiled and in a well-practiced move drew his Ruger .22-caliber pistol fitted with a suppressor, firing twice at close range into the startled guard's face.

Having disposed of the guard, the assassin slipped into Garrett's room.

General Gromyko had just drifted to sleep when his bodyguard, Boris Vladimirovich Petrov, gently awakened him.

"Sokolov has sent his plane from his sports team in Texas."

Gromyko had moved his quarters from the former Soviet embassy to a nineteen-room mansion on Pioneer Point, a scenic peninsula on the eastern Maryland shoreline where the Corsica and Chester Rivers merged. The main house was part of a forty-five-acre compound that contained two swimming pools, a soccer field, multiple tennis courts, and ten bungalows—all purchased in 1972 by the Soviet Union as a Chesapeake Bay "dacha" for its diplomats and visiting Kremlin dignitaries. The house had been owned previously by John J. Raskob, best known as the builder of the Empire State Building. Although the property was not legally sovereign Russian territory, under the Vienna Convention no one could enter it without permission, and any attack on its grounds was the equivalent of an assault on Russia.

Gromyko dressed quickly, tucking a PSM pistol, an easy-to-conceal handgun issued to top Russian diplomats, under his suit jacket.

Petrov was waiting outside his bedroom door.

"Did you do what I asked?" the general said.

Petrov nodded. "It's ready."

Four men were waiting for them in the house's grand foyer. Gromyko recognized Fedor Ivanovich Vasiliev, the Zasion commander in charge.

"Why are you here?" Gromyko asked.

"Moscow ordered us to escort you to your airplane in case the Americans attempt to detain you," Fedor replied.

"Moscow? Who in Moscow?"

"I received a direct order from your deputy Nikolai Kazakov."

The four soldiers split into pairs. Two fell in next to Gromyko, the other two next to Petrov. They were greeted outside by two drivers standing next to twin black Mercedes-Benz S Class sedans that had been lightly armored.

"General," Fedor said, "it would be better if Mr. Petrov rode in the second vehicle so two of us can ride comfortably with you."

"Tell me," General Gromyko said, "who does Kazakov report to?"

"Why, he reports to you, General."

"Then he has no authority over me, does he?" Gromyko replied. "Unless you wish to find yourself stripped of your duties, you need to acknowledge my authority. I decide who sits where and my bodyguard will travel next to me."

Without waiting for an answer, Gromyko and Petrov both took seats in the backseat of the first Mercedes.

"I meant no disrespect, General," Fedor said, slipping into the front passenger seat. "I simply thought it safer if two of us were in this car with you."

"Now you have offended Petrov," Gromyko chuckled. "Do you think he cannot keep me safe?"

The three other Zasion soldiers rode in the second Mercedes. The two-car motorcade exited the mansion's circular driveway, traveling along Corsica Neck Road toward the property's gated exit. Two of the compound's bungalows were now on the left side of the moving vehicles. To the right of the two-way road was an undeveloped plot covered with Atlantic white cedars and underbrush. It was a buffer to the Chester River.

As the lead car neared Towne Point Lane, the first intersection on the resort property, Gromyko announced, "I need an item from my suitcase in the trunk. Inform your men that we are stopping. No need for them to exit their vehicles. It will only take Petrov a moment to fetch it."

Fedor spoke through a handheld two-way radio. He started to turn his head so he could glance backward to address Gromyko when Petrov lunged forward from the seat directly behind him. He had put on leather gloves and drawn a garrote from his coat pocket. In a well-practiced move, the massive bodyguard dropped the wire over Fedor's head, pulling it taut around Fedor's neck. Petrov used his legs to thrust himself backward. The wire nearly decapitated the unsuspecting Fedor, who raised his hands to his neck in a panic much too late.

General Gromyko had drawn his pistol and now pressed it against the back of the driver's skull.

"If you want to live, keep your hands on the wheel and stare straight ahead," he warned.

A sliver of light from under the bathroom door in Brett Garrett's hospital room provided enough glow for the assassin to quickly survey his surroundings.

As expected, a patient was in the bed, but he was not the room's only occupant. An Asian woman was asleep under a blanket in a lounge chair near him.

The assassin would deal with her after Garrett. The killer lifted his left hand so he could compare a photograph of Garrett on his cell phone with the patient in the bed. It was his target. Satisfied, he lowered his cell while simultaneously raising the .22-caliber pistol in his right hand.

Thomas Jefferson Kim opened the bathroom door directly behind the assassin, startling both of them. Still wearing a sling from the bullet wound to his right arm, Kim yelled and lowered his shoulders, charging the surprised gunman. The impact caused both of them to bang against Garrett's hospital bed before they tumbled onto the floor.

Kicking his feet wildly, Kim scrambled to remain on top of the assassin while managing to grab his right wrist.

"Help! Help!" he hollered.

Now pinned to the floor by Kim, the assassin slammed his left fist against the right side of Kim's skull with dizzying force. A second blow was delivered to Kim's wounded right shoulder, causing him to yelp in pain. The killer's third left blow to Kim's jaw caused him to go limp.

Shoving Kim off his body, the assassin rose to his feet with his pistol aimed directly at the still-unconscious Garrett.

Boom!

The loud gunshot blast caused a confused look to appear on the assassin's face.

Boom!

The assassin shifted and aimed his handgun at Rose Kim, who'd cast off her blanket and fired her Glock semi-auto.

He pulled his Ruger's trigger.

Rose Kim had never been in a shoot-out before. She would later claim that the .22 round had barely missed her head. But everyone who had ever been fired upon believed he or she had been barely missed.

Boom! Boom! Two more shots—from Rose.

The assassin fell backward and hit the floor hard.

The FBI agent, who'd run toward the room when he'd first heard gunshots, shoved open the room's closed door but positioned himself along the hallway wall. As soon as the door opened, Rose Kim fired into the hallway, assuming the assassin had an accomplice. Her slug shattered the glass exterior of the office across from Garrett's room.

"FBI!" he yelled. "Drop your weapons!"

"It's me!" Rose Kim squealed. "My husband is hurt! I've shot a man attacking us."

"Put down your gun," he ordered. "Put it on the floor. Don't shoot me."

She put aside her Glock and hurried to her husband, still prone on the floor.

The agent edged his way around the corner, darted into the room, and immediately stripped the .22-caliber pistol from the assassin's hand. Kneeling, the agent felt for a pulse.

There was none.

Bodyguard Boris Petrov stepped from the first Mercedes into the morning darkness. The headlights of the second car some fifteen yards behind him caused him to blink and shield his eyes. He waved his hand downward, and the car's driver extinguished the front lights. None of the car's occupants bothered to exit.

Petrov opened the trunk and reached inside. When his hands emerged, they were holding a Russian-made RPG-7, a shoulder-fired, reusable antitank rocket-propelled grenade launcher. He spun, and before any of the soldiers seated in the Mercedes could undo their seat belts, Petrov fired. At that close range, the blast from the explosion knocked Petrov down onto the asphalt. Flying debris from the Mercedes flew in all directions. Everyone in the car was dead.

Inside the first Mercedes, the driver pleaded, "General, I'm only a driver. I know nothing about any of this."

"It's a pity," Gromyko said. He fired a round from his pistol into the back of the man's skull.

Stepping from the safety of the car, he called to Petrov: "Can you walk?"

Petrov used his palms to push himself onto his feet. He had been struck by shrapnel and his face was bleeding. He tugged a piece of chrome fragment from his left upper arm. Gromyko did not wait for him. He started walking toward the trees to their right. Behind him, the second Mercedes was burning, casting an eerie yellow light across the landscape.

Gromyko found the eighteen-foot-long fishing boat moored at an inlet on the opposite side of the trees where Petrov had said it would be. He climbed aboard and called to Petrov.

"Hurry or I'll leave you!"

The shell-shocked, bloody bodyguard came aboard. The general started the outboard and headed toward Chesapeake Bay.

Thomas Jefferson Kim had been knocked out by the assassin's punches, but he regained consciousness within seconds after the nurses took charge. They checked his heart rate and helped him into the lounge chair where Rose Kim had been sleeping only minutes earlier.

"I shot him just like you showed me," Rose Kim declared.

The FBI agent searched the dead man for identification. Nothing. He unbuttoned the man's shirt. A bullet-resistant vest. Three of Rose's shots were blocked there. The fourth had hit above the vest, ripping through the man's right carotid artery where it was connected to his brachiocephalic trunk.

Despite the melee, Brett Garrett remained unaware in his drug-induced sleep. If he had been semiconscious, what had transpired would have seemed to him much like a bad dream.

Forty-Four

The Day After

"The man who attempted to kill Brett Garrett appears to be Eastern European, but we have no other information about him," FBI director Archibald Davidson said. "No fingerprint matches, no facial recognition, nothing yet to identify him."

"Any idea how he entered the country?" President Randle Fitzgerald asked.

"None."

"What about Agent Mayberry?"

"She's still alive but has been put in an induced coma while doctors continue to try different levels of the antidote," Davidson said. He withdrew several photographs from a folder and handed them to Fitzgerald, who was seated behind his desk in the Oval Office.

"These were taken by the Queen Anne Sheriff's Department after gunshots and explosions were heard earlier this morning at the Russians' Pioneer Pointe retreat," Davidson explained. "The Russians refused to allow deputies or local Centreville Police Department officers to enter the compound. The enterprising sheriff used a drone to take these photos."

"What exactly am I looking at?" the president asked.

"A burning vehicle stopped inside the compound behind another luxury car with its doors open. General Andre Gromyko was staying at the property. The private aircraft that brought him to the U.S.—a jet owned by Ivan Sokolov—had flown in earlier from Texas apparently to transport the general back to Moscow. That plane left without him about an hour after these photos were taken."

"Texas?"

"Sokolov owns a basketball team based there," Davidson said.

"Your best guess?"

"Sokolov was getting out of the country to avoid us detaining him and the general for questioning." Davidson paused. "We've got no clue if he is still at that compound or even if he is still alive."

President Fitzgerald returned the photos to him. "What time were those aerial photos taken?"

"Shortly before six a.m."

"At eight this morning," the president said, "I received a telephone call from Russian president Kalugin. He immediately expressed his concern about the Senate attack. He then told me quite a story. He claimed a group of radicals had attempted to use poison gas to murder members of the State Duma in Moscow yesterday. He said his security people stopped them."

"I've not seen any reports about this. Has the agency or State confirmed the Moscow attack?"

"No. President Kalugin said he'd decided to keep it secret until after a thorough investigation. He then told me that he suspects General Gromyko was behind the attack in Moscow. In his words, Gromyko is a lunatic whose aim was to undermine both of our governments and cause us to go to war. He apologized for the general's actions but insisted that he had no idea about what Gromyko was doing."

"Sounds convenient. How did you respond?" Davidson asked.

"I said we were investigating the attack. That we took it extremely seriously and would take the appropriate action after we had gathered and evaluated all of the facts," Fitzgerald said.

"You believe Gromyko acted alone?"

"No, and the fact Kalugin called makes me think he knew and approved of yesterday's attempt. He's never admitted anything before about Russian poisoning. I'd say he is desperate to shift the blame and undermine any response we might make in retaliation. It wouldn't surprise me if he arrests some of his own people today and holds a show trial to convince the world the Russian Duma was threatened by Gromyko."

"Excuse me, Mr. President," Davidson said, "but it would be helpful if Director Harris would share his intelligence about Gromyko with the bureau and tell us what the hell he had Agent Mayberry and Brett Garrett doing for him. Garrett regained consciousness this morning, but he's refusing to answer any of Sally North's questions, claiming national security concerns. He just keeps saying, 'Ask Harris.'"

"I'll deal with Director Harris. Meanwhile, we need to know more about Senator Stone's legislative aide— the one who brought the poison in—and the woman in Antifa who was trying to take that case away from Agent Mayberry and release the gas. Were they sleeper agents? Can you find definite proof that this gas was made in Russia?"

"We'll get the facts, sir."

Moments later, as Davidson was leaving, he encountered Harris in a White House hallway.

"You've finished your briefing, I see," Harris said in a guarded voice. "Now it's my turn."

"Harris," Davidson said, "I've told the president that you've not been forthcoming with us. You're holding back information. I wanted to tell you that to your face. I wanted him to know that you have not been cooperative with us."

"If the president mentions it," Harris said coldly, "I'll respond." He stepped by Davidson.

Harris found the president waiting, still seated behind his desk. President Fitzgerald did not stand to greet him, nor did he respond when Harris said, "Good morning, sir!" Instead he nodded toward a chair across from his desk.

"What in the hell have you done?" Fitzgerald snapped.

"My agency has just helped prevent a catastrophe," Harris replied. "With assistance from Agent Mayberry and Brett Garrett, I stopped a mass murder."

"Davidson just told me that you've been holding back information and I know it's true because you've not told me a damn thing, either," Fitzgerald said. "You know that you're obligated by law to keep both me and Congress informed—something that you clearly have chosen not to do."

"I haven't disclosed information purely for national security reasons," Harris said.

"Where in the law does it say that you get to make that final decision? From the few facts that I've been able to glean, you used Agent Mayberry and Brett Garrett to operate an off-the books covert operation. You went rogue, and you hid it from all of us."

"It was the only way to protect Yakov Pavel," Harris replied. "If I'd told Congress, it would have leaked out. Surely you know that."

"Again, that's not a choice—not your decision to make. You can't arbitrarily decide what to tell and what not to tell, especially to me. You may be in charge of the CIA, but you still answer to the president and Congress."

"I was protecting you by going off the grid."

Fitzgerald leaned forward and glared at Harris. "No, you were not! You let your ego and your mistrust of Congress impair your judgment, and now you are self-rationalizing and self-justifying your actions by blaming others. Don't you dare try to claim that you were concerned about me. What you have done has undermined my administration."

Harris bristled but President Fitzgerald wasn't done.

"Harris, you're a liar," he said bluntly. He pressed a button on his phone that connected him to his secretary. "Please send in my guests."

Harris turned his head and saw a man and woman

enter the Oval Office. She was modestly dressed. Her blond hair was pulled back tightly in a bun. He was wearing a Capitol Police officer's uniform.

Harris didn't recognize either of them.

"My name is Elsa Eriksson," the woman said.

"I'm Jack Strong, but when I was a SEAL, everyone called me Bear."

President Fitzgerald said, "They have been telling me what really happened in Cameroon when Senator Stone's son was killed by terrorists. They've told me how Garrett and his fellow SEALs rescued a young girl named Abidemi who was being gang-raped, how those 'locals' who you described in your Senate hearing testimony were actually young girls. Mr. Strong—Bear—has relayed a conversation to me that he had with Brett Garrett that happened that night—about your granddaughter and how you had assured Garrett that you would have his back if he decided to rescue the children. You didn't, though, did you—have his back? Instead, you lied."

Harris remained stone-faced.

"Because you accused Brett Garrett of insubordination—of not obeying direct orders—he spent eighteen months in Leavenworth prison. He was dishonorably discharged. His career and reputation were destroyed. You did that!"

"I gave him a chance to redeem himself," Harris replied.

"Redeem himself? You're the one who needs redemption. Your hiding information from me has put my administration and me in a precarious situation. There are going to be investigations into everything that has happened."

"That's classified material," Harris said.

"Not for long. What you've done is illegal. I am not going to ask for your resignation. I am firing you because you deserve to be fired."

"You can't do that. You need me to deal with what happened in the Senate."

"I don't need you. I need to replace you with someone who is honest. And you—you need to hire yourself a team of really good lawyers."

Forty-Five

Three Months Later

B rett Garrett felt uneasy.

A taxi had dropped him at a gatehouse in the Round Hill neighborhood of North Greenwich, Connecticut, where a uniformed guard checked to ensure that Garrett was on Valerie Mayberry's visitors' list. Garrett was holding a bouquet of pink roses and alstroemeria that he'd bought at a grocery store.

Another officer in a golf cart drove him through meticulously groomed lawns along a winding driveway to the entrance of a fifty-room stone mansion built in 1909 on the fifty-acre estate. From its front stoop, he could see Long Island Sound.

"I'm Hannah Clements," a forty-something woman said after he'd entered the center hall, which had a

Bourgogne limestone floor and grand curved staircase and was decorated with Victorian-era furniture. She led him through French doors outside to a spacious terrace.

"Valerie's parents entrusted her recovery to us as soon as she was stable enough to leave the hospital," Clements said. "We are quite proud of our rehabilitation facility. We only accept fifteen patients so we can focus on individual needs and we've been rated one of the most successful in the world. This is your first visit, is it not?"

"Yes."

"Her parents are very protective and have not allowed many guests. Unless I'm mistaken, you may be the first nonfamily visitor. May I ask how you know Valerie?"

"We worked together before she was poisoned."

"Ah, so you are *that* Brett Garrett, the one I read about in the newspapers, just as I suspected." She nodded toward a woman sitting with her back to them, facing a formal English garden. "There's our lady."

He flinched. Garrett had not been warned that Mayberry would be in a wheelchair.

Clements noticed. "The chair is temporary," she said. "Actually, Valerie is making amazing progress. She is very determined."

"Yeah, you could say that," he replied, slightly smiling.

"I must warn you that Valerie still has difficulty speaking and she also becomes tired easily, especially after her morning sessions, so I must insist that your visit last no more than ten minutes.

He thanked her and walked over, taking a seat on the brick waist-high wall that edged the terrace so that he was facing Mayberry.

"Agent Mayberry," he said cheerfully.

Garrett handed her the flowers. She took them with her left hand, and he noticed her right was knotted awkwardly in a fist and lying on her lap.

"They said you're doing great with your rehabilitation. Very determined. I don't think they'll be able to keep you here for long, which is good news, because the bureau needs you back. Still lots of rabbits in the world for you to protect."

He grinned. She gave him a curious look. He wasn't certain she remembered her reason for joining the FBI.

She looked out over the gardens. He did, too. For several minutes. Peaceful. Silence.

"I never got to thank you," he said quietly. "You stopped a mass murder. Jumping into the Senate like you did, screaming about a bomb, blocking that hole with your finger. Brilliant. I probably would have been poisoned, too, if Makayla had wrestled that briefcase from you. Naturally, I deserve credit as well for throwing the gas mask to you. Probably the best pitch of my life."

He struggled to think of something else to say.

"Don't know if you realize how famous you are," he said. "Della has taped news articles about you on the wall right next to the 'Cash Tip's Pleas' sign in Baltimore. You're a real celebrity. I suggested they name an omelet after you." He laughed.

She continued looking out at the garden.

"Listen, Mayberry," he said standing. "My ten minutes is up, but I came to tell you that I'm going to get the bastard responsible and I wanted you to know something. Something I need to tell you. It's just not the bureau that wants you back. We're a good team, even if you do have a lot of really irritating habits. I'd like you back."

He reached down and gently placed his hand on her left shoulder.

"Thank you, Brett." Her words came out with a stutter. He realized that she'd never called him by his first name before. Glancing down at her lap, she added, "Your flowers suck."

She looked up at him and was smiling.

Thirty hours later, Garrett stepped from one of Kim's IEC jets onto the tarmac at the Bissau Airport in the

African Republic of Guinea-Bissau. Thomas Jefferson Kim was waiting behind the wheel of a Range Rover.

"Welcome to one of the world's most dangerous and utterly corrupt countries," Kim said. "Not many places to live when you're a Russian general hiding from the International Criminal Court and U.S. authorities."

"Gromyko isn't worried about being put on trial," Garrett replied. "He's looking over his shoulder for Russian Zasion forces. How'd you find him when no one else can?"

"I'm better than everyone else at tracking people," Kim replied as they drove from the airport.

"Have the other members of my team arrived?" Garrett asked.

"Brought them in yesterday. This nation is a haven for international drug smugglers, so cargo planes fly in and out daily without anyone paying attention. Everyone I've met here takes bribes."

He reached behind the front seats for a package that he handed to Garrett. "A little present I picked up for you." It was a SIG Sauer semi-auto with extra ammunition. "I know you lost the last one."

"I didn't lose it. Gromyko's goons stole it from me when I was ambushed on the train with Pavel and Peter."

The black oxide-coated handgun felt good in his grip.

"I want to remind you that Gromyko is living under the protection of a local warlord who helped lead a coup d'état against the last government," Kim said. "You have a limited amount of time to kill him. Otherwise, he'll call in reinforcements."

"It will be a piece of cake."

"I'm not a fan of cake," Kim replied.

"How reliable is your information about tomorrow?" Garrett asked.

Kim shrugged. "I paid a lot for it to a reliable source, but Gromyko could change his mind in the morning and cancel his trip."

"Between nine and ten o'clock. That's when he'll be on the move, right?"

"That's what I've been told. Get this: he'll be in a Mercedes-Maybach S650 that he bought off a local drug smuggler. In this hellhole," Kim said. "Tomorrow's our best chance to hit him. If he stays in his compound, you'd have to kill your way through a hundred mercenaries."

"How many bullets did you bring?"

It took them several hours to reach the remote area where Gromyko was hiding. The flat land they entered was barren at points, with only a few scraggly bushes surviving on the brown, dry dirt. Kim pulled off the one-lane road onto a dry creek bed, which they followed for several miles until they came to a more lush area with trees and overgrown bushes. He parked the four-wheeler in a grove of cashew trees, and they continued on foot, using a navigational GPS connected to an IEC satellite to guide them. They eventually reached a clearing about half the size of a football field in the African forest.

"Cost me a fortune to drop your teammates here last night," Kim said.

"Next time use Amazon Prime," Garrett replied.

"Funny," Kim grunted.

"You still got lots of money," Garrett said. "Stop crying poor."

They began unstrapping two pallets connected to parachutes. "Now the fun begins," Kim said. "Time to fire up MUTT-ONE."

Using a portable computer linked to his satellite, Kim started the engine of a robotic Multi-Utility Tactical Transport, called MUTT by the U.S. military, that he'd customized. It resembled an ATV but had been cut to about half that size. Kim had armed it with a DShKM, a new version of a heavy machine gun first manufactured by the Soviets in 1938 but still being used today by the Russian military.

"I've added remote-controlled laser-guided computer sights, GPS mapping, and gyroscopic stabilization," Kim said proudly. "Now some people mistakenly believe this weapon can fire U.S./NATO .50-caliber ammunition, but that's not true. The Russian military manual describes its rounds as being .51 caliber, just enough to prevent them from being interchangeable." He was enjoying showing off his customized weaponry. "I was able to get the records from the company that armored Gromyko's Maybach. His car was designed to withstand standard 7.62 mm NATO rounds, and a blast from two DM51 hand grenades detonated together. This Russian machine gun's ammunition will penetrate up to three-fourths of an inch High Hard Armor. Plus, MUTT-ONE will be positioned about fifty yards from the target. At such a close distance, the computer should be able to fire multiple rounds in such a compact grouping that if the first round doesn't do the trick, the following ones will be enough to penetrate and stop the Maybach's 621 horsepower V-12 engine."

Kim next started MUTT-TWO, which he drove remotely from its pallet.

"MUTT-TWO is armed with side-by-side, lightweight ASh-12.7 battle rifles. Favored by the Russians for urban combat. I bought the guns and ammunition from an arms dealer in Azerbaijan to make it appear this is a Russian attack."

Garrett glanced around the clearing, searching for

signs that would signal if someone else might have been there.

"Don't worry," Kim said. "I've had an employee watching this clearing nonstop since the drop." He turned his computer screen so Garrett could see it and increased its magnification. Kim waved and one of the two figures next to MUTT-TWO could be seen on the screen waving.

"Smile," he said.

It was dusk, and several bat hawks appeared chasing their dinners. "As you planned, we are about five miles from Gromyko's compound. The ambush site is about a quarter mile north in the trees."

"How's the ground cover?" Garrett asked.

"Yes, we really couldn't get a good feel for that from satellite imagery, but based on what we have been hiking through, I believe we'll be okay. There are enough trees and bushes here to hide the MUTTS, but not so much foliage to obstruct their rounds or prevent them from moving. Actually, they'll be able to move safer than you."

"You better head back to the Range Rover," Garrett said. "Just make certain you don't get lost or bitten by a snake or shot without me there to rescue you."

Kim said, "While you're ambushing Gromyko, I'll be controlling your teammates from the air-conditioned safety of my Range Rover miles away. In this scenario, who is more likely to need rescuing?"

General Gromyko had prepared his compound for a military assault. The razor wire fencing around it was buttressed with IEDs and monitored by motion detectors. Like all top Russian officials, he had stolen as much money as he could during his military service, and he had put his millions to good use hiring mercenaries and bribing the local warlord. His paid fighters lived in barracks near his main house, where he stayed with Boris Petrov, who had joined him in exile.

Garrett had easily identified the weak link in Gromyko's defenses. There was only one road leading in and out of his well-patrolled compound. The ambush site that Garrett had chosen was where the one-lane road was edged on both sides by trees and bushes. Plenty of spots to hide.

Nine a.m. at the ambush site and the road remained empty. A half hour later, still no sign of Gromyko. At ten, Garrett began to wonder about the truthfulness of Kim's paid informant—or had Gromyko simply gotten off to a late start or decided to postpone his trip? Garrett remained hidden in the tree line. He was sweating profusely under his heavy ghillie suit. He'd augmented his camouflage covering made of netting and loose strips of burlap colored to match the leaves, twigs, and ground around him with bits of branches. To pass the time, he watched a parade of ants inches from his face going to and from some food source, the workers returning to their nest with engorged bellies that they would regurgitate to feed those left behind.

At eleven, Kim spoke through Garrett's earpiece. "Satellite shows caravan leaving compound. Looks like we're finally a go."

A ruby-red Toyota Tacoma 4x4 with a heavy machine gun bolted on its truck bed was the first of three vehicles. Next was the Maybach, covered with dust from the unpaved single-lane road, and finally a half-ton troop carrier with what Kim estimated from his satellite viewpoint was at least fifteen armed men.

Kim had positioned his MUTTs some seventy yards apart in the forest that edged the vehicles' right side. It was important for Garrett, who was concealed on the road's left side, not to leave his position, which was tagged on Kim's computer screen, because the MUTTs would be firing across the road in his direction.

"Here we go," Kim said through Garrett's earpiece.

The cracking sound of MUTT-ONE's machine gun caused birds to abandon the trees. Three of its rounds hit the Maybach two inches behind its front wheel. The impact shook the entire car. Three more rounds aimed at those entry holes knocked the sedan slightly sideways, disabling it.

MUTT-TWO's machine guns sounded next, aimed at the troop carrier, causing the mercenaries aboard it to leap off onto the road. Some took cover behind the vehicle while others lay on the road in the knee-high grass that edged the one lane on both sides, providing twenty yards of clearing between the road and the forest. The fighter manning the U.S. military M2 machine gun on the Toyota's bed began firing indiscriminately into the trees in the direction of MUTT-TWO. His shots became erratic when the Toyota's driver suddenly began backing up, running the truck off the road next to the passenger side of the Maybach to shield it from the gunfire coming from the woods.

Kim zeroed in on the machine gunner and fired a burst of rounds from MUTT-ONE, killing him. Kim now concentrated his aim on the engines of the two still mobile trucks to prevent Gromyko from escaping in them. Neither the Toyota nor the troop carrier was armored, so their engines proved easy to destroy. Having disabled both, he unleashed MUTT-TWO's twin guns at the troop carrier, riddling its cab and puncturing its rear gasoline tank. The mercenaries who had been clustered around it ran, anticipating a probable explosion.

"Stay in the car," Petrov told Gromyko. He exited from the passenger side into the narrow space created between the Maybach and Toyota truck. Two mercenaries had unloaded crates from the Tacoma, which Petrov opened. Inside one was an assortment of Russian F1 and American MK2 hand grenades, purchased locally. He urged the two fighters nearest him to begin throwing them in the direction of fire. The second crate contained more lethal weaponry—RPO-A Shmel—disposable single-shot Russian-made rocket launchers. He grabbed one of the 93 mm–caliber tubes fitted with an RPO-Z incendiary warhead and fired it into the forest in the direction of MUTT-TWO. Unbeknownst to Petrov, Kim was in the process of moving both MUTTs. The fired warhead exploded, scorching the ground vegetation and downing three trees in a brilliant burst of yellow flames. But MUTT-TWO was untouched.

Petrov ordered his men to stop shooting, and for a moment, it was eerily silent along the road.

Having now been repositioned, MUTT-ONE unleashed a barrage of .50-caliber rounds at the Toyota truck, pockmarking its red exterior and shattering its glass.

A half-dozen mercenaries began running south up the road, abandoning the firefight. Others retreated to the grass on the left side of the road between the vehicles and the tree line where Garrett was hiding. He watched one fighter as he approached, seeking cover within a few feet of him. Garrett held his fire, not wishing to expose himself.

While the mercenaries were shooting into the forest from their hiding spots, Petrov remained upright, as if daring his enemy to kill him. He tossed aside the spent RPO-A Shmel and removed another one, which he shoulder-fired in the direction of MUTT-ONE to his left. Kim was already moving the motorized machine gun. Another thunderous explosion. Another fireball. More underbrush now in flames and trees toppled. More grenades thrown. It seemed impossible that any living being could survive the rocket blast.

Kim returned fire with MUTT-TWO stationed to Petrov's right, aiming his guns at the pinned-down mercenaries near the abandoned troop carrier. One screamed in pain when wounded. Kim moved his aim toward the Toyota, sweeping it with rifle fire, killing the two fighters throwing grenades from either end of it, along with the Maybach's driver, who had foolishly left the safety of the luxury sedan to help.

Petrov drew another RPO-A Shmel, this one loaded with a thermobaric warhead, which he fired at MUTT-TWO. The rocket flew wildly to its left, a mishap that accidentally had it striking the location where MUTT-

TWO was repositioning itself. A flash on Kim's computer screen confirmed its demise. With only the heavy machine gun still operational, Kim began pulling MUTT-ONE deeper back into the trees.

Petrov fired yet another rocket, causing a loud explosion and fire near where MUTT-ONE had been. To protect the mechanical killing machine, Kim did not give up its position by returning fire.

Again, Petrov ordered his mercenaries to stop firing and the ambush scene became quiet.

Petrov signaled his fighters to move from their hiding spots across the grass separating them from the forest. They walked gingerly toward the fallen limbs and still-smoking grounds that had been cleared by the rockets.

Petrov and one fighter remained behind to protect Gromyko, who emerged from the Maybach, thinking the assault had ended.

Having drawn back farther into the trees, Kim fired MUTT-ONE at the soldiers pursuing it, causing them to drop onto the forest floor. One of the mercenaries bolted toward the gunfire, heaving a grenade with all his strength.

It landed a few feet from MUTT-ONE's track plates. It exploded, destroying the tread, grounding the machine.

Kim waited as the mercenaries slowly edged forward. Waited until they were near enough to see that they had been fighting hardware. Having never seen such a machine, they grouped around it. Their leader raised his two-way radio to report to Petrov.

Kim pushed a detonate switch and MUTT-ONE exploded into pieces of deadly shrapnel.

The blast drowned out the suppressed double tap from Garrett's newly acquired SIG Sauer. He had fired after emerging from the forest and making his way across the grassy area behind the vehicles so that he was now less than fifteen steps from the Maybach's driver's side. His shots had hit their target—the mercenary who'd stayed behind with Petrov to protect Gromyko. He'd been standing at the front of the Toyota watching the woods when he was fatally wounded.

Petrov suddenly realized the retreating machine-gun fire and blast had been designed to draw his fighters away from the Maybach. He cursed for not paying attention to the woods behind him. His rear flank.

The broad-shouldered Russian tossed aside the spent rocket launcher and shoved Gromyko down toward the ground in the gap between the Maybach and the Toyota. He drew his Makarov pistol and turned to face Garrett, who was approaching from the vehicle's driver's side.

Garrett had removed his head covering. His head appeared out of proportion to the expansive ghillie suit that padded his frame. He could only see Petrov's head above the Maybach as the Russian glared at him across the luxury sedan's roof. Garrett's target was much smaller than what Petrov could see. The Russian raised his pistol to fire across the Maybach at the same moment that Garrett aimed his SIG Sauer. Only ten feet separated them. Garrett had once seen a lieutenant empty the clip in his semi-automatic pistol at a Taliban fighter who was shooting back at him in close quarters. Both missed. Hitting a paper target was different from firing at a man trying to kill you. But Garrett and Petrov were not inexperienced marksmen subject to panic. Neither flinched. Petrov's slug grazed the fringe on the right shoulder of Garrett's ghillie suit near his neck. Garrett's SIG Sauer struck the Russian in the center of his nose. He dropped.

Garrett hurried around the Maybach's trunk. Gromyko was crouched near the car's front tire, holding his PSM pistol.

When Gromyko had exited the car's backseat, he had left the passenger door open. Garrett ducked behind it as Gromyko began shooting. PSMs were generally loaded with rounds designed to penetrate Kevlar vests, but they were no match for the Maybach's armored door and bullet-resistant glass. Gromyko kept shooting until his gun was empty.

Garrett stepped from behind the passenger door and peered down at the general, who was still kneeling next to the front tire and clutching his useless weapon.

"I'm unarmed. I surrender," Gromyko cried. He dropped his pistol. "You can arrest me now." He held out his wrists.

In that moment, Garrett thought about Valerie Mayberry. He saw her sitting in a wheelchair, staring out at the gardens. He placed his SIG Sauer semi-auto on the top of the Maybach's roof.

"What did you tell me at the laboratory when you poisoned Yakov Pavel?" he asked rhetorically. "That Russian saying, 'He is brave when fighting against sheep, and when fighting against a brave man, he's a sheep himself'?"

From a slit inside his ghillie suit, Garrett withdrew his tactical knife. Using a blade made killing much more intimate than a bullet, much more personal.

And that was exactly what Garrett wanted.

A Partial Listing of Murders and Other Mysterious Deaths During the Putin Era

As this novel was going to press, General Colonel Igor Korobov, the Russian mastermind behind the 2018 Novichok poisonings in Salisbury, England, died under mysterious circumstances after being personally reprimanded by President Putin. According to press reports, Korobov emerged shaken and in sudden "ill health" after being admonished for mishandling the attempted murders of former Russian military officer and double agent for British intelligence Sergei Skripal and his daughter, Yulia Skripal. As in this novel, the Kremlin deals harshly in real life when those overseeing clandestine murder plots fail.

PUTIN CRITICS

Mikhail Lesin: Found dead in her Washington, D.C., hotel room in November 2015.

Alexander Litvinenko: Former KGB agent poisoned drinking tea laced with deadly polonium-210 at a London hotel in November 2006.

Anna Politkovskaya: Crusading journalist and author of *Putin's Russia*, in which she accused Putin of turning his country into a police state, shot point-blank in an elevator outside her apartment.

Natalia Estemirova: Journalist who uncovered human rights abuses by Russia in Chechnya, was abducted from her home, shot in head.

Stanislav Markelov and Anastasia Baburova: Human rights lawyer Stanislav Markelov represented Putin critics, and was murdered by gunmen outside the Kremlin. Journalist Baburova, walking with him, was fatally shot when she tried to help him.

Boris Nemtsov: Former deputy prime minister of Russia under Boris Yeltsin who accused Putin of accepting bribes from oligarchs, was shot four times walking home from a restaurant.

Boris Berezovsky: Russian oligarch who fled to Britain after a bitter dispute with Putin. Was unfortunate victim of a suspicious death at home in March 2013 after threatening to "bring Putin down."

Paul Klebnikov: Chief editor of the Russian edition of *Forbes* magazine who had exposed corruption of Putin's friends, was murdered during a drive-by shooting.

Sergei Yushenkov: Russian politician who founded a political party critical of Putin, was fatally shot in his face.

Yuri Petrovich Shchekochikhin: Writer and liberal lawmaker in the Russian parliament, Shchekochikhin died in July 2003 from a mysterious illness a few days before his scheduled departure to meet with FBI investigators. His medical documents have been "classified" by the Russian authorities.

JOURNALISTS AND WRITERS

2000

February 1—Vladimir Yatsina, Homicide
February 10—Ludmila Zamana, Homicide
March 9—Artyom Borovik, Homicide
April 17—Oleg Polukeyev, Homicide
May 17—Boris Gashev, Homicide
July 16—Igor Domnikov, Homicide
July 26—Sergei Novikov, Homicide
September 21—Iskander Khatloni, Homicide

October 3—Sergei Ivanov, Homicide
October 18—Georgy Garibyan, Homicide
October 20—Oleg Goryansky, Homicide
October 21—Raif Ablyashev, Homicide
November 20—Pavel Asaulchenko, Homicide
November 23—Adam Tepsurkayev, Homicide
November 28—Nikolai Karmanov, Homicide

2001

February 1—Eduard Burmagin, Homicide
February 24—Leonid Grigoryev, Homicide
March 8—Andrei Pivovarov, Homicide
March 31—Oleg Dolgantsev, Homicide
May 17—Vladimir Kirsanov, Homicide
September 11—Andrei Sheiko, Homicide
September 19—Eduard Markevich, Homicide
November 5—Elina Voronova, Homicide
November 16—Oleg Vedenin, Homicide
November 21—Alexander Babaikin, Homicide
December 1—Boris Mityurev, Homicide

2002

January 18—Svetlana Makarenko, Homicide
March 4—Konstantin Pogodin, Homicide

March 8—Natalya Skryl, Homicide

March 31—Valery Batuyev, Homicide

April 1—Sergei Kalinovsky, Homicide

April 4—Vitaly Sakhn-Vald, Homicide

April 25—Leonid Shevchenko, Homicide

April 29—Valery Ivanov, Homicide

May 20—Alexander Plotnikov, Homicide

June 6—Pavel Morozov, Homicide

June 25—Oleg Sedinko, Homicide

July 20—Nikolai Razmolodin, Homicide

July 21—Maria Lisichkina Homicide

July 27—Sergei Zhabin, Homicide

August 18—Nikolai Vasiliev, Homicide

August 25—Paavo Voutilainen, Homicide

September 20—Igor Salikov, Homicide

October 2—Yelena Popova, Homicide

October 19—Leonid Plotnikov Homicide

December 21—Dmitry Shalayev, Homicide

2003

January 7—Vladimir Sukhomlin, Homicide by police

January 11—Yury Tishkov, Homicide

February 21—Sergei Verbitsky, Homicide

April 18—Dmitry Shvets, Homicide

July 3—Yury Shchekochikhin, Homicide

July 4—Ali Astamirov, Homicide

August 10—Martin Kraus, Homicide

October 9—Alexei Sidorov, Homicide

October 24—Alexei Bakhtin, Homicide

October 30—Yury Bugrov, Homicide

December 25—Pyotr Babenko, Homicide

2004

February 1—Yefim Sukhanov, Homicide

May 2—Shangysh Mongush, Homicide

June 9—Paul Klebnikov, Homicide

July 1—Maxim Maximov, Homicide

July 10—Zoya Ivanova, Homicide

July 17—Pail Peloyan, Homicide

August 3—Vladimir Naumov, Homicide

August 24—Svetlana Shishkina, Homicide

September 18—Vladimir Pritchin, Homicide

September 27—Jan Travinsky, Homicide

2005

July 28—Magomed Varisov, Homicide

August 31—Alexander Pitersky, Homicide

November 4—Kira Lezhneva, Homicide

2006

February 26—Ilya Zimin, Homicide
May 4—Oksana Teslo, Homicide
May 14—Oleg Barabyshkin, Homicide
May 23—Vyacheslav Akatov, Homicide
June 25—Anton Kretenchuk, Homicide
July 25—Yevgeny Gerasimenko, Homicide
July 31—Anatoly Kozulin, Homicide
August 8—Alexander Petrov, Homicide
October 16—Anatoly Voronin, Homicide
December 28—Vadim Kuznetsov, Homicide

2007

January 14—Yury Shebalkin, Homicide
January 20—Konstantin Borovko, Homicide
March 15—Leonid Etkind, Homicide

2008

February 8—Yelena Shestakova, Homicide
March 21—Gadji Abashilov, Homicide
March 21—Ilyas Shurpayev, Homicide

August 31—Magomed Yevloyev, Homicide by police
September 2—Abdulla Alishayev, Homicide
December 30—Shafig Amrakhov, Homicide

2009

January 4—Vladislav Zakharchuk, Homicide
January 19—Stanislav Markelov, Homicide
March 30—Sergei Protazanov, Homicide
June 29—Vyacheslav Yaroshenko, Homicide
August 11—Malik Akhmedilov, Homicide
October 25—Maksharip Aushev, Homicide
November 16—Olga Kotovskaya, Homicide

2010

January 20—Konstantin Popov, Homicide
February 23—Ivan Stepanov, Homicide
March 20—Maxim Zuyev, Homicide
May 5—Shamil Aliyev, Homicide
July 25—Bella Ksalova, Homicide
August 11—Magomed, Homicide

2011

December 15—Gadzhimurat Kamalov, Homicide

2012

July 7—Alexander Khodzinsky, Homicide
December 5—Kazbek Gekkiev, Homicide

2013

July 9—Akhmednabi Akhmednabiyev, Homicide

2014

August 1—Timur Kuashev, Homicide

2016

March 31—Dmitry Tsilikin, Homicide

2017

March 17—Yevgeny Khamaganov, Homicide
April 19—Nikolay Andrushchenko, Homicide
May 24—Dmitry Popkov, Homicide
September 8—Andrey Ruskov, Homicide

2018

April 15—Maksim Borodin, Homicide

July 23—Denis Suvorov, Homicide

July 31—Sergei Grachyov, Homicide

September 10—Yegor Orlov, Homicide

Names taken from Wikipedia and additional media sources.

Acknowledgments

The authors wish to thank Joe DeSantis, who once again played a key role in thinking through, researching, and critiquing *Collusion*; and Eric Nelson, our editor at Broadside Books, an imprint of Harper-Collins. Their insights were invaluable.

In addition, Newt Gingrich wishes to acknowledge Herman Pirchner of the American Foreign Policy Council for his constant advice about Vladimir Putin and the modern Russian state; Terry Balderson, who continues to serve as our extraordinary guide to daily information on the Internet; Bess Kelly, who makes the trains run smoothly; Woody Hales, whose scheduling and travel coordinating are world class; Audrey Bird, who has become an amazing book sales entrepreneur; his daughters, Kathy Lubbers (also his agent for twenty years) and Jackie Cushman, and their husbands, Paul Lubbers and Jimmy Cushman, who have encouraged all his adventures; his grandchildren, Maggie and Robert Cushman, whose future safety keeps him focused on national security and politics; and his wife, Callista Gingrich, whose companionship and love make it all worthwhile and who continues to support him as she serves as ambassador to the Holy See.

Pete Earley wishes to thank his agent, David Vigliano of AGI Vigliano Literary Associates, Dan and Karen Amato, Gloria Brown, James Brown, LeRue and Ellen Brown, Bob and Mary Donnell, William Donnell, Amanda Driscoll, George and Linda Earley, Dr. Gary S. Fialk, David "Gunny" Gambale, Walter and Keran Harrington, Marie Heffelfinger, Geraldine Henryhand, Michelle Holland, Don and Susan Infeld, Sheriff Stacey Ann Kincaid, Merlin and Carol Leking, Julian and Natalie Levine, Bella Francis Luzi, Kelly McGraw Luzi, Bill and Rosemary Luzi, Ray and Julie McGraw, Dan Morton, David and Cindy Morton, Richard and Joan Miles, Jay and Barbara Myerson, Mike Sager, Jay and Elsie Strine, Lynn and LouAnn Smith, Dennis and

Suzanne Sorensen, Kendall and Carolyn Starkweather, Stephen Tausend, and Sharon Yuras.

He also is grateful for the love, advice, and always-inspiring support of his wife, Patti Michele Luzi; and their children, Stephen, Tony, Kevin, Kathy, Kyle, Evan, and Traci; and granddaughter, Maribella.

About the Authors

NEWT GINGRICH is a former Speaker of the U.S. House of Representatives, a Fox News contributor, and a #1 *New York Times* bestselling author. He is the author of thirty-six books, including the recent #1 bestseller *Understanding Trump*. He makes his home in Washington, D.C.

PETE EARLEY is a former *Washington Post* reporter, a Pulitzer Prize finalist, and the *New York Times* bestselling author of sixteen books. He lives in northern Virginia.

HARPER LUXE

THE NEW LUXURY IN READING

We hope you enjoyed reading
our new, comfortable print size and found it
an experience you would like to repeat.

Well – you're in luck!

HarperLuxe offers the finest in fiction and
nonfiction books in this same larger print size and
paperback format. Light and easy to read, HarperLuxe
paperbacks are for book lovers who want to see
what they are reading without the strain.

For a full listing of titles and
new releases to come, please visit our website:

www.HarperLuxe.com

HARPER LUXE

SEEING IS BELIEVING!